P9-CAZ-076

The Anvil

Dean Davies

Eloquent Books
New York, New York

Copyright © 2008 Dean Davies.
All rights reserved. No part of this book may be reproduced or transmitted in any form or by any means, graphic, electronic, or mechanical, including photocopying, recording, taping, or by any information storage retrieval system, without the permission, in writing, from the publisher.

Eloquent Books
An imprint of AEG Publishing Group.
845 Third Avenue, 6th Floor — 6016
New York, NY 10022
http://www.eloquentbooks.com

ISBN: 978-1-60693-003-8, 1-60693-003-6
Printed in the United States of America
Book Design: Bruce Salender

For my mother who lives in brightness;
For my brother and father who sleep
On the mountain they loved.

ACKNOWLEDGMENTS

Novels are not written in a vacuum. Writing is lonelier than martyrdom, and I suspect, without the support of many people, few novels would ever be written. *The Anvil* is no different. I have many people to thank: Ralph Davis, Fremont County Sheriff, Carl Kasperson of the Bonneville County Sheriff's Office, Rick Ohusman, of the Idaho State Crime Laboratory, and John Walker, Bonneville County Coroner, all of whom patiently and graciously took time to fill in gaps in my knowledge of police procedure.

My thanks to Tim Orr, a geologist at the Hawaii Volcano Observatory, with whom I had a delightful conversation, and learned much about volcanoes thereby. And incidentally, any errors are mine, not the fault of the men above.

A great shout of Thanks! to my tiny circle of readers at Muddy's Bar, who read the novel chapter by chapter, as it was written, and whose enthusiasm and interest constantly inspired and motivated: Mike Amundsen, Ted McIntire, Lynni Hincks, and not least, Tom and Kelly Dalik.

I cannot express the depth of gratitude for my family: Mic Rowberry and "Smoke" Whittley, Vietnam veteran brothers and *kola*, whose service to our nation continues to inspire and awe; I am humbled to have the friendship and love of such men; for my Uncle John Around Him for his many years of patient teaching that brought me to a little understanding, and great respect for the spirit world; for my brother Charlie White Buffalo, who kicked my ass when Uncle John wasn't around, and who, when he stopped laughing at my crude Lakota constructions, graciously corrected them; for my dear eighty-four year old mother, Jean, whose quiet, steadfast faith and love gave me strength and courage when there was none; for my daughter Caitlyn, whose unconditional love has always inspired and motivated me to try, at least, to make something of myself.

For my friend Nick—Nicole—well, she knows.

Finally, and not least, for my friend and personal assistant, Alyssa Rencher, whose meticulous attention to the tedious details of my daily life (dry cleaning, check writing, grocery shopping, ensuring a continuous supply of cigarettes) allowed me time to focus on writing. This novel would not have been written without her. Thanks Lys!

Makoce Waste
Thanksgiving Day, 2007

Table of Contents

Chapter 1

Jacob Two Feathers sat on an outcropping of broken black basalt. It was part of vast lava flows that had covered the land on four separate occasions in the last fifteen million years. This particular flow, partly buried by sand, sprouting sage and rabbit brush, had begun cooling a mere twenty centuries in the past.

He sat staring into what might have been a bomb crater, a deep depression almost twenty feet across and fifteen feet deep. It was actually the remains of a lava dome, formed by hot gases when the lava was hot and later collapsed when it cooled. Where he sat, the temperature pushed a hundred; down in the pit, among the broken blocks of basalt, and in the lava tube caves that threaded the desert, the temperature would be in the low fifties, cool enough to protect the rattlesnakes who would soon begin their twilight hunting. He looked toward the West.

The sun punched an incandescent hole in the sky, a hand's breath above the massive peaks of the Centennial Range, two hundred miles distant. They shimmered in the reflected heat from the black lava beds. Lavender now, in the growing evening, as the sun set, they would turn indigo, then black. By that time, the snakes would be in full hunt, and the sky will have turned to the absolute darkness of a night with no moon.

That he knew there would be no moon was characteristic of Jacob, for he was once a soldier and soldiers keep track of such things. After nearly twenty-five years as an army officer—fifteen as a Special Forces team leader—Jacob gave no thought to his automatic and routine knowledge of wind, weather, moon, and terrain.

He shifted on the rock, easing the familiar and comforting weight of the M1911A1 .45 revolver on his hip. It had been with him in Panama, Iraq, Mogadishu, and Afghanistan. It had saved his life and the lives of his team more than once. He knew there was no real need to carry it out in the desert where he now sat, but he would have felt naked without it.

Suddenly, he froze, dropped his eyes to the rocks beneath his feet. Without knowing how he knew, Jacob sensed the rattlesnake emerging from the rocks beneath him.

The triangular head and the first six inches of a very large rattler protruded from the rocks between his boots. While the tongue flicked this way and that, Jacob's hand moved slowly to the handle of the seven inch Yarborough sheathed just behind his .45. If he had to, he could take its head off with one lightning sweep of the blade.

"*Hau, misun,*" he whispered. "Hello, little brother." Slowly, the snake slid out of its den, carefully testing the air with its black, flickering tongue. Jacob tensed. Soon the heat sensors above the snake's nostrils would detect the large warm mass hovering above him. Either he would coil and strike or slither away. When all six feet of it cleared the rocks, it coiled and rattled, facing Jacob. Slowly, he eased the Yarborough out of its sheath. They stared at each other, snake and man, for a full minute before the rattler, sensing no harm, uncoiled and slipped silently into the tall bunch grass at the bottom of the pit. There would be rodents.

Jake smiled and relaxed. "*Toksa ake, misun. Pilamaya yelo.*" "See you later, little brother. Thank you." He looked again toward the mountains. The searing coin of the sun touched the peaks. "It's time," he said to himself.

He unsnapped the catches on the black nylon hard case sitting beside him, and withdrew the Knilling cello. He caressed the dark European maple, tightened his bow and began the Prelude to Bach's *Cello Suite No.1.* He segued into the traditional *Simple Gifts* and finally into the utterly inexpressible beauty of Tan Dun's *The Eternal Vow.*

He played for the father he never knew, for his alcoholic mother, dead in the ditch beside a dirt road on the reservation, for the women he had never loved, for each of his dead troopers, some resting in distant places; he played to the vast lava and sage desert, to the terrible majesty of the mountains, and when he finished the last lingering note, the sun slipped behind the Centennials. He embraced the indigo evening and its sweet coolness.

The cracked and broken lava dome on which he sat was a mote in the six thousand square mile Python River Plain, curving like a scimitar through the center of the state. The locals called it "The Anvil" because the sun beat mercilessly down upon the vast black lava fields like a blacksmith's hammer. In the summer the temperatures reached a hundred and fifty degrees

In earlier millennia, the plain had been dotted by marshlands and lakes, filling in the spaces where the lava flows had stopped. As the centuries passed, the climate warmed and the marsh and grasslands that supported the herds of mammoth, camel, and bison had dried up. The lavish herds perished and along with them, those who hunted them: the dire wolves, saber-toothed tigers, the terrible ancestors of the grizzly, and the American lion.

Eleven millennia ago man entered the Plain and began hunting the mammoth, the camel and the bison. He, too, became prey to the great predators, but unlike them, he did not perish when the hot winds came, drying up the lakes and blowing the sand into great dunes and into the cracks between basalt blocks.

Nine thousand years ago, when the Great Rift had opened up the plain like a splitting fruit, mankind had witnessed the terrifying spectacle of red lava flowing across it like blood.

The ancient ones called to him; somehow their flesh and minds still lived in a way that summoned him, even after eleven millennia. They had summoned him to the high sandstone plateaus of Colorado, to the dwellings nestled in Chaco Canyon, to the deep hidden places of Arizona. Now, surely as mammoth trumpeting, they had summoned him to the bleak sage and lava-covered desert of the Python River Plain.

It was a hostile place, an inferno of razor sharp, broken lava fields in summer, and a freezing treacherous expanse of snow hiding the crevasses and pressure ridges that can snap a man's leg, or back, in the winter. In the summer, the remnants of the last glacial winds swept from the vast mountains in the West, the Centennials, down across the sage and baking lava fields.

He had gone often, wherever he had been, to the bleak places where the People might have passed, searching hungrily for some sign of their passing: a chip of flint, the black glitter of obsidian, an arrowhead, a scraper. And now, he went often into the blistering heat of the lava fields, the furnace-like blast that can kill the unprepared and unwary.

Where the lava beds ended, and where the land had not been plowed, and if the spring had been wet enough, there grew the tall slender grasses among the sage, grasses sometimes as tall as his hip. Sometimes he simply sat at the edge of the lava, perched on a basalt bluff looking over the sea of grasses, searching the horizon. What he sought he did not know, but he caught himself hoping for a glimpse of mammoth herds, or the dark punctuation of bison against the page of the desert. Sometimes he merely listened to the hissing wind, hoping to catch a whisper of a voice uttered millennia ago, a cry of game sighted, or the laughter that arrowed out from camp fires at night. While other men dreamed of women, or power, or wealth, he dreamed smoke-clouded dreams of the hunt, of blood, and the dark dancing mysteries of death, and life.

He sighed, packed up the cello, and made his way carefully down through the sage and rock fall to the Hummer parked below. When he touched the ignition, it rumbled agreeably, like a huge, friendly beast.

Jacob threaded his way carefully through sand dune gullies. One had to be careful, for a myriad of tracks threaded through the sage and not all of them led back to the main road. It was easy to get lost or to get mired in the sand; he was grateful for the lumbering, powerful Hummer.

The track he wallowed on wound its way around the edge of the lava fields and down into a steep gully. Ordinarily only knee high, here sage grew the size of cedar trees, creating a hidden forest. The track tunneled through it.

It possessed an otherworldly, ancient feel to it, as though it had been present when the lava flowed. There was a mystery here, something remote, beyond the will of man, ancient from the dim mists of time, and surprising. He felt vulnerable, insignificant, even with all his years of combat experience. A jackrabbit froze in the headlights and then bolted. "Run, little brother, run." As the Hummer ground and lumbered its way back to the main road, Jacob wondered again at the power the desert held over him. He decided what most held him in thrall was much of the six thousand square miles of it remained unexplored.

True, Jeep trails skirted some of the lava beds but the vast lava flows themselves were virtually impassable except on foot. Walking on them was like walking on the rubble of a bombed-out, flattened city. Pressure ridges, collapsed lava tubes, collapsed lava domes all produced a minefield of treacherous blocks of basalt that could never be trusted not to shift if any weight were put on them. Cracks between the blocks required constant vigilance, for one misstep produced a broken leg or worse.

Crevasses—rifts that descended the depths of the lava bed and sometimes ran for hundred of yards—were especially lethal for the unwary. Barely the width of a man, they sometimes fell into the abyssal depths of the earth. A man could disappear without a trace, and no tracking device could penetrate the lava.

Yet somehow the People not only survived, but prevailed. They had mastered the brutal land, even over the giant predators, and made it serve them. They found water in the spring playas, and in hidden pools deep in lava caves when the land above was a blast furnace. And in some caves, they cached meat wrapped in woven sage mats on ice that persisted year around. Even with his years of military training, he would never know as much as they about survival in the desert. They had thrived; he could merely endure until he made it back to "civilization."

The phone in the Hummer rang, interrupting his reverie. He touched the Onstar button.

"I just put out a BOLO for a drunken Indian somewhere on the Desert Road."

Jake laughed.

"The complainant said the Indian was out there killin' things with his cello playing. Said he was armed and dangerous, and not to let him get a drop on you with his cello."

Jake laughed again. "Well, Sheriff," he said, "I'll keep an eye out for anybody fitting that description. So far, the most dangerous thing I've seen is a jackrabbit going thataway at warp speed. So, what's up, Tom."

"Where you at?"

"I'm just passing the cinder cone by the big dunes. I'll hit the oil into town in about ten. Why?"

"I'll tell you that at the Silver Horseshoe when you get there. You're buying."

"That's a rodge. I'll see you in about thirty."

Sheriff Tom Curdy had Jake under surveillance for the first month Jake lived in Python. The sheriff wondered, and naturally so, who the tall, long-haired Indian was, and what he was doing in Python. Sheriff Curdy might not have been so suspicious of the newcomer had he not been waging war on the drug dealers who grew marijuana along the river bottoms and along the ditch banks of potato fields. And although Python was a small, rural agricultural community, generally immune to big city vices, cocaine and meth, too, had begun to turn up in surprising amounts.

So who was this stranger who could afford to drive a new H2, pay cash for riverfront property, and build what looked like a three or four hundred thousand dollar complex of buildings, including a studio for sculpture. Indians don't ordinarily have that kind of money. Hell, not many people, regardless of race, do. He ran a check on the Hummer's North Carolina plate; it came up clean. A day later, Shirley, his secretary, stuck her head in his office.

"Hey, Tom. You gotta call on line one."

"Yeah, who is it?" He didn't look up from his paperwork.

"Says he's General Marcus Reilly—USASOC—whatever that means." She shrugged and left.

Sheriff Curdy knew exactly what it meant: United States Army Special Operations Command. Baffled, he punched the blinking "1" on his phone.

"This is Sheriff Curdy."

"Good morning, Sheriff. This is Mark Reilly with SOC back a Bragg. Rangers still leadin' the way, out there in the West?"

"Yessir, they are." Curdy swore under his breath, annoyed with himself for wanting to snap to attention. This was the fucking *Commanding General* of all the Special Forces Teams, Rangers, and Delta Forces in the *entire world.*

"Good. Says here, among other things, you were in on Binh Tay I back in '70. Also says here you got a bronze star."

"Yessir, that's right. General, why are you calling me? I'm too damn old to re-enlist and generals usually don't have time to chit-chat with aging rangers. And why did you pull my records?"

Reilly chuckled. "Call me Mark, Sheriff. As for your records, I wanted to see what kind of man I was dealing with. Pretty impressive. I'd like to make this a friendly phone call between two old rangers."

Curdy didn't know what to say. Finally, he said, "Well, O.K., but what did you call me about?"

"Yesterday, you ran an NCIC check on a friend of mine, and I was just wondering why you did that. He's not in any trouble, is he?"

"You mean the Indian?"

"Jake Two Feathers, that's right."

"But how did you know I ran a check?"

"You know better than to ask, Tom—may I call you Tom? Or would you rather I called you 'Mack?'"

Curdy rocked back in his chair. Mack was his handle in C Company, 75th Rangers. His buddies called him Mack, as in *Mack the Knife*, after the song by Bobby Darin, because he was constantly honing his K-Bar. He'd used it in Cambodia's Ratanktri Province in May, 1970 during Operation Binh Tay I. He'd gutted an NVA sentry who had come three steps too close to his hide.

"Listen, Tom, Jake's a special friend of mine and I try to keep an eye on him. His last tour in Iraq went sour and he wasn't the same after that. You know how it is. I don't think he'd lose it, but you never know. So, is he in any trouble?"

"No. At least none that I know of. We have been having a drug problem in my county, and I just didn't see how an Indian could afford to drive a new Hummer, buy waterfront property and build an expensive complex on it."

"You can if you put your twenty-five in, investing most of your money in stocks and bonds. Jake has no family. Was raised until he was sixteen mostly by his grandmother and grandfather. His grandfather was a Lakota holy man of some sort; his mother was a drunk who froze to death by the road in a ditch. But before she did, she had the sense to send him away to a foster home off the rez so he could get an education—high school at least. He joined us, the Army, I mean, when he got his diploma. Jake's special, very special. He's been on loan to the Company. Hell, I don't even know what he did."

"What happened in Iraq?"

"The boy shoulda got the CMH. He and two other members of his team were behind the lines spotting targets with a laser. Radar sites mostly. Anyway, they got ambushed by some Hadj. Wounded the other two pretty badly and Jake took a couple of rounds, too. He finished the mission, then carried his men out. God only knows how many pilots he saved by knocking out that radar."

"Christ. How did he carry two of them?"

"He leap-frogged 'em. He'd carry one for a ways, then go back and get the other one, and then carry *him* farther than he did the first one. I don't need to tell you how hard it is to hump over sand dunes.

Trouble was, by the time he got them to the extraction point, they were both dead."

Tom's throat tightened. He cleared it.

"So why didn't he get the Congressional Medal of Honor?"

"He refused it. Flat said he wouldn't take it. We forced a DSC on him, but he didn't show for the ceremony. Not too long after, he retired. So that's the story, Sheriff. He's an American hero, the real goddamned thing, and if he's in trouble, I want to know about it."

"Well, General, he's not in trouble with me. But I'll keep an eye on him."

"I'd appreciate that, Tom. Here's a number you can reach me at, anytime."

The Sheriff wrote the number down.

"And Sheriff, one last thing. Wouldn't hurt to have Jake on your side if things go to shit with the drug dealers. Think about it."

They said their goodbyes and rang off. Tom got in his cruiser and drove out to Jake Two Feather's place. Jake was watching the builders lower a log on the main house when the Sheriff pulled up.

"I'm Sheriff Tom Curdy, Mr. Two Feathers. I'd be honored if you would have a cup of coffee with me." And they did.

The main street of Python ran exactly eight blocks. The intersection at blocks three and four sported the only traffic light in the county. At ten p.m. it automatically switched from the usual red and green to a flashing yellow. The Silver Horseshoe, the "Shoe", in the lingo of the locals, sat on the corner of blocks four and five. It had been built at the turn of the century, when businesses tended to be housed in long, narrow, buildings, with a false façade.

The front half of the Horseshoe featured a dining room dressed in dark mahogany, complete with the cattle brands of the leading families burned into the paneling. The tin ceiling glittered in the light of chandeliers, fashioned from elk horn. Overhead fans sedately whispered, dispersing cigar and cigarette smoke no one complained about.

It was the age of the cattle baron and the menu was steak and steak, along with huge potatoes, locally grown, that were served fried, frenched, or baked.

The back half was the typical saloon of the West: mirrors, long mahogany bar, ornate colonnaded back bar carved from bird's eye maple. Over the years, as the economy changed, so changed the Shoe. Fewer steaks were sold; more hamburgers and chicken strips. Coin-operated pool tables replaced the ornate billiard and snooker tables; a postage stamp dance floor was nailed down; the place was rewired for amplifiers, lights and other electronic equipment used by three-piece country-western bands, which played only on the weekends.The men who trudged into the bar for their after-work beers wore baseball caps instead of Stetsons, scuffed and muddy ropers instead of polished Justins.

Three or four muddy pick-ups dozed in front of the bar; Tom's was the sparkling blue GMC with the silver Sheriff's Department logo on the door. Jake found the sheriff hunched over beer and peanuts at the bar. The Kettle brothers, Roscoe and Hebrew, scruffy-looking men in dirty bib overalls and plaid flannel shirts with the elbows torn out, shot pool in the background. Tom looked up as Jake walked in.

"Well, the agin' Indian finally makes it. I was about to organize a search and rescue."

"You know me, Sheriff. I always drive the legal speed limit."

"Yeah, well, that ain't fifteen miles an hour. What's the matter? Won't that fancy Hummer go any faster? Maybe it needs a shot of Viagra, like you." Tom howled at his own joke and Bill, the bartender, hooted.

"The usual, Jake?"

"Yeah, just coffee." Bill brought a heavy white mug, filled with thick black coffee. He set sugar and cream on the bar in front of Jake. The Sheriff snickered. Roscoe had come to the far end of the bar.

"How long have I lived here, Bill, three, four years?" Jake asked.

"Something like that, yeah."

"Have you ever heard me insult Barney here? Have you ever heard me say a single mean thing about his bullet?"

"No, Jake, can't say as I have."

"Didn't I give him a new bullet, out of my own stores, when he lost the one the city council gave him?"

Bill's eyes twinkled. "Yes sir, you did. I saw it myself, right here in the Silver Horse Shoe."

"Hey!" Roscoe yelled from the end of the bar. "Can I get some service, here?"

"Yeah, I'm coming." Bill rolled his eyes, and moved off.

"Bad enough I gotta drink in a place 'at serves stinkin' Indians, but I don't gotta put up with bad service. Me 'n Hebrew, we been comin' in here—."

"Can it, Roscoe," Curdy said. "You might just be too drunk to drive."

"Tom, let it go," Jake said softly.

Bill slid a couple of Buds down the bar. "Last one Roscoe. Time to go home after that one." To Jake : "Sorry."

"It's nothing," Jake said, smiling. "Not your fault. So, Barney," he turned to Tom, "What's up?"

Tom slid a small piece of paper across the bar. "These people came to see me today. Said they needed a guide to take them out on the Anvil." Jake read the names: Dr. Harald Haraldsen; Nicole Haraldsen. "Doctor of what?"

"I don't know. Archaeology, I guess. They're trying to find a place an old Mexican sheepherder stumbled onto years ago. They're staying down at Hootie's Motel. I didn't make any promises, but I said I knew a couple of people I'd check with." Tom paused to sip his Coors. "Tell you what, buddy," he grinned, "I'd like to be stuck on the Anvil with that Nicole. She's a real looker."

"She his wife?"

"No, daughter. Father and daughter team, I guess. She looks like she belongs in a penthouse in New York."

"How would you know what a penthouse babe looks like? The only place you've been besides Python is Viet Nam."

"I read *Playboy*."

"You mean look at the pictures?"

Tom shrugged.

"They say how long they wanted to be out?"

Tom shrugged again. "'Til they find what they're looking for."

"Just what I need," Jake said, "to babysit a couple of academics while they dig up my grandmother. No thanks." He slid the paper back across the bar.

"Said they'd pay real well." Tom grinned.

"C'mon, Tom. That place is damn dangerous, even for me. I don't want the responsibility. Besides," he said, "I have people over in Jackson Hole who are willing to pay a fortune for a Two Feathers sculpture. Real Indian art." He laughed, shaking his head. "Some people got more money than good sense."

Tom sipped his beer, and Jake finished his coffee, talking small talk.

"Thanks, buddy," Jake said, "but I'll pass on this one. See ya around." He rose and left.

The Sheriff drained his beer and got up to leave.

"Praise God Almighty! It don't stink in here no more," Roscoe said.

"Roscoe, the only thing that stinks in here is your mouth." Curdy shook his head and left.

Chapter 2

As Tom left the Silver Horse Shoe, Vassili Grubinich and his two associates pulled their Land Rover into Python's only other motel, the Best Western. They had flown a GulfStream G500 registered to Vantessa Mining Corporation from Madrid, where Vassili kept one of his many safe houses, to Mexico City and finally, Salt Lake. When the plane returned to Madrid, it would be repainted, re-registered, and Vantessa Mining Corporation would disappear. Customs had been well-lubricated before hand. No one saw Vassili, or his associates' faces.

Vassili Timofeevich Grubinich was born into the postwar hell that was the Ukraine, in Kiev in 1947. Though Vassili never knew him, before the war, Vassili's father, Stephan, was a respected mathematics professor at the University of Kiev. Fiercely nationalistic and independent, after the war, Stephan joined others in the Ukrainian intelligentsia in the doomed attempt to throw off Stalin's bestial rule.

Vassili was born on a stunning April morning, four months after the NKVD had come in the night for his father. Stephan was never seen again. Four years later, the NKVD would come again, this time for his mother. Years later, all Vassili could remember of his mother was a vague porcelain face framed by auburn hair, singing a lullaby in a language he could not remember. And a rage at being abandoned by a woman.

His principal training for life occurred in the State Orphanage for boys in Kiev where he was taken in the Spring of 1954. By the time he was six he understood perfectly that he could have anything he wanted—anything—if he were strong enough to take it, which at six, he wasn't. But he had inherited his father's intelligence which turned into a lethal cunning. At nine, he killed one of the older boys by poisoning his own thin cabbage soup, regularly stolen from him by the bully. He saw the rat poison in the basement furnace room where the bully and three others raped him.

When he left the orphanage at seventeen as a conscript in the cold war Soviet Army, none of the rapists still lived. One of them slipped in the shower and broke his neck; another fell on a kitchen knife, apparently stolen while conducting a midnight raid in the kitchen; a third hung himself from the furnace room rafters.

By 1970, Vassili had become an officer and team-leader in the then little-known *spetsialnoe naznachenie*, Spetsnaz. His ruthlessness and cunning served him well. By 1980 he was a KGB colonel leading a Spetsnaz brigade in Afghanistan. Working secretly under the KGB's Seventh Directorate, Vassili's specialty was anti-VIP activities: the abduction and assassination of political and military leaders. Whenever possible, Vassili and a hand-picked team abducted, tortured, and extorted money from the Afghan warlords and their masters, before he killed them. His preferred method of execution was the heated blade of a bayonet pushed slowly into the victim.

"The main thing is to make them die slowly," he told his men. "You don't want them to die fast, because a fast death is an easy death."

By the mid-nineties Vassili and his teams were working in Chechnya. *"Bespredel,"* he told his men, "no limits," meaning find the Chechen rebel leaders, find their money; use whatever means it takes. Then he demonstrated on a captured female Chechen sniper. He raped her savagely, then threw her out into the icy mud of Grozny's winter streets. He instructed his men to tie each leg to separate armored personnel carriers with cables. Later, when he was questioned by a visiting General, he shrugged. "There was a lot of blood, but the boys needed it."

Chechnya was good to Vassili. He netted just under 5 million dollars of the Muslim-backed Chechens, which he added to the 4.3 million he had extorted from the Afghans. The Islamists were smart enough to understand that he was better as a well-paid friend than as an enemy.

He and a few of his men retired from the Army and went into business for themselves. He expanded his repertoire into corporate kidnapping, blackmail, espionage, and assassination. His clients were international and respectable. He flourished, operating from several safe houses in Europe, and around the Mediterranean. He was welcome in Arab countries where few Westerners dared.

The "specially-equipped" vehicle had been left for them in the long term parking at the Salt Lake International Airport. The keys to the Land Rover had been left in a locker, along with maps to their destination. The keypad combination of the locker had been sent en route via encrypted e-mail, along with instructions to contact Les Fleurs d'Amour Floral Shop in London via Internet when he arrived. He was to inquire after black tulips.

A casual glance through the window of the SUV revealed equipment for a fly-fishing expedition: fly rod cases, waders, willow creels, fishing vests, sleeping bags, and a large white cooler.

Vassili immediately removed the heavy Kraft envelope from the glove compartment. It contained fresh passports, California driver's licenses, credit cards to match and Vantessa Mining Corporation I.D.s, identifying them as executives of the company. There was also fifty thousand dollars cash, in assorted small bills.

"Anatoly," he said, passing out the credit cards and I.D.s, "it seems you are Jeremiah Roberts, and you, Tolya, are Robert Jones, and I," he grinned, "am Michael Brewer. I am also the C-E-O of this company." They all laughed.

"Tolya, you drive." He studied the map for a moment. "We head north on Interstate 15. Remember, do not exceed the speed limit. After all, we are three executives on fly fishing trip. We are in no hurry. Relax."

Anatoly cracked a window and lit a cigarette. He offered Vassili one, who lit up and inhaled deeply.

"Anatoly," he said casually, "when we stop you will get rid of the Russian cigarettes and burn the package. If you make another mistake like that, I will kill you." He turned and stared at the man in the back seat. *"Da?"*

"Da."

"And no more Russian. Speak American."

"Michael," Anatoly said, "fuck off and die." The three of them roared.

It was well after eight o'clock when Vassili and his comrades pulled into the Best Western in Python. After they checked in, ("ground floor, smoking rooms,") they unloaded the camping and fishing gear, so they could get to the real gear concealed under the deck and side paneling in the cargo area: three Sig Sauer 9mm pistols, with suppressors, two 9mm Uzis, and for Anatoly, a *snaiperkaya vintokova Dragunova,* a Dragunov sniper rifle with a folding butt stock, shortened barrel, and a PSO-1 illuminated reticle. Anatoly kissed it and grinned, "With this, who needs a wife?"

There was an assortment of tactical knives, three pairs of small folding binoculars, a thousand feet of 250 grain det cord, half a dozen blasting caps, a small hand-held radio detonator, ten pounds of Semtex, a Garmin GPS, and a Motorola 9505 Iridium phone.

While "Jeremiah" and "Robert" cleaned and checked out the gear, "Michael"—Vassili—went to his room and logged onto the Les Fleurs d'Amour website. Under "Search by Flower," he typed "black tulips." After a moment, a blinking cursor appeared followed by,

ARE YOU IN PYTHON?
"Yes," he typed.
SUBJECTS IN HOOTIES MOTEL. NO MOVEMENT. SHERIFF IS SEARCHING FOR A GUIDE. WE CONTINUE GRAVITOMETER SCANS FOR EVIDENCE OF SITE. IMPERATIVE YOU DO NOT INTERVENE BEFORE WE LOCATE, OR THEY LEAD US TO IT.
"What then?"
TERMINATION MUST APPEAR ACCIDENTAL, AND THEY MUST DISAPPEAR WITH NO HOPE OF EVER BEING FOUND. THEY MUST **NEVER** BE FOUND.
"Have you deposited the down payment?
HALF OF YOUR FEE HAS BEEN DEPOSITED IN ZURICH. DO NOT, REPEAT, DO NOT TERMINATE WITHOUT OUR APPROVAL.
"Do subjects have military or survival experience?"
NEGATIVE. WILL SEND FULL DOSSIERS YOUR WEBSITE. MAINTAIN CONTACT EVERY TWELVE HOURS VIA WEB OR SAT PHONE. WE ARE MONITORING THEIR PHONE CALLS AND THOSE THEY CALL. URGENT INTEL VIA SAT PHONE. QUESTIONS?
"*Nyet*," he typed, "for now."

He logged off Les Fleurs and accessed his accounts in Zurich. Five hundred thousand dollars had just been deposited. Half of his fee for assassination. He smiled. All that money for doing such a simple and easy thing: kill. Who cares? He logged onto his own encrypted web site, and began reading the dossiers on Dr. Harald Haraldsen, and his daughter Nicole. He whistled at her picture.

"Give me an hour with that one. I *will* have an hour with that one," he corrected himself. An hour later, he emerged and rejoined his team.

He sat on the bed, lit a cigarette, and said, "Listen carefully, and I will tell you what we must do."

Two Feathers Gallery sat on ten acres of wooded land that ran down to the Python River. It was river bottom land, like Jake remembered from his childhood on the reservation. Here, stately cottonwoods sentinel the river, blaze green in the spring, yellow in the autumn. Thirty years before, the land had been owned by a nursery. They had planted blue spruce and pine, silver, and red maple, and for bloom in the spring and harvest in the fall, pear, apple, plum, and crab apple.

They planted more cottonwoods, added groves of aspen and then seeded grass over the entire ten acres. By the time Jake bought it, the trees had matured, and the grass lay thick and emerald. It was wooded, secluded, and sacred.

There are places on earth that are just that: earth, plants, rocks, trees. But there are other places, for those who can feel, that resonate with a certain depth, that seem to be clothed in a shimmering, radiant intelligence, a profound, sentient stillness, that knows and waits.

To Jake Two Feathers it was as clear as if a sign had been posted in the driveway: Sacred Ground.

The ten acres fell naturally into upper and lower halves. The lower half sloped gently down an expanse of broad lawn to a grove of old cottonwoods and then to the great river. Beyond the river to the West lay the Anvil. As he walked the property with the real estate agent babbling at his elbow, gooseflesh stood up the hair on his arms and down his spine. An eagle launched himself from one the cottonwoods.

Jake stopped, raised his hand in greeting: "*Hau, kola. Pilamaya yelo.*" Then he took a cigarette from his pack, broke the filter off, and tore the paper away from the tobacco. He sprinkled it on the ground.

"What did you do that for?"

"The eagle."

"Oh, where?" She turned around, looking. "I don't see it."

"I'll take it," he said, walking away. It was down there somewhere in the old grove of cottonwoods, the place where they performed their ceremonies. He could almost see them; he could almost hear the drums and the singing.

The real estate agent, breathless, ran to catch up with him.

"Great! We'll go back to the office and get the paperwork started."

"No." He began unpacking the Hummer. "Bring it out here. I'm staying out here tonight."

"But what about financing, and you—well, you don't own the property yet."

Jake looked at his watch. "It's ten o'clock in the morning. Bring me the papers and I'll write you a check. By sunset it will be mine."

"But we have to do a title search and we usually close in the title office."

Jake's eyes bored into her. "Bring them out here."

"Yes, well, O.K. I'll see what I can do."

After she left, he sat wearily on his sleeping bag. He knew he had been unreasonable. But he was so tired, so very damn tired. He had left Bragg in North Carolina six weeks ago, slowly working his way West, looking for a place to settle, a place to withdraw from the clamor of the world, a place where he could simply be. New Mexico, Colorado, Wyoming: he worked his way slowly through the vast spaces of the West until he found this place on a river at the edge of a great lava and sage desert. He would go no farther.

His last tour in Iraq had gone wrong, so terribly wrong. He'd lost men, and very nearly himself. Somewhere in his long years of military service, his soul had simply leaked away, leaving only a husk behind. He couldn't get the coppery stink of blood out of his nostrils, couldn't keep the explosions, the burnt, stinking bodies from his dreams.

Tomorrow he would build a sweat lodge, the way his Grandfather taught him on a similar cottonwood bottom a thousand miles away and years distant. And there, inside the dome-shaped lodge, he would pour water on rocks heated to incandescence to create the purifying steam, called Grandfather's Breath. He would sing the songs that bring the spirits. He would honor the dead, ask forgiveness of those whom he had killed. He would honor the ghosts of his own men. That was tomorrow. Today he would sleep.

He dragged his sleeping bag under a pine, unrolled it and flopped down. Before he dropped into sleep, he realized he felt safe. For the first time in decades, he felt truly safe. In his dream he saw spirits gathering around, warriors and women in ancient buckskin; he saw them gather in a circle around him, to watch as he slept.

Chapter 3

Vassili was shaving when the earthquake struck. Had he shaved with a safety razor instead of an old-fashioned straight razor (which he usually stored in his right boot), the sudden, sickening lurch of the earth would not have caused him any injury. As it was, the sudden and wholly unexpected tremor took him to his knees, toppled lamps in the room, and inflicted a gash an inch and a half long and an eighth of an inch deep in his left cheek. By the time he staggered to his feet, applied the wash cloth to his face, and stumbled outside, Anatoly and Tolya were already standing in the parking lot, along with a few other guests, gawking at the building. The tremor lasted twenty seconds.

Across the street, a fire hydrant geysered a stream of water twenty feet high and four inches thick. A blue sheriff's pick-up sirened past, overheads flashing. The manager stumbled out of the motel office.

"Are you hurt? Is anyone hurt—Oh, my God. Are you hurt, sir? We have to get you to a doctor."

"It's nothing," Vassili growled. "I was shaving. A scratch, that's all."

"But we need to get you to a doctor," said the manager, taking his arm.

Vassili shook him off. "I said it was nothing." To Anatoly and Tolya: "Get dressed. We have work to do."

"But sir—."

Vassili waved him away. "I'll meet you two in the restaurant in fifteen minutes." He strode back into the room, leaving the manager gaping.

The first thing he did was check the computer. He made sure the connections worked and he could log on to the internet. He finished shaving, expertly bandaged his face with several butterfly sutures, and met his team in the restaurant.

Tolya and Anatoly sat at the counter talking to a short, bald, older man, who wore a grease-stained apron. A young girl, maybe fifteen or sixteen, stood by, ready to take their order.

"Now you take the Hebgen Lake quake back in '59, now that was a quake. Killed twenty-eight people." He paused to light a cigarette.

"*Dad*, you can't smoke in here any more. They passed a law. Remember?"

"Shit, honey. I been smoking and cooking for damn near forty years. I'll smoke in my own restaurant, if I want to. 'Sides, ain't nobody in here but these two fellers and they don't look like they'd mind a little cigarette smoke."

Anatoly grinned. "No, we smoke, too."

"Well, there ya go. Anyways," he continued, "whole damn side of the mountain came down an' buried 'em all. This weren't nothing compared to that." He looked over at Vassili. "Wow! What did you do, catch some shrapnel?"

"No, I was shaving."

"Well, breakfast is on the house. You boys go on over and grab a booth an' Jolene here'll get yer order." He disappeared though some swinging doors into the kitchen, trailing a plume of cigarette smoke.

After they ordered, Vassili spoke quietly: "Tolya, after breakfast, you and Anatoly go rent another car—make it another SUV, different color. We will have to do surveillance, maybe in two places a once. Bring it back here so I will have a car if I need one."

Tolya eased out of the booth and retrieved the ashtray from the counter. He lit a cigarette. "So, what then?" He exhaled a cloud of blue smoke.

"We wait. They are trying to find a guide. We watch, we establish our cover as executives on a fly-fishing trip. One of us will always be watching, the other two will be around town asking questions about fishing, or out on recon. We need to know how the land looks."

Jolene emerged from the kitchen carrying their orders, followed by the old cook. Vassili waved him over. The old man grabbed a chair and sat.

"Where's the best place to go fishing?" Vassili asked.

"Well, hell. Damn near anywhere on the river. If ya just follow the river up you'll see signs that say 'Sportsman's Access'. Just follow any one of them and they'll lead you to the river. You boys up here fishin'?"

"Yeah, that and just exploring the country." Vassili mumbled through a mouthful of hashbrowns and eggs. "The lava flows. Is there anything interesting to see?"

The cook lit another cigarette. "Hell,ain't much out there except sand dunes, sagebrush, rattlers, and jackrabbits."

Jolene glared at her father. "You're gonna get us in trouble."

"A lot of folks come up from Utah with their dune buggies just tear up the dunes." He laughed. "'Course some of them get all tore up when they come flyin' ass off a dune into them lava rocks. Sheriff hauls three or four of them a year to the hospital. An' there's always somebody getting' lost in the caves."

"Caves?" Vassili asked.

"Yeah. There's a whole bunch a' lava tube caves out there. Some of them run for miles. I ain't even sure if they all been mapped."

"I would like to see these caves," Vassili said, forking up the last of his eggs. "How do we get to them?"

"Well, if I was you," the cook, whose name was Sam, said, putting out his cigarette, "first thing I'd do is go over to the BLM office an' get some maps. Some of them caves is marked. You git to the dunes by goin' up main street 'til you see the brown sign 'at says 'Sand Dunes' and turn left there. Just follow the road. But, if you boys—here, Jolene. Put my ash tray back under the counter, will ya? Thanks, honey. If you boys is goin' out there, be sure to take a lotta water. Gets hot as Satan's balls out there."

At that moment a Sheriff's deputy walked in. He frowned. "Sam, it's against the law to smoke in restaurants in this state." Sam looked at Vassili and his men, and back at the deputy.

"Ain't nobody been smokin' in here, Deputy." He looked back at Vassili. "You boys see anybody smokin' in here?" They shook their heads. "See?" Sam said. "Nobody smokin' in here." They thanked him for the breakfast and left.

Out in the parking lot, Vassili turned to Tolya. "Go get another SUV and bring it back here.

"What are you going to do?" asked Tolya.

"I am going to buy some flowers," Vassili said, stalking off to the room.

Jake had built three buildings on the land he named *Makoce Waste*, (pronounced Ma-*ko*-chay *Wash*-tay) the Good Earth. These were the main house or lodge, an eight-sided log building, aligned on an east-west axis so that the "front" door opened East and the "back" door opened to the West. The interior of the house was arranged around a central open fire pit. A large hood, suspended from the ceiling, carried the smoke outside.

In addition to the main lodge, he built a pleasant, airy gallery to display his sculpture. He cut large windows into the log building that drenched the sculptures in sunlight. Finally, tucked into the trees overlooking the cottonwood bottoms, he built his studio. In the summer he opened the large, overhead doors at both ends to admit air and sunlight, and so he could see the bottoms and the river.

Two Feathers Gallery employed one part-time receptionist, a bossy Japanese woman named Meij, who also served as his housekeeper. She badgered him continually about smoking and tracking the fine, flour-like dust into the house from the studio. He was concentrating on the delicate ribs of a soapstone feather when she interrupted him over the intercom.

"Mr. Jake, there's a couple of people here to see you."

"Good. Send them out." He had been expecting a couple from Jackson Hole who wanted to commission a sculpture. His heart sank when the couple turned the corner into the studio. "Damn." He swore under his breath. "Should have asked who it was."

The couple consisted of a tall, older man in his mid-sixties who wore khaki chinos and a safari jacket. Glacial blue eyes sized Jake up as they approached. But Jake knew they were the Haraldsen's by the woman.

She was a classic Nordic beauty: blonde hair cut short around a chiseled face with high cheek bones, her father's glacial eyes, square chin and sensuous, beckoning lips. The tailored black pantsuit did little to conceal the voluptuousness beneath. The hands were small, white, and with meticulously manicured red nails. When she saw Jake, her eyes frosted over and the lips compressed into a thin red line.

The older man extended his hand. "Mr. Two Feathers, I am Harald Haraldsen and this is my daughter, Nicole. The Sheriff will have told you of our inquiry." Jake shook the proffered hand, surprised that it was soft and slack.

"Then Sheriff Curdy also told you I'm not interested."

"He did. But please, just hear us out before you say 'No'." Haraldsen glanced at his daughter, then back to Jake.

Jake hesitated. "All right. Let's step into my office. His "office" was a small room in the corner of the studio. In contrast to the grit, dust, and rock chips that littered the studio, the office was meticulously clean. A picture of a newly born white buffalo calf, guarded by its massive mother, hung behind the desk.

"Have a seat," he said, indicating two chairs in front of his desk. They sat. Nicole picked at lint on the legs of her suit.

"Are you familiar with the archaeology of the New World, Mr. Two Feathers?"

"I know North America was thought to have been populated by people from northeastern Asia by crossing the Bering Strait about 11,000 years ago, if that's what you mean."

"That's exactly what I mean, except that I do not believe that is how the Americas came to be inhabited."

Jake shrugged, lit a cigarette, and sat back in his chair.
"As you may know," Haraldsen continued, "the first people were called Clovis—."

"Do you have to smoke that?"

"Nicole, please," Haraldsen said.

Jake settled deeper in his chair and smiled. "Yes, I do. Professor, you were saying something about Clovis."

Nicole snorted and launched herself out of the room.

Haraldsen shook his head sadly. "It's not you, or the cigarette, Mr. Two Feathers."

"Why don't you call me Jake."

"Thank you, Jake. Ah, I'm afraid Nicole is not in favor of this expedition."

"And why is that?"

Haraldsen stared at his hands as if he had never seen them before.

"You might as well know the truth. I am dying. I suppose Nicole thinks it's another wild goose chase, and I should be in a hospital."

"I'm sorry." Jake shifted in his seat. "What is it—what's killing you?"

"Brain tumor. Inoperable, or nearly so. One or two of those quacks think I may have a slim chance of surviving, but they don't know."

"I'm sorry," Jake said again. "Why does she think it's a wild goose chase?"

Haraldsen sighed heavily. "All my life I have been chasing all over the world trying to prove that the first Americans came not over the Bering Land Bridge, but from Europe."

"Europe!" Jake rocked forward in his chair. "As in skin boats? That's crazy."

"Not as crazy as it first seems. Think about it, Jake. Modern humans migrated by boat to Australia fifty to sixty thousand years ago. There was simply no other way for them to get there."

"But to sail across the North Atlantic in a skin boat? Doesn't sound reasonable to me."

"Not across it. On it. They might have come in successive migrations, using an ice bridge. Current computer models suggest during the last great ice age the Atlantic might have been frozen as far south as New England in North America. Wouldn't have been easy, of course. But possible."

"But what other evidence do you have to support your theory?"

"The Clovis point is the telling indicator of those first people, yet no Clovis points or any other evidence of their toolkits have been found either in northeastern Asia or in Alaska. If that's the way they migrated, then why haven't we found any points?"

"So where have they been found?"

The professor sprang from his chair and began pacing. "That's the point. By far the largest concentration of Clovis has been found in the Eastern United States. Again, if the Clovis People came across the Bering Strait and migrated across America why haven't we found more sites in Washington, Oregon, Idaho? Or in Canada?"

Jake shrugged.

"Furthermore," he took two quick steps to the desk, "look at these." He lay three arrowheads in front of Jake.

At that moment, Nicole came back in. "Don't let me interrupt," she said, and sat down. The two men stared at her for a moment, and resumed their study of the arrowheads.

"This is a typical Clovis point. You will note the fluted end."

Jake picked it up. "It's beautiful."

"Note also that it is bifacial, meaning it is chipped or knapped on both sides." Jake turned the artifact over and studied it.

"See how these reduction flakes were taken out of the stone?" The professor took his pen and pointed. "The grooves run all the way across the blade from one side to the other. We call it the *outré passé*, or overshot technique. See how thin the blade is? They were incredibly skilled flint knappers."

Jake grunted and stole a quick glance at Nicole. She wore what looked like a small ivory statue hung from a leather thong around her neck. She slid it back and forth along the thong.

"Now, look at this blade," Haraldsen said, pointing to the next arrow head. The only difference Jake could see was that the base of the Clovis point had shoulders whereas the one Haraldsen was pointing to had a rounded base.

"This is the laurel-leaf point dating from the Solutrean Period in Europe, somewhere between 22,000 to 18,000 years ago. It came from a site called LeRuth on the Vezere River in southwestern France. Take a close look at it, Jake; the knapping techniques are almost identical."

Jake studied the point for a moment. "O.K. So what? They are shaped differently."

"Ignore that for the moment. Now look at the last blade."

"I don't see any difference, except that it's made of obsidian," Jake said.

"That's exactly the point! It was found somewhere out there, on the Anvil."

"You mean this Solutrean point was discovered at a site somewhere here in America?"

"Not somewhere, but here on the Anvil."

"But how do you know that?" Jake stared at Haraldsen, then Nicole.

"Do you have time for a bed-time story, Mr. Two Feathers?" Nicole asked.

Then the earth rumbled, and a wave rippled through the room. The picture of the white buffalo calf flew off the wall smashing the glass and the frame. Jake's desk skittered across the floor. Jake bolted around it, grabbed Nicole, yelled at Haraldsen, "Outside! Now!"

As he hustled Nicole through the studio, several of Jake's soapstone and alabaster sculptures crashed to the concrete floor, firing shards of rock in every direction. Outside, another shock followed, slamming them to the ground. Then, silence.

Jake rolled over to look at Nicole. "You O.K?" She nodded her head "Yes."

"Professor, are you O.K.?"

Haraldsen nodded. "Wow. I didn't expect that. Does that happen often around here?"

Jake didn't answer, looking at the Gallery. "Meji," he said and took off running, shouting her name. Inside the Gallery, he found her standing, hands on hips, surveying the damage.

"Quit yelling," she said. "Look at this mess, just look at this mess." Several sculptures had fallen from their pedestals and shattered. Small pieces of alabaster and soapstone crunched under Jake's boots. Nicole and the Professor joined them. Jake kneeled down to where one of the broken sculptures lay. Before it shattered, it was an old Indian woman with a heavily creased face, sitting cross-legged, wearing a voluminous skirt. She cradled a small Indian boy in her lap. Both of them were laughing. The "Not for Sale" sign was still fixed to the base.

Jake tenderly began to gather up the pieces. Nicole kneeled beside him, and picked up the woman's severed head.

"She's beautiful," she said, handing it to him.

"Yes, she was," he whispered. "My grandmother."

"Then you're—." She stopped when he looked up, directly into her eyes.

His eyes were not black, as she had thought, but a deep chocolate, and they glistened with a pain and a love she was not prepared to see. She stood up quickly and walked back to her father.

"We should go."

Jake stood up and looked after her.

Haraldsen looked around the studio. "Yes, perhaps you're right. Jake, perhaps we should continue our talk tomorrow."

Meji began picking up pieces of alabaster.

"Ten o'clock at Sam's would be fine." Jake said, looking at the fragments in his hands.

Later, as they drove back to the motel, Nicole stared hard at her father. "Are you going to tell him?"

"No," Haraldsen replied, "not until we find it."

"But he deserves to know," she said.

"Nicole, we've been over this. Not until we find it." He turned away from her and gazed out the window at the passing farm land.

Chapter 4

Vassili had logged onto the Les Fleurs D'Amour site:

SUBJECTS IN CONTACT WITH POSSIBLE GUIDE NAMED JACOB TWO FEATHERS. HAVE INITIATED BACKGROUND CHECK, WILL FORWARD ANY INFORMATION YOUR SITE.

He logged off Les Fleurs and logged onto his own encrypted site. Jake's file was attached to a brief note:

UNABLE TO ACCESS COMPLETE MILITARY FILE ON SUBJECT. HE POSES AN EXTREME DANGER TO OUR ENTERPRISE; EXTENSIVE MILITARY AND SURVIVAL EXPERIENCE. USE EXTREME CAUTION.

Vassili read through the file carefully, and sat back. He cracked his knuckles. "I wish I had met you in Afghanistan. We could have danced the dance."

He stood and paced the room, stopping briefly to peer out the curtained windows. The enterprise had taken on an entirely new dimension. He walked back to the computer and stared at Jake's picture, memorizing it. "I look forward to meeting you, my friend." He logged off just as someone knocked on his door.

It was Anatoly, who held up a set of car keys. "It's the red Jeep Cherokee."

"I am going to do some recon. Get me a black box," Vassili said.

Anatoly stepped out to the Range Rover, rummaged around for a while and tossed Vassili a small black box.

The older Russian thumbed the phone book for *Two Feathers Gallery* and Jacob Two Feathers. Both showed 785 South River Road as an address. He took the keys, stopped off at the Motel office for directions to South River Road, and left.

He took the main road out of town. In front of him and sixty miles distant, the sharp spikes of the Tetons brooded on the horizon. He crossed the river, still swollen from runoff and turned left on a side road that followed it. He enjoyed the drive on the narrow country road.

Farm houses seemed to be spaced about every quarter mile. Sometimes farm dogs lay in wait, ears laid back, ready to chase his SUV. He came to a heavily wooded stretch of land and then a sign with an arrow: *Two Feathers Gallery*.

He turned in, parked, grabbed the small black box from the back seat of the jeep, stuffed it into his jacket pocket, and went into the Gallery. He wanted to see his kill.

Jake looked up as he walked in. "I'm sorry; we're trying to clean up some earthquake damage. We're not really open."

"I'm so sorry you had the damage." Vassili walked across the room, hand extended. "Michael Brewer."

Jake took his hand. "Looks like you had some earthquake damage, too."

"Nothing, just a scratch."

As Vassili expected, the handshake was firm and strong. As they made small talk, he studied Jake. His excitement and anticipation grew. There was a restraint, a kind of hidden intensity and intelligence in the man that Vassili knew could erupt in a fury of sudden, lethal violence.

Jake would have already subconsciously evaluated him, would even be doing it as they spoke, constantly scanning him for unusual signs or signals that telegraph a threat.

Vassili pointed to the Hummer sitting in the parking lot. Yellow, red, and white hand prints, surrounded by white dots decorated its flanks. "Is that your truck?"

"Yeah," Jake said, "why?"

"Forgive me, but what is the meaning of the hand prints?"

"Oh, those," Jake said walking to the window. "In the old days, Lakota warriors decorated their horses before battle to protect them. That's my horse." Jake laughed.

"Ah, very interesting. Well, thank you. I will come back when you are open."

He said his goodbyes and left. When he drew abreast of the Hummer he dropped his sunglasses. He kneeled down to pick them up with one hand, and with the other he swiftly attached a magnetic tracking device to the frame. The entire operation took less than five seconds.

As he drove back to the Motel, ripples of excitement coursed through him. First, he would disable Jake so he could watch while he dealt with Nicole, then he would kill Jake, slowly, so that as he died, Jake would submit, and accept the will and strength of a better man. Money was good, but this was better. He remembered the joy of his first kill in the orphanage, the surge of power and domination. He, little Vassili, had killed the school bully!

Roscoe got out of his truck, a battered and rusting seventies vintage GMC with wooden stock racks, and carefully closed the pole and barbed wire gate behind him. He had left the Kettle Ranch two hours before sunset and driven north along what the locals called The Red Road, "red" because the county road crews had used the red cinder from the nearby cinder cone buttes to gravel the road. It wound torturously through the northeastern end of the Anvil, threading its way around the lava flows like a red snake. Eventually, it crawled West toward Montana. Roscoe had just turned off onto a little used track.

He paused briefly to catch his breath after the exertion of closing the gate. To the West lay the immensity of the Anvil; it was bordered on the North by a great escarpment that was the southern end of the Island Park Caldera. It rose three thousand feet above the desert below. It had been formed 1.3 million years ago by a massive volcanic explosion that spewed ash over a thousand square miles and created a caldera thirty-three miles long and eighteen miles wide. By comparison, the largest volcano to erupt in the last two centuries at Tambora, Indonesia, was five times smaller.

Heaving his weight into the truck, he continued grinding his way toward the heights in the distance. Eventually he came to another track that wound its way around the edge and up the escarpment. As he climbed in elevation, the terrain changed. Sage yielded to lush and green meadows flourishing in the open spaces. Aspen, pine, willow, and alder grew on the steep sides of the caldera. Springs bubbled with the clear, pure water filtered through volcanic sands.

It was nearing dusk when he turned onto yet another track leading into a canyon with high, steep walls. A red-tailed hawk circled above. He came to a five strand barbed-wire fence and another pole and barbed-wire gate. A crudely lettered metal sign hung on the gate: NO TRESPASSING. Beneath it, the same hand had drawn a crude skull and crossbones.

Behind the fence lay a meadow thick with hip-deep timothy grass, ringed by aspens and alders. The track cut across the meadow and disappeared into the trees. The canyon veered to the left beyond the trees. The walls reached higher. A small stream burbled across the road. Full, now in the early summer, by August it will have dried to dust and sand. A faint breeze stirred the aspen leaves.

Roscoe got out of the truck and waited. He was tempted just to open the gate and go on in, but he knew better. He lit a Pall Mall and paced around the truck. Suddenly, a figure materialized from the grass in front of him. It wore an olive drab dew-rag around a skeletal skull and it was naked, ribs protruding, from the waist up, and streaked with black and green camouflage paint. It cackled, revealing two teeth missing in the lower jaw. It was also pointing an M-16 directly at Roscoe's chest.

"Goddammit, Uncle Zeb! Do you have to do that? You scared the shit out of me."

"If you was Cong you'd a' been dead ten minutes ago, boy."

"Well, I ain't Cong. Now open the gate an' git in. We got business to do." Zeb slung the M-16, undid the gate, waited for Roscoe to drive through and shut it behind them.

"Which way?" asked Roscoe.

"Take a hard right down th' fence line to th' creek. See them tracks the other boys made? Well, jest foller them. Don't stray more'n five yards either way. Got M-21's on both sides o' this track an' M-15's on th' main road. Ain't nobody gettin' in here."

"What's an M-15?" asked Roscoe.

"Shit, boy. Where you been? It's twenty-two pounds of HE—high explosive—to you. It'll blow the shit out of a tank. Kill everthang in it. An jest t' make certain ain't nobody sneakin' around, I got four or five hundred o' these little babies laid all around." He dug in the cargo pocket of his fatigues and produced a round, green plastic container about an inch and a half thick and three inches in diameter.

"What's that?"

"This here is a Chicom 72 anti-personnel mine, type C. These are the good 'uns. Know why?"

"No, Zeb, I don't."

"Shit, boy. You don't know nuthin'. Too bad you was too young for Nam. 'At was a good war. If you'd a gone with me, you'd know somthin'. Anyways, you try to find this little baby with a mine detector"—he held it up at eye level—"an' boom! It'll take your foot off up to the knee."

"Where do you *get* all this stuff?"

"I got my sources, boy. Don't you jest never mind. Good ol' friends o' mine. Nam vets, all of them. Shit, we'd a won 'at war if Westmoreland 'ad ever got his head outta his ass an' let us do it."

"Zeb, you mind putting that mine away?" Zeb had been waving it around while he was talking.

"Roscoe! Quit yer damn frettin'. Damn thang ain't even armed yet." He stuffed it back in his cargo pocket. They wound along the creek bottom, following a vague track made by other vehicles. Zeb peered up through the windshield.

"Nope. Ain't nobody gettin' in here. Got my Claymores up on th' ridge, all on trip wires. Overlappin' fields of fire. *Shee-it*. We gonna rock 'n roll now!" He cackled.

The track took a hard left. They eased down a steep embankment, crossed the creek and climbed up the other side. Another gate. Razor-barbed concertina wire, three coils deep, and six feet high, stretched in either direction. Beyond the concertina, in a clearing, stood an old weathered cabin, a corral that was falling down, and two or three faded and sagging outbuildings. The cabin, the corral, and the outbuildings were just visible over a ring of sandbags stacked four deep and chest high. Three trucks nosed in to the sandbags, ticking as they cooled.

"Beautiful, ain't she," Zeb said, as he slid out of the truck. "This here is Fort Fuck You." He cackled and slapped his knee.

"It might be beautiful, but it sure stinks."

"Hebrew's been a'cookin', Zeb said.

Roscoe looked at the trucks. "It don't look like Willie's made it yet. You better go lead him through."

The cabin that Roscoe entered had been a line shack for the sheepherders and cowboys back in his grandfather's day, when the Kettle Ranch prospered. It was a one-room cabin with a dirty plank floor, heated at one end by a fireplace of local basalt and at the other by an ancient black coal stove. A ratty overstuffed couch sagged against one wall. Above it hung a stained NVA battle flag, a gold star on a scarlet field. It irritated Roscoe, but Zeb wouldn't part with it, saying it was one of the spoils of war. He threatened to kill anybody who touched it. The thing about Uncle Zeb was, he probably would. You could never tell.

An American flag hung high on the fireplace. A black flag with a white closed fist encircled with a wreath of olive branches hung below it.

At the other end of the room, adjacent to the stove, a kitchen sink had been built into the wall; an old-fashioned hand pump sucked water from the well beneath. A greasy, curtained doorway next to the stove led to a pantry and another equally shabby curtain on the other side of the stove led to a small bedroom.

Four men sat around a scarred formica kitchen table in the center of the room, drinking from a bottle of Jack Daniels black. Two Coleman lanterns hissed from the rafters throwing deep shadows in the corners of the room.

Roscoe was greeted with a chorus of "Evenin' General," as he entered the gritty room.

"Evening, boys." He smiled and shook hands, delicately moving his ponderous bulk around the table. Except for his enormous girth, they were men who looked much like him. They wore heavy, scuffed boots, faded bib overalls or levis, faded and torn cowboy or flannel shirts. Two of the men grew scruffy beards, like Roscoe. The other two prickled with two days' growth of whiskers. The hair was generally uncombed and greasy; heavy calluses thickened their scarred hands. One spat tobacco juice into a styrofoam cup; the other three smoked generic cigarettes.

"What'd you think o' that earthquake, General?" asked a thin, sandy-haired man whose name was Earl.

"What I think," said Roscoe, reaching for a jelly glass, and pouring it half full of Jack Daniels, "is, it was the Word of God tellin' us of the battle to come. Fill 'em up, boys," he said, motioning with his glass. "Stop an' think about it," he said, staring at the floor, "we're seein' the signs. Everything is goin' to shit. This Zionist-owned (pronounced *Zeeonist*) government is leadin' us all to destruction. Why just look 'at all 'em stockbrokers, an' accountants; why, look at the corporations 'at have been caught stealing from th' American people." He paced, chin on chest. "Why jest look at how them Jew-owned corporations been sendin' all our good white American jobs overseas t' them slant-eyed mud people. Hell, you boys know how hard it is t' git a good job any more." He stopped and stared at them indignantly.

39

"An' you know who's takin' your jobs right here, boys? Do you?" He stared at each one of them. "It's them filthy Messican mud people! Not only is they takin' your jobs, but they's here *illegally* and the Jew-owned government ain't doin' nuthin' about it!"

He paced, thinking. Suddenly, he marched to the fireplace and pointed at the black flag.

"Do you see this, boys? It means 'white pride world wide.' That's what it means. An' we are gonna restore white pride in these parts, anyways."

Hebrew walked in the door, carrying a small cardboard box under one arm, bringing with him the smell of rotten eggs.

Earl wrinkled his nose. "Jesus, Hebrew, whyn't ye go git some clean clothes?"

"Hush up, Earl," Roscoe snapped. "Hebrew's doin' th' Lord's work. Hebrew, gimme that box."

Hebrew passed it over, and filled a jelly glass half full of Jack. "It ain't real fun, workin' in that shit, you know."

"How much is there?" Roscoe asked.

"A hundred and ten grams."

Roscoe patted the box. "This here's one of our weapons, boys. Methamphetamine. Meth." He strutted around the table nailing each of the men with his glare.

"We gonna hook them rich Jew boys an' girls an' bring 'em down. We gonna hook them Messicans, them niggers, them slant-eyed son a' bitches—all them mud people," he said, waving his free hand, "an' we're gonna bring back the respect for honest, God-fearin' white Americans. We made the world great, an' we're gonna keep it," he said, shaking a fist.

A scraggly-haired blonde man known as Willie burst into the room, followed by a Mexican boy about sixteen and an older woman. The boy's face bled from a deep cut under his left eye. Plastic cable ties cut into their wrists; duct tape sealed their lips. Both breathed heavily through their noses. Snot ran down the boy's upper lip. Zeb herded them into the room with the M-16 and kicked their legs out from under them.

Roscoe gently set the box on the table. "Well, lookee here." He looked from the Mexicans huffing on the floor to Willie.

"Well," he said softly, "you'd better have a damn good reason for bringin' 'em here, Willie, cause they ain't likely to leave."

"Shit, General, wasn't nothing else I could do. I was down in Mex-town tryin' to collect from Miguelito here—he been dealin' some stuff fer us—when *mamacito* comes boilin' outta th' trailer threatenin' t' call th' sheriff if I didn't pay her off. So I whacked the kid with my gun an' brought 'em both here."

"Take the tape off her mouth," Roscoe ordered.

Willie bent down and ripped the tape off. "*Cabron,*" she spit, and tried to kick him in the crotch. Willie kicked her in the stomach.

Roscoe kneeled on one knee. He twisted her hair until she looked up at him, choking and retching.

"Is that true, *mamacito*? Did you try to blackmail one of my soldiers?"

"Chinga tu madre!"

Roscoe slammed her head on the floor, and turned to the boy. He ripped the tape from the boy's lips. "You tryin' t' steal from us, boy?"

Miguelito shook his head vigorously. "No, senor, no."

Willie burst in: "Well, then how's come you didn't have the money? How's come you said you needed a couple of days? You spent it, didn'ja? Spent it on some greaser whore." Willie backhanded him, smacking the boy's face to the floor.

"Willie, Willie," Roscoe said, "'at's enough." To Miguelito: "Well, didja spend th' money? Didja?"

"No, senor. I can get it in a couple of days."

Roscoe sighed dramatically, and stood up facing the men circled around. "You boys think he stole our money?" There was a chorus of "Hell, yeses," and "Sure, he did."

Roscoe sat heavily on one of the kitchen chairs. He stroked his beard. After a moment, he looked up and said, "What we got here is clear-cut cases of blackmail, an' stealin'."

There was a chorus of "Yessirs."

"My granddaddy, Ezekiel, once caught a Mex sheepherder sellin' his sheep, an' claimin' the coyotes got 'em. You know what he done, boys?" He stood up, staring at the two on the floor.

"Well, he gathered all the he'p together so's they could witness Ezekiel's Law. That's what he done." He paused.

"Well, what was it?" Earl blurted out.

41

"Had him drug behind a horse one mile for every sheep he stole."

"How many miles was he drug, Roscoe?" asked Slim, another of the men.

"Six," Roscoe said. "He was drug six miles. Ezekiel hisself gave out the punishment, an' then give 'im a good Christian burial. I expect six will be good enough fer these two. Hebrew, you n' the other boys go fetch a coupla ropes. Take the Mex's with ya. Zeb, I wanna talk to you n' Willie." Hebrew and the other men shuffled out dragging the two Mexicans.

Roscoe walked to the table and poured another glass of Jack Daniels.

"Willie, since you brought 'em here, you kin do th' honors. Take 'em out on the road fer six miles, an' then drop 'em off in th' river in that deep hole under th' old black railroad bridge. I reckon they'll stay put down there. Ain't nobody's been found yet 'at's dropped off in there. Zeb, you go on an' change yer clothes, an' then give 'em to Willie here."

"My clothes? Well, jest why—?"

"Jest do it, Zeb. We don't want th' Sheriff findin' no traces of hair, or DNA, or whatever, if it should come to that. Go on, now; I'll git ya some new duds." Zeb disappeared behind the curtain.

"Willie, after you finish, get th' clothes from them other boys. Tomorra mornin', bright an' early, put all 'em clothes in yer truck and then burn th' truck."

"Burn my truck! Why, I ain't a' gonna burn—."

"Yes, you is, Willie, fer the same reasons I tole Zeb. Don't you worry none. The Python Brotherhood is gonna buy you another one about th' same age an' everthang, so's not t' attract too much attention. Do it out t' yer dad's ole place so's nobody'll see. Burn it good, Willie. We don't want no traces of nuthin."

"Yessir, General. I'll do like you say."

Zeb came out from behind the curtain, handed Willie a bundle of clothes.

"Them was my good cammos, Roscoe," he said, shaking his head sadly.

Chapter 5

"We were talking about bed-time stories." Jake had agreed to meet Nicole and the Professor for breakfast on the morning following the earthquake.

Haraldsen picked up his fork and began tracing patterns in the pancake syrup on his plate. "About three weeks ago a man of Mexican descent came to my office at the University. He had in his possession a small box of artifacts he wanted to sell to the museum that I curate. Of course, I loathe dealing with amateur pot-hunters, but I agreed to look at his collection."

"You guys finished? Can I take your plates?" Eveready Jolene. Haraldsen relinquished his plate.

"I'll bring some more coffee," Jolene said.

"You can imagine my surprise to see the blades I showed you yesterday. When I questioned him about their origin, he said his grandfather, a sheep herder, had become lost on the Anvil. The way the old man told it, he wandered for days, barely staying alive until he stumbled into a vast cave with a waterfall—."

"A waterfall!" Jake laughed. "A waterfall on the Anvil!"

"I told you it was a bedtime story." Nicole shook her head.

"Bedtime story or not," the Professor continued, "he stumbled into a vast cave with a waterfall. Apparently, the falls emptied into a pool with no outlet—the water just sank back into the earth again. The old man said near the waterfall was a room he called *el lugar de las calveras*, the place of skulls. It must have been a shrine or an altar, a sacred place of some sort. He said all along the back wall, behind a fire pit, lay a semi-circle of elephant skulls. Said there were other kinds of skulls, too, but he didn't know what they were. Did you ever hear of such a place, Jake?"

Jolene came by and silently refilled their cups.

Jake shook his head. "Frankly, the idea of a waterfall on the Anvil is as ridiculous as elephant skulls. It's a desert, for God's sake. And it's flat. The closest high ground is the Caldera on the North and the Centennials in the West. There's no place to fall. The closest rivers are miles away and there are certainly no rivers flowing across the Anvil."

"How about under it?"

Jake stared at Harald Haraldsen. "Professor, just how the hell would I know that?"

"That's exactly the point, Jake. No one knows if there is an underground river or stream out there. Jake," the professor leaned forward on the table, "the old man said the waterfall was in a *cave*. There are caves out there, aren't there?"

"Yes."

"Isn't it possible there is an underground stream that emerges briefly and then returns back into the earth—inside a cave?"

Jake and Nicole both stared at Haraldsen's left hand which had begun to twitch in an uncontrollable palsy. He withdrew it under the table.

"Well," he asked, "is it possible?"

"Yeah, I guess."

"Dad—."

"Nicole, I'm fine. My hand does that when I get excited. It's nothing."

At that moment three men entered the café. An older man led the other two. He was short and blocky, a man with almost no neck, muscular like a rhino. He wore his iron-grey hair closely cropped to his skull. The others, short-haired as well, were men whose faces one would instantly forget. They, too, were slim, muscular, and hardened. Jake recognized the older man as Michael Brewer. He waved; Brewer waved back.

Looking at the three of them a chime sounded in the back of Jake's mind. He came back to the conversation with Nicole and her father.

"Landmarks. Did he say anything about landmarks?"

The Professor hesitated. "He said the cave was located in the curve of a crescent-shaped island."

"A crescent-shaped island?" Jake looked to Nicole.

She shrugged.

"Jake, will you help us find it?"

He stared at the professor and then Nicole. "You're crazy. You don't know what you're up against, even if there were an 'island' out there." He stood up. "C'mon."

Outside, Jake opened the rear passenger door for Haraldsen. Beads of sweat had broken out on the older man's forehead and his face had turned a sickly, pale color, like dough.

"Professor, are you—"

"I'm fine. Let's go."

Nicole took shotgun. "Where are we going?"

"You'll see." Jake took a left at Python's only stop light and headed out of town. After about twenty minutes, they left the pavement and crunched along on the red cinder road. The road circled a cinder bluff that topped a rise. Just over the top, Jake pulled over and stopped.

Off in the distance, the Centennial range reared up, hazy and blue. From where they stood, the land fell away gradually into a great grey plain of sage, broken black basalt, and a few scattered pinyons. Jake pointed with a sweep of his arm.

"That's it. The Anvil. Six thousand square miles of broken lava, sage, cinder cones, and snakes. From here, it looks flat. It's not. That's basalt out there. When it cools, it cracks into blocks. Sometimes gas bubbles form in the lava creating domes. When they cool, they collapse. They look like bomb craters. Some of them are thirty feet deep. Out there, you climb out of one bomb crater and into another one—endless miles of them."

He looked at his watch. "It's eleven thirty a.m. It's probably ninety degrees where we're standing. By two o'clock the temperature out there will be a hundred and ten, maybe more. There's no roads except around the edges of the lava flows. Horses can't cross it; helicopters can fly over it, but they can't land. If you want to go there, you have to walk. Walking across that," he gestured again with his arm, "is like walking on a pile of bricks, only the bricks are two feet long and three feet wide and weigh a lot more than concrete. One misstep and you'll shatter a leg or break a back.

Out there you need a gallon of water a day to stay hydrated. Do you know how much a gallon of water weighs? Eight point three pounds. To say nothing of carrying every thing else you need—on your back. And you want me to simply lead you out there hoping to find something that resembles a crescent-shaped island? It's suicide. I might as well shoot you right here."

Haraldsen seemed to have recovered a little of his color and no longer shook. "Jake, we can hire a helicopter and fly it. If we can at least locate something crescent-shaped out there, will you lead us to it?"

Jake shook his head and took a couple of steps away.

The professor followed him. "Look, Jake, if we can find it, we can plot a course to it. We can use the helicopter to drop caches of water and food at certain points along the way. That will work, won't it?"

Jake turned as Nicole bent over to pick something up off the ground. When she did, the amulet fell out of her blouse. He stared, and then walked quickly up to her. "Can I see that?"

"What, this? It's just an obsidian flake."

"No, the carving." She took if off and handed it to him. The ivory had aged to a tobacco brown. The figurine had a head but only the vaguest suggestion of eyes, nose, and mouth. The breasts hung pendulously over a pregnant, swollen belly. Straight legs that tapered to a point.

Haraldsen walked over to where they stood. "That's a Venus."

"A what?"

"It's a so-called Venus. They were carved by prehistoric people in honor of the Earth Mother. See how the legs taper to a sharp point? We believe they stuck them in the ground in front of their dwellings. They are often found with mammoth bones they used for the frame-work of their dwellings—sort of like the willow frame of a sweat lodge."

"Where did you get it?"

"It was given to me by Professor Vernay. I helped him one summer at the LeRuth site in France. I gave it to Nicole. It's about nineteen thousand years old, by the way. Why?"

Jake handed it back to Nicole. "Just curious. We should go. It's getting hot."

"But what about my idea?"

Jake headed back to the Hummer. "I'll think about it," he said over his shoulder.

Rick Sanchez cruised South River Road cursing his rotten luck and his rotten life. If Bob Duncan—the Deputy who was supposed to work the swing shift—if his wife hadn't gone into labor with what, the fifth, sixth kid? then he wouldn't be on patrol and he could keep better tabs on his wife Jeannette. He was sure she was having an affair with that sonofabitch Lawrence Whitcomb, who owned Python Realty. Him and all his money.

"Jesus," he said out loud. For twenty years him and Jeannette had worked together to make a home for their two kids, Ami, sixteen, and Sean, eighteen. You didn't get rich working as a sheriff's deputy, but then few people in Python were, except Larry Whitcomb. Bald sonofabitch. He never could understand what women saw in bald men.

Everything was just fine until the kids got in high school and Jeannette started working as a receptionist at the real estate office. Pretty soon she started complaining about not having any clothes, and why couldn't they take any trips to Mexico, like everybody else? She worked later and later in the evenings saying she was "showing houses" because Larry was just too busy to handle it all. Once or twice she'd been gone all day Saturday, "working."

Lately, she'd been complaining about the house: it wasn't big enough; it wasn't new enough; it didn't have a nice enough yard. Why couldn't they get a hot tub? She even dropped a few hints about him finding another job. Jesus Harold Christ! He had seventeen years on the force. He was forty-four years old. He couldn't just up and find another job that paid a hundred grand a year. What the fuck did she expect, anyway? He shook his head sadly. What had happened to his high school sweetheart? The neat, white, three bedroom fifties vintage house on a cottonwood-lined street had been good enough before. What the fuck happened?

And Sean. My God. He could have had a football scholarship, but he quit football and everything else after his sophomore year. Came home one day with his eyebrow pierced and a "tribal" tattoo, whatever the hell that was supposed to be. Didn't look like anything to Rick, except trash. Worse yet, Jeannette sided with the kid, saying he was just "expressing himself." What? Expressing what?

"God help him, if he gets into drugs," Rick thought. "I'll beat him to death, and burn those baggy fucking pants." He didn't even want to think about the maroon mowhawk.

If that weren't enough, the light of his life, Ami, had missed several days of school this month. A couple of mornings he thought he'd heard her throwing up. Sweet Jesus! Not his little girl. What with everything else, he hadn't the courage to confront her. Maybe he just didn't want to know.

He looked down at the speedometer. Holy shit! He was pushing eighty coming into the right angle corner by the old black railroad bridge. Rick jammed the brake pedal to the floor and the rear end began to skid. He didn't even try to make the corner. Fortunately, straight ahead lay a dirt two-track that kids used to get under the bridge to party and make out. He cranked the wheel in the direction of the skid and caromed down the dirt track. The cruiser slid to a stop in a cloud of dust about ten feet from the bridge abutment.

He fell out of the cruiser, shaking. "Jesus fucking Christ," he thought, "I have got to get ahold of myself." Still weak in the knees, he walked around the car, checking for damage. A few scratches from the sage that bordered the narrow road.

Rick walked to the abutment and looked out over the river. Another hour and the sun would set. The massive iron girders of the bridge hung above him, vaguely threatening. Swallows darted here and there. Somewhere up in the girders a feral pigeon cooed. A coolness rolled off the river, bringing with it the faint scent of mud and fish.

The old bridge had been built in the thirties at a point in the river simply called "The Narrows." Here, eon after eon, the Python had cut a narrow chasm through the bedrock basalt. The surface of the river looked placid enough, but here the entire volume was constricted, shooting through the narrow chute between the rocks.

There were actually two rivers, one on top of the other one. The one above, the surface, purled languidly along, but the one below, about eight feet beneath the surface, tore savagely through the chute. No one caught in its treacherous and powerful currents was likely to come out, let alone alive.

The abutments had been built on the living rock about twenty feet back from the edge of the river. This is where the kids partied.

He wandered under the bridge, kicking through the trash: broken beer bottles, the remains of several campfires, plastic grocery sacks, empty beer cartons. He uncovered a used condom. He tried not to envision Ami, here under the bridge, with some pimply-faced kid with his ball cap on backwards. Someone had scribbled "Morgan, Class of '92" with red spray paint on a boulder. He sat down, shook a Marlboro out of its pack and lit it.

"Goddamn it, I just need to make more money. That's all there is to it. But how?" Rick shook his head. He didn't know. He looked down river.

The river opened into a wide bay once it shot past the Narrows, creating a backwater in the lee of the bridge. Here, the Python opened its great maw and released the contents of its journeying, trash, mostly: beer bottles, plastic jugs, odd bits of styrofoam, an occasional dead horse or cow, and great rafts of drift wood.

Where Rick gazed, an old cottonwood, uprooted from somewhere up-river, cast its limbs out into the current. Something white bobbed in its embrace. He stared at the tree and the white, well, pink/white object for a long while, lost in his own anguish, before he realized something wasn't quite right about what he saw. Was it a pig?

To get to the cottonwood snag he had to climb the railroad bed and fight his way through the thick willow underbrush on the other side of the bridge. From this angle he couldn't really see what it was. He crawled out on the tree on his hands and knees. He pulled a long stick out of the driftwood that had accumulated against the snag. He poked the pinkish-white bag. It seemed caught on something beneath the water. He poked it again.

It disappeared. When it popped up again, Rick stared at the shredded face. The flesh had been ground away to the bone on some parts of the skull. The chin, lower lip, and nose were missing altogether. A pair of hands, tied tightly with a thick hemp rope, floated languidly to the surface. The flesh under the arms and elbows was gone, like it had been sanded off. He screamed, half-fell, half-crawled back along the tree trunk to the bank.

Tom Curdy sat at the kitchen table, damp dishtowel wadded in his hand, studying his wife's ass. Ellie stood with her back to him at the kitchen sink, scrubbing the heavy, black cast-iron frying pan she had used to fry the chicken. She wouldn't let him wipe the frying pan with the dishtowel. "Makes the dishtowels black and greasy," she said.

They had begun doing the dishes together when they first married.

"Jesus," Tom thought. "How many years, now? Thirty-eight? Thirty-nine?" Even when they had fought bitterly, they always did the dishes after dinner. Ellie washed; Tom dried.

At some point, he couldn't remember when, he bought her the latest dishwasher for Christmas. It had all the bells and whistles:

settings for "normal wash"; "light wash"; "pots and pans"; "rinse and hold"—all that bullshit. They'd used it twice, and then went back to doing the dishes themselves.

When the kids were still home, after dinner, they'd be watching TV or doing homework. Then Tom and Ellie had the kitchen and the small, comforting talk of the day to themselves.

Ellie's ass hadn't changed in forty years. It was still round, small and taut. Not much else had changed either: hour-glass figure, a slim five six, one hundred and ten pounds. She wasn't beautiful the way a fashion model is beautiful. She was beautiful in a clean, simple way that just was: hazel eyes that smoldered grey, button nose, straight white teeth, peach complexion. Tom loved her hands: short nails, no polish; she had amazingly small, strong hands that deftly handled the routine horrors an emergency room nurse handles.

The hair had changed, though. He remembered when it fell in a blonde cascade off her shoulders and down her back. It was the first thing he'd felt brushing his face when he finally woke up at Brooke Army Medical Center after the mortar round shredded his right side near Pleiku, Viet Nam. She was leaning over the bed and her hair had drifted across his cheek.

"Welcome home, soldier," she whispered. And then she kissed him. What was once blonde and long was now short and showing streaks of grey, but as far as Tom was concerned it had turned from gold to platinum. He stood up from the table, slipped his arms around Ellie's waist, and nuzzled her neck.

She turned around. "My hands are wet," she said.

"I don't care. Hug me anyway."

She giggled. "What brought this on? Is that a banana? You better watch yourself, mister. There's laws against pornography in this state."

"It's O.K.," he whispered. "I know the sheriff."

"Well, in that case," she said, nuzzling up against him, "I can't wait to see what hap—". The phone rang.

Ellie laughed and slipped out of his arms. "Guess not," she said, handing the phone to Tom.

It was Bennie the dispatcher. Her name was Bonita Juarez, but everybody called her Bennie. Tom listened for a moment and said,

"O.K., Bennie. Call Joe and tell him to get the boat and meet us there. And you better call the coroner, too." Silence.

"Well, keep trying to find him. He's probably down at the Shoe. Thanks, Bennie. Yeah. Bye." To Ellie: "Rick Sanchez just found a floater under the old railroad bridge. Shit!"

Jake didn't have to unroll the small bundle of red cloth in his top dresser drawer to know they were the same. But he did.

He had dropped the Haraldsens off at Sam's Café, saying he'd get back to them in a couple of days. Haraldsen's idea might just work—if they could find the landmark—a big "if". They might even be able to find a place for the helicopter to land, though he doubted it. The expedition, however dangerous and foolish he thought it was, wasn't what was giving Jake pause. It was Nicole's Venus, or rather his Venus.

Jake sat on the edge of his bed staring at the tobacco brown figurine lying in the center of a square of red trade cloth. He found it on one of his many excursions on the Anvil. And until today, he hadn't really known what it was. He wasn't even sure if he "found" it, or if it was given to him. It happened like this.

Jake's grandfather taught him that whenever he ate a meal, he should set aside a small part of his food and water as an offering to the Creator, and to the spirits, in thanks for the abundance they provide. Often as not, he added a small pinch of tobacco, usually torn off the end of a cigarette.

On this occasion, he had camped in a small gulley near a cluster of pinyons. As he had done so many times before, he cleared a small space beneath one of the trees and laid out a slab of jerky, a few dried apricots, and from the old canvas water bag that was his grandfather's, poured a small cup of water. Then he sang a song, thanking the Creator for life, and health. He left the water bag lying on the ground near the offering. In the morning, the offerings of water, food and tobacco had disappeared, along with his grandfather's water bag. The Venus lay nearby.

Jake was not surprised the offerings disappeared. They often did. But the water bag? Was the Venus a trade for the water? He was certain it had not been lying there the night before. He wouldn't have missed it. He searched the area in ever-widening circles, looking for tracks. The difficulty was that there was precious little sand to leave tracks in. He gave up after he had searched a hundred yards out: not a blade of bunch grass bent, not a rock disturbed, not a single footprint, human or animal.

His grandfather would have said, "The spirits took it" and let the matter drop. But Jake knew full well that the spirits, if indeed it was a gift of the spirits, seldom gave without intention. Sooner or later the intention would be made clear, and he would have to do *something.* Jake just didn't know what. He had not been able, until today, to bring himself to think the thought that had lurked in the back of his mind: *What if it wasn't the spirits at all? What if the Venus had been left by a survivor of one those ancient tribes? What if a small group of them still lived, somehow, in the hostile and unexplored desert?*

He folded up the trade cloth, slipped the Venus in his shirt pocket, and shook the thought away. Someone would have stumbled on them by now. A sheep herder, a rancher, a hunter, a low-flying airplane: *somebody* would have discovered them. The Venus was a fluke, somehow. Maybe he just didn't see it the night before.

He wasn't sure what to do about the Haraldsens. He sure as hell couldn't take a sick man out on the Anvil. But what if there really were an important archaeological site out there? What if they were to find a shelter that showed signs of recent habitation?

And what about Nicole? He sensed her hostility. Why? She didn't even know him. There was something else at work, there, too. If he didn't take them, he was certain Haraldsen was crazy enough to try it alone. They would surely die.

He argued with himself all the way out of the house and down to the sweat lodge. He would do what his grandfather had told him: purify, pray, and ask Creator to make his purpose known.

Chapter 6

"So where is it?" Master Chief Joseph P. Landski, U.S. Navy Seal, retired, levered his 5'7", two-hundred-ten pound frame out of the Duramax 3500 that towed the eighteen-foot aluminum Search and Rescue boat. "I don't wanna put this pig in the water unless I have to."

Rick Sanchez pointed the direction of the snag. "It's bobbing out there about three-quarters of the way down that cottonwood snag."

Landski squinted into the ferocious glare off the water. "Yeah. I got it. Hell, I'll just swim out and get it."

"I don't know," Rick said. "The current's pretty treacherous; it's probably deep, too."

"Ain't as deep as the ocean," Landski said. He climbed in the boat, stripped off his levis and black tee shirt and began pulling on his wet suit.

Tom Curdy pulled up in a cloud of dust. "Hey, Rick," he said, climbing out of the truck. "What'cha got?"

Rick pointed again toward the snag. "Hard to tell. Looks like a juvenile male. Face is all fucked up. You can see it about three-quarters of the way down that snag."

Curdy shaded his eyes with his hand. "Oh, yeah. I see it. What do you mean 'face all fucked up'?"

A '72 white Thunderbird with a white vinyl top lumbered up and stopped, raising another cloud of dust.

Landski dropped down from the boat, wearing a pair of unlaced black sneakers to protect his feet. He held a dive mask and fins in one hand and a long black vinyl bag draped over his shoulder.

The county coroner, Morris—Mo—Creighton, climbed out of the land yacht. He wore tan dockers, a yellow and green Hawaiian shirt, and oxblood loafers with tassles.

"Nice tassles, Mo," Landski said. "Can I touch 'em?"

"Fuck you, Landski. Tom. Rick." He shook hands all around.

"So, Mo, what did you think this was, a luau?" Landski asked.

"I'm in the middle of a date, Landski. Some of us actually have a life."

"Yeah? What's he look like?" Landski asked, grinning.

"Like you, asshole, except bigger'n you, with a beard and no teeth." Creighton faked a punch, which Landski blocked.

"What did you mean 'face all fucked up'," Tom said to Rick. "I mean most of it ain't there," Rick said.

Tom asked Landski, "Where do you want to put the boat?"

"I don't. Shit, Tom. I'll just swim out and bag him and drag him."

Tom hesitated. "Well, I don't like it. You'll be out there without any backup."

"It's gonna be dark soon," Mo said. "We don't want to be floundering around out there after dark."

"He's right, Tom," Joe said. "Hell, by the time we get the boat in, it'll be dark. Then somebody'd have to baby-sit the body all night." He looked at Rick.

"All right," Tom said. "Let's try it. Just get the bag around him and Rick and I will get some boat-hooks and try and help from the snag." To Rick: "Grab a couple of boat-hooks, will ya? We'll see how far we can get out on the snag."

"What do you want me to do?" Mo asked.

"Just stand there and be pretty. You might get your tassles wet," Landski said, heading for the river.

Tom and Rick made their way up the railroad bed and fought through the underbrush. They worked their way out as far as they could along the snag. When they were in position, Landski breast-stroked toward the body. He carried the body recovery bag rolled up and slung across his back to leave his hands free.

The recovery bag is different than an ordinary body bag. It has holes in it to permit water to flow out, but still strain out any evidence on or near the body. Theoretically, all Joe had to do was slip the bag up around the corpse, zip it up, and tow the package ashore.

Holes or not, once it was opened and filled with water, the bag was heavy and it was still a tricky thing to tread water and slip the bag up around a corpse—without gulping mouths full of river water. Joe stopped swimming a few feet from the corpse and studied it.

Most bodies floated on their back or on their bellies—horizontally. This one seemed to be standing on something about five feet out from the tree. Joe didn't stop to think why it floated vertically, he just thought, "Well, it will be easier to slip the bag up."

Slipping his face mask on, Joe unslung the bag, unzipped it, and fitted the top part of it over the head and shoulders. His plan was to work the bag down around the body and zip it up after he had the feet in. He took a deep breath and ducked under the water.

Visibility was rapidly diminishing in the fading light. He could barely make out the ghostly grey limbs of the snag reaching out toward him. He sensed the deep water and sinuous power of the currents beneath him. He worked quickly, encasing the corpse in the black cocoon of the bag. It was when he tried to zip it up that he discovered the other rope.

A thick hemp rope tied the feet of the body together and angled downward underneath the tangled limbs of the snag. Joe surfaced.

Tom called out: "You O.K., Joe?"

"Yeah. It's hung up on something. Wait..." Landski dived again, trying to see what the rope was attached to. He swam down a few feet, grabbed it and gave it a heave. Something broke loose. As he kicked back toward the surface, the slack rope wrapped around his left leg. He kicked again, trying to free himself. He looked down between his legs and the diver's sixth sense told him that something awful, *some thing* hideous was now rising from the dark, cold deep to ensnare him.

And then the pale white form of what was once a woman rose languidly to meet him, her black hair unfurled like a pennant, the shredded remains of blouse and skirt trailing like confetti, arms outstretched like a lover reaching for an embrace.

Joe kicked savagely, trying to gain the surface, but unwittingly thrust his own head between the body of the corpse above and its bound, outstretched arms. He now carried the corpse on his back. He came up flailing, sucked a lungful of water, and coughed just as the dead woman surfaced in front of his face, close as a kiss. There were no lips, no nose, no chin, just the grinning rictus of death, and sightless orbs the color of plastic milk jugs.

He went under again, fought back to the surface, but the corpse's bound, cold hands choked him and he couldn't get a breath. The boat hook slapped his chest.

"Grab the hook! Grab the goddamned hook!" Curdy yelled. And he did. As Curdy pulled him to the snag, Landski heard someone scream, "Get it off me! Get it the fuck off me!"

Jake sliced the bloody kidney into small squares and scooped it into one of the four bowls arrayed on the counter. Before she left, Meji made Jakes's favorite, ham and lima beans. He poured a ladle of beans into another bowl, buttered a slice of bread and lay it in with the beans. Next, he sliced cantaloupe and watermelon. He put these in a third bowl along with a couple of cookies and peppermint hard candy.

"The spirits like sweet things," his grandmother told him. She leapt into his mind, a small, round-shouldered woman, who wore her iron-grey hair in a neat bun. Deep wrinkles scored the land around her eyes from laughing, which occurred often. Having nothing, she found joy in everything. She was the color of cedar bark and her eyes shined like chokecherries.

"The spirits like sweet things," she said. She tapped him on the nose with the wooden spoon, stained purple from chokecherry *wojapi*. *Wojapi* is a thick, sweet fruit pudding served with fry bread.

He wiped his nose with the palm of his hand and then licked it. "So remember when you do ceremonies to make sure to leave something sweet with the offerings," she said. Then she gave him the spoon to lick. He was seven years old, and his grandmother was cooking for a *lowampi* ceremony his grandfather was conducting later that night.

When she finished the *wojapi* and set it aside to cool, she began the laborious process of rolling the dough for the fry bread, which she cooked in a heavy, black cast iron pot on the coal stove. He got to cut the dough into diamond shapes. And if there were any dough left over (and there always was), the old woman made him sugar cookies.

"Thank you, *Unci*," he whispered.

He filled the fourth bowl with clear spring water, pumped from the deep well beneath the house. He floated three or four sage leaves on top of it.

Jake made two careful trips down the hill to the sweat lodge and arranged the offerings around the buffalo skull altar. He stood back and surveyed the sweat lodge and the altar, checking to make sure he had done everything correctly.

The fire pit, the altar, and the sweat lodge lined up on an East-West axis. Earlier, he'd stacked twenty-eight basalt stones in a pyramid in the fire pit and surrounded them with successive layers of split logs, creating a teepee of logs. Then, beginning in the West, he stood at each of the cardinal points around the rocks, and prayed to each direction, sprinkling a pinch of tobacco. Finally, again in the West, he sprinkled pinches of tobacco for *wanbli gleska,* the spotted eagle, *Unci Maka*, the Grandmother and *Tunkasila*, the Grandfather. Then he lit the fire. When the *tunkan,* or the grandfathers, glowed cherry red he would begin the Ceremony of Purification. Satisfied that everything was in order, he walked up to the house to wait for the stones to heat.

Jake made two more trips to the fire, adding wood each time. About dusk the rocks were ready. Naked, except for a towel wrapped around his waist, Jake used a pitchfork to stack fourteen of the stones in a shallow depression inside the sweat lodge, called the Grandmother. Then he carried a galvanized pail of water along with a ladle and set them inside the lodge. Finally, he dropped the towel, and crawled inside carrying a small rawhide buffalo hand drum, the Venus, and closed the flap, sealing the lodge.

He stuck the Venus in the earth in front of him, took a deep breath, and relaxed into the blood-red light and the blast of heat radiating from the stones.

He did nothing for a few minutes, except bathe in the heat and light, slipping into the sacred space and time of the Grandmother's Womb, which is what the lodge represents. When he felt centered, and in harmony with the lodge, he poured four ladles of water on the rocks saying, *Mni na ihe letahan. Oniyan tokeca, unkicupi k'ta ca, lecunkunpi. Wopila unkeniciyapelo.* "Grandfather, from these rocks and water, we will receive new life. That is why we do this."

Then he picked up the hand drum and began to slow beat of the first song of the ceremony:

Wakan Tanka, tokaheya cewakiyelo,
Grandfather, I acknowledge you first...

As he sang, he felt the spirits gather around him, like a cloak of feathers, touching and warming him, rustling, whispering in half-heard voices. And then the Power surged up from below, like a gush of warm water, rising in him, like golden liquid to meet the Power coming down from above. Jake sang the ancient song, but it was not him singing: *He was being sung* by the Powers engulfing him.

When the singing and drumming faded away, Jake poured more water on the rocks, creating the scalding steam called the

Grandfather's Breath. *"Hau, Tunkasila. Wopila ecici yelo,"* he said, "I send you thanks. *Omakiyayo.* Help me." Then he touched the Venus in front of him. *"Omakiyayo,"* he said again. And then he sat back on crossed legs, relaxed, and let himself slip into the glowing red spaces between the stones. The rippling heat faded and he slid into a deep darkness.

He was aware that he was walking through a velvety blackness. In the distance, here and there, flickered blue forms, formless forms, like changing cloud shapes, or a vaguely illumined banks of fog. Sometimes he heard a distant drumming and voices he couldn't quite understand. One of the cloud banks drew nearer, and nearer, and resolved itself into a mature Indian man. He wore his grey braids wrapped in red trade cloth and mink fur. The face was square, with straight planes dropping off high cheek bones; it was lined and dark, from too much sun and too many years. He was muscular, like a warrior is muscular: thick biceps, wide chest, and a ropy abdomen. A bone vest covered his chest and leather leggings sheathed his legs. Though no words were uttered, Jake understood him to be his father, from a time generations remote from his present life. The man's eyes found his, and gripped them, telling him to be strong.

And then he stepped aside, revealing the smoking, destroyed camp, tipis burning, women screaming, the earth littered with bodies like leaves. He ran though the camp calling her name, found the smoldering, stinking remains of their tipi. He cast wildly around, screaming her name and dashed toward the willowed creek nearby.

From the way the bodies lay, she had gathered the children, his two girls and his baby son, behind her and made a stand at the creek. She lay on her side, a great scarlet stain on the elk hide dress, an ugly black hole below her breast. Her head lay pillowed on an outstretched arm; the pale hand still clutched the knife that killed the blue-liveried trooper a few feet away. She had gutted him. The children lay behind her in a grotesque fan, shot in the back, apparently by another trooper.

Jacob heard a sound growing, not a howl, but a low moan that seemed to come out of the earth, an animal sound, nothing human, a soft wail of unutterable, disembodying grief. He gathered her in his

58

arms, crawled to where the children lay, tried to gather his family up and hold them, but they kept slipping out of his arms, limp and floppy; the children wouldn't sit up, their arms wouldn't stay around his neck. And all around the air writhed under the terrible lash of the sound that rose and fell like the wind.

He tried to wipe the scarlet slickness from his hands, but there was no where to wipe them that was not already scarlet; he tried to clean his children's faces, but only made them bloodier.

His wife, his beautiful wife, with the dark hair that fell to her waist, his beautiful long-legged, teasing wife, who drew him to and into her with those strong coltish legs, wouldn't stay on his lap, but kept flopping on her side, sliding away. Cante Wohitika Wi, Braveheart Woman. He tried to kiss her awake but she wouldn't kiss him back...

He sewed them into buffalo hides, built scaffolds for them on the side of a hill, overlooking the valley with its quivering aspens. Then he walked back to the ruined village where a knot of people waited.

They watched, silent and numb, as he soundlessly hacked off his long braids, slashed his chest and arms until the blood ran in scarlet rivulets. Then he cut the end knuckle from the little and third fingers of his left hand. They watched stoically as he traded hands with the knife and hacked the end knuckle from the little and third fingers of his right hand.

He threw the knife in the dirt at his feet. "From this day, I am called Cante Nica Wica, No Heart Man." Then he grabbed a fistful of mane on his pony standing by, vaulted up, and rode off across the prairie. The wasicu could no longer kill him; he was already dead.

He galloped, and galloped across the prairie until the lathered pony stumbled and threw him. He felt himself fly through the air and landed with a bone-jarring "thump" in the sweat lodge.

"*Mitakuye oyasin,*" he said, crawled out, and collapsed on his back. He held his hands up in front of his face: all his knuckles were still intact. He checked his arms and chest: he wasn't bleeding anywhere. He wiped the wetness from his cheeks, aroused himself stiffly and sat up. The fire had burned down to a glowing nest of embers, cradling the remaining fourteen stones. He piled more wood on the fire until it blazed.

"How do I know if I have a true vision, Grandfather?" Jake was eleven years old and his Grandfather was "putting him up on the hill"—taking him on his first *hanbleceya*, vision quest. They climbed the steep, rocky trail up the side of *Paha Sapa,* Bear Butte. The old man carried two wool blankets and four chokecherry stakes about three feet long. Black, yellow, white, and red flags were tied to one end of the stakes. Jacob carried his *cannupa*, what the *wasicu* call a "peace pipe," in the crook of his left arm.

The old man stopped, carefully set the blankets and stakes on the gravel, and sat on a boulder beside the trail. He could have been anywhere from seventy to ninety. It was impossible to tell by looking. He, himself, had no idea the year he was born, only that it was in the Fall, near the Greasy Grass River, many, many years ago.

His face was dark as elk hide, and etched with the gullies, ravines, and trails of long life. "People should look like the earth, when they get old," he said once, smiling. "I guess I'm doing pretty good." However eroded his face might have been, eyes sharp and restless as a crow's lanced out from under beetling white eyebrows.

His hair had long since turned white and he carefully arranged the two long braids on his chest as he sat down. A simple strip of red cloth tied the ends. The old man, whom people simply called "Robert," because he told no one his secret Lakota name, attended his hair very carefully. "Long hair is *wakan,"* he told Jacob, meaning "mysterious and powerful."

When his wife combed it out in the mornings, she meticulously cleaned the brush of any loose hair. She rolled it between her palms into a ball and gave it to him. What he did with it, no one ever knew.

"Never let a witch get a hold of even a single piece of your hair," he said. "They can kill you or one of your relatives with it." The young Jacob nodded, wide-eyed and serious.

The old man settled in on the rock and dug in the pocket of his blue and white checked cowboy shirt. Buffalo-colored hands, knotted like tree roots, dug out a sack of Bull Durham. He sprinkled a few flakes of tobacco on the ground, and rolled a cigarette which he lit with a kitchen match.

He inhaled deeply, and blew out a cloud of blue smoke. He seemed to sink inward, considering Jacob's question. Jacob sat cross-legged at his feet; he was used to long periods of silence when his grandfather was thinking. Ravens cawed overhead; the purple shadows that precede sunset lengthened.

"Lot a people come up here," he said at last, "and think they have a vision. Most of them are just imagining things. A true vision doesn't happen very often. Most people go their whole lives and never have one. So, sometimes they make them up in their heads.

A true vision happens when you are there in it, like you and I are here right now." He took a deep pull on the cigarette, rested his forearms on his knees and exhaled. "But even that," he looked up at Jacob, "doesn't guarantee a true vision. Iktomi is tricky. *Cante un wanla kin kte heca yelo,"* he said, touching Jacob over the heart. "You have to **be** it, **see** it with the eye of your heart. You will know a true vision because a true vision will tell you something about yourself or someone else that you already knew, but had forgotten."

He stared out at the valley below them. "We are spirit beings, *takoja.* We can live backward in the past or forward in the future, sometimes both at once. Spirits don't know time, grandson. Sometimes our spirit helpers will tell us, show us who we are, or why we are the way we are. Sometimes they will tell us what we must do. But always, they will tell us what we already know to be true in our hearts, because we have already lived it, but don't know it yet."

He pinched the end of the cigarette, and tore it open, sprinkling the remaining flakes on the ground. He tucked the half-burnt paper in his shirt pocket, and snapped the pearl snap. Then he picked up the blankets, and the chokecherry stakes, and resumed trudging up the mountain.

"A true vision isn't always a happy thing, *takoja,"* he said over his shoulder.

Jake shook his head free of memories. He could hardly doubt the trueness of his vision. He had carried the nameless, vague sadness, the sense of profound loss, all his life. The vision exhausted him, yet it was unthinkable to forget about the remaining fourteen stones. Once they are brought back to life, they must be used in the Ceremony. To do otherwise is to inflict grievous insult to the spirits. Yet, he simply didn't want to face whatever visions remained in the stones.

He had learned long ago not to ask "Why?" of the spirits. One simply accepted what was given. But he could not help wondering why they had chosen this moment to reveal the horror of the loss of his wife and children. What could they possibly have to do with a Venus carved thousands of years earlier? Or were they trying to tell him something about himself that he needed to know? He knew the questions would not yield to analysis. The best he could do is hope for illumination sometime in the future. Wearily, he picked up the pitchfork, and carefully stacked the remaining stones on the pile already in the lodge.

Again, the blast of heat and red light. He sensed the spirits crowding around him, filling the lodge with a palpable presence. He beat the slow, solemn cadence of the second song:

Kola le miye ca, wau welo,
Kola le miye ca, wau welo…

Friend, it is I, myself, I am coming,
Friend, it is I, myself, I am coming…

And slipped again into the red spaces between the stones.

He awoke, sprawled on the edge of a bluff, staring at a cloven hoof. He started, rolled away, and came up on his knees. The air around the figure standing in front of him shimmered. He seemed to be surrounded by a faint, rippling light; waves of power rolled out from him. He stood on the shaggy legs of a buffalo, but he had the arms, chest, and head of a man. The ivory horns of a stag sprouted from his head. A wolf-skin cape draped his shoulders; the silver tail hung behind his legs. A massive penis, thick as a sapling, and dark, hung in front.

Black unbound hair swirled over his chest and down his back. Small, grey feathers grew on the left side of his face, like the feathers on an owl's breast. The skin on the right side of his face was smooth, like a man's, but it was dark, mottled in the green and brown patterns of light under trees. They shifted in continual flux. A rattlesnake curled around his left wrist, and he held an eagle wing fan in his right hand. But the eyes were the thing.

They were human, but not human, neither grey, nor hazel, nor entirely gold, but all of them at once, shifting between the colors in response to some inner, unknowable purpose. They gazed at him from the depths of time, otherworldly and remote. He realized he stared at the Shaman of the Hunt, the Power to whom hunters pray.

He motioned with the eagle wing for Jacob to follow. They walked a few yards to where the bluff overlooked a broad green savannah, cut by a wide, clear river. Dark patches of varying shades of brown splotched the plain; Jacob realized they were vast herds of mammoth, bison, and elk. The river curved against the foot of the bluff, and nestled in the curve, lay a cluster of dome-shaped huts.

A cry echoed up from down river. In the distance, Jacob could make out three small figures struggling toward the camp. Two of them supported a third between them. They appeared to be half-carrying, half-dragging an injured person. Behind them and closing fast for the kill, raced two saber-toothed tigers. The big cats ran ahead of the group, and turned, cutting them off. Then they began circling, looking for an opening.

The party consisted of a man, a young boy of about thirteen or fourteen, and a pregnant woman. Her legs were slick with blood and fluid. A child was trying to be born on the open savannah. It was the air, heavy with the scents of blood and fetal fluids, that attracted the cats. The man faced one of them with a heavy spear, hafted with a long obsidian blade; the boy faced the other, with a similar, but smaller spear.

A dozen men from the village, all armed, were running as fast as their legs could carry them toward the surrounded family, shouting.

Suddenly, one of the cats charged the boy, who thrust with his pathetically fragile spear. The cat easily batted it aside, sunk its seven inch fangs in the boy's neck, and tossed him aside in a scarlet spray. The woman managed to stand and scream before the cat disemboweled her with a single swipe of his prodigious paw. When the man turned to defend his wife, the other cat sprang, sunk his fangs in the man's neck and hung on until the flopping stopped.

The baby lay in the grass, still attached to its mother by the blue, pulsing umbilical, until the cat crushed it in its horrible jaws and ran back toward the river. The villagers arrived in time to see the other cat disappear into the underbrush at the edge of the river with the body of the boy.

Jacob wanted to run away from the vision, wanted back in the sweat lodge, but the Shaman tapped him on the shoulder with the fan and turned him around.

Bitter cold bit though his flesh and stiffened his arms and legs. He stood in a gulley, surrounded on three sides by the snow-covered walls of black lava flows. Thick curtains of snow, driven by a howling wind, obscured vision farther than fifty yards. To his right, though the veil of white, Jacob saw that the ravine ended in the black, yawning arch of a low cave. To his left, Jacob heard the panting, labored breath and muted footfalls before he saw the people: a man and a woman on a dead run.

They wore heavy, dark furs, crudely cut into leggings and shirts. Each of them wore a short cape. The woman clutched a child of three or four, similarly dressed, to her chest. In his right hand, the man clutched a bundle of thin spears, or long arrows, and a narrow strip of wood. He carried a leather sack slung over his shoulder—heavy by the way it hung—and two or three other bundles tied around his waist. They were pursued by five hairy men, who were scrambling over the walls of the lava flow, and dropping into the gulley.

About twenty yards in front of the cave, the man turned, dropped the sack, fitted one of the shafts onto the stick, and threw it like a spear, using the stick as a lever. One of the pursuers grunted, and fell, the shaft sticking out of his chest.

The response was immediate and overwhelming. While the man struggled to mount another shaft in the thrower, one, two, three, long, feathered shafts punched him in the chest. He went down wheezing and gurgling, blowing a bloody froth from nose and mouth. The woman shrieked and crawled into the cave.

The pursuers closed rapidly. Three of them began stripping and plundering the body. One rummaged in the sack, and with a cry of triumph, held up a dark red haunch of meat. The other two began fighting him for it.

The fourth pursuer crawled in the cave after the woman. Shortly, a scream echoed out, and he emerged holding the child upside down by its legs. He swung it hard against the basalt, splattering blood and grey matter all over the stone. He tossed the child aside and went back for the woman. He dragged her out kicking and screaming. Once outside, he jerked her upright, and back-handed her once, twice, three times, until she fell on her back in the snow, trying to scoot away. He flipped her on her belly, tore the clothing away, and mounted her. When he finished, he produced a flint knife from among his furs, jerked her head back by the hair, and slit her throat in one savage slash.

Then he stood up, rearranged his firs, and walked to where his companions squabbled over the meat. He held out his hand. They gave it to him.

Jacob turned to the Shaman, who waved the eagle wing fan, and he fell into the darkness of the sweat lodge.

Jake slumped in the cooling sweat lodge, angry, frustrated, cold and puzzled. As a warrior himself, it was difficult to simply watch slaughter and carnage and do nothing, especially the wanton slaughter of a child. He was cold because the rocks had cooled, and along with them, the beads of sweat soaking his body. He shivered, both with cold, and with the intensity of the visions. He was puzzled, because he could see no connection between what he saw and the Venus sticking in the soil in front of him. He sighed, muttered *"Mitakuye oyasin,"* and crawled out of the lodge. To his surprise, the fire burned brightly.

Nicole Haraldsen sat staring open-mouthed at his nakedness. "I threw some more wood on the fire," she said. "It was almost out."

Chapter 7

Two thousand miles north and west of *Makoce Waste*, in the vast mountains of central Alaska, an unknown, and unnamed fault deep in the bedrock beneath the mountains, shifted upward, smashing the massive plate along the Denali fault line sixteen feet higher, and sliding it twenty-nine feet along the opposing Totschunda plate. The energy released was equivalent to exploding one billion tons of TNT.

Eight different mountain sides gave way, burying glaciers in the valleys below under fifteen feet of rock and ice. The earth under the Trans-Alaska pipeline shifted fourteen feet West. Seiche—earthquake-induced water sloshing—knocked houseboats off their moorings at Lake Union in Seattle. The seiche occurred as far south as Lake Pontchartrain in Louisiana. Seismic equipment at the University of Alaska in Fairbanks recorded the earthquake at magnitude 8.2. Shockwaves ripped eastward toward continental United States at 7000 miles an hour.

A hundred miles north and east of *Makoce Waste* most of the tourists in Yellowstone National Park slumbered. The parents who brought their children to watch Old Faithful, and perhaps see a bear, slept peacefully unaware of the incandescent sea of lava writhing beneath them.

Thirty-seven miles long and twenty-five miles wide, the Yellowstone magma body is roughly shaped like a banana lying on its side with the ends pointed up. The points of the banana lie a scant three miles below the surface, which, for most people, is closer than the nearest mall. The banana contains 3600 cubic miles of 2100 F magma. When Mount St. Helen's erupted in 1980, the total volume of the eruption was 2.4 cubic miles. The Yellowstone mass tries to force its way to the surface at pressure a thousand times greater than is found at the bottom of the Mariana Trench, 36,000 feet down in the Pacific.

The bedrock surrounding the magma body is plastic. But sometimes, at the boundary between where the rock is plastic and where it is unyielding, a crack occurs. Two days before the Denali earthquake, just such a crack occurred, fifteen miles northwest of West Yellowstone, Montana, at the Hebgen Lake Fault. As superheated magma wedged its way along the fracture, the rock above it rose explosively. Shock waves radiated outward toward Python in the south, and Yellowstone in the East, at nine times the speed of sound. Sensors registered the magnitude at 5.8. This was the quake that gashed Vassili's cheek and shattered Jake's sculpture. Then it stopped.

But as Nicole gaped at Jake, naked in front of the sweat lodge, the first pulse of waves from the Denali quake slammed the Hebgen Lake Fault and the Yellowstone volcanic basin almost simultaneously. Seismographs in and around Yellowstone immediately began recording swarms of small earthquakes at Norris Geyser Basin, Old Faithful, and West Thumb.

At West Thumb, Black Pool erupted with a column of water eighty feet high. At Old Faithful, Chromatic Spring and Beauty Pool, ordinarily clear, began boiling muddy water, with the domes of the boil reaching eight feet above the pools. At Norris Geyser Basin, near Pearl Geyser, a stream explosion blew out five hundred-sixty-three feet of trail, creating a new fumarole.

Black Growler Steam Vent fell silent. Norris Geyser Basin sank ten centimeters. Near the Hebgen Lake Fault, another quake occurred, approximately seven miles south of the previous one, measuring 4.8 on the Richter scale. Across the border, in Idaho, the land mass beneath the eastern edge of Henry's Lake rose five centimeters.

Telemetry towers at Bull and Greeno dutifully relayed data to a secondary collection tower at Montana State University, which then forwarded it to the University of Utah Seismic Stations in Salt Lake via the Internet.

For the last half hour, Dr. Gopal Deshpar—Desh—to his colleagues at UUSS—had been studying his golden retriever, Tambora. Desh was a small, dark Indian man in his early sixties. He was bald, with a fringe of white above his ears, and wore rimless glasses. The staff teased him occasionally, calling him "Gandhi," or "Mahatma." But he didn't mind, being the good-natured soul he was. Most of the time he quietly went about his business monitoring and predicting earth quakes and volcanic eruptions. But when he spoke in the wonderful, lilting tones of the British-educated Indian, his colleagues listened. He bought Tambora a year after his wife died.

He wasn't sure why he named her "Tambora," after the largest volcanic eruption in recorded history. There was nothing volcanic about her. She had the great-hearted, affectionate disposition of most retrievers, and seemed to live only to please him. She even developed a taste for the firey Indian curries Desh thrived on. She rarely barked, never shit in the house, and seemed content to lie at his feet in the evenings while he read, hoping for a belly scratch. Nevertheless, "Tambora" seemed to fit her. Maybe it was the yellow color.

Tonight she paced the floor, padding to the door and back again, whining. Once, she jumped up, put her paws on the window sill, and barked. Thinking she needed to go out, Desh led her to the back door and out into the yard. The Wasatch massif loomed high and dark behind them. Tammy merely whined and stared northwest, ears cocked forward. They went back inside.

His beeper went off. Desh turned it off, stepped into his study, and accessed the University's seismic station data with his computer. He whistled. "Big one in Alaska," he said out loud. "Big as San Francisco." To Tammy, who stood staring up at him: "Good girl, Tammy, that's a *good girl!*" He looked back at the computer screen. The phone rang. It was Charlie Parker, who was the lead scientist of the Yellowstone Volcano Observatory.

"Desh, you got this?"

"I'm looking at it now."

"What do you think?"

"Well, Alaska was big and set off the swarms in Yellowstone. We've got swarms at Norris, Thumb, and Old Faithful, and a 4.8 at Hebgen. Dramatic, but nothing unusual. Looks like a repeat of the 2002 sequence." A similar earthquake had occurred in Alaska three years earlier.

"Yeah, that's what I'm thinkin', too. Well, send some grad students up there tomorrow to document what kind of changes might have happened. Norris especially."

"Will do, Charlie," Desh said. "I'll be in touch."

They said their goodbyes and rang off.

"Just how did you know about that quake?" Desh asked of the dog.

What Tambora didn't know was that 600 cubic miles of magma had separated from the main Yellowstone mass and was slowly slipping back along a track it had taken 1.3 million years earlier. Back along the Island Park Caldera toward Python.

The motel the Haraldsens stayed in was named "Hooties" because its owner looked like a fat owl. His real name was Woodrow Gillispie. Woodrow's grandfather, Homer, had come to Python at the turn of the century, building the railroad that would soon ship thousands of cattle and sheep to the slaughterhouses east in Chicago. When the '20's roared in, dragging the Volstead Act in behind them, Homer Gillespie's life took one of those curious turns that often accompany what seems to be a small and insignificant decision.

Outraged that he couldn't get his usual pint of whiskey after sweating in the yards all day, he hitched a freight to Helena, Montana, where the boys there fixed him up with half a carload of Canadian whiskey. He only wanted a pint, but the offer was too good to pass up. The downside was that if he didn't pay for it in a month, someone would find his body in a ditch.

The cargo was loaded on a southbound freighter, but before it left, Homer sent a telegram to the yard Superintendent in Python, Greeley McNabb. Greeley, as yard Superintendent of the Oregon Shortline Railroad, and his brother Walter, as the Sheriff, were two of the county's leading citizens. Both of them allowed that "those frock-coated fools" in Washington had no business deciding whether an honest working man could have a drink.

Homer met the two of them at the railroad yard at three in the morning and a deal was struck. The McNabb brothers settled for twenty percent of the take each; Homer got sixty. Greeley would store it in the railroad warehouses, and Walter would quash any competition.

By 1925, Homer had become a rich, if penurious man, spending most of his time in the cigar-smoke-thick back rooms of the Silver Horse Shoe. But he was not idle.

As Americans took to the roads in their shiny new automobiles, increasing numbers of them passed through Python on their way to Yellowstone National Park. So, in 1926 on the corner between the first and second blocks of Python's main street, Homer erected the structure grandly called the "Yellowstone National Park Motor Hotel."

It was fairly innovative for its time. "L" shaped, it contained eight box-like rooms on one side, and six on the other. There was a grassy central courtyard, a couple of picnic tables, and a sandbox for the kids. There was a bath house with hot water and four outhouses tucked discretely out of sight.

Homer's wife, Elisabeth, long since grown waspish and thin with neglect,(she had a face like a straight razor) had, along with Homer's "milk-puking" son, Wilbur, then fifteen, assumed dominion. When the guests arrived in their model T's and later, model A's, it was Elisabeth who slid the register across the counter for the guests to sign, and collected the money: a cabin without a mattress rented for one dollar, a mattress for two people went for an additional twenty-five cents, sheets and pillow cases, an extra fifty-cents. People supplied their own blankets.

Having no husband to speak of, Elisabeth kept Wilbur, a pale, feral-looking boy with sharp teeth, close to her, for comfort. She taught him how to iron sheets, and make beds with hospital corners. Later, Wilbur learned to corner chambermaids on his own.

Homer died suddenly late in 1932. "Looks like his heart just gave out," Sheriff McNabb said sadly.

"Was he playing poker?" Elisabeth asked.

"Yes, ma'am, he was," Walter replied, fiddling with the hat, perched on his knee.

"I'll bet," she said tartly. "Haul him down to Whittaker's Parlor and I'll be there soon as I get my guests settled for the night."

The truth was Homer had been upstairs in the Shoe with his favorite girl, Flatnose Mary. Mary had discreetly informed Jake Macon, the Shoe's proprietor, of Homer's untimely and inconvenient death and Jake had just as discreetly summoned the Sheriff.

Walter had gone directly and quietly to Mary's room. Homer lay naked on the bed, looking pretty much like a beached whale. Folds of flesh fell over his crotch. Walter couldn't see a penis. He asked Mary what happened. She told him. Walter stood there studying the mound of flesh that was Homer Gillespie, idly wondering if he could blackmail a better cut out of Elisabeth. Flatnose stood there in panties and corset looking flat and disgusted.

"Put some clothes on, Mary," he said.

"Oh, yeah," she said, and began rummaging through a pile of clothes on the floor.

Walter shook his head. "How did you do it?" he asked.

"Do what?" Mary replied.

"Well, you know…" he tilted his head toward the body.

Mary snorted, struggling into a pair of bloomers. "It wasn't easy. Like riding a beach ball with a nipple. I earned every goddamned dime I pumped outta that fat, stingy son-of-bitch."

As the years wore on into the depths of the Great Depression, the fractured geometry of Elisabeth and Wilbur's lives solidified into the sharp, jagged angles of a bitter, defeated woman, and Wilbur's cruel, sexual hatred of life. He trapped a chambermaid in one of the rooms, beat her, and raped her. Elisabeth and Walter hushed it up, paying off the girl's parents.

Jake Macon of the Shoe, and all the other tavern owners in town, wouldn't let him set foot in their establishments. So, Wilbur took to disappearing for three or four days at a time, often returning in the early morning hours, sometimes bloody and scratched.

On a sunny June morning in 1937, Elisabeth awoke to discover a cardboard box on her front porch. In it lay a baby boy, with a note crudely scrawled in pencil: *"Here, this here is yourn. Take care of it."* Three days later, they found Wilbur's body floating in the Python. The cause of death was a shotgun blast, at close range, to the crotch.

Sheriff McNabb mounted a half-hearted investigation. Secretly, he was glad the fucker was dead. Saved everybody a lot of trouble. No one was ever brought to trial for the murder of Wilbur Gillespie. There's the law, and then there's justice. As far as McNabb was concerned, it had been done.

At Elisabeth's nasal, whining insistence, he also initiated a search for the baby's mother. That, too, led nowhere, which was surprising, considering the substantial sum the boy was likely to inherit on Elisabeth's death. She badgered Walter constantly about the progress of the search until one day, exasperated, he snapped.

"Goddamn it, 'Lisabeth. It ain't agin' the law to have a baby. It ain't agin' the law to give it up, neither. You and I both know that kid is one of Wilbur's by-blows. Now, he's your kin. Take care of him."

She sighed, dug down in the bedrock of her motherhood, and had him christened Woodrow Sharps Gillespie in the Presbyterian Church. "Sharps," after her grandmother, Eliza Sharps. "Woodrow Sharps Gillespie" had a nice, strong ring to it. She also changed her will.

But Woodrow was anything but strong. Born a raw, big-boned child with double chins, he kept them both all of his life. In fact, in later years, he added another wad of fat beneath the other two. He seemed to acquire fat by the mere act of breathing. By the time he was five, he stood just over three feet and weighed nearly sixty pounds, half again what most kids weighed. By the time he was seven, he stood five feet tall and weighed nearly a hundred pounds.

By then it was clear something was wrong with his eyesight: Woodrow kept bumping into things, and running his bicycle into fences, lamp poles, and other stationary objects. Elisabeth instructed Whimsey Cochran, the widow of a local farmer who committed suicide, whom she had hired to tend Woodrow, to haul him to the optometrist. A week later, Woodrow appeared at school wearing the spectacles with the coke-bottle lenses that, to the onlooker, so cruelly magnified his eyes. By the end of the day, Hootie was the name he would wear, like it or not, for the rest of his life.

In the curious pecking order of the public schools, Hootie had fallen from the little grace he had. He fell from the bottom rung of the white kids, through the various layers of the Mexican hierarchy, past the handful of black kids, who somehow slipped unnoticed, until it was too late, into the cracks of Python's social structure, past the one or two Indians who didn't count, to the very bottom.

It was the children of color who became his most savage tormenters, for Hootie could be mocked, slapped, bullied, and humiliated with impunity. He became their receptacle of shame, the same shame visited upon them from above, by their white classmates. Hootie never forgot, and never forgave.

Elisabeth finally gave up her stringy soul on a bitter cold January day in 1961. Hootie was twenty-four, and weighed in at just over three hundred pounds.

Since he wasn't sure Hootie could make it up the stairs to the second floor above the bank, MacNeish, of Robertson, MacNeish, and Lowell, brought the will to Hootie at the motel. It was duly read.

The next day, Amos Morton, president of the First National Bank, brought the necessary papers for transferring Elisabeth's wealth to Hootie. No one, except Amos, ever knew how much Homer and Elisabeth were worth. Hootie gasped.

The following April, the Yellowstone National Park Motor Hotel was razed, and a brand-spanking new brick, glass, and chrome eighteen-unit motel grew in its place. It was completed by August and the new neon sign read:

Hooties Motel
Clean Reasonable Rates
(No) Vacancy

Most evenings the "no" part of the vacancy sign remained turned off. It remained the only Motel in town until the Best Western moved in across the street in 1984.

Vassili, Tolya, and Anatoly sat in the lounge of the Best Western. The motel was "U"-shaped with three wings. Sam's Café and the lounge, dubbed "The Outlaw," occupied the wing nearest Main Street. The motel office, laundry, housekeeping, and janitorial areas occupied bottom of the "U", at a right angle to Sam's Restaurant. Twenty-four rooms, stacked two deep, took up the remaining wing. By five p.m. the pool in the courtyard usually swarmed with unattended, screaming kids, despite the sign that warned "No lifeguard on duty."

The three men had a clear view of Harald and Nicole's rooms at Hootie's across the street. It was no accident that they were having breakfast at the same time Jake and the Haraldsen's were. They tracked Jake's Hummer from *Makoce Waste* to Sam's on a laptop in Tolya's room. They waited.

Vassili studied a BLM map folded in half, like a newspaper. Anatoly was plugged into what appeared to be a Walkman; Tolya studied the chesty blonde bartender who was busily sliced limes and lemons. Three guys on vacation, relaxing.

About dusk, Nicole and the Professor emerged from the Professor's room, and walked across the street to Sam's. The parking lot at Hootie's began filling up with cars. Husbands and wives hauled luggage and herded children.

Nicole and her father took a booth, and studied the menus Jolene handed out. Vasilli kicked Tolya under the table, who stood up, put a light windbreaker on, and slipped across the street.

Virtually unnoticed in the parking lot commotion, he paused briefly in front of the Professor's room, as if he were fitting the key to the lock. It was an old '60's Schlage. With the slim jim, Tolya opened it as easily as most people open envelopes.

Once inside, he withdrew a small, black rectangular object from his pocket, along with a nine volt battery. He snapped the microphone onto the battery leads, fished around in his other pocket, and withdrew a small roll of duct tape. He lifted the heavy dresser a few inches out from the wall, and taped the package to the back of it. He hefted the dresser back into place.

Back in the lounge, Anatoly slowly spun the dial on the Walkman, apparently searching for a new radio station.

"Anatoly, when you can hear me, come to the window, and stand with your hands on your hips." Tolya repeated the phrase over and over until Anatoly appeared in the lounge window across the street. Tolya checked his watch: eleven minutes.

Vassili turned the map over and studied the other side of it.

Swiftly and professionally, Tolya searched the room, looking for anything that might provide a clue to the location of the site. He paused to scrutinize a topographical map. But it was simply a map of the area. No red "X." He found prescriptions for dilantin and oxycontin in the bathroom, but nothing behind the toilet tank. Eighteen minutes. He emerged from the room and dropped his sunglasses by the rented, white Ford Taurus. Five seconds and the magnetic tracking device clicked into place. The Haraldsen's grazed their way though house salads when Tolya dropped into the chair next to Vassili, who didn't look up.

"Hey, Julie," he yelled over his shoulder. "Vodka tonics." He made a circular motion with his hand. He glanced at Anatoly, who nodded imperceptibly. Bugged and tracked. Tolya resumed his fantasy of Julie.

Eventually, the three men filed into Sam's, had dinner, and retired to their rooms. About nine p.m. Tolya was about to draw to an inside straight when the laptop on the desk chimed. He snapped his fingers at Anatoly, who dialed Vassili's room.

"She's moving," he said, and hung up.

When Vassili arrived moments later, the three of them studied the blinking red dot moving across the map grid.

"How do you know it's just the woman?" Vassili asked.

"Because the old man started snoring fifteen minutes ago." Anatoly had been playing poker, still plugged into to the radio receiver monitoring Haraldsen's room.

"She's going to see the Indian," Vassili said.

"Maybe she's going to screw him into being their guide," Tolya said.

Anatoly smirked; Vassili ignored the remark.

"Do you want me to go out there?" Tolya asked.

Grubinich pondered the question a few moments.

"No," he said finally, "they can't do anything tonight, especially the without the old man." He walked to the door of the room, opened it, and turned with his hand on the knob. "After she returns, shut down for tonight. We begin again at six. Get some rest."

Jake was about to ask Nicole what the hell she thought she was doing intruding on his privacy when the earth rumbled and swayed. She jumped up, ready to run. It was over in eight seconds.

"What was that?" she asked.

Jake thought about saying, "Here's your sign," but he ignored her and turned around to pick up his towel.

While his back was turned, she saw clearly the two craters in his back: one on the left side just beneath his shoulder blade and the other on the right, about seven inches left of his spine, just above his hip. When he turned back around, she saw the corresponding small, white puckers that marked the entry of the bullets.

She also saw the thick slash that arced from just below his left collar bone to just above his right nipple. The fourteen year old Taliban fighter had been hiding inside the cave. The boy's father had lured Jake into it with promises of documents and computers left behind by fleeing Al Qaeda guerillas. The boy just wasn't good enough with a knife, and tried to make his fatal slash too soon. He missed Jake's throat, and Jake shot him with his .45. When the old man fell to his knees praising Allah for martyring his son, Jake slit his throat. What kind of father would wish that on his kid? Fucker.

In the flickering firelight, she also saw the thin white cicatrix circling his neck. Jake barely had time to get his left forearm up in front of his throat before the garrote viciously snared him from behind. His attacker was SAVAMA, Iranian Secret Police. Jake had just finished snapping a series of infrared photos of an Iranian nuclear site at Arak, about a hundred and fifty miles south of Tehran.

Then his sixth sense kicked in, the small voice all soldiers listen to. Without even thinking about it, Jake threw his left forearm up, took a step back and sideways, crouched slightly, rocked his right hip sharply, whipped out his Yarborough, and back-handed the seven inch blade into the soft flesh just above his attacker's pubic bone, pulling upward as he did. When the man gasped and dropped the garrote, Jake continued his pivot, flipped the knife over and rammed it savagely upward, through the soft flesh of the lower jaw and into the brain. Then he slashed the man's throat just to make sure.

The combat lasted less than thirty seconds. But it was long enough for the piano wire to slice Jake's forearm to the bone, and very nearly sever his external jugular.

Nicole stifled the unreasonable urge to reach out and touch the scars.

Wordlessly, Jake picked up the hand drum and walked up to the house. Nicole trailed behind. He took the short flight of steps up to the deck surrounding the back of the house two at a time.

As he opened the door to the screened-in deck, Nicole, still standing at the bottom of the steps, blurted out, "Look, I'm sorry. O.K.? I shouldn't have come out here. I didn't mean to intrude on your ceremony, or whatever. I just wanted to talk to you. I'm sorry. I'll just go."

Jake turned and glared. "You can't 'just go'. You made yourself a part of the Ceremony by walking down there while the fire was burning. The Ceremony's not over until we eat. You have to come in and eat." He opened the door and stood to one side. She hesitated, then bounded up the steps, and brushed in past him. Jake shook his head, and followed.

When Nicole stepped into his home, she wasn't sure if she stood in a cathedral, a museum, or an art gallery. From the outside, the house looked like a massive log Navajo hogan, except for the spacious windows that pierced the walls on each of its eight sides.

The interior of the house wasn't square and cut into little boxes, like *wasicu* houses; it was a tall two-storey cylinder. Nicole stood at the bottom of the cylinder. The walls curved away in either direction, enclosing a circular room a hundred and twenty feet in diameter. They also rose twenty-four feet above her head where eight massive wooden beams came together like a star. To her left, the arc of the wall slid past an open doorway and ended in a wooden stairway that disappeared behind a peeled and varnished log wall that divided the main room from the rest of the house. It extended three quarters of the way across the room, where it abutted a broad, wide staircase that led to a dining area.

A silver carpet covered the floor, silver as in moonlight, and the walls glowed ivory.

The huge room, with all its airy space, was impressive enough, but all the more so because of the central fire pit. A circular area, ten feet across and four feet deep, had been sunk in the main floor. There Jake had built a round, fieldstone fireplace, four feet in diameter and three feet high. A huge metal hood, like an inverted funnel, hung over it, venting smoke through the roof by a double insulated pipe. The pit was accessed by three sets of stairs, four steps each, on the North, West and South sides. He had built-in upholstered benches around the fireplace, creating a sitting area.

Jake eased past Nicole into the fire pit and threw some split logs on the embers already smoldering in the fireplace.

"I'm going to take a quick shower. Look around if you like." He bounded up the steps to the dining area, and disappeared behind the log wall.

A buffalo robe hung on the wall behind the fire pit. As she stepped down into the pit, she stopped, tapped the floor with her boot. She had assumed the flooring was some sort of black tile. But as she looked at it carefully, she saw it was bedrock basalt. Jake had built his fire pit on the living stone.

She walked around the fireplace to study the robe, which had been hung flesh side out. It was entirely covered with little pictures, each depicting a separate scene. Originally the stick men, women, horses, and buffalo had been drawn in bright colors, but they had faded over time. The hide looked ancient, and weathered. Two white wolf pelts flanked the buffalo robe, and higher on the wall, two heavy-looking spears crossed tips above the robe. They, too,

77

had acquired the dark patina of age, and the wood was stained darkly near the tips.

She recrossed the fire pit, still amazed at the basalt, and strolled to the left studying the sculpture displayed on short pedestals, and paintings hanging on the wall. One sculpture caught her attention. It was a small bronze about fourteen inches high. A soldier in battle harness and pack kneeled on both knees. His steel pot lay upside down beside him. An M-16 was slung over his shoulder and his head was bowed. Both arms stretched upward in supplication. The right hand clutched an eagle feather. The body of his comrade lay at his knees.

She browsed on, studying the paintings—all of them had Native American content—until she came to the open door. She peeked in. She saw wall-to-ceiling bookcases filled with books, a massive oak desk, two wing-back leather chairs, a cello on a stand, and another small traditional fireplace. She was tempted to go in, but didn't dare.

She turned and retraced her steps, heading toward the dining area. She was vaguely aware of a shower running somewhere in the depths of the house. She came to a low table. Jake had used river stones as book ends for the only three books on the table: Herbert Mason's verse narrative of *Gilgamesh*, Richmond Lattimore's translation of Homer's *Iliad*, and Robert Fitzgerald's translation of *The Odyssey*. Dog-eared and worn, they were the cheap paperbacks that college students buy, certainly not collector's editions. Curious, she picked up the *Iliad* and opened the front cover. There was an inscription. She glanced around to make sure Jake wasn't watching.

Jake,

Our capacity and skill in killing, when it is necessary, must always be tempered by an even greater restraint and compassion. A soldier must also be life's strongest defender, who, ironically, defends it to the death.

As commanders, we must always be aware that our decisions affect hundreds, even thousands of men whose lives are as valuable as our own. This is a book about war and rage, and its terrible consequences. It is also the seed-story of Western Literature. Study it. We'll talk. Happy Birthday!

Mark

She thumbed through the book's grimy pages. Here and there Jake had turned a corner down, marking a page, and she found comments scribbled in the margins of many pages, as well as underlined passages.

She picked up *The Odyssey*. Again, an inscription on the flyleaf:

Well, buddy, we made it. At times, I had my doubts. This is a story of a soldier trying to find his way home from war. Some scholars say it is the story of man's journey in Western Civilization. I don't know about that, but I do know soldiers have obstacles to overcome before they are really home. I'll be interested to hear what you think of Odysseus' journeying.

Welcome Home, glad you made it, Jake!

Mark

Again, she thumbed through the dog-eared, worn pages and toward the end, she found more underlined passages.When Nicole heard the shower turn off, she hastily put the book back. Five minutes later, when Jake stuck his head around the corner, she sat calmly in front of the fire.

"C'mon up," he said, meaning the dining area. When she walked past the table she saw Jake in the kitchen. He was barefoot, wearing a pair of levis and a white tank top. His hair glistened wetly. He gathered a plastic sack of hard rolls, butter, and a bowl of watermelon and cantaloupe slices in his arms. He put these on the table and then ladled beans and ham into paper bowls, which he put on paper plates.

"Have a seat," he said, serving her. He sat, tasted the beans, and nodded his head in approval. He tore a hard roll in half and buttered it. "Well," he said, "what's on your mind?"

Nicole reached for a roll, and began buttering it. "I don't want you to take my father on this wild goose chase."

"What made you think I was going to, anyway?"

Nicole sat back in her chair, looked him in the eye and said, "Frankly, because you're a mercenary, a soldier. You'll do it for money. This is my father's last chance to prove his stupid theory. What difference does it make to you whether he dies now or nine months from now? It doesn't even really matter if we find anything out there. You win either way. The trouble is, he'll probably die."

"Does this look like the house of a mercenary soldier to you?"

"So you have some talent, and expensive tastes. I know a lot of people like that. And I know your type; I was married to one."

"What type would that be?"

She finished chewing a mouth full of beans and bread before she answered. "The macho-Rambo type, finish the mission and all that. Trouble is everybody else pays. Wherever you guys go, somebody dies, and whoever waits at home lives in fear of the knock on the door."

Jake thought for a moment. He sighed. "Yes, people do die." He scraped the last of his beans out of the bowl. "You still married?"

She looked away. "No, the bastard died somewhere in Iraq."

"I'm sorry. Do you know how?"

"Yes, and I don't care. He didn't have to go; he could have stayed with me. His buddies were more important. It doesn't matter," she said, scraping the bottom of the bowl. "He's dead. History. I've moved on."

"I see that," Jake said. He speared a slice of watermelon with his fork and chewed his way through it, savoring the cool sweetness after the heat of the lodge. Nicole silently finished the other half of her hard roll.

"Just how sick is your father—on a day to day basis, I mean." Jake asked.

"Well, he's as sick as a man gets when he has a terminal glioblastoma eating away at his left temporal lobe."

Jake gave her the "I-asked-you-a-civil-question" look.

Nicole sat forward and rested her elbows on the table. "Most days he's his usual vigorous self. He's been tramping around the world all his life, so he's in good physical condition. About a month ago he started having seizures, and headaches, sometimes, in the mornings. He hasn't had a seizure since he started taking the dilantin. He's doing pretty good, really. But if he doesn't start chemo and radiation he's going to die. If you won't take him on this silly expedition, maybe I can talk him into going into the hospital." She sat back and looked at him.

"O.K.," Jake said. "I won't."

Chapter 8

"Jesus Christ, Hebrew! They found the bodies!" Willie had burst into the Kettle kitchen. Hebrew had just gotten up, and was sitting at the kitchen table scratching his ass, waiting for yesterday's coffee to heat up. Willie threw a newspaper down on the table. Hebrew read the headlines:

Sheriff Investigates Double Homicide

Willie paced back and forth on the worn linoleum whimpering "Oh, Jesus, they's gonna hang me; Oh, Jesus, they's gonna hang me."

"They don't hang people in this state, Willie." Roscoe stood in the doorway. "They shoot 'em, or poison 'em. You ain't gonna hang, Willie," he said, walking into the kitchen. "None of us is."

"But what are we gonna do, General? What if somebody down there in Mex-town saw me with 'em two?"

"Sit down, Willie, 'n have some coffee." Roscoe poured three cups of coffee and set them on the table. Then he dug around in the breast pocket of his bib overalls and produced a pair of reading glasses. He slurped while he read the brief article about the two unidentified bodies pulled from the river.

Hebrew stared into space, sipping his coffee. Willie fidgeted, running his fingers through his greasy hair.

Roscoe took the reading glasses off and folded the paper in half. "Well, did they?"

"Did they what?" Willie asked.

"Did anybody see you with the Mexes?"

Willie frowned, concentrating. Finally, he shook his head. "I don't think so. Ain't nobody lives real close t' their old trailer, down there by the river. Somebody might'a seen my truck comin' or goin', but no, I don't think nobody saw me standin' there with 'em."

"Well, then, you got nuthin' t' worry about, do ya?"

"Not if you say so, General."

"And I do say it, Willie. Th' only thing you got to worry about is goin' off panicky an' half-cocked." He looked at Hebrew.

"Hebrew, you'd best get dressed. We got to he'p Willie, here."
Hebrew had been sitting in his dingy, baggy long underwear. He
took his coffee and left.

"You never did have nuthin' t' worry about, Willie, You know
why?"

"No, sir, I don't," Willie said.

"It's 'cause God Almighty don't care a thing for them soulless
mud people, Willie."

"He don't?"

"No, Willie, He don't. You know why?"

Willie frowned. "No, sir, I can't say as I do. I don't think I ever
knew."

"Well, Willie, it's like this." Roscoe leaned forward in his chair.
"Says right in the Bible on the sixth day God Almighty created the
fishes, 'n the birds, 'n the beasts of the field and man and woman.
An' then He rested on th' seventh day. An' then it says right there in
the Second Chapter of Genesis that on the day after He rested, he
created Adam. Now those first men and wemmen were the mud
people, 'cause he made 'em outta the mud of Creation. Them
colored-skinned folks, them mud-colored folks, is jest like the
beasts. They got no more soul than that ole dog laying out there on
th' porch. Killing them Mexes warn't no different 'n swattin' a
couple of flies."

"It warn't?"

Hebrew came back into the room. He had slipped a pair of bib
overalls over his long johns, and wore a pair of heavy boots. He'd
washed his hair and slicked it back with water.

"'At's the truth, ain't it, Hebrew?"

"'At's the gospel, Roscoe," Hebrew said, filling his coffee cup.

"An' I'll tell you what else, Willie. You 'member the story of
Adam and Eve an' the Serpent?"

Willie brightened. He knew the answer to that one. "I shore
do," he said.

"Well, what nobody ever tole ya was that th' offspring of Eve 'n
the Serpent was Jews."

"She screwed a snake?"

Hebrew shook his head.

Roscoe stared at Willie for a moment. "No, Willie, she didn't
screw no snake. Satan appeared to Eve first as a Serpent, then as a

82

man, an' seduced her. An' th' offspring of Satan an' Eve was th' Jews."

"Oh," Willie said.

"Now, Willie, pay attention. Th' real Israelites, th' true, white sons of Adam and Eve, well, there was twelve tribes of 'em, an' one tribe wandered off. 'At's the lost tribe of Israel. Ya follow me, Willie?"

"Yes, sir, I do."

"Well, 'at lost tribe went north from Israel and eventually wound up in Europe. They crossed them big Caucasian Mountains an' that's why white folks is called "Caucasian." An' since most of our foremothers, and forefathers come from Europe, us good white Americans is the true descendents of th' lost tribe of Israel. An' that's the God's pure truth. Ain't it, Hebrew."

"'At's the God-honest pure truth, Willie."

"Well, I'll be," Willie said.

"Now, Willie—here, Hebrew, gimme some more coffee—let me ast you somethin'. How long did you work for old man Horton up at th' sawmill? Thanks," he said to Hebrew, taking back his cup.

"I worked there seventeen years, 'n never missed a day's work."

"An what didja do there?"

"Why, I run a forklift."

"An' when old man Horton sold 'at mill t'at big corporation outta Seattle, how long was it 'til you got laid off?'

"'Bout six months."

"An' what reason did they give?"

"They said they hadda downsize."

"An' last fall, when they was hirin' agin, didja apply for work?"

"Why, shore, I did."

"How's come ya din't git on, with seventeen years experience, 'n all?"

Willie stared at the floor. "I don't know, Roscoe. I jest don't know." He shook his head sadly.

"Well, how much was you makin' when you worked there?"

"I was makin' my union wage: seventeen dollars an' twenty-eight cents an hour. I was worth it, too."

"I'm sure you was, Willie. Do you know how much 'at very same job, drivin' th' very same fork lift is payin' today?" Willie shook his head.

"Seven dollars an' ten cents an hour. Do you know who is drivin' 'at lift?"

Willie shook his head again.

"His name is Pedro Wetback."

"No." Willie said.

"Yes." Roscoe sat back, scratching his beard, studying Willie. "Hebrew, sweeten Willie's cup."

Hebrew opened the cupboard behind him, pulled out a bottle of Jack, and poured a shot in Willie's coffee cup. Roscoe shook his head when Hebrew offered him the bottle.

"Now, Willie, you got to see the big picture in order t' understand this great work we're a-doin', an' why it's so important. Jest a second; I'll be right back." Roscoe heaved his bulk out of the chair, and disappeared through the doorway.

Willie looked at Hebrew, who shrugged.

Roscoe returned with a magazine, opened to an article titled, *Petroleum Industry Rakes in 10 Billion in Profits.*

He slapped the magazine down on the table in front of Willie. "See this, Willie? Them oil corporations make more 'n three months than some countries make th' whole year. They doin' that while us folks have t' take th' food outta our kids' mouths t' fill up th' truck t' git t' work. Who do you suppose owns them corporations, Willie?"

Willie shook his head.

"Why them Jew stockholders back East in Boston, 'n New York, 'n Philadelphia. So what we got here, Willie, is th' filthy offspring of Satan 'n Eve robbin' us blind on th' one hand, an' the soulless mud people on t'other, stealing our rightful jobs 'n paychecks."

Roscoe leaned forward and tapped the table with his finger. "They's allied agin' us, Willie. Th' enemies of God Hisself is allied agin' us."

Willie gasped. "'At ain't fair. 'At ain't right, Roscoe."

Roscoe shook his head sadly. "No, son, it ain't. An' 'at's why we're preparin' for a war 'at's comin' 'tween us an' the ZOGs."

"What're ZOGs?"

"Zionist-Owned-Government, Willie. Zionist-Owned-Government. Ain't that right, Hebrew?"

"Shore as hell is, Roscoe." Hebrew sweetened his own coffee from the bottle on the counter.

"An' Willie, 'at's also why sellin' Hebrew's pastries t' all them Jew kids an' mud kids is important. If you want t' take a tree out, you gotta chop at th' roots. Weaken it, first. An' Willie, little by little, we're a doin' it. Them pastries you sell, Willie, he'p th' cause. Little by little, we're buildin' an arsenal out t' Zeb's, n' one day, th' Python Militia is a gonna sweep th' streets a Python clean again."

"'At's right," Hebrew said.

"But, what about the Sheriff?" Willie asked.

"Th' Sheriff ain't got God on his side," Hebrew answered.

Roscoe got up and walked to the kitchen window and looked out. Willie's truck sat next to Roscoe's old GMC. He whirled, took two steps, and slammed a fist the size of the end of a railroad tie into Willie's face, knocking him out of the chair. Willie slid up against the kitchen cupboard, bleeding from the nose and mouth.

"Jesus E. Christ! What 'n th' hell got into you, Roscoe?" Hebrew had jumped and spilled his coffee.

Roscoe grabbed Willie by the shirt front and yanked him up. Willie shook his head, trying to clear it, and managed to splatter blood all over Roscoe.

"Goddamnit, Willie! I tole you two days ago t' burn 'at truck and everthang in it. You got to *think,* boy, 'er you're gonna git us all kilt. *Think,* boy. What if somebody did see ya with them Mexes, er saw yer truck. What if they tole th' goddamn Sheriff? Hell, boy, they could be lookin' fer 'at truck right now. An' you led 'em straight here!"

"Oh, God, Roscoe..." Willie wiped his nose with the back of his hand, smearing a streak of blood across his face.

Roscoe stepped to the window and looked out again.

"General, I'll go burn 'at truck right now."

"No, Willie," Roscoe said turning, "it's too late fer 'at now." To Hebrew: "Take th' truck an' lead Willie out t' the old sheep cave, way out there. Member? Where grandpa usta pen up th' sheep, 'n shear 'em?"

"Yeah. I 'member."

"You kin drive his truck all th' way in it, 'n hide it there. Ain't nobody comin' on our property without our say so. It'll be safe 'ere. An here..." Roscoe dug deep in his bib overalls and produced a thick roll of one hundred dollar bills wrapped with a wide rubber band. He counted out twenty-five and handed the wad to Hebrew.

"When ya finish, take Willie down t' old Buster Walthrop's used cars 'n buy 'im another truck 'bout th' same as this un."

"General, I'm sure sorry--."

"Nevermind 'at now, son. Jest git goin'."

Roscoe stood on the porch and watched them convoy across the desert, trailing a plume of dust. "'At's twice, Willie." He shook his head and went inside.

Sheriff Curdy scanned the faces staring at him. Bennie Juarez, Tom Landski, Mo Creighton, Bob Duncan, his chief deputy, Hal Lindsay, Nick Greenwood, and Sheri MacDougal, deputies, all stared back at him. Sanchez was home sleeping after the swing shift. One other officer, Amil Jackson, who worked the graveyard, should have been home sleeping, but stayed for the morning roll call, and the scoop on the floaters.

Looking at them, Tom permitted himself a small moment of pride. The Python County Sheriff's Department was small, but dedicated, well-trained, and professional. And being small, there weren't any secrets. It hadn't taken long for news of Landski's panic to get around. To their very great credit, none of the deputies or other staff had said anything to him, or thought less of him. Being choked by a rotting, cold corpse would shake anybody.

The only weak link in the department was Rick Sanchez. Law enforcement officers are only too human, and Tom knew the kind of pressures a marriage going sour put on a man. He didn't meddle in the private lives of his officers, but he'd heard the rumors, like everyone else, about Jeannette. And he'd seen the anger, and irritability in Rick. He was a pressure cooker that wouldn't take much to explode. Not good for a man who carries a 9 mm Glock.

Tom knew what he owed to Ellie, and their marriage. Like many Viet Nam Vets, he had started the long, slow, slide on booze and drugs when he got back to the world. He drank to sleep, to avoid the nightmares, which came anyway; he took pills to wake up, and so he could drink more. He refused to talk about the war, and sometimes even denied he'd been there. He'd come home in the early morning hours off a drunk and Ellie would find him in the shower, lying in the bottom of the tub, crying.

She worked, rose with the kids, sent them off to school, while Tom played musical jobs. It came to a head eighteen months after he came home. He had finally stumbled home after a three day drunk and passed out on the living room floor. He hadn't shaved or bathed in a week. When he came to, Ellie was sitting on the couch watching him.

He sat up, wishing he had a glass of water to flush the dead cats out of his mouth. "Get me a glass of water, will you, hon?"

"No, Tom, I won't."

"Well, what the fuck's the matter with you? Never mind, I'll get it myself."

He got up and stumbled into the bathroom. Ellie followed him.

"You're what's the matter with me. The kids saw you on the living room floor this morning. They wanted to know what was wrong with you, Tom. So do I." She leaned against the door jam.

He drank a glass of water, then filled the glass up again.

"Tom!" She cried out. "I don't know how to help you. Tommy, baby, I don't know what to do." She beat on his chest with her small fists, slid to the floor, sat with her back up against the bathtub, sobbing.

Tom slid down beside her, buried his face in his hands and wept. "Ellie, I don't *know* what is happening to me; all I want to do is run away and drink."

"Tom, you can't. You just can't." She cradled his head on her shoulder, rocked him while he wept. After a while, she kissed him on the forehead and said, "There's somebody here to see you."

Tom looked up at her and said, "Who the fuck would want—." A shadow fell across the doorway.

The man who filled the door frame stood six-four and wore a black motorcycle jacket, white tee-shirt, levis, and heavy boots. Bronze-brown skin glowed, revealing his Cherokee-Hispanic origins.

"Hey, Mack," he said, grinning. He held something in his left hand, concealed beneath his jacket.

"Shota! You son of a bitch!" Tom grinned through the tears streaking his face.

"What'chu doing, down there on the floor, boy?" Ain't no place for a Ranger." Tom made to get up.

"No," Shota said, "I'll come down." The two men hugged each other, slapped each other on the back, and sat back beaming.

The three of them sat in a circle on the bathroom floor. Shota withdrew a fifth of Jack Daniels Black and set it on the floor.

"Shota—." The brown man cut Ellie off with a fierce "I-know-what-I-am-doing" look.

"God, yes," Tom said, "let's have a drink," and reached for the bottle.

Shota's dark hand clamped down on it. "There'll be time enough for that, brother, but first you gotta hear what I have t'say." His obsidian eyes stopped Tom dead.

"Oh, fuck! Don't start, Shota."

"Hold on, now, brother. I ain't gonna say anything you don't already know. Am I right?"

Tom sat looking his hands, clenched on his lap.

"You got to talk about it, Mack. You got to get it out. You got to tell your woman here, what's eatin' you alive. Haven't said a word, have ya."

Tom shook his head. "I can't," he croaked.

Shota reached out with a hand on Tom's shoulder; Ellie took one of his hands.

Tom glared, first at Shota, and then Ellie. "I don't want to talk about it. Goddamnit! I don't want to talk about it." He tried to stand up.

Shota ripped his tee-shirt up, revealing the half-inch wide, jagged scar that ran diagonally from his belly button up to his arm pit. "You can start by telling her how I got this," he said.

Tom sat, staring vacantly at the scar.

"If you don't, I will," Shota warned.

Tom stared directly ahead. "I can't."

"We was on a recon about fifteen klicks outside a Pleiku. Word was there was a big NVA buildup and we were supposed to check it out. Well, they were buildin' up, all right, 'n we walked into the Mother of All Ambushes. Mortars, RDP machine guns, AK 47's...it was a regular killing field. This—he traced his scar—was compliments of 60 millimeter mortar shrapnel, an' about three 7.62 rounds. Felt like getting' whacked with a baseball bat real fast, bapbapbap."

Ellie looked away, choking back a sob.

"Ellie, you got to stay with me. You got to hear this for his sake, 'n for your sake. Now, look at me."

Ellie looked up, wiping her eyes with her palms.

"You got to be there, to understand. But I'll try to explain it, anyways. I was sneakin' along an' all of a sudden smacksmacksmack—sounds like slapping cold steak with the flat of a knife—when the bullets hit, an' then the explosions of the mortars, smoke and flame and dust. Shit, I couldn't figure out what happened. I couldn't hear, couldn't breathe. But I could smell the goddamn cordite—gunpowder. It coats your tongue, and the back of your throat. And somewhere far away I hear this screaming."

He stopped, gazed up at the ceiling, drew a deep, ragged breath, swallowed.

"I tried to get up, but I couldn't. I just lay there feeling the wet on my sides and legs and smelling this stink, kinda like shit—it's a warm, moist, animal smell—like shit, and blood and something else. Somebody long ways away was screamin' and I wanted him to stop, an' the explosions to stop, so I could just lay there an' go to sleep, you know. But he wouldn't shut up. It was me."

He picked up the bottle of Jack, hefted it, stared at it. "Shit, Mack, some days I just wanna drink this whole fuckin' jug." He shook his head.

"Well, anyways," he continued, "I was laying there when out of th' smoke and dust, Mack, here, just appeared. I mean he was just *there.* An' all this time shrapnel was whining by and AK 47 rounds are whipping, and buzzing like hornets. Well, he grabbed me by the collar and drug me outta the line of fire. He plugged me up the best he could. And I'm sitting here, now, alive, Ellie, because of him." He kicked Tom's toe with his boot.

She squeezed Tom's hand.

"But here's what you don't know, sugar. This man, here, your husband, went back into that hell three more times an' did the same thing for three other brothers, before he got nailed by that Chink 60."

A sob escaped Ellie's lips.

"That's right, honey. He got fragged trying to save his brothers. He's a hero, but he don't feel like no hero, do ya, Mack."

Tom sat silently, staring at his hands, gritting his teeth.

"The thing is, Ellie, he ain't thinkin' 'bout the four of us he yanked outta there. He's thinkin' 'bout the two he didn't. That right, Mack?"

And then a thin, animal sound seeped between the clenched teeth; the small, tiny cry of a dying thing lapped over the dam holding back the black waters of his unutterable anguish. And then the dam itself crumbled, folded in on itself, and the blocked, dark water burst out.

Tom lay on the bathroom floor, heaving the great, racking sobs of killing sorrow.

Shota rose quietly, gave her a card with his phone number, and silently departed, leaving the bottle behind.

Ellie sat with him, rocking him on the bathroom floor, until the heaving died away in a long, slow, sigh. Then she stripped the stinking clothes from his body, stripped herself, and put him in the shower. The two of them lingered in the steaming water, she kissing Tom's own cruel scars, he chanting, "I'm so sorry, baby; I'm so sorry, baby." And so Tom Curdy began the long journey home from war with a woman's kiss.

"Hey, Tom!" He heard the voice from a great distance. "Tom, buddy." Landski waved his hands; snapped his fingers. Tom came back from the shower to the room of assembled officers.

"Oh, sorry," Tom said. "Everybody here?" he asked. They all looked at each other, then at him, nodding.

"Well," he cleared his throat. "By now you know about the two John Does we got outta the river yesterday. Here's where we are: Yesterday evening about twenty-hundred hours, officer Sanchez discovered the body of a juvenile male, probably fifteen or sixteen, in the Python River, near the Narrows Bridge. In the process of recovering the body, Officer Landski subsequently discovered a second body, a middle-aged woman, fortyish, tied to the first body. Time in the water about twenty-four hours. That right, Mo?"

"About, yeah." Mo shifted in his seat.

Both subjects appear to be of Hispanic origin. No identifying papers. Nothing. Cause of death appears to be the result of massive trauma caused by being dragged behind a motor vehicle."

"Jesus," Sherri gasped, "how do you know that?"

"Mo," Tom said.

"Because one of the victims was tied at the wrist with heavy hemp rope, and the flesh had been abraded from their underarms, faces, thighs, backs, and heels. We also found red cinder, typical of the Red Road imbedded in the remaining flesh. Somebody dragged those two to death, and threw them in the river."

To Tom: "You gonna try to get Mary over here to do a reconstruction?" Mary was an artist who occasionally helped out the PCSD with sketches of suspects. She lived across the Tetons in Jackson.

"We'll try, but don't expect much. Bob, I want you to call Mary, and ask her to drive over and see what she thinks. I don't know if she can do much—not much left of their faces. Tell her we'll pay her per diem for the drive over."

Duncan nodded, writing in a notebook.

"Bob, I also want you to get on the Tri-County network an' see if there's any missing persons bulletins that might identify these two."

Nick Greenwood piped up. "Any evidence where you got them out of the river?"

"Not that we could see last night. It was getting too dark. But Joe, take Sherri with you, and you and Sherri and Mo go back out there and finish working the crime scene. Bobby Wilson and the boys at the State Police kept it secure last night, and," he looked at his watch, "they're probably waiting for some relief. Mo, you're gonna get the prints to AFIS, right?"

"Yeah. If we get good prints."

"How soon is the pathologist coming up?"

"He said last night he'd be here this afternoon," Mo said.

"Hal and Nick, I want you to check out the West Road that runs up along the river by the bridge. I don't know what to tell you to look for, but look anyway. Tire tracks, footprints, you know the drill."

To all of them: "Unless somebody reports these people missing or we get good prints and luck out, this could be a tough one. Let's crack."

Shirley, a part-time secretary, stuck her head in the door. "Tom, PHARK's on the phone."

"Shit!" Tom swore. "Tell him I'll call him back in about twenty minutes.

PHARK was the department acronym for Herb, The Public Has A Right to Know, Witherspoon, the editor/publisher of the *Python Gazette*. He was a pain in the ass who still wore bow ties, tweeds, and a frumpy straw hat with a card proclaiming "Press" in the hatband. Tom suspected he still smoked Chesterfield straights.

Tom went back to his office and punched the intercom button. "Shirley, when Rick comes on shift, ask him to step in and see me before he goes on patrol. Right. Thanks."

He swiveled around in his chair to face the credenza behind his desk. On it were pictures of Ellie and the kids, and the unopened bottle of Jack Daniels—the one Shota left behind. Every day the choice was the same: Ellie and the kids, or the bottle. He'd have a talk with Rick to see how things were, and then send him nosing around the *barrio* to see what he could turn up.

Two wolves, silver in the faint moonlight, of Makoce Waste, loped past the sweat lodge, now quiet and dark, up the grassy slope and slipped into Jake's house. They stopped where Jake and Nicole had stood hours earlier. The two wolf skins behind the fire pit rippled.

The male, slightly larger than the female, bounded right, up the stairs to the dining area. The female loped left, up the wooden stairs and into Jake's bedroom.

"We're here," she said in Jake's mind. She jumped up, putting her front paws on the edge of his bed. He felt the weight of her, and a soaring joy, along with a sense of safety and belonging the wolves brought with them. The big male padded into the bedroom, and he, too, jumped up, put his paws on the edge of the bed.

"Hau, Isnala Mani, hokahey! She wants you." The wolves dropped off the bed, loped from the room. Jake's white wolf spirit flowed from the bed, and followed.

He paused at the edge of the deck. The two wolves waited, standing shoulder to shoulder, below on the grass. He looked out over Makoce Waste, the grass, the trees, the river, and the great desert beyond, silver in the moonlight. He filled his deep, clean lungs. He took in the rich loamy scent of the earth beneath the grass; the dry, dustiness of the mice beneath the steps; the pungent, clean bite of the pines; the soft, powdery sweetness of the aspens; the thick, meaty flavor of the squirrel the owl perched in the cottonwoods gulped; and the mossy, liquid trail of fish and mud rising off the river.

He tipped his head back and howled the long, trailing cry of the wolf at the fingernail moon. Then he leaped off the deck into his two companions, bowling them over. Jake crouched on his forelegs, head low, tail high and wagging. The big male recovered himself, lunged at Jake, who took off like a shot, racing away. The female ambushed him from behind, sending him rolling. She padded a few feet away, and stood, grinning over her shoulder. The male blind-sided her, knocking her back into Jake. He nipped her shoulder, leaped straight into the air, and pounced on the male, who stood stupidly grinning, tongue lolling. The female jumped up quick, nailed Jake from behind, and they all fell in a pile of wagging tails, and licking tongues. Jake snuggled down between them, heady with the scents of fur, warmth, and wolf.

The owl dropped the squirrel carcass, hooted her disapproval at the foolishness, and silently winged away into the darkness. The three of them lay for a while, reveling in the rich scents of earth and grass, and of themselves. Then the big male jumped to his feet, looked across the river, and said, "Hokahey!" He led, the female followed, and Jake brought up the rear. They loped toward the river, leaped down the embankment, and without any hesitation, trotted across the water, their paws dimpling the surface. Across the river, they passed a farm house, and a terrier yapped, banging the end of his chain.

"Be quiet, little brother," the big male said, and the yapping subsided into a whine.

When they reached the edge of the desert, they broke into the loping run wolves use to cover great distances. On and on they ran, skimming the sharp, broken lava, deep into the desert under a razor-thin moon. Once they spooked herd of antelope sleeping in the grassy bottom of a lava dome crater. The herd jumped and spilled over the lip of the crater like coffee poured from a cup. They ran a safe distance and turned to look, large liquid eyes glimmering in the starlight.

"Not tonight, brothers," the big male said.

On and on they ran, eating the miles with long graceful strides, until they came to a large lava dome rising out of the desert floor like a mushroom cap. When they reached the top, they sat, and looked below.

A narrow corridor of basalt led to a wide, low cave. A faint flicker of firelight licked the entrance. His companions turned to him and said, "Toksa ake, Isnala Mani," and melted into the darkness, leaving Jake alone on the dome. He waited, staring at the entrance.

Then the air shimmered; the lava, the pinyons, and the sage, shifted, separated, and coalesced into the form of a woman standing beside him.

She wore the kindly, weathered face of a grandmother; the flesh around her eyes spiderwebbed when she smiled at him. She touched him with a soft, warm hand and he quivered.

She wore a white buckskin dress; long fringes danced from the sleeves. Her hair was parted in the middle and two long grey braids hung over her breasts. She carried a sprig of sage in her left hand.

For a long moment, she stared at the cave, and finally looked back at Jake with a great, sad face. She sighed. "They are the last," She said. She stuck the spring of sage in his fur. "It's up to you." The air shimmered, and she dissolved away into the earth from which she had come.

Jake bolted upright in bed, and stared at his hands. They were the ordinary hands of a man. He looked around the room: the bedroom was the same as it always was. Out the window, in the East, the sun pinked the tips of the Tetons. He flopped back down reliving the crystal clarity of the dream / vision / experience — whatever it was.

His brother and sister wolves had summoned him, calling him *Isnala Mani*, Walks Alone, and he had answered. It seemed so natural, so right, as if being a wolf were his ordinary state, yet here in the clear light of morning, he was undeniably a man, the same old Jake Two Feathers.

And the Grandmother. She was not his maternal grandmother, but *the Grandmother*, and she had summoned him to make a choice: to protect—. Jake cringed inwardly at his own stupidity. Of course. All the people in his sweat lodge visions had needed protection from something or someone larger and stronger than they were.

In the oblique and subtle way of the spirits, the Grandmother reminded him of who and what he was: a warrior, whose duty it was to protect the old, the young, the weak, the infirm.

Jake leapt out of bed, threw on some sweats and a pair of moccasins, and trooped through the dew-wet grass to the grove of cottonwoods. He searched beneath the trees and found the squirrel carcass about where he thought it would be. He went back to the house, into the bedroom, and checked the clock on the night stand: 7:45 A.M.—too early to call Haraldsen. He would take a quick shower and then call. He started to straighten the bedding and stopped. A sprig of sage lay among the rumpled sheets.

Nicole was going to be one pissed-off white woman.

Chapter 9

Vassili Grubinich had just stepped out of the shower when his laptop chimed. He padded across the room bare-footed, with a towel wrapped around his waist: an e-mail from Black Tulips. He logged on and read:

INTERCEPT ON HARALDSEN'S PHONE REVEALS TWO FEATHERS AGREED TO GUIDE. EMPHASIZE THREAT TO PROJECT. WE MUST CONSIDER TERMINATING HIM.

Grubinich grunted, thought for a moment, and typed:

"Have you located the site?"

STILL SCANNING WITH GRAVITOMETER. EXPECT RESULTS WITHIN ONE WEEK.

"First, contract calls for termination of two individuals. A third will require additional payment, with half in Zurich account. Second, if reasonably sure you will locate site, suggest termination all three." He sat in his towel, staring at the blinking cursor. He sat a full minute before the reply came:

NEGATIVE ON ALL THREE. TERMINATE TWO FEATHERS. NO WITNESSES. NO QUESTIONS. IT MAY BECOME NECESSARY TO INTERROGATE THE HARALDSENS.

"As you wish. And the money?"

AN ADDITIONAL $250,000.00 USD HAS BEEN DEPOSITED TO YOUR ACCOUNT IN ZURICH.

"With an additional $750,000.00 due when the contract is fulfilled?"

THAT IS CORRECT.

"Pleasure doing business with you."

WITH YOU, AS WELL. HOWEVER, YOU ARE AWARE OF SANCTIONS ENFORCED FOR BREACH OF CONTRACT?

Grubinich laughed out loud, and typed:

"Yes, of course. Not to worry." He'd like to see them try.

ELIMINATE THE GUIDE WITHIN ONE WEEK.

"I will eliminate him when the time is appropriate; that is my call, not yours."

JUST SEE THAT IT IS DONE QUICKLY. OUT.

Grubinich logged off. The phone rang.

"The Indian is moving," Tolya said.

"I'll be there in five minutes."

"Son-of-a-bitch! That son-of-a-bitch!" Nicole sat on the edge of her father's bed in a tee-shirt and levis, hair dripping.

Haraldsen had summoned her to his room after Jake called with the news he would guide them."What do you mean, Nicole. He's going to help us."

"Help us what?" Nicole fired back. "Help us kill you? Great. He said he wouldn't do that."

"What do you mean, 'He said he wouldn't do that?'" Haraldsen stood up from the chair and joined Nicole on the edge of the bed. "What did you do?"

"I went to see him last night to ask him not to take you out on the Anvil."

Haraldsen threw her a withering look and started to stand.

"No! Listen to me." Nicole pulled him back down on the bed.

"Dad, you're dying. Don't you get it? If you don't start chemo—surgery—something, you are going to die. And if you go out there—," she flung her arm toward the Anvil—"you will die."

"Nicole. Nicole, look at me."

She stared at the bedspread, tracing patterns with a red fingernail. He tilted her chin up towards him with his palm.

"You're right. I *am* going to die." He dropped his hand to his lap. "It doesn't matter what I do, honey, whether I go or whether I don't. I-am-going-to-die." He pulled a leather thong from around his neck. A red felt bundle dangled from it. "Look at this," he said, and unwrapped the felt.

The object lying in the center of the red felt was a prehistoric knife. The handle, which was dark brown mammoth tusk, had been hafted to a blade, about four inches long. But the blade was unlike any blade anyone had ever seen, including Haraldsen, with his many years' archeological experience. It was shaped like a willow leaf, slender and delicate, slightly convex on both sides, and tapered to a sharp point. But it showed none of the usual grooves of a knapped blade; it was perfectly smooth, perfectly polished to its finished shape. And it was crystal clear, glittering, except for a few dark inclusions of carbon.

"*Look* at this, Nicole." Haraldsen held the knife reverently in his palms. "It represents an entirely new order of technology among ancient people. Proof positive of ancient people using diamond technology. The only way this could have been made," he held it up with one hand, " the *only* way this could have been made is by using one diamond to shape another. Incredible." Haraldsen shook his head, eyes glittering. "Think of the size that diamond crystal must have been."

Nicole stared at her father. "But how do you know it came from the Anvil?"

"I don't, Nick, but the bone carbon-dates at 10,700 years. And look at the shape of the blade: same shape as Solutrean points. Don't forget, the Solutreans were the first, the *first* to make quantum leaps in blade technology."

"But is it worth risking your life?"

"Nick, it *is* my life, my whole life. Do you think I want to end it in a hospital bed puking my guts out on chemotherapy, with tubes and needles sticking out of me, sucking on a respirator? No thanks. With any luck, I will die out there, after we've found the site, and I've excavated it. And you've pocketed two or three pounds of these diamonds. He carefully wrapped the knife back up in the red felt.

"Dad, I make six figures at Merrill-Lynch. I don't need money. I need you."

"And you have me, Nick, as I have always been—not in some damn hospital bed. "Here," he said, handing her the bundle, "just in case something does happen to me, you'll have this. It's worth its weight in diamonds." He grinned. "Wear it around your neck; there are people who would kill for it."

Someone knocked on the door.

"There's Jake. Nick, we're about to make the discovery of the century." Haraldsen rose to answer the door. Nicole hung the blade around her neck.

"He's across the street," Tolya said. The three of them, Vassili, Tolya, and Anatoly stood around the laptop. Anatoly had abandoned his headset, monitoring the room, to watch the locator on the laptop. He had not heard what had passed between Nicole and Harald.

"Anatoly, get on your head set," Vassili ordered. "We must know what they are planning and when." To both of them: "We have a new task. We must take out the Indian."

Tolya grinned.

Jesus Romero sat patiently in a stand of willows bordering the Python River. He was quite comfortable nestled in the willows, for, in his fifty-seven years, he had often found refuge among them along the Rio Grande, the Rio Bravo, the Hondo, the Arkansas, Colorado, and now the Python, Rivers.

Most often, the thick stands of slender, lance-leaved bushes hid him from the green and white SUV's of the INS, but there had been other times when the friendly thickets and rivers had hidden him from assorted sheriffs and from the officials of one very nasty prison in Georgia.

Jesus Romero did not consider himself a criminal, but rather a gentleman traveler, a sojourning philosopher-poet, who, according to the mutability of fortune, was occasionally obliged to indulge in minor pilfering, pick-pocketing, and robberies of the harmless sort. He abhorred violence, preferring to practice the arts of love, and his occasional brush with the law usually stemmed from something involving a woman, like having money to pay her.

In truly dire circumstances, and when he wanted to hide, he found small out-of-the-way ranches or farms to hire himself out to, which benefited from his considerable knowledge of horses, cattle, sheep, and pigs. Jesus had not yet sunk to the level of tending chickens.

He had gained his considerable knowledge of livestock in the Northern Mexican state of Coahuila, where his father moved from ranch to ranch as an itinerant *vaquero*. Jesus naturally adopted the trade, and might have stayed happily at *El Rancho Moreno*, had not *el jefe's* daughter, a comely black-haired wench, turned up in a family way. He was forced to flee for the sake of his precious *cojones*, if not his life. He had been fleeing, more or less, ever since.

Under different circumstances, he might have enjoyed lying in the willows, relishing the fine, clear weather of a June afternoon, perhaps even composing a few lines of poetry in the spiral notebook he always carried, along with two stubby pencils.

But Jesus was worried. He had arrived two nights ago in time to see the vanishing tail-lights of a pick-up truck. He wasn't quite sure, but he thought Rosa and her son, Miguelito were in it. He had met Rosa several months earlier in the local cantina, *El Guerro Negro*. They shared a pitcher of sangria; Rosa flirted; Jesus responded; a price was negotiated; they retired the short distance to Rosa's trailer by the river, and Jesus became a regular—when he possessed the funds.

Over the months, he developed an affection for Rosa, and eventually their relationship creeped beyond the merely professional. Their pillow talk covered a wide range of subjects: their early lives in Mexico, their separate adventures with the INS, stupid *gringos*, and Rosa's fears about her son, Miguelito.

He said he worked for the *gringo*, Willie Jensen, but gave only vague answers about what, exactly, he did, when she questioned him. He slept late in the mornings, hung around pool halls when he was awake, and seldom came home before three or four in the morning, yet always seemed to have money. Occasionally, Willie's battered Ford pick-up rattled down the short lane to the trailer, where Miguelito and Jensen held short conferences, always shielded from Rosa's eyes by the truck.

"I think he is selling the *gringo's* drugs," she confided.

And so, when Jesus saw Rick Sanchez's cruiser thump down the lane and into the yard, his heart sank. Something had happened, but what?

Sanchez went to the door, knocked, and when he got no answer, walked around to the back of the trailer.

Jesus dug out his little notebook, scribbled something, darted out of the willows and left a slip of paper under the windshield wiper on the driver's side.

Later, walking through town, Jesus saw the headlines through the window of a coin-operated newspaper box. He shook his head sadly; it was time to move on.

Rick Sanchez drove his cruiser in the gravel parking lot of *El Guerro Negro*, turned the ignition off and sat. He tried to sort out the conflicting emotions that savaged his mind.

"Things goin' O.K. at home?" Tom had asked.

"Yeah, why?" Rick answered.

"Well, you've seemed a little irritable and preoccupied for the last three or four months, Rick." Tom sat back in his chair. "Seems like something's been eating at you. Anything I can do?"

Sanchez schooled his face not to react, but inwardly he cringed. Was he that obvious? He shook his head. "No, nothing in particular. The usual hassle with the kids." He shifted uneasily in the chair in front of Tom's desk, embarrassed.

"Yeah. I know." Tom grinned. "They can be the shits. Makes you wonder why you had 'em. Well, you're a good cop, Rick. I just wanted you to know that if you need anything—time off—my door's always open. We'll work something out."

"Thanks. I'm O.K.," Sanchez answered.

Tom moved on to the subject of the two floaters.

Rick sat in the cruiser, listening to the ticking of the engine cooling. The two things that held his life together, his family and his job, were unraveling around him, and there was nothing he could do about it. He tried to shake the shame he felt; maybe he *was* a loser. What kind of man would take his wife back—even if she had cheated on him? But he knew he would, gladly, if he could only see the love and admiration in Jeannette's eyes he had once seen.

He tried to curl up around her last night in bed; she pushed him away. This morning her eyes dripped with contempt.

He pounded the steering wheel with his fist. He *had* to get her back! He just had to! But he didn't know how. Well, he knew how: money. He just didn't know where to get the money.

And Curdy. The Sheriff had as good as admitted he knew about Jeannette and implied Rick wasn't doing his job. Fuck him. He lay his life on the line every day for the miserable salary he got. If he were paid a decent wage, he wouldn't be in this fix. Fuck Curdy. Fuck this job. After seventeen years, they owed him. He fumed for a moment staring at *El Cantina Guerro Negro.*

It occupied the corner lot of a seedy, weedy, mostly uninhabited block on the outskirts of the city most people unkindly called "Mex-Town." Black, stylized Aztec warriors flanked the door to the white stuccoed building. Above the door, green, arching script spelled out *"El Cantina Guerro Negro."* On either side of the door, barred windows looked out on the parking lot. In one window, a blue neon sailfish advertised *Cerveza Pacifico;* in the other, a red neon parrot perched on the final "a" of a blue neon *"Corona."* Two wretched-looking day laborers sat on a wooden bench beneath the windows watching Rick. He got out of the cruiser and crunched across the gravel toward them.

"What the fuck you lookin' at?" he growled.

They grinned, and shrugged.

"*Levantarse ahora!*" he yelled. "Stand up! *Saque su identificación!* Take out your indentification."

The two men quit grinning and hastily reached for their wallets.

Rick hovered over them, hands on hips, bristling. One of them showed him a current driver's license, the other a state I.D. card.

He returned their wallets and said, "*Salgas de aqui,* get out of here!" The two took off, leaving half-finished beers on the bench. He felt like kicking the front door in, but opened it instead, and marched in.

Hector Enrique, the proprietor and bartender, a huge man with a Poncho Villa mustache, and black, slicked-back hair, slouched behind the counter, resting the two logs of meat that he called arms, on the bar. A toothpick stuck out the corner of his mouth.

"Ricardo," he said, tilting his head toward the departing men, "how come ju run off my customers?"

"Because I felt like it," he said, straddling a stool. "And don't call me 'Ricardo.'" He slipped a couple of one dollar bills on the counter.

Hector heaved his bulk off the bar, reached into the cooler, extracted a *Corona*, and set it in front of Rick, sliding the bills back toward the law man. He leaned against the back bar, crossed his meaty arms, flicked the toothpick to the other corner of his mouth.

Rick lit a Marlboro with his zippo, took a deep pull on the beer, and set it down, slowly twirling the bottle.

Hector stared at him, waiting.

The front door opened, momentarily flooding the dim interior with light. When the two men saw Rick sitting at the bar, they backed out, closing the door behind them.

"What 'chu want, *Rick*. Ju bad for business," Hector said.

Rick took another long pull on the bottle. "Gimme a shot of *Cuervo*."

Hector poured the shot, picked up the two one-dollar bills, and said, "I need two more dollars."

Rick glared at him, fished out the two bucks and threw them on the bar. He tossed down the shot and followed it with a swig of beer. "You hear of anybody missing down here?"

"Missing? What 'chu mean 'missing'?"

"Missing. Absent. Not where they're supposed to be. Gone. Nobody's seen 'em. Understand?" Rick dug down in his pocket, produced four more dollar bills. "Gimme another shot."

Hector poured it from the bottle into the empty shot glass on the bar, collected the bills. "People come, people go." He shrugged his massive shoulders. "Ain't seen Rosa in a coupla days."

"Rosa?"

"*Si.* Rosa Gonzales. *La viuda verde.* Lives in that trailer down by the river with her son. Usually she's in here alla time. Ain't seen her in a coupla days." Hector shrugged.

Rick eyed Hector for a long moment, finished his beer, and put out his cigarette. "It's against the law not to report illegal immigrants."

Hector gave him the "Yeah-so-what?"look.

Rick turned on his heel and left. Hector flipped his departing back the finger, and began wiping down the bar.

The trailer Hector mentioned was only about four blocks from the bar. It sat at a forty-five degree angle to the river. A thick brake of willows bordered the water and made a sort of fence for what could loosely be called a front yard. A worn footpath led down-river to the crumbling remains of the once teeming stock yards. Generations of Pythonians had used it to walk to work in more prosperous days. Now, generations of illegal *vaqueros*, sheep herders, and farm hands used it to slink through the city to the greener labor markets in Montana.

Rick parked the cruiser and got out. The place certainly looked deserted. He walked up the rickety wooden steps, opened the storm door that had the lower panel kicked out, and knocked. After a minute he knocked again. Rick didn't hear any movement inside.

He made his way around to the back of the trailer hoping to find a window to look in. He found a blue nylon milk case in the weeds and stood on it, peering through what was the kitchen window. A half-empty bottle of *Tecate* sat on the tiny kitchen table along with a black plastic ashtray half-filled with butts, and a pack of generic cigarettes. He tapped on the window and waited. No response. He jumped down from the milk case and made his way back around front.

Well, it looked lived in. Maybe they just weren't home or away visiting relatives or something. Two days didn't make for missing persons. Rick was already sitting in his cruiser when he saw the note. He climbed out and retrieved it from the windshield. It read, *Willie Jensen took them.*

Chapter 10

Gopal Desphar walked briskly from the conference room, carrying a pile of computer print-outs clutched to his chest. A mob of excited graduate students followed him out of the room buzzing about the quake in Alaska, and its possible effects on Yellowstone. Four lucky ones, two young men and two young women, whom Desh suspected had become items in grad school, had been assigned to leave immediately for Yellowstone. The mob went one noisy direction, while he went to the peace and quiet of his office.

Desh spent the next two blissful, uninterrupted hours pouring over the telemetry from Yellowstone. It was as he had told Charlie Parker: pretty much the same scenario as the big quake two years earlier in Alaska. The swarms had subsided overnight, and even though there was a new fumarole, such changes were to be expected. By its very nature, volcanic activity was inconstant and difficult as hell to predict. He had instructed the students to check out the Hebgen Lake Fault, too, and to leave some gas sensors along the fault line. Desh was curious to discover if there was any magma activity. All in all, the telemetry, at least, showed nothing significant had changed in Yellowstone, a burp, maybe, but nothing more.

One detail nagged him, though: the ten centimeter drop in elevation of portions of Norris Geyser Basin. A ten centimeter drop of approximately 500 acres wasn't much, but still, it was significant. What had happened? If the magma pod had changed shape, migrated, or risen toward the surface, there would be a corresponding bulge elsewhere. But there wasn't—at least none the telemetry showed.

The problem was confounded by the fact that the drop might not have anything to do with the magma pod; it might have been the result of a change in the hydrolic system underlying the geyser basin. He just couldn't know. Maybe the grad students would turn up something. He set the problem aside, and began working on his recommendations to the Advanced National Seismic System Conference, coming up in July. The Intermountain West Region needed more equipment, and stable funding.

Over the night and while Desh worked, the five centimeter rise in the landmass at the eastern margin of Henry's Lake had strangely subsided. That no notice was taken of its rise and fall was largely because no technology had been installed in the area to sense such events. Yet, even if there had been sensors, the quick rise and fall would have baffled scientists. What they couldn't know was that the six hundred cubic mile pod of magma had changed shape and was now a river, and had dived deep into the earth below the Island Park Caldera. There, like a hunting snake, it would seek the fissures, faults and lava tube tunnels from which it had come a million years earlier.

Willie Jensen was down on his knees beside his truck, apparently stuffing tools, or something, underneath the front seat when Rick Sanchez pulled into the yard in his cruiser. Jensen pulled his head out of the truck, saw the overheads on the cruiser, and leaped to his feet looking wildly about for someplace to run. One of his eyes was plum-colored and almost swollen shut. A white strip of adhesive tape held the bridge of his nose together. He stood there, trapped against the open door of the truck.

Sanchez eased out of the cruiser, and walked slowly toward Willie. "What's the matter, Willie. Did I scare you?"

Willie looked longingly toward the front seat of the truck, then back at Rick.

"You wanna step away from the truck, Willie?"

Jensen looked again at the front seat, and back at Rick. His face was the color of dough and his eyes grew wide and luminous. He seemed to be looking at the horizon behind Rick's shoulder.

Sanchez took a step forward, and assumed a shooting stance, his hand on the holstered Glock. "Don't do nuthin' stupid, Willie; I just wanna talk."

Jensen's attention snapped back to Rick. "Talk about what? I ain't done nuthin'."

Sanchez shuffled a couple of steps closer, maintaining his shooter's stance. About eight feet separated them. "Stay cool, Willie." He unsnapped the safety catch on the holster. "I just wanna talk about Rosa Gonzales."

Jensen dived for the cab of the truck. Sanchez whipped out his pistol, moved in and clubbed Willie on the back of the neck, just as

Willie reached for the .38 lying on the seat. Jensen crashed to his knees, dropping the gun. Rick back-handed him with the barrel of the Glock. A jagged red tear appeared on Willie's cheek.

"You wanna pull a gun on me—you little prick." Sanchez clubbed Willie again with the Glock. Willie lay under the open door of the truck, moaning.

Rick holstered the Glock, flipped Willie over on his stomach, handcuffed him, slammed the door closed and sat Willie up against the side of the truck. Willie sat there groaning, bleeding on his shirt.

The radio in the cruiser crackled to life: "Unit 26, what's your 10-20?"

Rick keyed his shoulder mike, "Dispatch, I'm code 6 at the end of Walnut, checking out a trailer." He didn't fucking feel like telling them where he was.

"10-4."

He slapped Willie a couple of times to wake him up. When Jensen had come back around, Rick hauled him over to the cruiser and threw him in the front passenger seat. Then he walked around, slipped in the driver's seat, lit a Marlboro, and said, "O.K., Willie, you got five minutes."

Jensen tried to wipe some of the blood off his cheek on his shoulder, but only succeeded in smearing it. Silence.

Sanchez turned in his seat, left hand on the steering wheel, holding the Marlboro between his fingers, and stared at Willie. "Look, you little fucker, I'm trying to give you a break here. I know you had something to do with Rosa Gonzales." He looked at his watch. "You got four minutes before I haul your ass down to the station and charge you with first degree murder as a hate crime."

"It warn't me," Willie whined. "It was Roscoe 'n Hebrew. They had me do it. I didn't mean t' kill anybody."

Rick laughed out loud. "Didn't mean to kill anybody? Christ, Willie! I'd hate to see what you do to people you *mean* to kill. You dragged 'em, didn't ya? Dragged 'em death and then threw them in the river." Rick laughed again. "Didn't mean to kill anybody." He shook his head.

Willie just sat there, bleeding.

"Why'd you kill 'em, Willie?"

"'Cause that goddamned spic kid was a stealin' our drug money, an' th' ol' lady wanted to blackmail us t' keep quiet."

"How much drug money, Willie?" Sanchez took a deep drag on the Marlboro, blew out a cloud of blue smoke. Willie sat there.

Rick punched him on the shoulder. "How much goddamn money, Willie?"

Willie recoiled from the punch. "Well, I don't know—fifteen, twenty."

"Fifteen, twenty what?"

"Fifteen, twenty thousand a month—from my three guys."

Rick whistled. "And Roscoe Kettle put you up to this?"

"Hell, yes," Willie sniveled. "It was him started th' whole thing."

Rick Sanchez reached for the mike, keyed it, released it, and sat back in his seat.

Willie squirmed, trying to get comfortable. Hard to do, sitting in a car seat with his hands handcuffed behind him.

Rick keyed the mike again, saying, "Dispatch, I'm going to be code 7 for about forty-five minutes." Code 7 was "out to lunch."

"10-4," came the reply.

Sanchez turned on the ignition.

"Where we goin'?" Willie asked.

"We're gonna go see Roscoe," Rick smiled. "Maybe I can help you out of this mess, Willie."

The Kettle homestead lay in a curve in the river about five miles from downtown Python. There, what had begun as a modest ranch house, became a sprawling structure, with rooms added haphazardly as Ezekiel's family and fortune grew. Sadly, by the time Roscoe and Hebrew came into sole possession of the family mansion, it had taken on an air of dilapidation and neglect. The steps leading to the sprawling front porch sagged; the roof had long since drooped with age and an accumulation of moss and lichen. Most of the white paint had peeled off, leaving a sullen, weathered grey structure.

The house itself lay at the end of a quarter mile dirt lane, lined with half-dead cottonwoods. A thick hedge of lilacs hid the house from the lane. Rick crept down the lane and parked the cruiser behind the lilacs, out of sight of the house. He pulled his Glock, and marched Willie swiftly and quietly up to the back door. He paused only briefly to kick it in, and shoved Willie in before him.

Roscoe and Hebrew had been sitting at the kitchen table reading newspapers when Willie flew through the door, stumbled, fell flat on his face, banging his already broken nose, and breaking a tooth. He lay there moaning and groaning, bleeding again.

"What the hell—?" Roscoe started to stand.

"Sit down Roscoe, and put your hands where I can see them. You, too, Hebrew."

The Kettle brothers carefully lay their hands on top of the newspapers.

"You gonna arrest us?" Hebrew blurted.

"No, he ain't gonna arrest us, Hebrew," Roscoe said, staring at Rick steadily. "He'd a already done it, and he wouldn'tna brung Willie. He wants t'make a deal. Ain't 'at right, Rick?" To Willie: "Willie, shut up yer damn moanin." Willie lay prone, one cheek on the floor. A little pool of blood accumulated under his chin.

"Your boy, Willie, here, spilled his guts," Rick said. "I know all about Rosa Gonzales and the drugs. I know enough to get you two death by lethal injection. Now we can either get on with this arrest or we can talk." Rick waved the Glock at them. "It's up to you."

"How much?" Roscoe said.

"Five thousand a month," Rick said.

"So, when do we kill him?" asked Tolya. Anatoly had donned the headset, listening to the conversation in Haraldsen's room. Vassili had walked to the window, thinking. Tolya followed.

Vassili looked at his watch. Nine-thirty Mountain Time. Four-thirty PM in Lisbon. "We don't," Vassili said. "Stay with Anatoly. If they leave, follow them. I will make some phone calls." He strode out of the room, leaving a disappointed Tolya behind.

Back in his room, Vassili activated the satellite phone, dialed a number. After a long moment, he heard, "*Da.*"

Speaking Russian, he fired his instructions to the person three thousand miles away. He terminated the call, then dialed another number, this time to Salt Lake.

Jake pulled the Hummer into the yard at *Makoce Waste*, turned it off, and sat. For the past two days and the better part of the evening he and Haraldsen had poured over topographical maps of the Anvil, trying to locate a sickle-shaped island. They could identify elevations easily enough, but none of them were sickle-shaped. The old Mexican might have been fooled by the way vegetation grew, the way the shadows lay, or he might have simply been delirious. Jake wondered what he had gotten himself into. Nicole listened in, but sat in the corner, brooding.

They had located three possibilities, though: elevations roughly oval in shape that Haraldsen called *kipukas*. *Kipuka*, Jake learned, was the Hawaiian term for "island," and a *kipuka* was an island of lava created when a slight rise or hill in an older lava flow was surrounded by a new, younger lava flow. *Kipukas* were often covered with more mature vegetation. Unfortunately, the topo maps revealed nothing about vegetation. They would have to fly the desert. He'd call his chopper pilot buddy, Harlow Ramsey, in the morning.

Jake went in the house, heated up a bowl of leftover beans, took a quick shower and went to bed.

Jake and his teammates Rico Dominguez and Shea Hardesty lay buried atop a sand dune. Below them, an Iraqi radar installation showed little activity except for an occasional sentry making his rounds, and the radar dish revolving. The installation, and the trucks with the twin S-125 Neva missles glowed an eerie green through the night vision goggles.

Jake's headset crackled. "Sphinx, this is Swordsman. Do you copy."

"Swordsman, Sphinx. Copy five by five, over."

"ETA two minutes. Light 'em up, will ya."

Jake punched Rico, who was manning the laser, in the shoulder, and said, "Swordsman, roger that, illuminating now." As he spoke, Jake heard the distinctive sound of an AK 47 bolt slamming a round in the chamber. "Stupid bastard," Jake thought as he rolled over, pulling his .45, "why didn't he have one already locked and loaded?"

Jake jerked awake from his dream. The sound he heard wasn't from his dream: it was somewhere in the house. He grabbed his Yarborough from under the pillow, and slid out of bed. He lay the pillows end to end and threw the covers back over the bed.

Downstairs, the two men dressed in black BDU's, balacavas, and wearing night vision goggles stood stock still, listening. One of them, beyond belief, dropped the knife he used to jimmy the sliding glass door. Stupid. Stupid. Stupid. When they heard nothing upstairs, they moved out, one going left, past the study, the other heading right, up the stairs past the dining room and through the kitchen. Both routes would eventually lead to one of the two doors that led to Jake's bedroom.

Upstairs, Jake slipped into a walk-in closet, and closed the door, except for a crack, and crouched, waiting. He had begun to think he was imagining things when he heard the faintest whisper of a shoe on the carpet. Moments later, a black-clad figure slid past his hide, carrying a small pistol at port arms. Jake watched as the shooter aimed at the lumpy bed and the pistol spit four times: two shots center mass and two shots to the head. As the fourth shot hissed, Jake leapt out of the closet, clamped his left hand over the shooter's mouth, jerked his head back, and plunged the Yarborough into his neck midway between collarbone and chin, pushing outward as he did. He heard a soft "pop," and felt a hot spray on his hands and forearms.

A second attacker stepped though the other doorway and fired twice before he realized Jake had pivoted and used the first shooter as a shield. As his shield, bleeding out and loosing consciousness, began to slump, Jake shoved him two steps forward into the second shooter, who fired another round. Jake reeled a step back from the jack-hammer impact of the slug. His left side went numb. As the second shooter stumbled under the weight of his comrade, Jake stepped right and toward him, hooking his throat beneath the chin with the Yarborough. He heard a whistle, and gurgling as the man dropped to the floor, thrashing.

Jake fell, flat on his ass, next to the night stand. Molasses. He was trying to move through a sea of molasses, thick and syrupy. The phone was somewhere on the nightstand; it took hours for his hand to move, to search, to find the receiver. The green numbers faded out of focus, back into focus, out, in. Out. In. His finger seemed as big as a baseball bat, and fuzzy, as he carefully, slowly depressed the keys: nine, one, one. A familiar voice answered.

"Bennie," he said thickly. "Bennie, thish iss Jake." He felt so goddamned tired. He wanted to sleep. "I'm shot. Call Tom." Then he toppled over on his side. The last thing he heard was Bennie's tinny little voice screaming from the handset on the floor.

Chapter 11

Tom Curdy had just settled in around the delicious curves of Ellie's backside and was trying to decide on what strategy to use to turn her on. But Ellie, as familiar with the man as she was her own hand, had already detected the subtle movements of his body that signaled an amorous assault. She couldn't help grinning.

She wasn't especially interested in sex; she was bone-weary from a brutal day in the ER. It was brutal because they lost Angelina Maria Valdez, fifteen, to a meth overdose, and Ellie couldn't put the sight of the girl convulsing, then stroking-out on the table, out of her mind. Angelina went rigid as a post, her eyes snapped open wide, and then the light faded.

They tried heroically. They always did. Bones—Dr. Michael Purser—called it at 5:36 pm MST. He snapped off his purple exam gloves, threw them on the floor, gathered himself together, and marched out to where the family waited.

"What the hell," Ellie thought, "maybe it will get my mind off of it." She rolled over. "Wanna get laid, cowboy?" she asked.

"Well, yeah," he whispered. He had just begun to kiss her, when the phone rang, shattering the mood like a baseball thrown through the window.

"Jesus Christ!" He reached for the phone with one arm, hung on to Ellie with the other. "This is Curdy, and this better be goddamn important."

Ellie felt him stiffen, heard the sharp intake of breath and the tight, choked voice.

"How bad is he?"

Ellie sat up, turned on the lamp on her side of the bed. Tom had turned as pale as the lampshade.

"What do you mean, you don't know?"

Silence.

"Goddamn it, Bennie! Get every fucking body up and get them out there. Everybody. Get Creighton up, call the ER and have Bones waiting…well, goddamn it, call 'em again! I'm on my way."

Tom leapt up, struggled to pull on his pants with his one free hand.

Ellie got out of bed and asked, "Tom, what is it?" just as he threw the phone in the general direction of the night stand.

"Somebody shot Jake." He choked on the words.

"How bad is he?"

"Don't know, ambulance isn't there yet." He had pulled his boots on and struggled with a shirt. Then Ellie watched as he dug in the back of the closet, produced a black short-barreled twelve gauge shotgun and began ramming shells in it.

"Tommy!"

He stopped, and stared at her, with the gun tucked in the crook of his arm. Ellie walked around the bed, took the gun away from him, laid it on the floor, and slapped him on the chest with the flat of her small hand.

"Tommy!" She said again, then she put her arms around his waist, pressing herself against him. "You don't need that, baby. This isn't Viet Nam."

Tom clung to her. "Jesus, Ellie. Who would want to shoot Jake?"

"I don't know, " Ellie said. "Just go and do your job. And leave that street cleaner here."

Tom released her, strapped on his gun belt, and paused at the door of the bedroom to look back at her.

"Go on," she said, "I'll meet you in the ER."

Tom went.

While Jake lay bleeding on the floor of his bedroom, it rose from abyssal depths like a thousand-tentacled beast. It sought its way through the cracks and fissures in the rock above, driven by the hellish heat and pressure below. A thousand times it divided, slipping through cracks as fine as a hair; a thousand times it merged again, filling the larger fissures with its lethal presence. Upward and upward it rose, expanding in volume and force until it broke through the topsoil halfway down the western slope of the Island Park Caldera.

The hiss and slightly sulfurous odor startled a snowshoe rabbit, which loped a few hundred feet down the mountain and hid in a hollow, thick with wild cherry and buckbrush. His rustling startled a covey of six blue grouse which clucked, and waddled to the other side of the thicket.

Heavier than air, the beast above poured out upon the slope like an invisible avalanche that filled the hollows and glens with a deadly mixture of carbon dioxide and hydrogen sulfide. The grouse and the rabbit crouched dumbly in their hiding places, trying to breathe, until they died, kicking, from suffocation.

It swept down the slope, extinguishing the life of every living thing, until at last, at the bottom of the Caldera, where the mountain met the plain, it passed silently through a campground, pausing to fill in the low places, and out onto the Anvil, where it dissipated in an early morning breeze.

After Rick Sanchez left with the fifty crisp one hundred dollar bills stuffed safely in his pocket, Roscoe sent Hebrew to take Willie home. They had patched him up again and pulled the broken tooth, figuring it was easier to pull it than fix it. Hebrew held him down while Roscoe applied the vise grips to the tooth. Willie howled, but it was over in ten seconds. He looked like a hillbilly, anyway; a missing tooth completed the image. Willie insisted on keeping the tooth, vowing vengeance on Sanchez. Roscoe snorted, telling Willie to get the hell on home and to swish his mouth out with whiskey every so often.

Roscoe was glad when they were gone. He had far more important things to think about than Willie's tooth, like the phone call he was afraid to make, but had to. If the man he was about to call wanted Roscoe dead, Roscoe would simply disappear and no one would ever discover what happened to him.

As far as the citizens of Python were concerned, he was simply a harmless business man, moderately successful, a man who minded his own business and who did not call attention to himself. But the truth was that beneath the mild, milk-toast persona lurked a twisted and vicious soul, a soul that seethed with hatred for any person of any color or race, other than white, Anglo-Saxon. And he was connected.

Roscoe himself did not understand completely the extent of the secret network of cells similar to the Python Brotherhood that infected the western and southern United States. But he knew they were many and they all operated in much the same way: the sale of drugs, especially to people of color, and most especially to the sons and daughters of the wealthy, funded caches of firearms which were secretly stored away, waiting for the day when the cleansing of the Country had come.

A third of the money Roscoe and his boys collected went to the Man, the other two-thirds paid their salaries, bought guns and ammunition, and more drugs. Roscoe knew something else, too, that the rest of the boys didn't know: those who did not keep the secrets of the Organization did not live, for the Man had at his fingertips some of the most cruel and bloodthirsty enforcers in the nation. He had only to summon them, and summon them he would, if the secrecy were threatened.

Rick Sanchez had waded into deep and bloody waters and the blood was his own. Willie was simply stupid, and his stupidity would cost him his life, too. As he dialed the number, Roscoe tried to shake the snakes writhing in his belly.

A voice answered with a single word: "Yes."

Roscoe cleared his throat and said, "We have a serious problem."

"Tonight. Usual place. Usual time." Click.

Roscoe stared at the silent hand set, then hung it up gently. He wiped his face with a dirty bandana handkerchief; he hadn't realized he'd been sweating.

"Isnala Mani," the Voice said. "Hokahey!" He struggled to awake from the dark, syrupy depths. It was so peaceful, there, floating, slowly spiraling down, down. He didn't know where he spiraled to; he didn't care.

"Hau! Isnala Mani! Hokahey!" He opened his eyes. Far, far above him, a light grew larger and larger as he was drawn into it. The darkness turned from black, to brown, and faded until he lay, resting on a bed of white light. Gradually, the brightness dimmed and he found himself staring at firelight flickering on the ceiling of a cave. With the firelight came the deep, burning pain in his shoulder. He gasped, sat up, and came face to face with an enormous grizzly bear, who stared at him through luminous yellow eyes.

He looked around the cavern. He lay between the great, curving tusks of a mammoth skull. A fire burned at his feet, and beyond the fire, a ring of shadowy figures, some with spears, danced and chanted. His two wolf friends paced back and forth, throwing huge shadows on the wall.

The Shaman appeared from behind the huge bulk of the bear, leading a woman holding a wooden bowl. The Shaman went to his left side and kneeled by the bear; the woman walked on his right side and kneeled behind him. She put her right arm across his chest and drew him back until he rested his weight against her, then, with her left hand, she forced him to drink the vile, bitter liquid in the bowl. He choked, but relentlessly, she held the bowl to his lips until it was empty.

Jake's lips and tongue went numb and the cavern began spinning. The Shaman began a low chant, and waved his eagle wing over the wound in his shoulder. The woman tightened her grip across his chest.

The bear came, first sniffing the wound, then cleaning it with his rasping tongue, probing deeply into the torn flesh. The pain came in rippling waves and brought tears to his eyes. Then the bear stopped, raised one massive paw heavenward with the first six-inch claw extended. And then he plunged it into the wound, digging to where the bullet lay. Jake cried out, gasped, and struggled, but the woman held him tightly against her breasts. As he felt himself losing consciousness, the grizzly withdrew the claw, with the bullet adhering to it. The woman leaned over him, and kissed him, and when she did, the Venus she wore around her neck fell across his chest. He tried to speak but couldn't. The woman, the cave, the Shaman, the bear, all receded in the distance, and suddenly, he was back—back in himself, in his time, and aware of someone standing next to him.

Tom paced up and down under the fluorescent lights of the waiting room. Sheri MacDougal sat on one of the hideous hospital green vinyl chairs flipping though a dog-eared, out-dated *Cosmopolitan*. He had left Bob Duncan in charge at the crime scene at Jake's house after it had been secured and a preliminary investigation begun. He had called in the boys from the state crime lab. Didn't make sense. Why would two professional hit men try to take out Jake?

He looked up as Ellie and Bones stepped into the room, still dressed in surgical greens. Bones swept off his surgical cap and held his hand up to forestall the flurry of Tom's questions.

"He's going to make it and no, you can't see him. He's lucky, that Indian. The bullet entered just below the collar bone, nicked the first rib, but basically passed over it, instead of shattering it. He a' had a lung full of bone splinters if that had happened. Nicked the maxillary artery, though; that's what caused all the bleeding." Bones shook his head. "Who would want to shoot Jake?"

"I don't know," Tom replied. "I'm hoping he will be able to shed some light on that question." He put his arm around Ellie, who drooped, and kissed her. It was almost two in the morning.

"Why don't you go on home, baby. I'll be along in a bit."

Ellie shook her head and kissed him. "Don't be too long. You look beat."

"I am," he said. To Sheri: "You might as well go home, too, Sheri. We'll have a big day tomorrow." After Ellie and Sheri walked away, Curdy turned back to Bones.

"I want to see him," he said.

Bones stared hard at Curdy. "You're not going to leave until you do, are you."

"Nope."

"Oh, Christ! Come on, then. But don't you try to wake him up."

"I won't, Bones, I just want to see him."

Curdy took off his Stetson as he entered the ICU. He exhaled a long breath of air, stepped up to the bed and the form, dark against the white sheets. Jake's long hair lay in a thick black cascade down the pillow and disappeared under his left shoulder. His shoulder and chest were tightly bound with dressings.

Curdy felt Bones's hand on his shoulder.

"He'll be O.K., Tom. Ten minutes, then go home and get some sleep. Doctor's orders," he said softly, giving Tom a firm squeeze.

"Thanks, Bones," Tom whispered. He didn't look up, but stared at his friend. *Kola*: that was the word Jake used to greet him. He had explained that the word was usually translated "friend," but in the old days, the Lakota restricted its use to those warriors whom you knew would go back onto the battle field to get you, even if it might cost them their own life.

"A man doesn't have very many *kola* in his life," Jake told him. "Three, maybe four—five at most."

Tom had struggled all night with the volcanic emotions unleashed by Jake's wounding. Their source was the constellation of feelings summoned by one word: soldier. When Jessica Lynch told the special ops team, "I am an American soldier, too," every veteran in the nation wept, and understood.

In the curious transubstantiation of war, every soldier becomes the other: to leave your brother behind is to leave yourself behind, lost in the unthinkable horror of never going home again, never to see wife, son, daughter, mother, father, to never see the beloved faces that lock life in its orbit. And when your brother lies bleeding on the scarlet field of war, his blood is your own, and if he dies, a part of you dies, and can never, never be summoned to life again. And so Tom Curdy stood at the bedside of his *kola*, unable to hold the tears in check, feeling the same old rage, the same old impotence, and in the mysterious and curious way of soldiers, vaguely guilty that he had let this happen to one of his own.

"You gonna stand there sniveling all night, or are you going to go home and get some sleep. You sure a hell aren't doing me any good." Jake's voice was weak and hoarse, but steady.

Lost in his own anguish, Tom had not seen Jake open his eyes.Curdy burst out laughing, and soon Jake was laughing, too.

"Ow," he said, rubbing his chest.

"You son-of-a-bitch," Curdy said. "You scared me."

"Yeah, well, most Rangers are pussies," Jake croaked. He held out his hand for Curdy to shake. "Go on home, Tom; we'll talk tomorrow."

Curdy shook the hand and donned his Stetson. "Tomorow," he said, and turned on his heel. When he reached the door, Jake called out, "Hey, Tom."

Curdy turned, "What?"

"Thanks."

Curdy nodded, and left.

For a while, Jake tried to fight off the haze of anesthetic hangover, but eventually, he gave up and slipped back into sleep.

Tom's route home took him past *El Guerro Negro* which he would ordinarily have driven past without a thought. But this night, he glimpsed the glimmer of a brake light behind the darkened building. Tired as he was, he wheeled the cruiser around to investigate. To his surprise, Roscoe's old GMC was parked next to an equally battered eighty-three Buick. The driver of the Buick apparently had his foot on the brake.

Tom dismounted the cruiser and approached the passenger side of the Buick. He tapped the window with his Magnalite. Roscoe rolled the window down. Tom shined the light in Roscoe's face, then bent over to see who was in the driver's seat. He was surprised to recognize the man sprawled there, a meaty hand on the steering wheel.

Tom stood up. "Can I ask what you boys are doing here?"

"We're doing business," Roscoe said. He spit out the open window.

"That may be," Tom said, "but you're trespassing on whoever owns this bar."

"No, we ain't," said Roscoe, "cause my associate here owns this here bar." He pronounced 'associate' to rhyme with 'gate.'

Tom bent down and looked past Roscoe to the man in the driver's seat. "That right? Do you own this bar?"

"'At's right," the man said. "Me'n Hector go a long way back."

Tom straightened back up, looked at Roscoe. "Roscoe, next time, do your business in a place and at a time that doesn't look quite so suspicious."

"I'll do business where an' when I want, Sheriff." He spit out the window again. Tom turned on his heel and left.

"That was unfortunate for the Sheriff to see the two of us together. Do you get my meaning, Roscoe?"

Roscoe looked out the window at the darkness. "Yessir, I reckon I do."

"Can I count on you for that, Roscoe?"

Roscoe sighed. "Yessir, you can."

Ellie was dozing when Tom got home. She awakened when he crawled into bed. She sat up and turned on the light. "You bullied Bones into seeing Jake, didn't you."

"Well, I don't think 'bully' is the right word. He simply saw the futility of saying 'no' to me." He grinned.

Ellie snuggled up. "I'm glad he's O.K. I'm glad you have Jake as a friend, Tom."

Curdy kissed the top of his wife's head. "He's more than a friend, baby. He's...well, he's like Shota. He's been there and done it."

Ellie looked up at her husband. "Speaking of Shota, what do you hear from him?"

Tom stroked Ellie's hair, laughed. "He's in Mexico, down on the Baja with Joanie, layin' in the sun, eatin' fish tacos. He wants us to come down in September." Ellie sat up.

"Oh, Tom! Could we? In forty years we've never done anything for ourselves. Tommy," she pleaded, "let's do it. For once, let's let duty go to hell. Tommy," she kissed him, "Tommy, take me to Mexico, lay me down on the beach and make love to me."

Tom laughed. "Well, since you put it that way..."

Ellie yanked on his arm, grew serious. "Promise me, Tom." He held up two fingers in the Boy Scout salute. "Promise."

"Good. Let's go to sleep." She slid down in bed and turned over. When she didn't feel him slide down next to her, she sat up and said, "What?"

"Something else strange happened."

"What?"

"Roscoe Kettle and another guy were parked behind Hector's bar 'doing business' at three o'clock in the morning."

"Who was the other guy?" Tom told her. "Stranger even yet," Ellie said. "Do you think it was weird sex?"

"No," Tom said. "They were hiding something."

"Let's go to sleep, baby," Ellie said, sliding down in the bed, and turning over.

Tom snapped the light off and snuggled up. "Where were we?"

"Tom, stop! I'm too tired. Tommy, stop...damn you!" She rolled over and kissed him.

Later, much later, she mumbled, "Are we really going to Mexico?"

"Naw," he said, "I just wanted to get laid."

She rolled over and slapped him.

Vassili sat in the darkened motel room flipping the safety catch of a sig sauer 9 mm pistol on, off. On. Off. His cigarette flared redly as he sucked hard. On. Off. Mikhail and Ivan had been with him in

Afghanistan, then Chechyna. He had sent Anatoly and Tolya to find out what they could. There was a soft knock at the door.

"*Da.*"

Tolya and Anatoly stepped into the room, turning on the light. They stood facing him. "The Indian is alive in the hospital," said Anatoly.

"Mikhail?"

"*Nyet.*"

"Ivan?"

"*Nyet.*"

Vassili jumped up cursed in Russian, paced the room, waving the nine around. "Both of them! He killed them both! I will kill him myself with my bare hands." He glared at Tolya and Anatoly. They shrank back a little, knowing the consequences of Vassili's rages.

"On the Anvil," he said, "I will shred his flesh with these two hands."

Chapter 12

By the time Tom got to his office in the morning the news of Jake's shooting had already spread all over town. Ambulance drivers and EMT's went home to tell their wives and sisters of the grisly spectacle of blood-splashed walls, black-clad strangers wearing night vision goggles, and a pool of blood, thick as pudding, beneath the unconscious Jake.

Even the deputies, used to the carnage of automobile accidents, had never seen anything like this, and wondered aloud about the identity of the men who lay tangled together, their slit throats smiling the hideous parody of smiles. Hal Lindsay, who accompanied the bodies to Whittaker's Parlour, where they were stripped for identification, fingerprinted, and meticulously examined for evidence, described in detail to his wide-eyed wife, Julie, the thick, muscular torsos almost entirely tattooed with elegant and strange-looking cathedrals, religious imagery, and animals.

His description ignited a weird lust in Julie, who tore off her nightie, and worked Hal into a lather. When he was finally permitted to sleep, he dropped off, vaguely hoping for some new carnage within the week.

In a town of fewer than six thousand people, the small, ordinary scandals of life provided nourishment for weeks of chewing and ruminating in Python's cafes, bars, barber shops, offices, and church basements. The two dead Mexicans, and now Jake's shooting, were feasts beyond imagining.

Although most of the citizenry knew who the tall, dark-haired Indian was, they did not *know* him. For most of them, he was remote and distant as the President. Rumors about his military record, his wealth, and how he got it, flourished, then hardened into a larger-than-life myth.

Speculation about the motive for Jake's shooting ranged from simple burglary:

"Well, if they was just robbin' 'im, why was they wearin' 'em fancy night goggles?" one objector to the bulgary theory asked.

"Well, you damn fool, so's they could see the money an' jools!" to vengeance:

"Payback, 'at's what it is, sure as hell. Hell, I heard he was in th' Mid-East n' Russia assassinatin' 'em ragheads 'n commies for th' CIA. Somebody's getting' even, 'at's whut it is."

"'At's right," another voice piped. "Ain't safe havin' him around. What if they'd a' tried to blow 'im up while he was in the Shoe, er someplace? He's dangerous, I tell ya." The others at the bar murmured their assent, nodded their heads wisely.

Had Jake heard the stories, he would have laughed.

When Tom arrived at the Python County Law Enforcement Center, three reporters, including PHARK, waited for him. He waved them off and asked Shirley, his secretary, into his office. After the door was closed, Shirley said, "PHARK's been waiting for an hour."

"Yeah, O.K.," Tom said, hanging his Stetson on the coat rack. "When you go back out there, tell them both the two unidentified Hispanics, and the shooting of Mr. Two Feathers are under investigation and as of now, we don't have any new information for them. I'll probably hold a press conference tomorrow."

Tom dug around in his wallet, produced a gold credit card. Shirley looked puzzled when he handed her the card. "Take this," he said, " and book Ellie and I two first class seats to Loreto, Mexico on... ." He swiveled around in his chair and studied the calendar above the credenza. "Book us out of here on the fourteenth of September, returning October first."

"Why, Tom, what brought this on? You've never taken a vacation in the ten years I've been here."

"Yeah, well, Ellie and I aren't getting any younger, and it's time to live a little. All this death makes a guy think."

Shirley grinned. "Consider it done."

"You still have Shota's number in Mexico—the one I gave you in case anything happens to me?"

"Yes, I do."

Tom winked. "I need to consult a weapons expert on the pistols we found at Jake's—never seen handguns like them before. Shota's pretty good on military weapons; maybe he can help. Anyway, get him on the horn for me, will you?"

Shirley nodded. "Anything else?"

"Yes, there is. Are Bob and the boys all here?"

She nodded. "Mo called and said he'd be here in ten minutes. Oh, and Rick Sanchez called in sick."

Tom had picked up the toxicology reports on the two Mexicans that Mo had apparently left on his desk. He paused shuffling through them. "Sick, huh?"

"That's what he said."

He fiddled with a paper clip for three or four seconds, then put Sanchez out of his mind. "Well, call Mickey Crosgrove and ask him if he will help out if we need him." Cosgrove was a retired Salt Lake City detective who lived outside Python on the river. He spent the winters tying dry flies, the summers using them on the cutthroats in the river.

"Done," Shirley said. "Anything else?"

"Yeah. Ask Bob to bring me one of the pistols we found out there last night."

Shirley got up to leave. "You want the door open or closed?"

"Closed." Tom grinned. "Call Shota first, will you?"

Shirley exited, firmly closing the door behind her.

Tom swung around in his chair, and studied Ellie's picture on the credenza. A fierce joy rose in him. There comes a moment in every man's life, when, if he is lucky, for an instant, he glimpses all the years of his life at once, as though it were a picture, as though he were seeing the sum totality of how well he had actually lived. It is as though the gods, in a moment of revelation, carry him to a pinnacle above the plain of his life, where he may see it all at once, and judge whether he has lived his life well and wisely.

He realized he and Ellie had done it: they had lived through a war, and the fall into despair, but they had pulled out of it with the sinew and muscle of their love. They had raised two children who were now sterling young adults, responsible for themselves and capable. Ellie had dedicated her life to healing; he to justice and righting the wrongs no one else could.

They had not spent their lives in the unquenchable thirst for wealth, nor in great cities, as large and important people, but in the small island of their community, where they had stood for something good, and life was better for those who passed within their light.

The best part of his life was his life with Ellie. She had taken the raw ore of his outrage against senseless death and suffering, passed it again and again through the crucible of her love, and refined him into the simple, honest gold that he was. It was her constant and unremitting love that had hammered him into a man other men admired, and other women trusted. And he wanted to tell her, thank her, somehow, for joining her life with his.

He had two bodies, and a *kola* whom someone had shot. He would right these wrongs, somehow, and take his woman to Mexico, and after that, maybe even retire so he could spend the remaining years of his life, thanking the woman who had helped him make so much of his. Why hadn't he thought of this before?

His phone rang. It was Shirley: Shota, line "1". Tom punched the blinking "1". They traded "sonofabitches," and other insults, then Tom told him of his plan. Shota was ecstatic, saying he'd have the boat waiting in Loreto. Tom hung up, grinning. Life, in spite of all the senseless evil, was good.

There was a tap at his door.

"Come."

Bob Duncan entered, carrying an evidence bag with a pistol in it, and another small evidence bag with spent cartridges, along with a pair of latex gloves, and a file folder. "Damned if I know what this gun is—never seen anything like it. The cartridges, either." They were about a third longer than most pistol cartridges.

Duncan handed the two evidence bags to Tom, who donned the gloves and examined the gun. "I'll be damned. Looks like this thing has a two part barrel. Looks like the breech and the chamber recoil inside the frame." Tom returned the weapon to the evidence bag. "We'll ask Jake. Maybe he'll know something about it. What else you got?"

Just then, another rap came at the door.

Tom yelled, "Come on in!"

The door opened and Mo stepped half-way into the room, and turned to speak to someone in the lobby, his hand resting on the door knob. "I know, but PH—Herb, we've got our hands full right now. You'll know as soon as we do." Mo walked the rest of the way into the room, closing the door behind him. He shook his head as he sat down next to Duncan.

"You gotta hand it to him," Mo said.

"What?" Tom asked.

"Herb. He doesn't give up easily, does he?"

"Neither do wood ticks," Duncan said.

Tom smiled. "So where are we, Mo?"

"Well, the state crime scene boys are wrapping it up, dotting all the 'i's' and crossing the 't's'. Aside from who those two jokers were, and what their motive was, I'd say it's pretty cut and dried; looks like a clear case of self-defense to me. I'll convene a coroner's inquest late next week—depends on how Jake is."

"That's pretty much the way I see it, as far as Jake goes," Tom said, "but somebody has to answer for an attempted murder charge."

"Damn straight," Duncan said.

"Tom," Mo said, shifting in his seat, "these guys were heavy hitters. I mean heavy-duty world class pros. They're way out of our league, like not even from the same planet. Chances are we won't be able to identify them—through Interpol, maybe, if we're lucky."

"World class or not, they're not above the law in Python. Do what you have to do," he said, speaking to both Mo and Duncan.

"What did you think of the tattoos?" Mo asked.

"He hasn't seen them yet," Duncan said.

"What tattoos?" Tom asked.

"These," Duncan said, walking around the desk and opening the folder with the eight by tens. Both Mo and Duncan looked over Tom's shoulder as he leafed through the photos.

There were full shots of each man's torso, both front and back: they were almost completed tattooed. What looked like a Byzantine cathedral with five onion-shaped spires completely covered one man's chest. Epaulettes had been drawn on his shoulders. A blue shield lay in the center of the epaulettes; three diagonal arrows lay behind a white parachute that ran diagonally the opposing direction. A gold eagle with red and white wings had been superimposed on the parachute. The number '103' was written in an arc at the top of the shield.

A large, ornate cross decorated the other man's chest, along with five pointed stars that covered each nipple. Spiders crawled up the inside of both arms. A sun set (or rose?) behind low hills and a sky filled with birds on one forearm and a black tulip blossomed from the other. A tom cat snarled from his belly. He, too, wore epaulets, but his bore grinning skulls and the number '103'.

"Beats the shit outta me," Tom said, closing the folder.

"Let's see what Jake has to say," he said, standing up.

"Forty-one hundred, right? Can you deliver it today? No, it has to be delivered and set up today." Rick was talking to a hot-tub dealer in Jackson.

"Look, if you can deliver it today, set it up, and have it running by tonight, I'll buy it, cash money; if not, forget it." He paced the floor. Jeannette had gone to "work," and the kids had left for school.

"Yeah, O.K. I'll pay the two hundred delivery charge. Just have it set up and hot by six tonight...O.K., I'll settle for seven-thirty, eight o'clock." He gave them the address in Python.

"I'll be waiting. Yeah. Cash. In hundreds. Right. Bye." He rubbed his hands together gleefully. He might just get laid tonight.

Nicole Haraldsen started to apply lipstick, then angrily wiped it off. "What the hell was she putting make-up on for?" There wasn't a man within five hundred miles she cared to impress. She studied herself in the mirror. She had begun the downward slide on the back slope of her thirties, but she still looked damn good. A few tiny lines at the corners of her eyes, but not much else. She turned sideways, and studied her profile. Flat tummy, voluptuous breasts, still firm and round. The levis she had wriggled into this morning fit perfectly, molding her buns into perfect moons, not that she gave a damn.

What was the point? Here she was, sitting in the corner again, while the men decided what to do. And she would dutifully sling her pack and trudge off after them, just like her mother had done, until the trudging landed her at the bottom of an icy, silt-filled river somewhere in the Yukon.

She had decided early on in her life that she wouldn't be like her mother, who seemed to live only to support her father in his escapades around the world. She would have her own life and roots, belong somewhere, actually own furniture in a house instead of camp stools, and a tent hastily erected in some god-forsaken, insect-infested spot in bum-fuck no where.

The routine of her childhood had always been the same: she spent her summers at whatever dig her father was either directing or working on. The winters she endured at schools in cities where he held temporary teaching positions. She seldom spent more than one year at a school, just long enough to make friends and then give them up when the family moved on to the next dig.

When she was little, and later, in junior high and high school, what she wanted most when she sang in choirs, or performed in school plays, was to look out in the audience and see his face, beaming at her. But he was never there. She had grown up with the vague impression that there was something flawed in her that was the cause of her father's indifference, but she could never determine what it was.

She was hard at work in her second year with Merrill-Lynch when the phone call from Whitehorse, Canada came. Her mother had taken one of the boats and gone out for supplies. They found it, its hull holed and the boat shattered, along with water-soaked packets of provisions littering a five-mile stretch of river. Of Jessica Marie Haraldsen and her Inuit helper, they found nothing.

She spent a month with him, vainly searching the river, and later, endured as long as she could through his deep despair and despondency. "No," she said, finally and firmly, to his many entreaties to return home and help him with his work. No. She would not be her mother for him or any other man.

In the years that followed, they achieved an uneasy peace, he, throwing himself utterly and wholly into the work of proving the New World was populated by prehistoric emigrants from Europe, and she, orchestrating a meteoric rise in the quicksand of corporate America. She grew to despise most of the women, and all of the men she worked with. The women were weak and greedy, willing to do almost anything to ensure their access to wealth and power.

The men either tried to trap her into dependency or negotiate her promotions with the universal coin of corporate sex. She did neither. Instead, she made herself the most successful broker in the Company. Nicole possessed an uncanny weather sense regarding the winds of the market. She just seemed to know when to sail and when to find a hurricane hole and wait. Even her enemies, and there were many, could not dispute her skill.

She tried, half-heartedly, to become interested in one or two of the men who crossed her path, but none of them possessed any real substance, beyond their blind desire for wealth and power. They didn't seem to be able to *do* anything besides wear expensive suits, hunch at their computers all day, and occasionally fly off to exotic places, where they experienced carefully choreographed "adventures."

Scuba diving, rock-climbing, jungle, desert, and arctic survival skills were not electives in the Haraldsen household. By the time she was eighteen, Nicole had belayed down glaciers in Tierra del Fuego, dived for artifacts off the Yucatan peninsula, run untamed and unnamed rivers in Chile, and Argentina; she swung from jungle vines in Brazil and played with the children of "head-hunters." She spent one summer dodging grizzlies and mucking in the caves on Prince of Wales Island off the coast of Alaska. She had climbed the Alps in Italy, Austria, Switzerland. She had sifted dirt on two different digs in southern France.

When she was sixteen she gave her maidenhead to a chocolate-skinned Mexican laborer who was possessed of a dazzling smile, and a strong back. He didn't speak English; she didn't speak Spanish, but they understood the universal signals of desire well enough. This, on a sultry night in the remote mountains of Baja California. Her father never noticed.

By the time she was twenty, she was fluent in French, Spanish, and Portuguese.

The two or three men she did encounter in corporate America she discarded soon after she took them to bed, bored and disappointed.

Then Rafe happened. Major Raphael Cardoza. He was not the kind of man one usually ran across at corporate cocktail parties, but there he was, resplendent in his dress blues, with the salad of his campaign ribbons all over his chest. His meticulously tailored uniform was razor sharp, as one would expect of a Green Beret. He ignored her for the first half of the evening, which, she hated to admit, attracted her to him. Nicole was not often ignored by men.

In the last half of the evening she learned that he was soon to retire from the military to start up a global security service for corporate executives operating in the hot spots of the world. Rafe and six of his special forces buddies were to be the core of the new corporation, called "Securacorp." Well, they had the credentials, and Nicole knew the clients. The match seemed inevitable.

But Rafe, as she soon found out, not only feared no one and no thing, and despised those who did, but he was also a hopeless adrenalin junkie. Soon he had her skydiving, racing Harley Davidsons, and bungee-jumping. Their bedroom became an arena for a kind of savage sexual combat. Nicole loved it, and they were married within six months.

At first, life with Rafe "the Strafe," (when she asked one of his buddies why they nicknamed him "Strafe," he gave her a cold look and said, "You don't want to know.") was exhilarating and exciting. There was always something in the mill: races, jumps, dives; he taught her basic hand-to-hand, how to fire revolvers and close-quarters shotgunning; she learned to fight and defend herself with a knife. She began to wonder if she were being trained for combat.

When Securacorp began protecting executives, Halliburton in Iraq, for example, it became clear that Rafe simply could not stay in the office. He insisted that he had to be "on the scene," and "in country" to oversee the success of his new corporation. But Nicole sensed that his real reason was to be with his men in the middle of the action. The adrenalin high was something no woman could give him—especially after they were married.

The car Rafe, two of his team members, and two executives were riding in was ambushed with machine-gun fire, and RPG's. The Land Rover with the five burning, charred bodies aired on CNN.

Nicole endured the military funeral, accepted the thanks of a grateful nation, the American flag, and a presentation case with miniatures of Rafe's decorations. She threw them on the top shelf of a closet she stored old clothes in.

Two years later her father called: "Terminal glioblastoma in the left temporal lobe, inoperable." Life just kept getting better and better. But he had, at last, stumbled on unimpeachable evidence to support his theory. But he needed her help, if he were to prove it to the world before he died.

Nicole studied the face staring back at her in the mirror. She had sworn not to be her mother, yet here she was about to follow her father onto a desert that would likely kill him, maybe even her. But what choice did she have? He was her father. In spite of the tension between them, she loved him. At some deep level, she reluctantly admitted that her difficulty with men was that none of them ever measured up to the man her father was. And although she resented him bitterly for never giving her the stability and nurturing she needed as a child, he had given her a most marvelous and enviable childhood.

She knew as well, though she couldn't bring herself to admit it, that she liked the ripple of Jake Two Feathers' muscles against her when he picked her up, and carried her out of the studio during the earthquake. Her father was not a man who hunched and pecked at computers; neither was Jake Two Feathers.

"Nicole! Nicole!" It was her father, pounding on the door. Hastily, she threw on a white silk blouse over her naked torso, and answered.

Haraldsen stood there pale-faced and sweating. "We have to go," he said. "Jake's been shot."

A chill seized her, and suddenly, she felt like crying.

Jake had been transferred from ICU to an ordinary hospital room. When Tom and Mo knocked softly on the door to his room, Meiji opened the door a crack. "Go away," she said, "he's sleeping."

"Meiji, who is it,? Let 'em in." Jake was still hoarse, but his voice was stronger.

"Now, see what you've done?" She glared at Mo and the Sheriff, but she opened the door and stepped aside. "You woke him up."

"Meij, go home and get some sleep; I'm O.K.—really, I am." After protesting loudly and "Call me if you need anything" she left.

"How long she been here?" Tom asked.

"I don't know; most of the night, I think." Jake yawned. "Sorry. I'm a little groggy yet."

Bones stuck his head in the door. "Fifteen minutes, boys. That's it. Fifteen." The door closed again.

Tom laughed. "Looks like you're well taken care of."

"There's no shortage of that," Jake said. "God, I hate hospitals."

"Jake," Mo said, "tell us what happened." Jake recounted the events of the previous evening as well as he could.

Tom took the pistol out of the evidence bag and passed it to Jake. "This is what shot you. Ever seen anything like it?"

Jake examined the pistol briefly, then handed it back. "Yeah, it's Russian. It's a PSS."

"PSS?" Mo asked.

"Pistolet Sptsialnyj Samozaryadnyi." Jake surprised them both by what sounded like flawlessly pronounced Russian. "The KGB and Spetsnaz use them. It shoots a special 7.62 cartridge that traps the hot gasses inside the cartridge, so you don't need a silencer to have a silenced weapon."

Tom stared steadily at Jake.

Mo handed Jake the photographs in the folder. "These are the guys that tried to snuff you. These tattoos mean anything to you?"

Jake leafed through the pictures, pausing now and then to study them. He passed the folder back to Mo. "Russian prison tattoos."

"What?" Tom blurted. "Russian prison tattoos?"

"Yeah." Jake said. "Russian has more people in prison than any other country in the world—about thirty million people. There's an entire subculture in the prisons. Those tattoos tell other prisoners who the person is, how many years they've served, what they're in prison for, who to fuck with and who not to fuck with. There's some fairly bad boys in Russian prisons. And girls."

Mo selected one of the photos and held it up for Jake to see. "What do you make of these epaulets? Does the parachute and the eagle mean anything to you?"

Jake hesitated. Finally, he said, "Yeah. It's the unit patch for the 103rd Guards Airborne Division. They were an elite airborne division that fought in Afghanistan until the end of 1989."

"So these guys are ex-military, and have served prison time in Russia?" Mo asked.

Jake shrugged. "Probably."

Tom knew better than to ask, but he did anyway. "How do you know all this, Jake?"

Jake's eyes locked with Tom's. He smiled. "Don't ask me and I won't have to kill you." They all laughed.

When the laughter died away, Tom shifted in his chair. "Jake, why would the KGB, or Spetsnaz want to kill you? What motive could they possibly have?"

Jake shifted a little in the bed, transferring some of his weight to the uninjured shoulder. He thought for a moment. "Well, they're probably not active military. I'd say they're mercenaries of some sort—maybe with connections to Russian mafia. And I haven't the faintest clue why they would want to kill me." He shook his head. "Doesn't make sense to me, either."

"Revenge?" Tom asked.

Jake shifted again in the bed, drew one of his legs up to his chest. "Nah. That's not professional. Wouldn't serve any purpose, even if anybody had a reason for revenge. Which they don't, as far as I know."

Bones marched briskly into the room without knocking. "Time's up boys. I need to examine my patient, and then he needs some rest."

Tom started to say something and Bones interrupted him. "Out. Now." Tom and Mo went meekly, promising to return.

Tom and Mo rode silently back toward the Law Enforcement Complex. Tom shook his head. "Doesn't make sense, Mo. Somebody paid a lot of money to have those two imported to Python. To Python of all places!"

"Do you think Jake is telling us everything he knows?"

Before Tom could answer, the radio crackled: "Unit 10, code two to Cascade Campground. We have multiple DB's." Tom keyed the mike, "10-2. We're on the way. Creighton is with me." He hung the mike back up, looked over at Mo. "Shit! Shit! Shit! What is happening around here?" A code 2 was "proceed immediately without siren"; a "DB" was a Dead Body.

Chapter 13

Bones and the nurse, an attractive red-head named Sheila, carefully removed the dressing on Jake's shoulder. The doctor scrutinized the wound, gently probing here and there. Then he gently pulled Jake forward so he could examine the exit wound on Jake's back.

"So far, so good, Jake. No sign of infection. How's the pain?"

"Take me off the pain killer, Bones; it's makin' me loopy, and I need to think."

"You sure, Jake? That's gonna hurt like hell." He began redressing Jake's shoulder.

"Yeah, I'm sure. How long before I can get out of here?"

Bones thought for a moment while he applied surgical tape over the clean, sterile dressing covering the bullet hole. "Three weeks, maybe four. We need to make sure that artery doesn't break loose again. Then a month or two in therapy." He shook his head. "Theres' gonna be some muscle loss, Jake; I'm sorry." To Sheila: "Hand me that chart, will you? And unhook the Demerol from the IV. Thanks." She did as he asked.

"What is all that stuff?" Jake asked, looking up at the IV tree.

"Ringer's lactate to keep your blood volume up, and to keep you hydrated, some powerful-broad spectrum antibiotic, and glucose to keep you fed. Just a sec," he said as he made notes in the chart. "We'll give you forty-five minutes," he continued, "without the Demerol. If the pain gets too severe, just ring for Shelia and she'll fix you up. And keep that shoulder still as you can. We don't want that thing breaking open."

"Thanks, Bones. How 'bout some real food, starting with a cup of coffee?"

"If you're up to it, it's O.K. by me," Bones replied, making another note in the chart. "Tell Shelia what you want for breakfast."

Jake told her.

Bones closed the aluminum cover on the chart, slipped his pen back in his pocket. "Any questions?"

Jake shook his head "No."

"Then I'll check on you this evening. You're a lucky man, Jake," he said, shaking Jake's hand.

"Depends on your point of view," Jake said.

"I'll be back with your breakfast," Shelia said, as she walked out with Bones.

Jerram Hartigan flopped on the floor of the lava tube cave, shook his water bottle, and drank the last remaining drops.

He couldn't stop shivering. The temperature had to be nearly freezing. He looked around. He couldn't see more than ten feet in either direction; the batteries on his headlamp were almost drained. What he saw was the same thing he had been seeing for the last three (four?) days: rockfall from the ceiling of the cave and a sheet of ice, thinly coated with a layer of dust.

He had driven up from Salt Lake City, stealing a little time for himself. His wife, Chantal, had just given birth to their second set of twins, and between the stress of the impending births, and working the American Express customer service phone lines, he'd had it.

The Church demanded much of his time, as well. But Bishop Hartigan felt he had done his duty, at least for the time being. Four kids and a wife were enough. He paid his tithes, counseled the wayward, preached on Sundays, and provided for his family. And now that Chantal had been successfully delivered of the second set, Jerram felt he needed a break.

Besides, the house overflowed with gushing women, ("Oh, aren't they *darling*! You are *sooo* blessed!") busy plastering tiny pink bows on the bald heads of his tiny, red daughters. He loved his babies; he just couldn't stand all the cooing and mooing women. At the moment, he wondered if he would ever see any of them again.

He had driven through Python in the early morning hours, through the silent, empty, darkened streets, past the sand dunes that were the last dusty remnants of the lakes and marshes of the Holocene ten thousand years in the past. He threaded his way out onto the Anvil, choosing one sandy track after another, one fork in the sand over another, until at last he broke against an impassable wall of basalt twenty feet high and stretching as far as he could see in either direction. As nearly as he could reckon, he was about seventy-five miles into the Anvil.

The mouth of a large cave, black in the early morning light, loomed darkly in front of his Isuzu Trooper. It had been formed two thousand years ago when a river of incandescent pahoehoe lava bled on the land like an open wound. Eventually the top of the flow cooled and crusted over. When the source of the lava exhausted itself, the empty tube remained.

Jerram Hartigan was the professional archaeologist's worst nightmare. That he had navigated unerringly to his cave was no accident. He had been here many times before. Although Hartigan styled himself an amateur archaeologist, he was, in fact, a plunderer, looting the caves of any artifacts he could find. He had no compunction whatsoever against digging random potholes and screening the earth for what it had protected for thousands of years. His basement in Salt Lake was a gallery of stolen metates, points, knives, scrapers, a few fragments of bone, woven sage mats, and sticks that might have once been arrows.

On this morning, in his haste to get into the cave, Jerram decided just to grab his safety helmet, headlamp, and a bottle of water. He'd leave his pack in the Trooper, and set up camp later.

A year ago, when he had begun excavating, Jeram didn't know just how far the lava tube extended; he only knew the vast, mostly unmapped, network of caves that threaded the Anvil sometimes ran for miles. Over the course of a year, he had worked his way, digging here and there, about a hundred yards in.

Ordinarily, most artifacts were found near the cave entrance, twenty or thirty yards in. But in this cave, he continued to find obsidian chips and flakes, and one or two broken points beyond the usual perimeter of occupation. Encouraged, he had continued his random digging.

After six months, he made a most marvelous discovery. The dust-covered floor sloped upward for about ten yards then leveled off again, about five feet higher than it was. When he began a new hole, the blade of his trenching tool chipped ice, instead of soil. He was standing on sort of a mini-glacier, five feet thick, that had existed in this cave, insulated from the heat above, for who knew how many thousand years. He swept the floor of the cave (actually the dust-covered surface of the ice) with his headlamp. The light revealed the usual rock fall, but also what appeared to be lumps under the carpet of dust. When he swept off the layer of dust on one of the lumps, he discovered a hard, leathery mass, wrapped in a woven sage mat, desiccated by the cold dry air.

He turned it in his hands, examining it. A brown stick protruded from one end; what looked like a knot on the end of the stick, protruded from the other end. The narrower end looked like it had been smashed, or snapped, leaving sharp spikes of wood, that threatened to stab him if he weren't careful.

Holy God! When Hartigan realized what he held in his hands, he dropped it, staggered backward a couple of steps, and wiped his gloves on his jacket. It couldn't be! He stepped forward a couple of steps and picked it up again. But it was. My God, it *was* what he thought it was: the mummified front quarter of a deer, or maybe an antelope. The "stick" was bone. He lay it aside and quickly brushed off two more of the remaining lumps. They, too, were parts of animal carcasses, hacked apart and left on the ice. Since he didn't know what to do with them, and obviously couldn't take them home, he left them where they lay.

Methodically, he began sweeping the surface of the ice with a small whisk broom. Almost immediately, he uncovered a stone axe, roughly the size of the palm of his hand. It had sunk into the ice, but he soon chipped it out using the blade of his trenching tool. He hefted it. Two, maybe three pounds of glittering black obsidian. Shaped like a thick leaf, it was sharper on one side than on the other. He stood there, holding the axe, thinking.

He stepped over to the cave wall, looking for niches and crannies that someone might hide something in. Although the walls were essentially smooth, occasionally cracks occurred as the lava cooled. He had examined ten feet of the wall when he found it: a musty leather bundle stuffed in a crack about six inches wide. His hands shook so badly he could hardly pry the stiff, parchment-like leather open. When he did, an assortment of obsidian blanks, a core of obsidian, a couple of egg-shaped hammer stones, five or six perfectly knapped blades, and three or four antler tines fell into the dust. Jerram let out a cry of jubilation. He had found a toolkit, intact, just as it was left, maybe a thousand years ago, maybe ten. Who knew? All he knew was it was his! He quickly gathered up the spilled items and returned to the mouth of the cave, where he could study them in the sunlight.

In the ensuing months, Jerram had returned to work this cave, again and again. Confident that no one had discovered evidence of his "excavation," he left tools and a few supplies hidden along the edges of the cave, like the ancient people before him.

But on this morning he found the tools and supplies buried under new rock fall. The earthquakes had opened up an entirely new lava tube, roughly parallel to the one he was working in. And it was pristine. The ice lay glittering in the beam of his headlamp, coated with only the thinnest coat of dust, untouched for a thousand? two thousand? ten thousand? years. Unhesitating, he plunged in.

The new cave was huge—maybe twenty yards across and twenty or thirty yards high. The bottom third was ice. It looked as though a small river had been running through it and suddenly froze. He looked right, then left. He stood at the deepest point of a sweeping arc, the point of the new gallery that came closest to the old cave. A scant ten feet had separated them.

He stepped out to the center of the ice and turned slowly with his arms open. "I name this cave 'Hartigan's Cave,' as is my privilege as its discoverer." Then he stepped to the wall and crudely scratched "Hartigan's Cave," along with his name and the date with his pocket knife. Then he had to slump down on the ice, sit a minute, and collect himself. He realized he was the first human being to set foot in this cave in thousands, perhaps ten thousand years, if, in fact, a human had ever set foot in it at all. Now he knew how Hillary felt at the top of Everest. The first! He was the first! When he was calmer, he stood up on rubbery legs. He looked right and then left, his headlamp sweeping the darkness like headlights on a car. He chose left, and strode off into the darkness, heady on the drug of discovery.

One of Hartigan's assumptions was that the new lava tube would eventually breech the surface somewhere. His other assumption was that there was only one lava tube: the one he was in. Neither assumption was entirely correct.

He had trudged, slipping often on the ice, about a quarter mile when he encountered the first fork. Here, two smaller lava tubes converged to form the larger one. He took the one to the left. He had gone about another quarter mile when he encountered yet another tube joining the one he was in. And so it went until he had taken five or six of these forks. None seemed to lead out.

He had taken his watch off so he had no idea how long he had been in the caves. Weary and a little afraid, he sat down on a block of basalt to think. The beam of his headlamp swept around him as the looked first, over his shoulder, and then to his front. The light seemed small and fragile in the thick weight of the darkness surrounding him.

It occurred to him that he had been steadily walking uphill—not a steep grade—but a gentle slope. He had been following the lava tubes back to their source! Obviously, he would have to turn around and go back the way he came. The down side was that he couldn't remember which of the forks he had taken had been a "left," and which had been a "right." Undaunted, he turned and started back. At each intersection, he thought he had taken the fork that would bring him back to his old digs. What he didn't know was he was actually stumbling deeper toward the heart of the Anvil. At some point in his three or four day ordeal, he panicked and ran, shouting "Help! Help! Can anybody hear me! Is anybody out there?" Then he tripped and fell, smashing his shoulder against the sharp edges of rock fall. He sat there, crying like a child, until he cried himself into a fitful sleep.

He dreamed he saw himself as another spelunker might see him years hence: a withered, mummified version of himself, lips drawn back in the feral smile of the shrunken and dried, his legs and arms drawn up to his chest, leathery and brittle, like crossed sticks. The nightmare woke him, and he moved on in the ever diminishing circle of his light, until he could go no more.

So he flopped on the floor of the cave, and leaned against the rock fall. His headlamp dimmed, barely keeping the utter darkness of his entombment at bay. As a Bishop of the Church, he had often described, in glowing terms, the bliss of eternity and the heavenly kingdom. He had been sealed in the Temple—guarantees both of his eternal life and of being joined, eventually, with Chantal and his children. But now the concepts seemed alien and remote, ridiculous in the face of the darkness and crushing weight of the surrounding basalt. He didn't think he deserved to die, not this way, slowly perishing of starvation, and thirst. It was unlikely he would even be found.

The headlamp dimmed, flickered, and went out. Utter darkness leapt at him, like a ravening wolf. He removed his safety helmet with the headlamp on it and set it down. There was nothing to do but wait for death. He supposed he should try to leave some kind of last message for Chantal and his kids, but he had nothing to write with and nothing to write on. He might try scratching something on the wall, but he couldn't see. Exhausted, he simply lay down on the ice, hoping he would freeze to death. Mercifully, he drifted off into an uneasy sleep.

He awoke with a start, clawing at the darkness. He had dreamed a snarling, slavering cave bear was about to clamp its hideous jaws around his head. He stood up, stamping his feet, flapping his arms, trying to restore circulation and a little warmth. He took a few tentative steps in the direction he had been going when his light failed. Walking was difficult enough when he could see; he tripped over a boulder and fell almost immediately, scraping his forearms and knees on the basalt boulders. Well, then, he would crawl. Slowly, like a blind man, he felt his way across he rock fall, crawling on his hands and knees. He looked behind: utter darkness. He looked ahead: the same.

How long he crawled he did not know; both his knees and both of his hands were slick with blood. The lava tube curved downward and to his left, and he had been crabbing along the smooth wall, leaning into it for support when it suddenly disappeared and he fell into empty space. He screamed and flailed, landed on his back with a sickening crunch on a smooth, hard-packed floor. A flour-fine dust billowed around him. He heaved, trying to get his breath back, choked, then coughed, and waved his hands in front of his face.

He had fallen into another tunnel, and in the distance, he saw a circle of light, which, from where he sat, looked about as big as a quarter.

"Oh, thank you, God. Thank you!" he yelled, jumped up and ran toward the light. He ran about thirty yards before he stepped out into empty space and fell again into abyssal blackness. Blinded by the light, he had not seen the yawning hole in the cave floor. He slammed into a mound of something that felt like sand, rolled about ten yards, fell again, bounced off a shelf of basalt, and fell another fifteen feet, this time into the light. He landed on his belly. When he looked up, he saw the large arch of the cave entrance, sunlight, and the bleak, black lava and sage landscape of the Anvil. The light pierced him painfully, and he shielded his eyes with an upraised hand.

Ten yards to his left, the remnants of a fire smoked lazily, and filled the cave with the resinous scent of juniper.

"Fire?" he thought. "How can there be fire here? There's no one out here."

Then something seized his neck from behind with a paralyzing, crushing, grip. It stood him up, ran him to the wall, smashed his skull once, twice, three times on the basalt. The first time he saw stars, the second he felt the bones of his skull give, and he didn't feel the third.

A raven sat in a pinyon tree on the valley floor below the lip of the cave. He had just finished pecking on the bones, skins, and whatever else looked like edible morsels tossed from above. He looked up as the body sailed from the cave, turned lazily end over end, and crashed in the bone pile littering the ravine. He sailed down to investigate. To get to the eyes first was the thing.

Chapter 14

YOUR FAILED ATTEMPT TO ELIMINATE THE INDIAN HAS CAUSED CONCERN AMONG THE MEMBERS OF THE CONSORTIUM. SOME OF THEM ARE SUGGESTING WE CANCEL YOUR CONTRACT BEFORE ANY FURTHER ATTENTION IS AROUSED.

Vassili stared at the blinking cursor, resisting the impulse to smash the laptop into poker chips. Even the people he often worked for seemed to think real life happened like they saw it on television. They had no idea that the outcome of operations like the assassination of Jake Two Feathers often depended as much on luck as on skill—especially an operation involving close quarter combat at night. He was not often in the position of defending himself, and it annoyed him.

"What did you expect? Assassination usually does arouse the attention of the police. If you didn't want the risk, you should never have ordered it. The Indian got lucky."

A DEAD BODY IS ONE THING; THE BODIES OF TWO ASSASSINS IN THE CUSTODY OF THE POLICE ARE ANOTHER. IT WOULD BE MOST UNFORTUNATE FOR YOU IF THEY WERE TRACED TO YOU, AND THEN TO US.

"Mikhail and Ivan were two of my best men. Have some respect for the dead; they were with me a long time."

WE DO NOT HAVE THE LUXURY OF SENTIMENTALITY. CLEAN UP THIS MESS WITH THE INDIAN IN SUCH A WAY THE POLICE ARE SATISFIED. HE MUST BE KILLED BEFORE HE LEADS THEM OUT ON THE THE ANVIL.

"The Indian will be killed when I decide to kill him, and when the time is right."

DON'T PUSH US TOO HARD, VASSILI. YOU ARE PERFECTLY AWARE OF THE RULES.

"I have never failed you in the past, and I will not fail you now. The Indian cannot be killed until he gets on to the Anvil. The hospital and the town are too small. We have already aroused too much attention. We must wait until he is alone with the Haraldsen's. He would not need to be eliminated at all if you would locate the site. Have you?"

OUR AERIAL SURVEYS HAVE NOT PRODUCED CONCLUSIVE DATA.

"In other words, 'No.'"

THAT IS CORRECT. WE ARE STILL SEARCHING.

"Contact me when you have something more than threats."

Vassili clicked out of the e-mail and sat back. When this assignment was completed, it might not be a bad idea to teach the Consortium a lesson on the perils of screwing with him.

The coffee that came with breakfast was the color of weak tea. He peered into the cup, and looked up at Sheila.

"Give it to me," she grinned, "I'll get you some from the nurses' station. We know how to make coffee."

"Thanks," he said. "Thick and black."

"Gotcha. I'll be right back."

He lifted the silver cover off the plate. Underneath lay two pieces of what looked like yesterday's toast, a couple of greasy sticks (bacon?) and a yellow glop.

Sheila came back with the coffee.

"The chicken that laid this must have been one sick chicken," Jake said, poking the mass with his fork.

"Give me that," she said, sweeping up the plate and the cover. "I'll be back."

He tasted the coffee tentatively. Thick and black as promised. He lay there, savoring the coffee, wishing he could have a cigarette.

She returned twenty minutes later. "Try this," she said, removing the cover with a flourish. There was a thick slice of pitt ham, three eggs over easy, three slices of freshly buttered toast, and an assortment of those little square packets of jam. The edges of the eggs were brown and crisp.

"I didn't know if you used this, so I brought it just in case." She produced a bottle of Tabasco from her pocket.

"Yeah, I do." He smiled. "My compliments to the chef."

"Thank you." She nodded and grinned.

"Did you cook this?" he asked.

"Yeah, well, there are perks to being in a small hospital. Besides, I know what a man likes." She blushed and developed a sudden interest in the IV tree. Jake studied her.

A mass of coppery, shoulder-length hair framed a square, strong face of porcelain skin, dotted by a few freckles. Eyes, blue as a robin's egg, studied the levels in the IV bags. A few laugh lines etched the corners of her eyes. He could never figure out why older women hated those lines. To Jake, they signified a woman who had lived, endured, and attained some maturity. He found the slight creases around her eyes appealing. Jake pegged her at early forties.

A slender nose swept down to full, lush lips—eminently kissable lips. She wore little make-up, a shadow of auburn eyeliner, a touch of color on the eyebrow, and a glisten of blush on her lips. He realized the blush had just been touched up.

"Did you know the average American marriage lasts two and a half bottles of Tabasco?" he asked, picking up the fork in his right hand.

She laughed. "No, I didn't."

Jake stared at the ham. The surgical dressing bound his left arm and hand to his chest. "Uhh... ."

"Here," she said, "let me help you." She sat on the edge of the bed, cutting the ham. "So how many bottles of Tabasco did yours last?" she asked.

Jake laughed. "About half a bottle—no, maybe a quarter."

"What happened?" she asked, carefully slicing the rind from the pieces of ham.

Jake shook his head. "I came home from Panama and she was in bed with another man."

She handed him the fork. "Ouch. That must have hurt."

"Did, but after a while I figured it was good to find out early. Can't be with someone you can't trust."

"No, you can't," she said, crossing her legs and smoothing the white skirt of her nurse's uniform.

"Sounds like the voice of experience," Jake said through a mouthful of egg and toast. "So how many for you?"

"None," she grinned. "He didn't use Tabasco. He didn't do much of anything else, either."

"So how long were you married?"

She sighed. "I stuck it out for twenty-three years, until my son went to college. By then, I'd had enough."

"Enough of what?"

Sheila laughed. "Enough of nothing."

They talked small talk until Jake had eaten about half the ham and most of the eggs. Then he pushed the tray away and slumped back against the pillows. To Sheila's eye, he had grown noticeably paler.

She cleared the breakfast tray away and asked, "How's the pain, Jake?"

"It's getting there," he said.

She slipped a syringe from her other pocket, and injected its contents into the I.V.

"Demerol?"

"Yeah," she said. "Just enough for you to relax and get to sleep." She reached out and held his hand briefly. "Nice talkin' to you, Jake."

"Yeah, thanks for the good service."

She released his hand and left. Jake slipped into a hazy sleep; he dreamed an Iraqi in a black and white *kaffeyia* was using him for target practice.

Gopal Deshpar waited until he was sure the Utah State Highway Patrolman had turned around and driven south, back toward Ogden, before he floored the white suburban and accelerated to ninety-five. He had tried to explain that he was on his way to find out what had happened to his four dead students, but the state bull was unsympathetic. Desh had wasted half an hour and gotten a speeding ticket for all his persuasiveness.

He had asked the Sheriff (Cordy? Currey? Curdy?) not to move the bodies until he got there, saying he'd leave immediately and be there in four hours. The Sheriff said he'd wait as long as he could, but when the crime scene techs finished, the bodies would be transported.

"What was the cause of death?" Desh asked.

"Too soon to tell," the Sheriff said. "Looks like they died in their sleep."

Desh had a terrible feeling he knew the cause of death. And if he were right, these four deaths might be multiplied ten thousand times.

It was mid-afternoon by the time he found the turn-off marked by the wooden Forest Service sign, "Cascade Campground .... 6." He followed the twisting red cinder road over a series of roller coaster sage hills that led toward the escarpment towering above the plain of the Anvil. He passed a chain of small ponds hedged in by thickets of willow and alder. The Forest Service sign read "Bead Lakes." He rounded a corner and broke into a broad graveled parking lot. He saw two ambulances, two PCSD cruisers, a blue Duramax 3500 with the Sheriff's department logo, an official-looking white van with State of Idaho plates, and a white suburban that matched the one he drove.

The campground nestled in a lovely glen of old aspens, each as thick as a man's waist. Yellow crime scene tape cordoned off the area where two small tents had been pitched. Desh parked and made his way toward the tents where he saw a group of men talking. He was soon stopped by a bull of a man wearing levis, a revolver, and a short-sleeved khaki shirt with a deputy sheriff's badge and a brass name tag that read "Landski."

One of the men in the group, the one wearing the Stetson, looked up as Desh approached Landski.

"Joe!" he called. "It's O.K." He motioned Desh to join the group. "Dr. Deshpar?" He held out his hand. "Just in time. We're getting ready to transport the bodies."

Desh shook his hand and the hands of the other men standing around. He looked at Mo Creighton, the coroner. "Have you established a cause of death?"

Creighton glanced at Tom, then back to the small mahogany-colored man. "Too soon to tell, really, but—doesn't make sense—I'd say they suffocated in their sleep."

"You might be right," Desh said. "May I see them?"

Tom interrupted Mo before he had a chance to respond: "Dr. Deshpar, I know these were your students, and you are naturally concerned, but you seem to be awfully interested in what killed them. Do you know or suspect something we should know?"

"I'd prefer not to speculate until I see them and have a chance to examine the area."

Tom stared steadily at the little man. "All right, Doctor, we'll play it your way. But don't withhold anything from us we need to know."

"That is precisely why I have come—to make certain you *do* know everything."

Tom led the way down to the first of the two pup tents. He hesitated before he lifted back the flap. He turned to a technician who was packing up his equipment in a Halliburton case. "O.K., Jim?" The technician looked up and nodded "Yes." Tom held back the flap. Desh got down on his knees and looked in.

The crime scene techs had peeled the sleeping bag back to reveal the boy and the girl naked, entwined in each other like lovers. The boy lay on his back with his left leg crossed over the girl's legs. She lay across his chest, head nestled under his chin. Both lay with their arms outstretched, as if in crucifixion. From where he kneeled, Desh observed the cyanosis—bluing—of the lips and beds of the nails. He stuck his head in the tent and inhaled noisily.

"Jesus Christ," Mo muttered.

"Mr. Creighton, would you mind joining me?" Desh asked. The British lilt to his voice made it sound as if he were asking Mo to tea.

Creighton looked at Tom, who shrugged. He dropped to his knees and stuck his head in the tent.

"Smell," Desh commanded him. Creighton took a deep breath. "What do you smell?"

Creighton stared at Desh in disgust. Both the victims had voided their bowels when they died. "Shit, that's what I smell."

"That, but something else, too. Try again. Try to distinguish other odors."

Creighton hesitated, then did what he was told.

"Well?"

"Rotten eggs. There is a faint odor of rotten eggs."

"Just so," Desh said, backing out of the tent. He dusted his hands off daintily and turned to Tom. "I think you will find that they died of suffocation all right, but also of hydrogen sulphide poisoning."

"Hydrogen sulphide?" Mo blurted. "Where the hell would that come from?"

"It's one of the gasses emitted by a large magma body nearing the surface."

"Are you saying a volcano is going to erupt?" Tom asked.

"I wish I knew," Desh answered.

For the tenth time, Rick Sanchez checked the thermometer floating in the hot tub. He had sent the two kids to spend the night with their friends, saying he and their mother needed a night alone. They bitched about not being allowed to sit in the new hot tub so he let them get in, even though the temperature was only 90 degrees.

Then they bitched about it being too cold. So he made them get out and sent them off.

The thermometer read 103. Perfect. Now if Jeannette would just get home. Rick stepped inside. The kitchen clock read 8:30. He strolled into the living room and stood looking out the front window.

He saw a placid, comfortable street lined by ancient cottonwoods. They had been planted mid-century and had grown to gigantic proportions, with girths four or five feet in diameter. Their roots buckled the sidewalks in many places.

The houses, too, had been new in the post-war boom of the late forties and fifties. They were the modest bungalows and cottages of railroad workers, barbers, hardware and drugstore owners, dry goods dealers, and clerks. Most wore layer upon layer of white paint, and nearly all of them looked alike, with the wooden steps that led past two square pillars to the tongue and groove porch, usually painted battleship grey. Single car garages nestled next to the house at the end of a one-lane driveway. They were the peaceful, solid houses of hard-working, respectable people who publicly minded their own business, and gossiped over the back yard fence.

Rick was standing at his front window, watching the gathering dusk, when Jeannette's grey Ford Taurus swept up the street and into the driveway. She got out of the car and tried half-heartedly to pat her hair back into place. She usually wore it up in a weird do of blond ringlets, but most of it had fallen out. She gave up and marched resolutely up the steps. When she came through the front door and saw him standing in the living room, she stopped short.

"What are you doing?" she asked, trying to fix her hair again.

"Waiting for you."

"Why?"

"I thought we could sit in the hot tub."

"Yeah, right," she snorted, and marched down the hall to the back of the house where the bedrooms lay.

Rick trailed along behind her, like a puppy, and followed her into the bedroom.

"No, really. Come out back and look. I bought one today."

She kicked off her shoes, unclipped the earrings and began unbuttoning her blouse. She stopped half-way down the buttons.

"Well, that's nice if you did, but it's about ten years too late. I'm tired; I want to take a shower and go to bed. I ain't in the mood for hot tubs and romance."

"Well, Jesus, at least come and look at it."

She shook her head and moved past him down the hall toward the bathroom. "A hot tub ain't gonna fix nuthin' between us, Rick." She closed the bathroom door and the lock snicked into place.

He retreated to the deck, where he sat deep into the night, smoking one Marlboro after another.

Nicole and her father had waited all morning, trying to get in to see Jake. They had watched the Sheriff and another man come and go, and a couple of nurses scurrying about performing their morning nursing duties. The only information they could get was that he was in stable condition and resting. No visitors. Immediate next of kin only. Nicole thought about saying she was his sister, but they would never believe her.

Haraldsen fussed and fumed his way through the outdated magazines in the waiting area, gave up, and began pacing. He was obviously worried that Jake wouldn't be able to lead them onto the Anvil.

"Typical," Nicole thought, watching him, "the dig is more important than the people."

He had grown pale, and kept his hands in his jacket pockets so she couldn't see the palsy. Or maybe that's how he kept the shaking from himself. About one in the afternoon she finally convinced him to go back to the room and take a nap. She would stay behind to try to see Jake.

After her father left, Nicole approached the nurse's station. An older, plump woman with rosy cheeks hacked away at a computer and a red-haired nurse thumbed through her charts.

"Excuse me," Nicole asked, "can you tell me when Jake Two Feathers might be receiving visitors?"

The older woman turned and looked at the red-head.

The red-head looked Nicole up and down and asked, "Are you next of kin?" Her eyes flashed like Gillette blue blades.

"No. Business associate."

"What kind of business?"

Nicole suddenly became acutely aware that she was wearing a thin white silk blouse, levis, and no bra. "So that's how it is," she thought. She stood a little straighter and thrust her chest up.

"Jake and I are close business associates. We are working on an important archaeological surveying and mapping project that just may save priceless artifacts and change the archaeological history of the New World. So if he's not dying, I'm sure he'd be glad to see me."

"Who's not dying?" Bones had cruised up silently in his usual uniform: boat shoes, levis, tee shirt, and tweed jacket.

"Miss—what did you say your name was?—wants to see Jake. She's a 'close business associate.'" Sheila rolled her eyes.

Nicole offered her hand to Bones. "Nicole Haraldsen."

Bones shook it, trying heroically not to stare at her chest. "Michael Purser. They call me 'Bones.'" To Sheila: "Well, how is he?"

"He ate about half of his breakfast. But the pain was getting to him, so I gave him Demerol."

"How long ago was that?"

Sheila looked at her watch. "About two hours ago"

Bones turned to Nicole, and taking her arm, walked down the hall toward Jake's room. "Let's see how he is." Bones beamed.

Nicole slipped her arm in his, and smiled. "I really appreciate this, Michael."

Sheila watched them go. "Men are such pigs," she said, shaking her head.

The older woman looked over her readers at Sheila. "You just figuring that out?"

Chapter 15

Bones paused at the door to Jake's room, and cracked it open. He let it slide softly closed and turned to Nicole. "Looks like he's still sleeping, but I'm sure he'll wake up fairly soon; you can go in and wait if you like." He flashed Nicole his most alluring smile.

"Thanks," she said, patting Bones on the arm. "I promise not to wake him." She slipped through the door, leaving Bones gawping in the hall.

Jake heard he distinctive sound of a AK-47 bolt slamming a round in the breech. "Why didn't the stupid bastard have one locked and loaded?" he thought, as he rolled over, drawing his .45. The heavy Colt bucked in his hand twice, and the Arab went down in a flurry of robes, but not before the jack-hammer punch of a 7.62 slug flattened him against the dune. He sat back up in time to see another Arab topping the rise of the dune, spraying Shea and Rico with a lethal volley. They jerked like puppets and lay still. He pointed the .45 toward the Arab and emptied it. "Shea! Rico!" He began crawling toward them, and a terrible sharp pain lanced up from his right side. "Shea! Rico!" He kept on crawling, ignoring the sticky wetness in his crotch, and the piercing, numbing pain.

"Jake?" Nicole had come to the bedside when he began yelling and writhing in his sleep. She touched his shoulder. Jake's hand shot out like a cobra's, seizing her neck in a crushing grip; simultaneously, he came up on one knee, and slammed her down across the bed, choking the life out of her.

"Aake! Aaake!" she choked.

When the red mist cleared from his eyes, he let her go, stunned at what he had done.

She jumped up massaging her throat. "Jake, guys like you are dangerous bastards." She grabbed her purse and bolted out the door, running into Sheila.

Jake was still up on one knee in the bed.

"Jesus, Jake. What happened?" She came bedside to help him lay back down.

"I was having a nightmare. She woke me up."

"And?" She tucked the sheets back around him.

"Never wake a vet up unless you do it with a broom handle."

The forty-five minute drive from the Cascade Campground to the Python County Law Enforcement Center was a quiet one for Thomas Curdy and Morris Creighton. Each man wrestled with the horrific consequences of a major volcanic eruption.

They had talked quietly and privately with Deshpar, away from the other men at the crime scene. Desh explained that the students probably died from carbon dioxide and hydrogen sulphide poisoning—two heavier than air gases—emitted when large magma bodies passed close to the surface, "close" being a relative term.

The gases had simply flowed down the ravine above the campground, and settled in the low places until the morning breeze dispersed them. Unfortunately, the students pitched their tents in one of the lowest places.

He filled them in on the quake in Alaska, the ensuing activity in Yellowstone, and what the students were doing in the first place. And no, he didn't think a major eruption was eminent. But it was possible, he said. They just didn't have enough information, yet.

Desh didn't mention that the existence of these gases miles away from Yellowstone didn't make sense to him, and he had no idea how to account for their presence. Either a new magma mass was approaching the surface from deep in the mantle, or something had happened in Yellowstone that the sensors hadn't detected. Large bodies of moving magma cause earthquakes. Aside from the usual small swarms in Yellowstone, there was no evidence of an impending eruption.

Still...four students lay dead from gases that spilled out somewhere up the side of the caldera.

The three of them agreed to keep the suspected cause of the deaths quiet, pending the outcome of the autopsies, and further monitoring of the Caldera. Desh did his best to downplay the idea of a large, eminent eruption: there just wasn't enough evidence to support it. There might not even be an explosion, like Mount St. Helen's. The lava might just break through the surface and flow across the land, like it had several times before, creating the Anvil. He just didn't know.

But try as they might, neither Tom nor Mo could shake the horrifying vision of a supervolcano erupting in their backyard. They parted company in the parking lot of the Law Enforcement Center. Mo went home; Tom trudged into the building.

Shirley looked up as he entered and said, "Tom, you better read the *Gazette*. I put a copy on your desk."

"Why?" he asked.

"Just read it," she said. "You'll see."

The *Python Gazette* lay unfolded on his desk. The headline read:

Terrorists Attack Python Residents

The article speculated that for some unknown motive, two of Python's undocumented Hispanic residents had been brutally murdered and implied a link between those two deaths and the shooting of Mr. Jacob Two Feathers of South River Road.

The article went on to describe, in great detail, the clothing, tattoos, and weaponry of the two dead assailants. The principal evidence for labeling them "terrorists" seemed to have been the clothing, and the tattoos.

The article implied that the Sheriff, Tom Curdy, had deliberately withheld information from the press vital to the safety of the citizens of Python.

Tom stuck his head out of his office. "Shirley, please call PHARK and tell him I want to see him *now*."

Ten minutes later Herb Witherspoon walked through the front door of the Python County Law Enforcement Complex. Herb was a seedy, paunchy man in his early sixties. Had it not been for the baggy grey flannel pants, the non-descript blue shirt, the maroon and green checked blazer, he could easily pass for an aging dishwasher. What was left of his long, stringy, sandy hair was yellow, like the nicotine stains on the first and middle fingers of his right hand. A thin turkey neck sprouted between slumping shoulders. A small head and a long, narrow face perched on top of it.

"He wanted to see me," he said smugly, pointing at Tom's door. He smiled a nasty, triumphant smile, revealing small, yellow teeth.

"Do go right on in," Shirley said.

Herb rapped loudly, and entered without waiting for a reply. He left the door open. Five seconds later, Tom appeared at the doorway, smiled at Shirley and quietly closed the door.

Thirty-six minutes later (Shirley timed it), PHARK left. He seemed confused, eyes unfocused, pale, slouching out the door.

Two minutes later, Tom emerged from his office, whistling *Camptown Races.* He grinned at Shirley, who was gathering her things to leave for the day.

"Tomorrow morning, first thing, make an announcement that there will be a press conference, here, at eleven o'clock. Thanks. Have a great evening, Shir." He tipped his hat and left, whistling.

"'Night, Tom," Shirley said to his departing back. She waited until he was out the door. "Yes!" she shouted.

Early the next morning, Olivia Haglund sat at the receptionist's desk of the Python County Hospital contemplating her wickedness. Reveling in it, actually.

Olivia had turned sixty-three in May; she had been sentenced, for some reason unfathomable to her, to endure forty-three of those years as Rupert Haglund's wife. Her marriage had been an arranged one, arranged by the two Mormon Bishops who were Olivia and Rupert's respective fathers. It satisfactorily joined two sections of prime river-bottom farm land into one grand and profitable farm.

The elder Bishops, along with their worn-out wives, had removed to town the better to wage religious war against encroaching Catholics and Presbyterians, as well as luxuriate in their two-thirds of the profits. The task of ensuring those undiminished profits fell to Rupert and Olivia. The task of raising four children—three girls and a boy—as well as satisfying the perverted and sometimes downright cruel, needs of Rupert, fell squarely on Olivia's shoulders.

Fortunately, she was a hefty woman, big-boned, wide-shouldered, with beamy, capacious hips, a vast field for Rupert's plowing. And plow he did, often and cruelly.

As soon as the girls blossomed enough to attract his feral eye, she contrived to send them off, one by one, to various schools, away from Rupert's stinking fingers.

The boy, Judah, grew into a younger version of his father. As soon as he could, he took a wife, moved down the road a mile, and vigorously began practicing the sins of the older generation on his own.

The wickedness that Olivia contemplated was Rupert's sudden death in February.

It happened like this. The man was possessed by a nearly sexual obsession for pork chops, which he devoured with a noisy, liquid intensity. On the evening in question, Olivia sat at her usual place at the dinner table, watching in horror and disgust as he practiced what can only be called a perversion of eating. He looked up and caught her staring.

"What're yew lookin' at?" He dropped the bone he had been sucking on. It clattered on the plate.

"Nothing," she said, expecting a cuff on the head. She quickly focused her attention on the puddle of creamed corn on her plate. She was surprised when no cuff came and the sucking noises continued, along with the sound of rending meat. Rupert had begun on his third pork chop, which he liked to eat with his hands, like chicken. She looked up when the sucking, chewing noises became gagging, choking noises.

Rupert had reared back in his chair, waving a half-eaten pork chop like a baton. The other hand clutched his throat. He grew red in the face; his eyeballs popped out, looking to Olivia for help.

Her first impulse was to panic, to pound Rupert on the back, as she had her children. She half rose in her chair, then sat back down. A great calm descended upon her. She folded her hands neatly in her lap, and crossed her legs at the ankles. She stared Rupert down, pinned him with a stare leaded with forty-three years of cruelty.

His lips turned blue. He jumped up, grabbed her by the shoulders; she flicked him off, like a horse flicks off a fly. He flailed around the kitchen and fell; the heels of his heavy boots drummed the floor.

After a while, she stood up, scraping the legs of the chair on the linoleum, and took a step toward him. She bent over and peered at the body.

"Rupert?" When she got no response, she nudged him with her shoe.

"Rupert? Are you dead?" Silence. She choked out a sob of joy, giggled, pirouetted around the kitchen like a girl, and called 911.

Olivia roused herself from memory. A fierce joy seized her. She was glad he was dead: glad, glad, glad! The Lord gave her an opportunity and she took it. And now He was giving her another one: Lawrence Whitcomb of Python Realty had called to say he had investors interested in buying the farm, which was now hers, free and clear. The figure he quoted for the thousand plus acres of river bottom approached the astronomical—at least it seemed so to Olivia.

She wrote the price per acre on her desk pad and multiplied it by 1280. The six figure number scared her. What would she do with it all? Not give it to Judah, that's for sure.

Olivia took a sip of coffee—another symbol of her freedom. Coffee and tobacco were forbidden by the Church. She laced the coffee with thick cream and sugar, reveling in the delicious wickedness she felt. She thought she might even try cigarettes, but she would have to work up to that. She would have to find someone to buy them for her, because if she bought them herself, it would soon be all over town that Olivia Haglund was smoking.

A polite cough summoned her from her reverie. She had been so preoccupied she had neither seen nor heard the massive Indian. Tall as a moose and thick as a grizzly, he seemed to fill the entire reception area. He wore a black, tattered cowboy hat with a low, sweat-stained crown. The brim had been flattened and shaped to a "V" in the front. An eagle feather sprouted from a beaded hatband.

Two fierce black eyes studied her from a brown, moon-shaped face. A toothpick jutted out between surprisingly full and feminine lips. A faded red sweatshirt with the sleeves cut off, clung to the elephantine chest.

The toothpick flicked to the other side of his mouth. "What room's Jacob in?"

Olivia collected herself enough to answer. "You mean Mr. Two Feathers?"

"Yeah. That's him." The Indian spoke in curious, clipped, nasal speech. English did not come easily to his tongue.

Olivia shuffled some files on her desk, wishing Sheila were here instead of off in one of the patient rooms. She wasn't supposed to let anyone in to see Jake, but she was afraid to say "No" to the monster facing her. "Aahh, one-oh-one at the end of the hall."

He whirled silently and headed back out the front door. A faded and rusting '72 Ford pickup blocked the drive in front of the door. A bundle wrapped in an old grey and white blanket sat upright on a lawn chair in the bed of the truck.

The massive Indian opened the front door of the hospital, hollered, "*Hokahey!*" and waved "C'mon!" with his hand. His twin bailed out of the driver's side of the pickup, gently lifted the bundle out of the truck, and set it down on the sidewalk.

A wizened, ancient woman about four and a half feet tall emerged from the folds of the blanket. She produced a stick, adorned with eagle and red-tailed hawk feathers, and pecked her way through the door. The two goliaths flanked her.

Sheila emerged from old Mr. Pedersen's room, one-oh-nine, in time to see the strange procession of Indian trolls and a dwarf in a blanket pass by.

"Can I help you?"

Toothpick barely glanced at her. "Nope." They continued tapping down the hall. Sheila raced around and positioned herself in front of them.

"Visiting hours don't start until seven p.m. You can't just come barging into this hospital. Who did you want to see?" She knew it was a stupid question; it was perfectly obvious who they wanted to see. But she asked it, anyway.

They ignored the question and tapped relentlessly forward. When they came to Jake's room, Toothpick said, *"Leci."*

Sheila spread-eagled herself across the door.

"You cannot go in here!"

Toothpick nodded to his twin, who gently picked Sheila up and set her aside. She ran off down the hall hollering for Olivia to call Bones and the Sheriff.

The commotion woke Jake and he sat up in bed in time to see TP open the door, and the old woman pecking toward his bed. She dropped the blanket that had all but concealed her face and hair.

The leathery, oval visage puckered with the seams and pleats of long life. She smiled a toothless smile, and reached out with a withered, gnarled hand, small as a child's, to pat him on the cheek. The hand was warm and soft as silk. She wore her hair pulled back and braided into a single thick braid, white as clouds.

"Isnala Mani," she said. And then she launched a barrage of growling words. He could understand only a few of them.

Jake held up his hand. "Wait," he said. "Hau, hau." He shook each of their hands. "Thank you for coming, but I don't know who you are. I can't understand her," he said, looking at Toothpick.

The old woman looked at Toothpick and made a couple of quick, swiping motions with her hand.

The huge Indian took his hat off, and assumed a kind of slouch-hipped awkward stance. "This is your grandfather's second cousin, Wilma Slow Horse. I am her great grandson, Wilbur, and this is my brother, Wilmer. She is *winyan wakan.*" He paused, screwing up his face, as if in deep and painful thought. "She is medicine woman?" The statement was made as a question, as though he were asking Jake for the correct translation.

"Yes. I understand those words," Jake said. "But I can't understand many of her other words."

"Ummm." Wilbur shifted his feet uncomfortably, looked at the floor. "That's because she uses a lot of, ummm, old words, that nobody understands anymore."

Jake nodded; his lips formed an "Oh." "Why did she call me *Isnala Mani*? My name is Jacob Two Feathers."

Wilmer fired a question at the old woman in deep guttural language.

She snorted and fired right back, though her answer was much longer. She stared at Jake.

Wilbur shifted again, redistributing his great weight. "She says that is what the, ummm…" His eyes rolled up to the ceiling as he sought the words. "Ahh, she says that is what the First Ones called you—."

The old woman interrupted him with a short volley of sharp words. An ancient leather satchel hung from her shoulder; she rooted around in it.

He fired back a short, annoyed volley.

"But why have you come?" Jake asked.

"The old woman had a vision, and they told her to come and heal you."

"Come and heal me," Jake repeated.

"*Heceteu,* Wilbur said, shrugging, "that's the way it is."

The old woman produced a bundle of sage and a bic lighter from the sack. She fired a command at the brothers. They started to pick up the bed, discovered it had wheels, and rolled it to the center of the room.

Sheila flew in the room in time to see the old woman preparing to light the sage.

"What are you doing?" Sheila screeched. You can't do that! There's oxygen in this room!"

The old woman torched it. The sage smelled surprisingly like marijuana. When it billowed smoke, she danced around Jake's bed singing in a high, singsong voice. When Sheila tried to snatch the bundle away, Wilmer gently, but firmly embraced her from behind.

"Stop this!" Sheila yelled. "The Sheriff is on his way; you will all be thrown in jail! Jake! Tell them to stop."

He shrugged. "They're doing a healing ceremony." He shrugged again. Off in the distance, sirens wailed.

The old woman completed four circuits around the bed and loosed another volley of gravel-language at Wilmer and Wilbur.

Wilbur looked at Jake. "She says we have to go outside."

Jake shrugged, smiling. "Lead on."

The two boys pushed the bed. The old woman led, singing, with the sage bundle held aloft. Sheila trailed behind.

When they breeched the front doors they were greeted by the sound of twelve gauge shotguns racking rounds in the chambers. Bob Duncan, Hal Lindsay, and Tom crouched behind two cruisers and Tom's pick-up, using the vehicles for cover.

"What did you tell them?" Sheila asked Olivia, who had followed them out the door.

Olivia clasped her hand to her breast. "Why, I told them terrorist thugs raided the hospital to kidnap Jake!"

"Chrrriistt!" Jake said, shaking his head.

The old woman began to sing a mournful song.

"What's she doing?" Sheila asked.

"She's singing her death song," Wilbur replied. "She thinks they're gonna kill her, like at Wounded Knee." He joined her, followed by Wilmer.

"Oh, hell," Tom said, and stepped out from behind the truck. "Put the guns down, boys. What's going on, Jake?"

"A healing ceremony."

"A healing ceremony?"

"Yeah," Jake said. "A healing ceremony."

Bones roared up on his Harley, jerked his helmet off and rushed up. "What the hell is going on? Olivia said terrorists attacked the hospital. And who are these Indians? What is Jake doing out here? Tom, what's going on?"

"A healing ceremony."

"A healing ceremony?"

"Yeah."

"Well, I'm sorry I missed it, Bones said.

Chapter 16

Jake sat on his deck looking over the lush grounds of *Makoce Waste* and the river beyond. It was his favorite time of day, the two hours before sunset, when the hot breezes that blew in from the desert died, and the light changed from white to gold. The emerald leaves of aspen and cottonwood burned with an amber glow, and a muddy coolness crept up from the river. The new hatch of insects swarmed above it, bright points of spinning light. The river itself poured on, like liquid metal, rose-gold in the coming sunset.

A week had passed since the fiasco at the hospital. When the situation finally got sorted out and the guns unloaded, Tom and the deputies helped push Jake's bed behind the hospital to a grove of aspens where Wilma Slow Horse finished the ceremony.

Things nearly came to blows again when the old woman ripped the dressings off Jake's wound and packed it with the brownish-green wad of herbs she had been chewing on. Bones and Sheila had to be restrained by Wilbur and Wilmer. Tom didn't know what to do: no laws had been broken, but he wished he could call the police and let them handle the whole brouhaha. Jake lay there, amused and proud to be an Indian. Bones plastered new dressings over the goo, swearing he was no longer responsible.

When it was all over, Wilma patted Jake on the cheek, smiled, and said, "Now you be good. Four days—you leave this place. Be all well." As soon as Wilma left with the goliaths, Bones nagged Jake to change the dressing and "Get that shit out of there." Jake smiled, and shook his head "No." The goo stayed. Whether it was the goo and the ceremony, or Jake's naturally vigorous health was never known, but at the end of four days even Bones had to admit the wound had healed beyond expectation.

Of the vision that had driven Wilma Slow Horse to ride nine hundred miles in the back of a broken down Ford F-150 to perform a healing ceremony, she either couldn't, or wouldn't, say very much.

It had taken her by surprise, as visions often do, as she stared into the fire that heated the *tunkan*, the sacred rocks used in the sweat lodge. Wilma and the boys had been preparing an *inipi* ceremony in an attempt to help a young woman with a difficult childbirth.

The tobacco-colored face, gouged and slashed by unknowable years and distances, appeared in the flames, and drew her down unfamiliar, ancient spirit trails to the entrance of a cave on a brutal desert, where, at twilight, the gnarled and shrunken shaman who wore the face that drew her, conducted his own ceremony.

His appeal was a simple one, as old as the first stirrings of human consciousness: it was an appeal for help in the face of a destruction, larger, stronger, more powerful than all the remedies the merely human can bring to bear upon it. When men have no where else to turn, they turn to god.

In the veiled way of a shaman's world, Wilma was permitted to see the small clan for whom the prayers were made. There were not more than thirty of them, clad in the rough-tanned skins of bear, elk, and deer. And of the thirty, only nine were women of child-bearing age, and worst of all, only four were children. One of them, a four or five year old girl, sheltered against the knee of the old shaman.

It was unclear to Wilma just what the exact nature of the threat to these people was, save that unless someone or some thing came to help them, they had but one alternative in the attempt to save themselves. In a moment of sickening horror, Wilma realized what it was: they would sacrifice the child to the forces that orchestrated their fate. Life for life.

No words passed between them. In the way of the spirit world, the two of them simply *knew* and *understood*. Wilma knew herself to be among the First People, the Ones from whom all others like herself had come. She heard the name *Isnala Mani* in her head; she saw his face, knew where he was, and what was required of her. She also knew that the explanation "Why?" was beyond her, and not for her to question. The Great Mother, who was the source of all life, and the receiver of it in death, shuttled her threads where She chose, coarse as they sometimes seemed to be.

She told none of this to Jake, saying only that the *Oyate Tutewoiecicu Hinsma* had called her. Jake and Wilbur struggled to translate the unfamiliar words, but they made no sense. The best they could come up with was "Hairy Feed-Themselves-with the-Nose People, which was nonsense. They gave up trying.

Wilma insisted that Jake was to go West. "*Wiohpeyatakia*," she said, "in the direction of the West." He pressed her, but that's all she would say, aside from the fact that the errand was urgent.

Jake insisted on leaving the hospital four days after the ceremony. Bones and Sheila resisted, of course, but relented when a grim Meij turned up carrying a change of clothes.

The first thing he did when he got home was prepare a small offering of jerky, dried fruit and tobacco. He carried them down to the sweat lodge and left them on the altar, giving thanks for his life.

The second thing he did was check out his bedroom. He was surprised to find new carpet laid and the walls freshly painted. The room smelled faintly of paint. Meij had turned down the bed and was fluffing the pillows.

"Wow!" he said. "Did you do all this Meij?"

"Me and Mr. Tom and Mrs. Ellie. Mr. Tom, he don't want you coming home to no blood."

"Thanks, Meij." He stood awkwardly in the center of the room; he didn't know what else to say.

"I make *miso* and *tonkatsu*; no more hospital food." She pointed at the bed. "In."

"No way, Meij. I've been flat on my back for six days. You cook and I'll play." He left the room before she could argue, fetched his cello from the study and walked out on the deck. He sat, wiggled the fingers of his left hand. "It's the shoulder, not the hand," he reminded himself. He tightened the bow, took a deep breath and launched into O'Connor's *Appalachia Waltz*. "A little rusty, but O.K.," he thought to himself.

When the last notes faded away, he sat back in his chair, rested the cello against his shoulder and sighed. He lived; he survived again. For now.

Aside from the obvious, the attempt on his life nagged him. What was most disturbing was he didn't know why anyone would want to kill him. Even in the murky world of special ops and intelligence, there were rules. Among professionals, the first was no killing without a purpose. Killing occurs when there is no other choice, when state secrets are threatened, or someone in the state apparatus is threatened enough to be damaged if certain information becomes known by the adversary. Jake had no intelligence on anyone or anything that mattered anymore. He hadn't even been involved in the last four years of duty.

Revenge simply wasn't a motive. To kill out of revenge was to invite disaster, for the other side would likely respond with savage force, killing as many assets of yours as it could. Good operators were far too expensive to cultivate, train and effectively field. The task often took years to accomplish. Both sides knew it. No, it wasn't revenge.

The Russian connection made no sense, either. Jake had served two tours of duty in Afghanistan. During the first, in the eighties, he helped train and equip the *mujahideen* freedom fighters who were resisting the Russian invasion. The second tour had nothing to do with the Russians. He spent his time rooting Taliban out of caves, trying to find the elusive Bin Laden. He could think of nothing in either tour that would provoke an attack, especially years after the events.

If his would-be killers were Russian mafia, (and Tom hadn't proved that they were) the puzzle was even more baffling. Jake wasn't a threat to anyone or anything—at least that he knew of—and he certainly hadn't done business with Russians, mafia or otherwise, after the fall of the Soviet Union. Yet in some way he had become a threat to *someone, somewhere*. The only thing he could think of was his new connection with the Haraldsens', but that made no sense, either.

He looked up when he heard a familiar *whop, whop, whop, whop* in the sky. The Huey arrowed out of the sunset, circled at tree top level, and settled in at Makoce Waste. The sleek olive chopper wore a black horse-head logo with the words, *Black Horse Aviation*. As soon as the blades spooled down, the cargo door slid back and Haraldsen emerged, followed by Nicole and the pilot.

Frustrated by Jake's convalescence, Haraldsen had taken it upon himself to hire the helicopter to begin searching for the "island." Black Horse Aviation was the only game in town and the pilot, Harlow Ramsay, was a friend of Jake's. Harlow had called Jake in the hospital and Jake had filled him in on the proposed expedition.

"Meij!" Jake hollered. When she appeared in the doorway, he said, "We've got company. Put the *miso* and the *tonkatsu* in the fridge; I'll eat it tomorrow. Better call out for a pizza. Put this in the study, will you?" He leaned the cello toward her.

Meij took the cello and wandered into the depths of the house muttering something about "rest."

Jake watched as the three of them walked up the gentle slope to the house. Harlow Ramsay, "Ram," to Jake and Tom Curdy, had flown with the 7th Calvary in Viet Nam. Though he was in his mid-fifties, he marched up the slope with a ramrod straight back, and a distinctly military stride. Haraldsen and Nicole struggled along behind. Ramsay wasn't even breathing hard. He leapt up on the deck, hand outstretched to shake Jake's.

"Heard you gave those Russkies a Brooklyn shave," he said, grinning.

"They didn't give me much choice, Ram," Jake said, shaking his hand.

"Well, you know what they say about pissing like a puppy when you run with the big dogs," Ram said, sitting down. "Fuckers got what they deserved. So, how you?"

Jake grinned. "Winged, but I can still fly."

"Atta boy, Jake!" Ram pointed his chin toward the Haraldsens. Harald had stopped for a breather. Nicole stopped with him. "Where'd you get those two?"

Jake studied the pair catching their breath. "They found me."

Ram dug in the pocket of his flight suit, and produced a pack of Camel studs. He shook one out and tapped it against a Zippo that bore the familiar black and yellow patch of the First Armed Cav Division. He lit it and exhaled slowly. "Well, buddy, this is your show and you can do what you want to, but if I was you, I'd leave the old man at th' motel. Ain't no way he's up to hiking across th' Anvil."

"Yeah. I know. But I can't leave him behind. He'd just follow."

Haraldsen and Nicole resumed their trudge up the slope. Ram studied Nicole. "She's a piece a work, ain't she? Mark my words, Jake,"—he pointed at Jake with the Camel between his first and second fingers—"there's some steel in those panties. Didja poke her yet?"

Jake laughed. "I don't think that's an option."

"Well, don't," Ram said. "A woman like that will swallow a man whole n' spit 'im back up in little bloody pieces."

The Haraldsens stopped twice more before they finally reached the deck. The old man's face glistened with a sheen of sweat and his face was the color of newspaper. His left hand quivered uncontrollably; his eyes ticked. Nicole guided him to one of the chairs on the deck.

"Meij! Meij!" Jake hollered. She appeared, read the situation at a glance, and disappeared without a word. She returned momentarily with a glass of water and a covered laquer bowl.

166

Haraldsen took the glass, mumbled thanks. His hands shook so badly he sloshed water on the deck. He managed a few sips, sat back in his chair, and took a deep breath. "I'm O.K.," he said, "I'm O.K. I think I took a little too much dilantin."

Meij stepped forward, pointing at the bowl. "Dlink *miso*, Mr. Lrarlsen. Feel much better." *Miso* was Meij's cure for everything from herpes to heart disease. Haraldsen took it, nodded his thanks.

Nicole lay a hand on her father's shoulder, peering at him intently. "Dad?"

He took another sip of water and waved her off. "I'm fine, Nicole. Just let me rest a minute."

Jake and Ram exchanged glances. Jake shrugged. When he looked at Nicole, she gave him the "you've got to put a stop to this" glare.

They sat there, slyly studying Haraldsen to see if he really was "O.K." After a glass of water, and half a bowl of *miso*, the shaking subsided, and his color improved a little.

The doorbell rang. Meij disappeared into the house, and returned a couple of minutes later. "Pizza's here," she announced, carrying two large pizzas which she put on the table.

They munched through the pizzas; Jake and Ram tried half-heartedly to maintain a conversation; Nicole sulked; Haraldsen nibbled a slice of pizza, and seemed to continue recovering.

After the pizza mess was cleared away, Jake lit a cigarette, leaned back in his chair, and looked at Ram. "Well?"

The pilot dug in the cargo pocket of his flight suit, produced a map, and spread it out on the table. Haraldsen and Nicole looked on as Ram briefed Jake.

"The three sites you wanted to check out are approximately one hundred fifty miles out in the northeast section of the Anvil. They are all located within a fifteen mile radius of this butte, called Black Butte." He tapped the map with a slim silver pen. "We didn't see any formations even remotely resembling a crescent, but some of those *ki—?*" He looked at Haraldsen.

"*Kipukas.*"

"*Kipukas.* Right. But some of those *kipukas* are pretty heavily wooded with pinyons so it's really hard to tell how they might look from the ground."

"Can we land anywhere close?" Jake asked.

Ram grimaced. "That's the problem, Jake. The nearest I can safely land is about here." He tapped the map again. "Which is about fifteen kilometers from the nearest site, and oh, I'd say about twenty, twenty-one kilometers from the farthest. The LZ is just a lava flow, looks like a frozen river, but it's fairly smooth. You *could* set up a base camp here, and hike to the sites, but it would be a hump. And Jake," he said looking up, "I haven't seen terrain chewed up like that since the B-52s flew arc-light missions in Nam."

He pointed at the map again with his pen. "Take the nearest site, here. You can't see it on the map but the terrain is a combination of cinder fields and collapsed lava domes. Some of those pits must be twenty, thirty feet deep—well, I guess you would know, wouldn't you? You've been out there."

Jake nodded.

"A man in great physical condition," Ram continued, "might make seven, eight miles a day, but that's a big 'if.'" He looked at Haraldsen. "No offense, Mr. Haraldsen, but I just don't think you've got it in you." He looked to Jake. "And buddy, in your condition, I'm not sure you do, either." He started to say something to Nicole, but the look on her face stopped him. "I don't know, Jake," he said, "there's a reason most of the Anvil is unexplored, and the terrain's the reason. That out there was hell in the making, and it still is."

Jake stood up, leaned over the map, and thought for a moment. He looked up at Ram, Nicole, and finally Haraldsen.

"You got plenty of money?" he asked Haraldsen.

"My life's savings," the old man said.

"This that important?" Jake asked.

"Jake, you can't be ser—," Nicole hissed.

Jake silenced her with a hand held up, palm out. He stared steadily into Haraldsen's glacial blue eyes.

"Yes."

"All right, then," Jake said, looking at the others, "we leave in two weeks." To Nicole: "I assume you know how to outfit an expedition?"

"She does," Haraldsen answered, looking at his daughter. "She's been on enough of them."

Chapter 17

Across the river, Anatoly centered Jake's head in the crosshairs of the Dragunov sniper rifle. He had changed the scope to a night vision scope, and Jake glowed an eerie green.

"Range," Anatoly whispered.

"Two hundred-six meters," Tolya whispered back, looking through night-vision range finders. He looked to Vassili, who had been listening to the conversation on the deck through a parabolic mike. Vassili stared at his men, who waited for his command. At his signal, Anatoly was to kill them all. He looked back across the river.

Jake looked at Ram: "You in or out?"

"I'm in if you're in."

"Nicole, you in or out?"

She stood up. "I think we should talk ab--."

Jake cut her off. "We're going. Are you in or out?"

She crossed her arms, fidgeted on one foot and then the other, glowering at Jake. "I'm in," she said finally.

Jake turned to Haraldsen. "Ram's gonna be flying a lot of trips ferrying supplies, so I hope you have deep pockets. JP-4 isn't cheap." To Meij: "Meij, would you run Mr. Haraldsen back to the motel, please? He needs some rest and I need to talk to Ram and Nicole."

Haraldsen started to protest, but Jake interrupted. "Harald, get some rest. We're just going to talk about getting organized for the next week." Jake smiled. "Go on; you're not going to be left out of anything."

Meij took the old man in tow and they left.

After they had gone, Jake sat back down and looked at Nicole. "O.K., let's hear it."

"What's to hear? Were you listening to him?" she nodded at Ram. "My father can't make it. Yet you're going to take him out there, knowing it will probably kill him."

Jake stared at her for a long moment. "Nicole, sit down, please."

She glared, hesitated.

"Please," he said pointing to a chair.

She sat.

"Yes, I am going to take him, and yes, it might well kill him. And if you care about him, you will help."

"Vassili!" Tolya hissed. He gestured with both hands, giving him the "Do-we-take-the-shot-or-not?" look.

"*Nyet.* Not yet. Anatoly," Vassili whispered, "relax a moment."

Anatoly lowered the weapon, disgusted, and disappointed.

"Help you? Why the hell should I help you kill my father?"

"Ram and I have seen a lot of men die."

Ram nodded, lighting another Camel.

"Most of them died," Jake continued, "doing a job they didn't want to do, in a place they didn't want to be. They wouldn't have ended their lives the way they did, if they'd had a choice."

Jake paused, lit a Marlboro. "How a man finishes his life is important, Nicole, maybe as important as how he lived. Which death do you want to give him? The one doing what he's always believed in? Or the one shitting himself in a hospital bed?"

She stood up, walked to the rail of the deck and looked out across the river into the night.

Jake got up, went to the rail, and stood next to her. He looked across the river. "There's something out there; I know it."

"What makes you so sure?" she asked.

"Two reasons," Jake said. "Whatever it is, somebody is willing to kill me to prevent us from going out there. The very fact that someone *is* willing to kill tells me that there is something out there, something very important, and related to what we are trying to find."

"What makes you think that?" Nicole asked.

"Nothing else it could be," Jake said. "The question is, what is so important that the Russian mafia wants to prevent us finding?"

"Russian mafia? You've got to be kidding!"

"No, Nicole, I'm not. I doubt if Tom will ever be able to prove they were Russian mafia, but I know Russian prison tattoos when I see them. The men who tried to kill me were elite paratroopers turned mafia. I fought against them in Afghanistan. They are very, very bad boys." He walked back to the table and sat down. "Do you know something about this site you're not telling me?" He gazed at her steadily.

She pushed off the railing and sat down across from Jake. She lay both hands flat on the table and leaned toward him. "You know as much as I do. And Jake," she said slowly and quietly, "I-don't-even-want-to-go-fucking-out-there. Remember?"

He sat back in his chair, glanced at Ram, who shrugged. He looked back to Nicole, who sat eying him coolly, arms crossed across her breasts.

"You said there are two reasons. What's the second?"

"This," he said, taking his Venus out of his pocket and tossing it to her. He had been wearing it the night of the attack and the leather thong was black with blood stains. It was almost identical to the one Nicole wore.

She picked it up. "Where did you get this?"

"It came to me," he said, and then he told her the story.

"And you think this validates my father's claim?"

"I think it means there's a mystery about where it came from and who brought it. I'd like to find out."

"What are you saying, Jake?" Ram asked. "Are you saying you think there's people out there? A lost tribe or something?"

"I'm saying I don't know, but I'd like to find out."

Nicole fell silent, fingering her own Venus. Jake and Ram talked a while longer, then Ram and Nicole left in the chopper, leaving Jake alone on the deck. He massaged his wounded shoulder, and went to bed.

Before he turned the lights out, he tucked the Yarborough under the pillow, and made sure a loaded twelve gauge shotgun lay within reach. Just because they failed the first time didn't mean they wouldn't try again.

Vassili, Tolya, and Anatoly eased out of the thicket of willows bordering the river, and slipped back to where they had hidden the red Cherokee.

"They don't know where it is," Vassili said. "We will wait, and watch until they get in place. Then we will follow. *Da?*" His men shrugged, loaded the equipment.

"I could have taken them all," Anatoly grumped.

"If they had told us were the site is, I would have let you." Vassili grinned.

While Jake, Ram, and Nicole sat on the deck talking, the "Man" sat in his small, dingy office. He lived in a suite of grubby rooms at the back of his business, which he rarely left. On this night, he sat at his massive roll top desk. The desk itself was a relic of a bygone era, gouged and scratched by long decades of life, its cubby holes stuffed and plugged with notes, papers, and envelopes wrapped in rubber bands. Cardboard boxes of yellowing business papers surrounded it, like a fort. Here and there, where the boxes had not yet been stacked to the ceiling, white styrofoam containers held the drying and crusty remains of dinners sent over from Sam's Café. He sat in a pool of light cast by a single small bulb in a goose-neck lamp.

He was the bloated spider at the center of an invisible web of drug dealers, gun runners, the occasional whore, and if circumstances required, murderers, and aside from Roscoe, no one else in town knew it. One of the purposes of his organization was retribution for wrongs done to him long ago by the people of Python. The knowledge that just beneath the surface, unknown to the publicly pious, self-righteous, sanctimonious town folk, he ran an organization that used their weaknesses and vulnerabilities against them, pleased him greatly.

His mind flickered and pondered. Up until a couple of weeks ago, murder had not been necessary. And it probably hadn't been necessary then. A little money and an invitation to leave town would have sufficed. But the Man knew that the men he used to achieve his ends possessed the crude mental processes of the ignorant and the angry. When they were afraid, they were as dangerous as wounded buffalos. He used this knowledge, too.

Roscoe was a pompous fool, weak in the way bullies are weak; Willie merely an idiot. And now, the problem of Rick Sanchez. The man laughed out loud. People in general are such fools! He chuckled, wondering who was stupider, Rick or Jeannette: Jeannette for thinking she could screw Larry Whitcomb out of his wealth, or Rick for being in love with his own illusion.

There would be more demands for even greater amounts of money. This he knew surely as he knew his own face. Sanchez would have to go, but in a way that would be final, without suspicion. A plan began to form in his mind. It could be done, but

Tom Curdy would have to help him. The Man chuckled again. Only Curdy wouldn't know it.

He roused himself and walked to the closet at the back of the room, opened the door, and tripped the latch on the inside above the lintel. The back wall slid to the left, revealing a darkened room beyond.

The secret room with its cleverly concealed door had been built by the Cabinet Maker of La Paz. His name was Emiliano de la Vaca but he was Argentinean, not Mexican. Born in Buenos Aires, he came to manhood building the same exquisite cabinets, armoires, and jewelry boxes as had his father and grandfather. But unlike them, he came into manhood during the time when Argentina opened its arms to embrace the Nazis fleeing from a devastated Europe, and the hangman's noose. Most of them possessed a desperate need for places of concealment. Emiliano became the master of concealed compartments, hidden safes, secret rooms, and even concealed escape tunnels.

Although his business brought in much profit and more status than a lowly carpenter could ordinarily hope for, Emiliano's misfortune was the beautiful woman with a love of gold. And since he knew where the treasure trove of the Third Reich lay, it was only a matter of time before jewels, gold, and cash began disappearing from the great, but anonymous houses of Buenos Aires.

He had no choice but to abandon his love and flee for his life, and although he managed to spend a few relatively safe years in La Paz, the Nazis were as ruthless and relentless in their search for him as they had been the Jews.

Just how Emiliano, by then a broken and haunted old man, came to land in Python, the Man never knew. Emiliano simply appeared one afternoon, begging for work. He was hired to do handyman labor about the premises, but at half the wages of a white man.

Over the months and years, an unlikely "friendship" developed between the two. The Man would never admit publicly to being a "friend" to a greaser, but in private, they were cordial enough, and he eventually learned Emiliano's story. By then the fruits of his vengeance had begun to ripen and he, too, had need of a secret room. Thus it was built by the Cabinet Maker of La Paz, who, shortly afterward, fell in the Python in a drunken stupor, and drowned.

He stepped inside, flipping on the light. Here lay the reward of his life's work and the source of his deepest, most profound, almost sexual, satisfaction. Shelf upon shelf lined the walls, each one stacked full with bundles of crisp one hundred dollar bills, ten thousand dollars to the bundle. A massive stainless steel table stood in the center of the room; the table was necessary, for the shelves could not bear the weight of the gold: rows and rows of one ounce ingots, fifteen to a stack, tube after tube of one ounce double eagle gold pieces, twenty to a tube.

The floor space in a third of the room housed the armory: rows of AK-47s, and M-16s stood in wooden racks like platoons of soldiers. Two .50 machine guns mounted on tripods bristled in one corner, in another, half a dozen M-79 grenade launchers rested in their own rack. Cases of ammo stood nearby.

He browsed along the shelves, occasionally flipping through a bundle with his thumb, as though he were quickly counting it to make certain each one totaled the ten thousand it was supposed to. He turned to the table, and stood, studying the rows of ingots and tubes of gold. While he did not caress them, exactly, he fingered them tenderly, a touch here, a touch there. He exhaled a great sigh of satisfaction before he moved through the rows of weapons, inspecting them like a general. Occasionally he stopped, picked one up, cocked, and dry-fired it, to make sure it worked properly. He ran his hand lovingly over one of the .50's.

The room smelled faintly of cosmoline, gun oil, and the dry, musty scent of used bookstores.

Satisfied that all was as it should be, he turned out the light and exited, sealing the room behind him. The plan he formulated while he wandered in the treasury would work. But, as with most things in life, timing was everything. He would lay the ground work by preparing Roscoe and the others, then he would act. He went to his unmade bed and slept a deep and untroubled sleep.

Three hundred miles to the south, Gopal Deshpar sat in his comfortable condominium in Salt Lake. Tambora lay beside the chair and Desh idly scratched her ears, thinking. Not thinking, really, but stewing. Although the deaths of the four grad students rocked the University community, when he presented the case to extend gas and seismic monitoring equipment south and west toward Python, his request was denied. The phenomenon that produced the gasses that killed the students was dismissed as an "anomaly," and besides, there was no other hard evidence to indicate a sudden presence of magma. There just wasn't the evidence of an imminent threat that justified emergency funding.

The scientist in Desh agreed with them. There really wasn't enough hard data: the deaths of four students, the presence of lethal gasses. That's all. No quakes, no sudden hydrothermal activity, no rise in landmass. It *was conceivable* that a large pocket of poison gas, for reasons unknown, had suddenly found its way to the surface. It *could be* a one-time occurrence.

But Desh's intuition gnawed him like puppies chew shoes. The problem was that without ground-based GPS sensors, gas emission monitors, and seismic monitoring equipment, he was blind. He had no way of knowing what was happening under the Anvil, until it was far too late.

He stood and walked across the room to study the sculpture on the mantle above the fireplace. A bearded figure wearing a short kilt rode a donkey. He wore a wreath of ivy leaves in his hair, and carried a hammer and blacksmith's tongs. The sculpture was an anniversary gift from his wife. It represented the Greek god Hephaistos, the blacksmith god, whose forge was the heart of a volcano. His Roman names were Volcanos, or Vulcan. Desh ran a finger lightly over the figure. "What are you up to?" he whispered.

Chapter 18

The mid-morning sun cast the shadow of the helicopter on the broken lava field below. It raced ahead of the chopper, dipping into the collapsed lava domes, darting up again as the Huey sped across the fractured terrain at 125 miles an hour.

Two weeks had passed since the meeting on the deck. Jake had left the equipping of the expedition to Nicole and her father and the ferrying of it to Ram. He had put himself into training, running five miles a day and lifting weights. The shoulder still bothered him; not nearly enough time had passed for it to heal, but he had little choice; Wilma Slow Horse's vision nagged him.

Jake sat in the co-pilot's seat, studying the map Ram had given him. He looked up and out the Plexiglas windscreen. "So where's Black Butte?" he asked.

Ram pointed a Nomex-gloved hand toward the horizon. "We're about a hundred and forty miles out, which is almost to base camp. Base is at twelve o'clock from where we are now. The closest site is about fifteen miles from base at one o'clock. I labeled it 'Alpha' on the map. 'Bravo' would be at one-thirty; Black Butte, you can't quite see it from here, is at two o'clock, and 'Charlie', the site furthest from base, is at about two-thirty. Black Butte, by the way, ain't much of a butte—just mounds of cinder. All four sites, as you can see on the map, make a slight arc running southwest to northeast. Must be a fault line running through there. We'll fly recon before we land so you can see the lay of things." The chopper took a hard dip to the right, as Ram changed headings to fly the arc.

After about ten minutes, Ram changed course again, this time to the left.

"Charlie coming up on your right," he said.

And indeed, from the air, the fault line slashed the land like a knife cut, and the connected the landmarks.

At some point in the remote and distant Holocene, the skin of the earth simply split, spewing lava and creating towering, wickedly sharp hornitos—lava spires—from the lips of the gash. Ages passed. More pahoehoe ran like a river surrounding the existing flows, and where the land was not submerged, *kipukas* formed.

A'a lava, a slower, stickier lava, oozed from other fissures, cooled, and exploded from the trapped gasses, creating acres of razor-sharp rock fragments, volcanic glass, and cinder.

Ages more passed. The winds that blew the sand from the evaporating lakes blew seeds as well. Eventually, enough seeds and soil accumulated to produce the silver growth of sage and the dark green buds of pinyon trees. That any of it happened at all amazed Jake. "*Maka kin hecela te han yunkelo,*" he said.

"What?" Ram asked?

"I said, '*Maka kin hecela te han yunkelo*—only the earth lasts forever.'"

"Meaning?"

"Ram, men come and go; governments come and go, civilizations rise and fall, but that down there... ."

Ram grinned. "What's this? You becoming a philosopher in your old age?"

Jake grinned back. "Yeah. I guess so. But look at it, Ram. God, it's beautiful, in its own savage way. The rules are always the same; you can count on them; there's no treachery, no betrayals, no technicalities to get the pussies off. It's not like men, or women, or ass-kissing commanders, or politicians. Dependable, I guess. If it kills you, it's nothing personal. Just means you weren't strong enough, and smart enough. Or lucky enough," he added. "And it's always just 'there'."

"That's not it, Jake. Well, maybe that's part of it, but the real reason you love it is because it's something to fight against, and the stakes are high. You need an enemy, Jake, somebody or something to pit your strength against. Think about it. You been fighting all your life, the kind of fight that takes all your strength, all your skill, all your nerve, all your brains to win. And if you don't win, you die."

Jake grinned. "Now who's the philosopher?"

"No, Jake, I'm serious. I've thought about this a lot. When I was in Nam, I occasionally flew medevac."

"That was some heavy shit."

"Yeah, it was. But a lot of pilots didn't want to fly anything else. Those Hueys came back looking like swiss cheese, stinking of blood. Had to douche 'em out with buckets of water. But they did it again, and again, and again. Why? Because they wanted to. And then they came home and got married, and went back to school or began flying milk runs for corporate geeks. They got old, fat and bored. Because nothing else in their grey, tedious lives was ever as important—*they* were never as important—as when they flew those missions, me included. War ruins you for anything else, Jake. At least then you can be a man, or at least some of us can."

For a minute, the two men sat silently gazing at the land passing beneath them.

"Site 'Alpha' coming up on your right," Ram said.

Jake studied the landscape below. Alpha was not a single butte, but a series of three or four low cinder cones arranged in a semi-circle. A river of lava surrounded them, and flowed south and eastward toward the base camp. From the air, the lava looked like a flow of dark fudge, criss-crossed with hairline cracks.

"See those cracks down there?" Jake asked.

"Yeah. What about 'em?"

"They're actually crevasses—like in glaciers. They're only three or four feet across, but some of them are six, seven, eight hundred feet deep. You don't want to screw up jumping across one of them. Even if you survived the fall, you would be wedged in tighter than the Bishop's ass."

Ram laughed. "Wouldn't want that!"

Jake grinned. "So where's base camp?"

"I was just about to show you." The chopper made a steep, sharp turn to the left. "Dead ahead, about twelve clicks."

Jake grunted. The flight roughly followed the path of the river of lava that flowed from the southern edge of site 'Alpha."

Ram had flown Nicole and Haraldsen out the day before to set up camp, and earlier in the week they had cached water and food at mid-points between camp and each of the sites. The caches made it possible for them to trek with much less weight. Carrying enough water was the problem. So while Ram hovered the chopper, Harald and Nicole lowered ten gallons of water, and half a case of MRE's with a couple of packs of Marlboros for Jake tucked in each case. Then they marked each stash on two hand-held GPSs, one Jake's, the other Nicole's.

The great river of pahoehoe lava that flowed from the southern tip of the fault line was three hundred yards wide and fifteen feet thick. It ran like a vast ribbon south, then curved lazily east. Successive flows of younger lava had flowed across it, pocking its surface with broken lava domes and fields of cinder. It was these successive flows that made it impossible to land the Huey and establish a base camp closer than twelve kilometers to site Alpha.

Where the broad, rippled flow turned east, it had, for some inexplicable reason, divided into two smaller streams, one curving southward again, the other continuing east. Harald and Nicole set up a base-camp in the sandy soil between the two forks of lava.

It was a perfect place for camp. A small ravine led from the top of the lava flow into the fork, making it easy to carry supplies. Since the camp lay fifteen feet below the lava, it escaped the wind that blew incessantly. Harald and Nicole had pitched a larger tent, that served as storage for supplies as well as mess hall, command tent, and sleeping quarters for Harald. They pitched two smaller tents for Nicole and Jake farther down the ravine, tucked in under a small grove of three pinons. Still farther down the ravine they set up two privacy tents: one for a chemical commode, and the other as a solar shower.

As Ram circled to land into the wind, three small figures emerged from the command tent: Harald, Nicole, and Ram's daughter, Cherie. By the time the blades spooled down, the three of them stood waiting.

"Dad! Dad!" Cherie yelled, and ran to hug her father. At sixteen, she was one of those girls that older men gawked at and said, "They didn't make 'em like that when I was in High School."

The mane of chestnut hair had been pulled into a pony-tail that hung to the middle of her back. She had Ram's deep blue eyes, her mother's lush Italian lips, high cheek bones, and an oval olive face. She wore a pink tee shirt beneath the bib overalls that helped conceal the premature lushness that drew men's eyes. A pair of scuffed black Doc Martin's kicked up the dust as she ran to her father.

Ram beamed. "How's my girl?"

"Great, dad." To Jake: "How's the cripple?"

"Cripple? I'm not too crippled to spank you!" He swatted her on the butt as he hugged her. Jake held his "niece" at arm's length. "You're a pain in the ass," he said, grinning.

"I hope so," she said, "especially for you." Cherie threaded her arms through the arms of the men as they marched lockstep toward the Haraldsens, who couldn't help smiling at the reunion.

Suddenly, she broke loose from them, saying, "Oh, Dad! Look what Harald gave me!" She withdrew a small Solutrean point tied on a length of artificial sinew from under the pink tee.

"You mean Mr. Haraldsen?" he said, as he peered at it.

"Yeah. Him." Cherie pointed her chin at Harald. Ram took a swat at her, but she dodged. "And," she said, "he said if we find the site I can help excavate it."

"Yeah, well they gotta find it first, and right now, missy, you have a helicopter to unload."

"Dad!" she moaned, "I've been helping; I've already broken two fingernails!"

"So, go break two more."

"I'll help," Nicole said, stepping forward. "C'mon, Cherie, won't take long." She walked past Ram saying, "She's a great girl."

"Thanks."

Ram, Jake and Harald inspected the camp while the girls unloaded additional cases of MRE's, a few groceries in sacks, two large white coolers packed with ice, and additional gallons of water.

After Harald had taken the men on a tour of the camp, Jake turned to Ram. "Looks like home to me!"

About ten the next morning, Ram lay inside the tail assembly of the Huey, trying to spot a reason for the rattle in the linkage he'd heard when he and Cherie flew back to Black Horse Aviation. Cherie, still in her bib overalls, but with a white tee, squatted at his feet, tool chest at the ready.

"Damned if I know what it was," Ram mumbled.

"Maybe you just need to get your hearing checked, Dad. You are getting on in years, you know."

"Yeah, 'n you're about the right age for a convent, too. So keep it up, girlie. We'll see how you like going around dressed like a penguin for the rest of your life."

"Oohh. Does that mean I never get to have sex?"

Ram began backing out of the crawl space. "You can't have sex anyway until I'm dead. So you loose either way, buckaroo."

"Well, in that case, I better go get some this afternoon and hope you don't find out."

"Keep it up, *chica*. I am a personal friend of the Pope."

"Hey! Anybody here?" A silhouetted head appeared at the edge of the cargo bay.

"Yeah!" Ram yelled. "Be right out!" He made 'move!' 'move!' motions with his hands to Cherie. She scrambled out of the Huey.

Ram caught a glimpse of Cherie being held, hands behind her back, by a tall thin man, before the blow from his blind side knocked him on his face on the concrete of the hanger. He rolled over, started to get up, and a second blow flattened him again. Two men grabbed him by the arms, hustled him to a nearby chair and secured his arms behind him with a nylon cable tie. Dazed, Ram shook his head sideways to try to clear it. Droplets of blood flew both directions. His nose was broken. He watched helplessly through a haze while the men bound Cherie's arms behind her and duct-taped her mouth. An open-handed slap rocked him back in his chair.

A burly, muscular man with close-cropped grizzled hair stepped in front of his chair. He jabbed the first two fingers of his right hand at his own eyes and said with a thick Russian accent, "Look at me, Major Ramsay."

Ram's eyes flicked upward.

"Good. My name is Colonel Vassili Grubinich, late of the Russian KGB." Vassili paused to light a thin, dark cheroot. The stench of cigar filled he hangar. Vassili puffed, paused, studying Ram. "I tell you that," he continued, "so you will know I am professional and do not play games with you."

"What do you want?" Ram croaked.

"Good. What I want, Major, is for you and your daughter to show me where, precisely, the Indian has gone. If you do, no harm will come to either of you."

"Fuck you. I'm not showing you squat. And you know I won't," he added.

Grubinich paced in front of Ram as he talked. "No, of course not. You are an American soldier—a good one. I read your file."

Grubinich drew a bayonet from his boot and tapped Ram on the cheek with the flat of the blade. *You* would not betray a comrade. I could torture you for hours, perhaps days, before I got something from you. I know that. However... Tolya..." Grubinich lifted his chin toward Cherie.

Tolya, who was standing behind Ram's chair, whipped out a small caliber pistol and shot Cherie in the thigh. She screamed through the duct tape and her leg buckled. Her eyes rolled white and wide. Anatoly jerked her upright. She stood on one leg, blood puddling on the floor beneath her Doc Martin.

Ram lunged to get to Cherie, but Tolya whacked him with the pistol and he fell back into the chair.

"You bastard!" Blood dripped into one of Ram's eyes from a cut on his forehead.

"You see?" Grubinich asked. *"Do you see what happens if you do not give me what I want?* Fortunately, Tolya is very good shot. It is only a flesh wound. Anatoly," Grubinich lifted his chin toward the girl. Anatoly stood her firmly on one leg and swiftly applied a compression dressing on the wound. Then he took his place behind her once again, holding her up.

Grubinich opened both palms in a gesture that said, "Well?"

"All right, all right, all right." Ram slumped in the chair. "Bring me a map; I'll show you where they are. Just don't hurt her any more."

"Major, major. You know that will not work. You will accompany us; in fact, you will fly, while Anatoly entertains Cherie in the back. You will fly us to the site, or.... " He paused. "Yes, I remember now. Did I not read that American intelligence officers threw uncooperative Vietnamese prisoners out of helicopters? Yes. You will fly. No tricks. Or "phfssst," out she goes. We will give Cherie flying lessons." He ground the cheroot out under his boot. "Well, major?"

"I'll do it. I'll do it," he said, looking up. "But if you hurt her again, I swear to God I'll find a way to kill you."

Vassili laughed. "Be my guest." He bowed low. "Tolya! Anatoly! Get the chopper out and fueled up. We are all going for a ride."

Chapter 19

Harald Haraldsen stopped, took off his straw panama hat, mopped the sweat out of his eyes with a red bandana and stooped to pick up a piece of the clinkery slope he struggled to ascend. The chunk he picked up reminded him of the cinders he used to take out of his father's coal furnace. Black, glassy, iridescent, the fist-sized hunk of volcanic glass and ash didn't weigh much, but its edges were sharp enough to flay an ungloved hand.

"Dad, you O.K.?" Fifty yards up the slope, Nicole had turned back, watching him. Jake had apparently already topped the rise.

"Yeah." He peered up at the sun, shading his eyes with the hat. "Christ!" he thought to himself. "Seven o'clock in the morning and already hot as hell." He turned and looked back down the slope toward base camp. Half a mile distant, it shimmered in heat waves. He had wanted to see Nicole and Jake off by walking a short way with them. Now he wasn't sure it was such a good idea. The half mile hike back to base camp seemed an awfully long way.

"Dad? You coming?"

"Yeah, I'm coming," he yelled back. He put his hat back on and trudged the rest of the way to the top. Jake and Nicole sat just under the lip of the rise. Nicole read her GPS: "Looks like our heading should be about 275 degrees West."

"Yeah," Jake replied. "But that's how the crow flies. We may not be able to fly like crows. Look." He handed her the field glasses. "Look about half a klick out. From here it looks like a thin black line. Through the glasses you can see it for what it really is: a crevasse, which we may not be able to jump." He shook his head. "We'll have to wait until we get there. We may have a long detour."

Haraldsen squinted. He could just make out the jagged black line they were talking about. The land between them and the line was pocked with the deep craters of collapsed lava domes. The huge slabs of basalt had fallen in upon themselves lining the bowls with unstable and treacherous plates of rock. Sage and sometimes even pinons grew in along the sides and in the bottoms of the craters, obscuring their view of what, exactly, lay in the bottom, and how deep it actually was.

Since the craters collected rainwater and snow melt, the sage that gained a toe-hold often grew to five or six feet tall, and if it grew thickly, it presented a practically impenetrable barrier of tough, woody limbs. And snakes. Rattlers favored the shade and cool depths of the thickets. Staring at the tortured land, Haraldsen doubted they would make three kilometers on the first day. Alpha lay fifteen clicks somewhere out there in the shimmering heat waves.

Jake stood and hefted his pack. Nicole stowed the GPS and hefted hers as well. Jake turned to Haraldsen and held out his hand. "You'd best get back before the heat really hits." He squinted looking up at the sun. "We'll probably lay up somewhere when the afternoon sun gets dangerous. A cave, if we're lucky. Anyway, we'll try to call you when we stop for the night and give you an approximate location. So, keep your cell charged up and close. That is if we have service out here. If you don't hear from us, don't panic. We'll try again when we find some higher ground. See ya." Without another word, Jake turned and marched off.

Haraldsen gave Nicole an awkward hug.

"Don't say it," she said. "I'll be fine. You get out of this heat." She turned on her heel and fell in behind Jake.

He sat down on the lava field, and watched as they picked their way across the broken terrain. He watched until they disappeared into a vast crater, then heaved himself up and slowly made his way down the slope toward base camp.

"Tom, you'd better take line one." Shirley had barged into his office without knocking, something she just didn't do.

Tom looked up from his paperwork. "Why? Who is it?"

"Won't give his name. Says he knows the drug dealers and where they cook the stuff."

"O.K. Tell him I'll be right with him, but before I pick up, I want Bob Duncan in here and—is Hal Lindsay around?"

She nodded 'Yes.'

"Good. Get 'em in here quick." After the two men filed into his office, Tom set the phone to speakerphone, and punched the blinking "1."

"This is Sheriff Curdy."

"I hab son informacion por ju."

"Who is this, please."

"My nane no es importante. I know the *bastardes* who kill Rosa an' where they make the drugs."

"Alright. Who is it and where."

"The Kettle brothers. They make the drugs in the old cabin up Five Mile Canyon. Sonthing beeg es goin' to habben. They make much drugs and hab beeg meeting Wednesday night. They all be there. You catch them."

"Why are you telling me this?"

"Rosa was my fren'."

"How do you know all this?"

"You catch them all." The connection went dead.

The Man sat back in his worn, ancient office chair, and peeled five one hundred dollar bills off the wad in his hand.

"You did good," he said, laying them in front of the dark-skinned laborer who sat nervously across the desk. "Now, if I was you, I'd load up my wife n' kids n' move down th' road. That away, if any of this leaks out, I'll know it wasn't you, an' I won't have to come a-killin' 'em kids. *Comprende?*"

"*Si, jefe.*" He twisted an old baseball cap in his hands.

"You *do* believe I *will* kill that woman of yourn n' 'em kids."

"*Si, jefe*, I do."

"Good. You get on, now." The laborer scurried out.

The Man dialed another number. A pause. "Roscoe, get Hebrew out to Zeb's an' start cookin'. We got a big deal comin' down, an' we need a lot of product." Pause. "Don't be askin' me a bunch of questions. Just do it. An' another thing. You boys is goin' to be introduced to one of the men who founded our organization. 'At's right, you is. So, I want every man we got to be at Zeb's Wednesday night, about eight. He wants to talk to you all about what's about to happen all over this country." Pause. "Just do it, Roscoe, an' make sure everybody's there. Right."

He hung up, sat back in his chair. So far so good. He dialed a third number. After three rings, a voice answered, "Yes?"

"I need you here tomorrow daybreak. Bring your equipment."

"O.K." The line clicked dead.

By the time Harald shuffled back to camp, his hands quivered and his head felt like a split melon. He washed down a couple of oxycontin with some water, and lay down on his cot. He prayed nothing would break loose in his head. Not now. Not when he was so close.

He lay, staring at the ceiling of the tent, listening to the whining wind, and the occasional snap of the canvas. He dozed. Hours passed.

Haraldsen jerked awake, startled and confused by the *whop, whop, whop* of the Huey. It didn't make sense to his drug-numbed mind. Why had Ram returned?

He staggered out of the tent in time to see Ram and Cherie, hands tied behind their backs, file down the ravine accompanied by three men. Two of them carried Uzis with silencers.

"Run! Run, Harald run!" Ram yelled.

The tall thin man clubbed Ram to the ground with the butt of his Uzi. He fell into Cherie, who stumbled and rolled to the bottom of the ravine, helpless to catch herself with her arms tied behind her. She lay in the grit, sobbing silently.

Stunned into action, Harald ran toward Cherie. The thick, heavyset man, with short, grizzled hair, blocked his path. Without a word, Vassili bitch-slapped Harald to the ground. Harald sat up, dazed, shaking his head. Vassili slapped him again with a slap that rang like a pistol shot. Then he grabbed Harald by the shirt collar and dragged him into the tent, where he threw him in a camp chair and cuffed his hands behind him. Tolya and Anatoly soon followed, dragging Ram and Cherie. They were thrown in the dirt.

Harald sputtered. "Who...? Ram? What's goin on?" He looked up at Vassili? "Who *are* you?"

Vassili smacked Harald with a vicious back-hand, rocking him back in the chair. Then he pointed the first two fingers of his right hand at his own eyes.

"*Look at me*, Professor."

Harald looked up.

"Good. Who I am doesn't matter. Where the Indian went does. Where did he go? Tell me."

Haraldsen mustered up a "fuck you" look. "I will not; it's none of your business."

"As you wish." Vassili lifted a chin toward Cherie. "Tolya... ."

As Tolya withdrew the small pistol from his shoulder holster, Ram came to his knees and lunged in front of Cherie.

"No! God, no! Alpha! They probably went to site Alpha!"

To Harald: "Tell them! They went to Alpha, didn't they?"

Vassili turned to Harald. "Well, professor?"

Haraldsen stared at Cherie. She sat in the sand with one leg curled up underneath her, her wounded leg straight out. She nestled her head against Ram's chest, sobbing quietly through the duct tape. Ram's eyes pleaded. For the first time, Harald saw the bloody dressing applied over the bib overall pant leg. Tolya cocked the pistol with a loud "click."

"Yes," he said quietly. "They left for Alpha this morning."

Vassili's eyes flicked to Tolya. He de-cocked the weapon.

Grubinich lit one of his nasty cheroots, exhaled a cloud of blue smoke, studied the glowing end. "And where is this 'site Alpha'?"

Harald squirmed in the chair. The cable ties cut painfully into his wrists. "There's a map on the table behind me. It's marked." Harald stared at the sand.

"Good." Vassil's eyes flicked to Tolya. He lifted his chin toward Ram and Cherie.

Tolya and Anatoly stepped to Ram and Cherie.

"C'mon. Up," Anatoly said, grabbing Ram by the armpit. Ram and Cherie filed out of the tent, prodded by the Uzi Tolya held by a sling over his shoulder.

"To the right," he said. They walked through the heavy sand past the two smaller tents, past the two privacy tents, until they came to a small opening in the grove of stunted pinons.

"Stop," Tolya ordered.

Vassili studied the map. "This is site Alpha?" He held it up for Haraldsen to see.

"Yes."

"And these other marks. They are additional possible sites?"

"Yes—what are you doing with Ram and Cherie?" Haraldsen blurted.

"They are no longer your concern. How long have they been gone?" A puzzled look from Haraldsen. "The Indian and your daughter—how long have they been gone?"

Ram turned to face Tolya. "Untie me."

A look of amused disbelief crossed Tolya's face. "You kid me, yes?"

"No. I want to embrace my daughter. You can allow that, at least."

Tolya thought for a moment, shrugged. He flipped the safety on the Uzi to "off," withdrew a wicked black switch blade from his pocket, flicked it open. "Turn around." Ram turned and presented his hands to Tolya. He felt the nylon part and stinging as the blood rushed into his hands.

Ram drew his daughter to him, and turned her so her back was to Tolya. Tolya stepped forward and cut the bands on Cherie's wrists. "*Da?*" he asked.

"*Da,* thank you," Ram replied. He gently peeled the duct-tape off her mouth.

"Daddy…?" she wailed. She tried to turn to see Tolya. Ram wouldn't let her turn. He held her in a tight embrace and whispered, "You are the brightest, the best, the most glorious thing that has ever happened to me. You made my whole life worth living—." Then the nine millimeter slugs tore through their bodies.

Chapter 20

"Well, what do you think?" Tom sat back in his chair, lit a Camel. They weren't supposed to smoke in the Law Enforcement Complex, but most of the deputies smoked. Tom couldn't see any reason to add to their already stress-filled jobs by making them go outside like animals to smoke.

He, himself, refused to accommodate the politically correct war on tobacco. As a result, morale was higher, and his officers worked much more efficiently. In fact, it saved his department a lot of lost man-hours, and stress.

Bob Duncan shrugged. "Worth checking out."

"Either of you know the cabin he was talking about?"

"Yeah. I do," said Lindsay. "It's an old line shack old Zeke Kettle and his boys used back in the day. I'm pretty sure I could find it. It's at the base of the Caldera way the hell and gone out there."

"How about the DEA? Do we need some back-up?"

"The first thing we better do is some recon. Try to find out if they're cookin' up there," Duncan said.

"Alright," Tom said. "Today's Monday. You two take off and do the recon. But make like hikers, or sheepherders or something. See if you can find definite evidence of probable cause. I'll alert Judge Reilly, and Phil Jenkins at the DEA, just in case. If you find something, we'll get a warrant, and bust 'em Wednesday night. Just look. And try not to be seen." Tom stood up.

"Let's get to it."

Alfonso de la Chevera stood, scraped the remaining beans and bacon from the tin plate into the small campfire. He wiped it clean with a paper towel and stowed it in the battered plywood camp box that sat just out side the flap of the grungy white canvas wall tent.

Unlike the other sheepherders of the vast Miliken Ranch, who used the familiar covered wagons with thick, fat tires as their camps, Alfonso was forced to pack tent and supplies on horseback. The terrain of the Anvil would permit nothing else. Indeed, most places would not permit horses at all.

Alfonso was a patient man in his early forties. He had learned his trade in the severe deserts of Northern Mexico and so was at home on the vast furnace of the Anvil. He was also a careful man who thought things through before he acted.

He had learned early in life that to be conspicuous was to invite trouble, so when the Miliken foreman asked if any of the shepherds were willing to work the Anvil, he had volunteered. His *compadres* shook their heads sadly. No one had ever been able to find a way through the myriad of flows, caves, and crevasses without losing most of their sheep. But to be out on the Anvil from late April to early October was to be invisible to the white and green SUVs of ICE.

And so, every year for the last six years, the *jefe* drove Alfonso to Cascade Campground where they unloaded Alfonso's horse, a pack horse, a blue healer named Pero, and two weeks' supplies. And every two weeks thereafter, *jefe* delivered the same ration of coffee, flour, beans, salt pork, fresh fruit and sugar. Over the years, Alfonso had discovered routes accessible, but just barely so, by a four wheel drive truck. As he moved his sheep farther and farther into the desert, he and the *jefe* had worked out places where they met to resupply. Still, he sometimes had to backtrack ten or fifteen miles.

His summer journey inscribed a vast circle on the face of the desert. From Cascade Campground, he led the sheep first north by northwest eventually circling around to where he began. His slow, patient exploration had not only saved the lives of many sheep and earned him the admiration of the *jefe*, but it also led to the discovery of many remarkable things on the Anvil, most notably, where water was to be found.

So far as he knew, he was the only living man who knew the location of the spring where he now bedded his sheep. He discovered the emerald pool that welled up underneath a basalt overhang while trying to find a wayward ewe. The spring was not large: about the size of a ten by twelve room, but it was deep, clean, and pure. It rose up, spilled into the desert a few yards, and disappeared, a mystery.

On this morning, Alfonso rummaged in his duffel, withdrew a bar of Ivory soap, a clean towel and a wash cloth. He liked to be clean as the next man, and he was on his way to his first bath in a month. He stripped off his dirty clothes, wrapped the towel around his waist, donned his boots with no socks, and hiked the short distance to the pool.

Ringed with horsetail rushes and cattails, the pool smoked in the mid-morning sun. He dropped his towel, shook off his boots, and dived in.

He surfaced, looked around, puzzled. He had expected the shock of an icy pond, but found the water bathtub warm. He swam around a while, luxuriating in the gentle warmth and wondering why the water was so warm. It had been icy in the years before. He noticed some spots were warmer than others. He swam to one of the warmer spots and dunked his head under, trying to see the cause.

He had no time to scream. The tongue of live steam licked up from the depths and enveloped him, instantly cooking the flesh from his bones.

The dog whined and paced along the rim of basalt. He barked and ran away when the spring came to a full boil.

"How long have they been gone?" asked Vassili.

"I don't know. I was asleep. Three, four hours, I guess," answered Harald.

"Anatoly, get the packs and the phone out of the helicopter." As Anatoly left to do as he was bidden, Tolya returned.

Vassil raised his eyebrows. Tolya nodded slightly.

"What did you do with them!" Haraldsen shouted. "You didn't hurt the girl... ." He paled when he saw the look on Tolya's face. Then he threw up on the sandy floor. Vassili stared at him in disgust. He stepped out of the tent, away from the stench of vomit, signaling Tolya to follow. Anatoly shuffled down the ravine, wearing one military-looking pack, carrying the other two and the satellite phone.

"Anatoly," Vassili said, taking one of the packs and the phone, "Tolya and I will follow the Indian and the woman. If we are lucky, we will catch up to them tonight. If not, tomorrow. You stay here with the old man. Do something about the bodies."

They filled the camel-backs on the packs with water, and set off across the desert at a brutal pace. Anatoly peered up at the sun, grateful to be left behind. The temperature had to be close to 110 degrees F.

He returned to the tent, groaning at the stench of vomit, finding Haraldsen bent over with his head between his knees, retching.

Anatoly rummaged around in the supplies until he found a metal cup and some water. He cut Haraldsen loose.

"Here, wash your mouth out," he said, handing him the water. "A shovel—do you have a shovel?"

Haraldsen nodded, choked a little on the water, and pointed to the back corner of the tent.

"Stand up," the Russian ordered. Haraldsen stood. "Strip down to your shorts." Haraldsen hesitated. "Do it!" Anatoly said, pulling a .45 out of his shoulder holster. While Haraldsen stripped, Anatoly retrieved the shovel, from the back of the tent.

Haraldsen stood there in his boxer shorts, a skinny old man; flaps of loose skin hung down from his arms; he had no buttocks, only protrusions of bone.

"Put your boots back on." Anatoly leaned on the shovel while Harald grunted, wheezed his way though lacing his boots up. He handed Harald the shovel. "Scoop up that mess you made and take it away from the tent. I'm not sleeping with puke."

Nicole paused for a breather in the shade of a basalt overhang. She mopped her forehead with the *kaffiyah* Jake had given her to keep the sun off. She stood in the bottom of a collapsed lava dome. She peered up at the sun and then the collapsed side of the dome. She had lost track of the number of domes like this one she had climbed down into and up out of again.

They were the remnants of large bubbles formed by gasses in the lava. When they cooled, they simply cracked and collapsed in on themselves, lining the remaining bowl with huge, treacherous plates of basalt. The plates that lay in direct sunlight radiated heat like stove tops, and one could easily cook eggs on them.

She shrugged off her pack, and sat in the shade for a moment, flexing her back and shoulder muscles. The middle of her back felt like someone had stuck a knife in it. Jake had already scaled the twenty foot wall of broken basalt, and disappeared, but she didn't care. She needed to rest. She sipped a little water from the camelback, dug her GPS out of her pack. In four hours plus of hiking they had covered 3.8 kilometers, but most of it was up and down, in craters and out of craters, rather than straight line distance. Felt to her like fifteen miles. The temperature function told her the ambient air was one one five degrees F. She thought she was in pretty good condition, but four hours a week at the gym hadn't prepared her for this. For the first time in a long time, she wished for a cigarette.

"Nicole?" Jake's voice echoed of the walls of the crater.

She stepped out into the sunlight. She looked up, shading her eyes with a hand. "Yeah. I'm here."

"Are you hurt?"

"No, I'm just resting a little. I'll be up in a minute."

"Do you want me to come down?"

"No, I don't want you to come down," she yelled, slipping into her pack, "I'll be right up." She chastised herself for showing weakness. She had been determined to keep up with him, as she had Rafe. But she had to admit, Jake Two Feathers seemed to be made of something other than flesh. When she reached the top, she found him sitting, studying the panorama in front of them with compact field glasses. He sat with his legs dangling into a vast crevasse; it was eight or ten feet to the other side. There would be no jumping this one—at least not here.

The first three they encountered presented no great obstacle; they simply leaped across the two or three feet of space to the other side. Nicole sat down next to Jake and tossed a pebble into the abyss. She didn't hear it hit bottom.

"How deep do you think this is?"

He continued scanning the landscape in front of them. They sat on the high edge of a great valley that sloped gently south and west. The rift that produced the sites they were to investigate formed the other high ridge. In between lay a vast valley of of black, broken a'a lava, flows of ropy, entrail-like pahoehoe lava, sage, pinyons, prickly pear cactus, and a kind of dry bristly grass.

"Hard to say," he said at last, dropping the glasses to his lap. "I hear some of them are seven, eight hundred feet deep—deep enough you don't want to fall in." He studied her for a moment. "You O.K?"

"Yeah. O.K. as I can be, out here in this bake oven."

Jake stood up, shouldering his pack. "Yeah. We need to find a place to hole up out of this heat." He gave her a hand, pulling her up.

When she had shouldered her pack, he pointed across the valley. "Look. See those black cones. The ones on the far right?" She nodded. "That's site Alpha," he said. "Near as I can make it, it's about twelve klicks. We're not going to make it today, so we'll follow this crevasse south until we find a place to jump it. We'll hope that's not too far. After we get across, we'll look for a place to hole up and sleep for a while."

"Whatever," she said.

They marched off.

Two hours later, Vassili and Tolya came to the overhang Nicole had briefly sheltered in. Both men panted; sweat streamed off their faces, and soaked their shirts.

"Look," Vassili said, pointing the barrel of his Uzi at Nicole's tracks. "They've been here."

"Da, Tolya said, flopping down in the shade. "Vassili Timofevitch, I cannot keep this up much longer. We need to rest."

"Ten minutes," Vassili said, flopping down beside him. "I want to catch them today." He took a small sip from his camelback. "You can rest when you are dead."

After Harald shoveled the puke from the tent, Anatoly took his boots away from him again and tied him back in the chair.

"What are you going to do with me?" Harald asked.

"Shut up," the Russian answered, peering out the tent at the sun. He wiped beads of sweat on his forearm, turned, stepped to Harald's cot and lay down, cradling the Dragunov rifle across his chest. He clicked the safety to "off."

"Get some sleep," he said. "You will need it."

While the men dozed fitfully in their own sweat, like a cutting torch, the sun burnt a downward arc in the blistering sky. When the sun was half-way to the western horizon, Anatoly stirred, cut Haraldsen loose.

"Get up!" he commanded, and prodded Harald with the gun barrel.

"Where are we going?"

Anatoly answered with a vicious backhand which sent Harald sprawling out of the tent onto the burning sand.

"Get up," Anatoly said again, and tossed the archaeologist's boots and a shovel on the ground beside him. Anatoly paced impatiently while Harald struggled into his boots.

They found the bodies as Tolya had left them, father and daughter entwined in a last embrace. Puddles of blood blackened the sand beneath them, and flies had begun to collect.

Haraldsen fell to his knees, retching and crying at the same time. Anatoly tolerated it for a minute, then kicked Haraldsen in the ass, saying "Get up, old woman! Get up and dig!" As he kicked Harald a second time, the ground beneath him rumbled and swelled like an ocean swell. He staggered, stumbled.

In a flash, Haraldsen came to his feet, swung the shovel at the Russian. The back of it "whanged" the side of Anatoly's face with a metallic clang, and he dropped like a pole-axed pig. Haraldsen dropped the shovel and took off running down the ravine, clad only in boots and boxer shorts.

In the thirty seconds it took Anatoly to recover his senses, Haraldsen wheezed and pumped away about forty yards down the ravine. The Russian shook his head to clear it, spit some teeth, and scrambled up the basalt barricade hedging the ravine, to gain the high ground.

By the time he centered the cross-hairs of the sniper rifle on Haraldsen's head, Haraldsen had stopped running, confused, about eighty yards out, turning first one way, then the other. From his higher vantage point, Anatoly could see what stopped the archaeologist: a deep crevasse, about fifteen feet across, blocked his path. Anatoly squeezed the trigger. A pink mist bloomed above Haraldsen's head, and he toppled into the abyss in front of him.

Chapter 21

Jake was becoming worried. The attempt to find a way across the crevasse had led them much farther south than he imagined it would. They had trekked the edge of the abyss for over an hour and had not yet found a place to jump it. Until they did, they were forced to trudge, unprotected, in the relentless, blistering sun. He looked back over his shoulder. Twice Nicole had fallen farther and farther behind and twice he had to stop to let her catch up. She had fallen behind again, trudging heavily, not really picking her feet up. He cursed under his breath. They had to get out of the sun and fast.

A low hammock of sand and a dry, brittle grass rose in front of him. The blades of windblown grass carved concentric circles in the sand. It sucked at his boots like wet concrete as he humped the dune, dripping sweat. When he crested the low rise his heart leapt: twenty yards away the crevasse closed to a gap of about seven feet. He turned and hollered at Nicole, who seemed to be wandering erratically.

"Nicole!" He waved. Slowly, she seemed to become aware of his voice. "Nicole! Over here!" he yelled again. She came to, and marched his direction.

Jake heaved his pack across the expanse, backed up about ten yards, imagined he was in high school doing the broad-jump, and flung himself toward the yawning abyss. The tips of his boots gripped the lip of basalt and he pushed off, sailing above an eight-hundred-foot deep crack in the earth. His boots slammed the basalt; he fell forward, skinning his knees and hands. He crouched there for a moment, catching his breath, and breathing a sigh of relief.

When he turned, he saw Nicole poised fifteen yards from the lip of the crevasse, breathing deeply, readying herself for the jump. She dug in, leapt forward in a sprint, but she foolishly forgot the sixty pound pack on her back. Jake knew she wouldn't make it. As she launched herself into the air, he lunged to the edge of the crevasse. She was two feet short of the edge and falling. She didn't scream, didn't say anything. She stared at him helplessly.

"They're cookin' up there, sure as hell." A sweaty Hal Lindsay flopped in one of Tom's chairs; Duncan flopped in the other one.

Tom grinned, looking at the stained armpits and sweaty faces of his deputies. "You boys have a hike, didja?"

"Yeah—about a ten mile forced march," Bob said.

"Well?" Tom asked.

"We hiked from the Red Road up the side of the Caldera to where the property begins. It's fenced and posted, so we had to work our way around the east side of the canyon. That's the downwind side. Stinks to high heaven up there. Roscoe and Hebrew's trucks were both there and from what we could see through field glasses, looks like they have a couple of ammonia tanks and a whole lot of garbage—sacks 'n shit. Probably wrappers and empty Sudafed packages."

Tom held up his hand, punched a button on his phone. "Shirley? Find out if any ammonia fertilizer tanks have been stolen in the last couple of days, will ya? Thanks."

Lindsay took off a salt-stained dew rag and draped it over his knee. "The good news is that canyon is a box canyon. Once we start the bust and block the road, they don't have any way out."

"The bad news," Duncan said, "is the place looks like a fort: concertina wire and sandbags chest high around the main shack."

"That's Zeb's doing. Crazy old Viet Nam bastard. See any guns, as in machine guns."

Both the men thought for a moment. "No," Duncan said at last. "But that doesn't mean there weren't gun mounts that we couldn't see. You don't think they have that kind of firepower up there, do you?"

Shirley stuck her head in the door, and read from a piece of paper in her hand. "Two tanks reported stolen last night."

"Thanks, Shir. No, I don't," Tom said, lighting up a Camel. "But I wouldn't put it past Zeb to have a couple of fifties stashed, just in case. The place is fortified for a reason. They mean to fight it out; they have to if they're trapped. You two go get some topo maps and start drawing a plan. I'll call Reilly for the warrant, and we better bring Jenkins and the DEA in. Sounds to me like we need all the fire power we can get.

As she fell past, Jake lunged again, and seized the two front shoulder straps of Nicole's pack. Both of his elbows banged the raw basalt lip; he lay on his belly holding her up like he was starting a bicep curl. The veins in his forehead and biceps bulged; a pain seared his shoulders. For a moment, he simply lay there, holding her above the yawning darkness below.

She seemed to know not to panic, not to try to climb up his arms, not to struggle, or scream. She hung suspended from Jake's arms like a side of beef on a meat hook. The *kaffiyah* had fallen down around her shoulders; a lock of blonde hair fell across a turquoise eye. The lush, rich lips parted slightly; she breathed in tiny little pants.

"Don't let me die," she whispered.

Unaccountably, Jake wanted to kiss those lips; he realized he always had. He felt himself weakening, but some raw power, some beast stirred deep within, uncoiled, and rose up.

He growled as he leaned slightly to the left, drew his right knee up under him; leaned slightly to the right, drew his left knee up, and heaved her up and over the lip of the crevasse.

They fell backwards, Jake lying on his back with Nicole on top, both of them panting great heaving breaths. After a while, he slid the shoulder straps off her shoulders, tossed the pack aside. She clung to him, arms around his neck, burrowing her face under his chin, pressing her body against his.

After their breathing eased, they sat up, Nicole sitting between Jake's outstretched legs. She brushed the hair out of her eyes, sighed.

"What's that white thing under your shirt?"

"A sports bra."

"Take it off," Jake said. "You won't be as hot, and you'll breathe easier."

While Nicole turned her back to strip off the bra, Jake rummaged in his pack, and removed the camelback bladder. "Let's get some water on you," he said, and soaked the back of her khaki shirt while she buttoned up.

"Thanks, I feel better," she said.

She leaned back against his chest. A small, hot wind blew across the desert, cooling them both a little. The dry grasses whispered in the sand, and the sage rattled. Jake put his arms around her, and their fingers entwined. The heat beat down relentlessly.

"You feel like you can move on?"

"No. Not yet," she said, lifting her lips up toward his. Jake's lips met hers halfway, and they kissed a long, needy kiss that surprised them both.

"Ughnh." Nicole made a small animal sound.

Jake lit a Marlboro and sat silently, brooding, staring at the sand, drawing circles with his finger.

A long moment passed. Jake alternately drew circles, stared at the horizon.

Finally, Nicole blurted, "What?"

His face cracked into an uncharacteristic boyish grin. "I'm trying not to say something stupid, like 'What took you so long,' or 'Where have you been all my life?'" He giggled. "Hell of a time for a kiss. You just almost died; we're sitting out here in the middle of a desert, five degrees from heat stroke, and we're making out."

Nicole giggled. "You got my bra off without any trouble."

"If I had known it was that easy, I'd have done it a long time ago."

"Pig."

"Witch."

"Prick."

Jake tossed his cigarette, threw his leg over hers, and pinned her under him in the sand. "Bitch," he whispered, and kissed her again.

"Dr. Deshpar?" The grad student knocked politely and stuck his head in Desh's office. "You asked to be informed of any activity south of Yellowstone?"

"Yes." Desh looked up from the interminable paperwork of a professor-scientist.

"Well, it's not much—" the student held up a wad of printouts—"but the Big Grassy Butte station recorded a 4.9 about half an hour ago."

Desh held out his hand. "Let me see."

While Desh studied the printouts, the grad student located the small triangle that marked Big Grassy Butte station on the map behind Desh. "Big Grassy Butte is here, sir."

Desh swiveled around in his chair, grunted. "Thank you," he said, dismissing the student. "Good work."

He swiveled around again, studying the map more carefully. Big Grassy Butte lay twenty-five miles south by southwest of Cascade Campground. If he drew a line from Cascade Campground to the epicenter of the quake and continued southwest, the line bisected Craters of the Moon, where, fifteen thousand years ago, the Yellowstone Hotspot was located. At least six different times in the last fifteen thousand years, the earth opened up at Craters of the Moon, and along the path of his imaginary line, spewing thousands of miles of lava.

Desh snatched up his phone, dialed a number, hung up. He shuffled though the printouts. Of course there were no ground displacement numbers: there were no GPS's out there. He had thought to argue again with the powers to be in the University, but he had no proof, no ground displacement figures, to argue an eruption. But Desh's instinct told him that somewhere out on the Anvil, the earth was beginning to bulge, or soon would, and no one would know until it was too late.

The gentle rocking motion of the earth broke Jake and Nicole from their embrace. Jake sat up. "That's happening entirely too often." He stood up, and pulled Nicole up with a hand, and looked around.

"Why, what does it mean?"

"I wouldn't put it past this place to have another eruption."

"How often does that happen?"

"About every two thousand years."

"How long's it been since the last one?"

"About two thousand years."

"Great," Nicole said, picking up her pack. "What we need is a little more heat."

Jake shaded his eyes against the westering sun. He pointed. "Alpha is northwest of us, now. We'll follow that lava flow toward the foothills over there, and hope we find a cave." He turned and looked at Nicole. "You O.K.?"

"Yeah, I think so. I just gotta get out of this heat and rest for a while."

"We should be able to find some place to hole up along the edge of those foothills. I make it a klick to the foothills, maybe a little less. But once we hit that lava flow we have to cross it quickly.

The Anvil

Temperature out there is a hundred and twenty, maybe thirty. You sure you're up for this?"

"I have to be; I'm going where you're going."

Chapter 22

Vassili Grubinich threw himself on his hands and knees at the edge of the crevasse Nicole and Jake had crossed a scant hour before. As he stared at the sand between his hands, sweat dripped off his nose, speckling the sand with dark polka dots. A wave of nausea washed over him, threatening his consciousness. His head pounded; his vision darkened, then returned. He licked chapped and cracking lips, permitted himself a sip of water. His chest heaved, sucking in great draughts of air.

He glanced back the way he had come. No sign of Tolya. They had come at a lope, unerringly following the track of their quarry. Half an hour ago, he'd heard a cry, and looked back to see Tolya fall. He had pressed relentlessly on. Tolya knew the rules; either he would get up and follow or he would die. That is the way it had been in Afghanistan; that is the way it would be here: only the strongest lived.

Ten minutes. He would wait ten minutes. Vassili lay back on the hot sand, resting on one elbow. He saw the cigarette Jake had thrown down, picked it up, sniffed it. Fresh.

Vassili heard a noise behind him. It was Tolya, who stumbled and staggered over the small hill.

"Tolya!" he called.

The Russian soldier staggered over to where he lay, and collapsed in front of him, heaving and sweating. He used precious water in his camelback to dampen Tolya's head and shirt.

"*Dyakooyu*," Tolya mumbled.

"*Bood laska*," Vassili returned.

The men lay silently, recuperating as well as they could in the blast furnace breeze. After a while they stirred, sat up.

"We have gotten soft since Afghanistan, Tolya Andreyovitch."

"No, Vassili Timofevitch; we have gotten old."

Vassili snorted and laughed. "Men like us don't get 'old', Tolya."

Tolya shrugged. "We died long ago; we just don't know it."

"Then let us live in death," Vassili said, rising. He scanned the horizon, shading his eyes with a hand.

He turned back to Tolya, and extended a hand to help him up. "We will move more slowly, more carefully, now. They will try to find a cave to get out of the heat, and to rest for the night. That is where we will catch them. *Da?*"

"*Da.*"

Nicole struggled along behind Jake, praying she wouldn't faint. The had been walking for about an hour, on a northwest course she assumed would take them eventually to Alpha. They had woven their way down through short, scrubby sage and plates of jagged, upturned   basalt to where a river of solidified lava stretched northeast. It would have been easier walking if the lava had been smooth, but it had a ropy, entrail-like surface, like piles of gut laid side by side. She kept tripping and stumbling. The surface radiated heat like a plate of steel. The soles of her boots burned. Her lips had cracked and begun to bleed a long time ago. She trudged along behind Jake, staring at the lava at her feet.

Suddenly Jake pulled up sharply, and pointed off to their left. He croaked a word. Nicole couldn't see anything but a depression at the edge of the flow. To her, it looked like a shallow bowl, ringed with sage. But Jake made a bee-line for it, and she followed his sweat-soaked back. Rounding the edge of it, she saw what he apparently already knew. A hole in the earth simply opened up revealing a dark tunnel large enough to drive a bus in. She felt cool air radiating from the depth. They scrambled down the scree of basalt blocks to the bottom.

Tall grasses grew there, waist deep, resembling a sort of pampas grass, and surprisingly, ferns in the shaded entrance. Where the floor of the tunnel was not covered with rockfall from the ceiling, it was compact and sandy. The air smelled vaguely musty, animal-like and moist. It was deliciously cool. Jake heaved his pack off and sat on a block of basalt.

"This is what we were looking for," he grinned.

Nicole heaved her pack off and sat beside him. "But what is it?"

"It's a lava tube. Desert is threaded with them. Around here, the earth just opens up and spews out lava. When the surface of the lava cools, it keeps flowing underneath, forming these tunnels. Some of them run for miles. And sometimes, the ceiling caves in, revealing them. Look behind you."

Nicole turned. The tunnel curved gently to the left and out of sight. "Looks like a big spider hole." She shivered.

Jake grinned and began rummaging in his pack. He handed her a couple of MRE's. "Why don't you cook some supper, and I'll set up camp. We'll stay here, tonight, and move on tomorrow."

"Yes, sir." She saluted.

Jake busied himself clearing a space to throw their shelter halves down. Nicole studied the two MRE's Jake had given her, plus the two she dug out of her pack.

"Which do you want?" she asked. "Ham and shrimp jambalaya, beef steak with mushroom gravy, beef stew, or pork chop, chunked and formed in Jamaican style sauce with noodles."

Jake laughed. "Can't see myself drooling over formed pork chop in Jamaican sauce. I'll take beef stew."

Nicole decided on the jambalaya, though she expected no great gastronomic treat, but she wasn't into red meat, let alone red meat that had been on the shelf for months. She opened the heating packets, slipped the MRE pouches into them, but hesitated when it came to adding the water necessary to activate the heaters. Her camelback was two thirds empty.

"Jake, how much water do you have left?" He was busy leveling the floor with a small trenching tool.

"I don't know; take a look at my pack—throw me your shelter half, will you?"

She looked. His was almost empty. "Jake, I don't think we should use the water to heat these things up. We're too damn low on water." She dug in the bottom of her pack and threw him the shelter half.

He stopped what he was doing and checked the camelbacks. He dug in the bottom of his pack and produced a quart canteen of water. He thought for a moment, and looked up. "Good thinking. Just set them out in the sun; they'll heat up quickly enough."

When she returned he sat studying his GPS. "You stashed water and supplies at Alpha, right?"

"Yeah. We entered the waypoints on both GPS's. Waypoint 1 is halfway to Alpha. Waypoint 2 is Alpha; waypoint 3 is halfway to Beta, and so forth."

Jake took a deep breath, exhaled slowly. "Well, according to this, Alpha is thataway (he pointed roughly left of due North), six point seven klicks on course 3-2-6, which means the nearest water is a day and half away, if we're lucky. And we have a little over a quart of water between us. Should have about a gallon apiece. Which means," he grinned, "we'll just have to swap spit when we get thirsty."

"Eeyuu. Yuck." She made a face.

"Here, let's try it," he said, kissing her. She fought him for a moment, then relented, and kissed him back.

"Wasn't that bad was it?"

She shrugged. "Weelll, no, but I got more tongue than water. You're disgusting."

"Hey, I'm just a macho warrior Indian. What didja expect?"

"A little more finesse, like this." And she showed him.

After a while, Jake came up for air. "You're right, I need some lessons. We better eat that crap out there in the sun; we're going to need more energy than either one of us has."

Nicole fetched the MREs from the sun, while Jake unrolled their sleeping bags on the shelter halves. They sat cross legged on the sleeping bags. After a couple of bites Nicole asked, "Well, how's your beef?"

"Well, won't take too much to make a turd; it's already half-way there. How's yours?"

Nicole snickered. "Not like any jambalaya I ever had—same as yours. I think I'll skip to desert and try the energy bar." She pried open the orange foil rectangle labeled "New Millennium Energy Bar, Orange Natural Flavor." She broke a corner off the orange-greyish slab in the packet, and chomped away while she read the label. "Let's see, it contains flour, sugar and more sugar. Great." She stared at Jake. "And you guys win wars eating this crap?"

"Hey, you've never had the green eggs and ham in C rations. Those were reeaaallly good. You better eat some more of that," he said, pointing his chin at the jambalaya. "It will keep you on your feet." He lit a Marlboro, exhaled a long blue plume of smoke, and lay back on the sleeping bag.

Nicole chewed her way through several more plastic spoonfuls of jambalaya. When Jake glanced at her she was smiling a secret little smile.

"What?" he said, exhaling again.

"Ugh! Enough!" she said, setting the package down. Then she leaned over, took the cigarette from Jake's fingers, and took a puff. She coughed, and handed him back the cigarette, scowling. "I forgot how nasty those things are."

Jake shrugged. "So what was so funny?"

She drew a knee up under her chin, hugged her leg and looked at Jake coyly. "You surprised me. That 'swapping spit' remark. It was so out of character for you."

Jake sat up. "Why?"

"Humor. Hu-*mor*. You're usually serious as Custer at the Bighorn."

"Well, you haven't exactly been Carol Burnette, yourself."

"I don't breathe well in testosterone-infected atmospheres."

Jake stared at her.

"What's the matter? Don't know what 'testosterone' means?"

Jake opened his mouth, then closed it.

"Why Jake Two Feathers, you do such a good imitation of a gold fish." She snickered. "What else do you do?"

"I'll show you," he said, grabbing her by the shoulders, shoving her down on the sleeping bags. "I'll show you." When he had her pinned, he tickled her mercilessly.

"Oh, no! Jake! Jake, stop!" She howled helplessly. "Jake! Stop!" Then she froze beneath him, and the laughing died in her throat. He rolled off her to see what she stared at.

Vassili Grubinich stood there with Tolya, grinning. He racked a round in the 9 mm Uzi he pointed at them.

Jake jumped up, glanced toward his pack with the shoulder holster and the .45 draped across it, ten feet away. Grubinich followed his glance.

"By all means, try for it," he said. His eyes hardened, flicked to Nicole, who stood up, straightening her clothes, flicked back to Jake.

"Your name's not Brewer, is it?"

"Tolya," Vassili said, lifting his chin at the two of them. Tolya stepped forward, tied their hands behind them with nylon cable ties. Then he began searching Jake. The first thing he took was Jake's Yarborough. Jake ignored him, staring at Grubinich.

Vassili lit a cheroot, and walked around behind Jake.

Tolya stepped aside, began patting Nicole down. His hands lingered over her breasts, crotch. He looked up at her, smirking. Nicole bit her tongue, stared straight ahead.

Without any warning, Grubinich smashed the butt of the Uzi into Jake's back, above his left kidney.

Jake grunted, went to his knees.

"I will tell you my name, but only so you will know who killed you." He kicked Jake in the back, slamming him face flat on the sleeping bags. Grubinich whipped the bayonet from his boot, straddled Jake, grabbed a handful of hair, jerked his head back, exposing the throat. Vassili lay the point of the blade above Jake's jugular.

"No!" Nicole yelled.

Tolya backhanded her. "Shut up!" A thin line of blood leaked from the corner of her mouth.

"My name is Vassili Grubinich, Colonel, *Komitet Gosudarstvennoy Bezopasnosti,* Seventh Directorate. You owe me two lives, and I am going to take them from you slowly." He paused, tapping the point of the blade against Jake's throat. "But not yet."

He walked behind Nicole, grabbed a handful of blonde hair, and twisted it, forcing her to face him, their lips almost touching. "And you, *zaichic,* we are going to have a lot of fun together," he whispered. He caressed her cheek with the bayonet. "We will get to know each other very, very, very well."

He tossed her aside. "But not yet." He sheathed the bayonet.

He stepped in front of them both, and stood, gloating. Grubinich tossed Tolya the Uzi. Then he clapped his hands and rubbed them together. "First, we will find the diamonds. *Da?*"

Jake struggled to his knees, grimacing in pain. "Don't know anything about any diamonds." He looked at Nicole, who had fallen to her knees. She kept her head down, avoiding his gaze. "As for your two goons, well, they got what they deserved."

"As will you—Tolya, their feet."

Tolya stepped forward, pushed them to lying positions, and secured their feet with cable ties.

Grubinich jerked his head toward the entrance of the cave, signaling Tolya to follow him. They stood, talking quietly, while Vassili fished around in his pack for the sat phone. After a minute's conversation, Tolya re-entered the cave, began rummaging through Jake and Nicole's packs.

Nicole lay facing Jake's back. He stared into the darkness of the lava tube, thinking furiously. "Diamonds? What diamonds?"

Nicole scooched up against him. "I'm sorry, Jake. I wanted to tell you."

"Not now," he snarled. "If I can't figure a way out of this, we're dead."

Tolya, jumped up and savagely kicked Jake in the stomach. "No talking!"

Grubinich, came back in time to see Jake retching from the kick. He looked at Tolya quizzically. Tolya shrugged. "Whispering," he said.

Vassili cuffed Nicole up side her head. "It's not polite to whisper," he said. "Did you find them?" he asked Tolya.

"*Da.*" Tolya handed Vassili the two GPS's. He fiddled with one of them for a moment, stepped over to where Jake and Nicole lay. He drew his bayonet, and kneeled beside Jake.

The bayonet was a 1968 SVD Dragunov bayonet: 5 7/8 inches of carbon steel, honed to glittering sharpness. Jake lay on his side, staring down the tunnel. The Russian rolled him to his back, tapped his thigh thoughtfully with the flat of the blade. Grubinich patted Jake's shirt pockets, withdrew a pack of Marlboro reds, and lit one up with a silver Zippo. The Zippo bore the sword and shield emblem of the KGB. He exhaled a plume of blue smoke, looked at the cigarette appreciatively, and asked, "Those waypoints, what do they signify?"

Jake stared at the ceiling of the cave.

The tapping became for rapid.

Grubinich took a deep drag, exhaled slowly, looked at Nicole, back at Jake. He sat back on his ass, cross-legged in the dirt.

"Tolya!"

Tolya snapped to. "*Da?*"

"Did you get the water from their packs?"

"*Da.*"

"Food?"

"*Da.*"

"*Khoroshiy.* Now go see if you can find some firewood."

"*Da.*" Tolay slung his Uzi and marched out, shaking his head. The fools should just tell him what he wants to know. They always did, in the end, anyway.

Vassili turned his attention back to Jake, who lay uncomfortably on his back with his hands wadded up underneath him, bound by the cable tie.

"What do the waypoints signify?" He tapped Jake's shin with the flat of the blade.

Jake stared at the ceiling.

Grubinich laughed, casually slit Jake's pant leg from the knee to mid-thigh.

Nicole watched in horror, as the Russian casually folded back the cloth, drew the point of the blade down Jake's thigh. A thin line of red appeared.

"This is ridiculous, *moy drug*; you know I will get the information I want; we are soldiers, *da*? You know what happens.

You, I will hurt only for my own pleasure. She," he pointed the bayonet at Nicole, "will tell me what I want to know, and you will watch as I cut off her nipples, then slice steaks off then rest of her breasts. Then I will use your leg as a cutting board, as I cut off her fingers, one by one." He giggled. "She will not be able to grab your cock, eh?"

Jake lifted his head up, drilled Grubinich with his eyes: "Untie me and try it."

Grubinich threw his head back in a throaty laugh, then spoke with a lethal flatness, "We will locate the diamonds, then *vnebrachnyy rebenok*, we will have our dance. You will beg me like a little boy to end your pain." He reached over casually and unzipped Jake's trousers.

"Waypoints two, four, six and eight are the locations of possible sites; one, three, five and seven mark half-way points from base camp. We cached water and food." Nicole sat there, pale and quivering.

Vassili, looked to her, grinning. "Good. What, exactly, are we looking for?"

Nicole stared back at him, impassive, blankly. "A sickle-shaped landmark, with a large cave and a waterfall inside. That's the story we were told." She broke eye contact, looked away.

Tolya came back with an armload of dead sage and pinyon branches, threw them down at the entrance of the cave.

Vassili stood up, laughing another throaty laugh. "Pain is part of the game—for the loser. He knows this." He laughed again, and walked away toward Tolya.

Chapter 23

He decided he would provoke Brewer, or whatever his name was, into killing him before he started in on Nicole. Jake wasn't particularly squeamish, but he just didn't want to watch. He'd had enough of it in his life. There had been plenty of torture and cruelty in Mogadishu, Afghanistan, and Iraq. Better to die and get it over with.

There is a line men of war sometimes cross, a line from which there is no return. Something in them snaps, and morality, what little remains in a theatre of blood, slips its leash. Cruelty sometimes serves a purpose when the lives of hundreds, perhaps thousands of men, hang on a slender thread of information, known or not known. But sometimes, in some men, the pleasure of inflicting pain becomes a drug as addictive as heroin, and as compelling. If not the pleasure of pain, then the pleasure of raw, unrestrained power, the terrible knowledge of omnipotency without retribution, becomes the awful elixir that drives life and inflicts death at whim, and without thought or remorse.

Jake had watched such tendencies develop in some of his own men—Special Forces—operating for weeks and months hundreds of miles and light years away from any civilizing authority. The men themselves became as harsh and severe as the jungles or deserts surrounding them. The snake shows no compassion to the rat, nor the leopard to the monkey; daily death becomes the natural order of life, and men become as inured against the pain and death of their own species as fish to other fish.

Jake had seen the flat, reptilian stare in Grubinich's eyes before. It was a gaze entirely void of any humanity; there was nothing human to which one could appeal. It was the black, abyssal stare of the shark before he rolls and strikes.

Nicole, in her naiveté, had sought to save them with the information she gave. But she had actually condemned them to a slow and painful death, especially herself.

Men like Grubinich hardly cared about sex; they used it in the most sadistic ways possible to achieve the levels of degradation and humiliation, as well as the domination and control they so desired.

Jake didn't want to watch what he was certain Grubinich would do to her; but in his present circumstance, he was powerless to prevent it.

A woman can get into a man, eat at him, until he is little more than an empty bag of desire. It begins deep in the loins, an ache rising up until it dissolves sinew, bone, and organ; it consumes common sense; it eats at him until there is nothing left, only the fire of her beckoning in the flames of his own pyre.

Jake wasn't quite to this point, yet, with Nicole, but he knew he wasn't thinking straight about her, either. He wanted to be furious; she lied to him about the diamonds. She had betrayed his trust, a thing not easily given, nor regained, once it is gone. But he felt neither anger, or betrayal, only nauseating fear in the pit of his stomach. And impotence. He couldn't protect or trust the woman he so badly wanted to cherish.

He lay on his side, staring into the dimness of the lava tube thinking these thoughts. He was mildly surprised the Russians had left them alone throughout the afternoon. As he lay there, he realized he stared at a pathway through the rockfall on the cavern floor. If he had been standing up, he might not have noticed the subtle ways a rock had been moved here, or piled there to make walking easier.

Moreover, he also realized that as he had lain so furiously thinking, he had noticed what appeared to be a bundle of sticks stacked against the wall where the boundary of daylight and dark occurred. Why a bundle of sticks? They had to have been put there on purpose. In his present situation, the question was academic, but he formulated a theory, anyway.

He heard the heavy footsteps of Grubinich approaching, but he gave no outward sign that he heard, and steeled himself against the torture to come.

But Grubinich merely kicked the sole of his boot and said, "Tomorrow we will find the diamonds. If you do well and help us, I will kill you both quickly. If not... ." He let the sentence hanging and walked back to where Tolya squatted by the fire.

"Jake. Jake," Nicole whispered, nudging him awake from behind. In spite of himself, he had dozed off after Grubinich promised a quick death. He had no idea what time it was, but darkness had fallen, and he couldn't see a thing. He lay on his side, still. Nicole had slid down his backside until his hands rested in the hollow of her throat. He felt her warm, moist breath on his wrists.

"What?" he whispered back.

"Put your hands down inside my blouse. There's a knife hanging from a leather thong. It's wrapped up in a cloth."

"Whaat?" he whispered.

"There's a goddamn knife hanging inside my blouse; it's wrapped up in a piece of cloth." She scooted up, forcing his hands down between her cleavage.

His palm brushed a nipple. He hesitated.

"Lower," she whispered harshly. A stirring and a mumbling came from the front of the cave. Jake froze. After a moment, when he heard no further sound, he continued groping and found what felt like tightly rolled cloth. He pulled it out of the blouse.

After he struggled with it for a while, he managed to slip the cloth off. He felt the smooth bone of the handle and then a stinging when he sliced one of his fingers. "Son of a bitch," he muttered. Then he flipped the knife over one hundred and eighty degrees so the edge rested against the nylon tie binding his wrists. He was surprised when it parted easily and his hands broke free.

He quickly and quietly sliced the tie binding his feet, then freed Nicole. With a glance toward the cave opening, he took Nicole by the hand and whispered, "Quiet. We're going into the cave. Put your heels down first."

He slipped the leather thong around his neck and the knife inside his shirt, crouched low, and began sweeping the area in front of him with his free hand, feeling his way into the cave, trying to remember the details of the path. It was difficult to estimate distance in the absolute darkness, but when he got even with where he hoped the sticks lay, he dropped Nicole's hand, stopped, and whispered: "Stay here. I'll be right back."

"Jake! Where are you going?"

"Shhhh," he whispered back. "Just stay here. Don't move."

She crouched where he left her, fighting off panic. What if he didn't come back? That and a dozen other equally frightening thoughts raced through her mind. After a while, she heard the muffled, woody knock of wood on wood and then a sort of clacking sound, like a stack of broomsticks being gathered up. Then Jake was back, his breath hot on her ear.

"When I turn around, grab ahold of my waistband. We're moving out."

"Jake, what….?"

"Shhhh…," he whispered harshly. "Just follow me." She grabbed the waistband at the small of his back and followed, in the crouching, thigh-burning stoop that allowed Jake to feel his way ahead. Walking by braille.

He lugged the sticks under one arm and swept the other in an arc in front of him. After a while he realized the path they followed hugged the smooth wall of the tube. He stopped, stood up. The cave curved gradually to the right; he figured they had gone far enough to be out of Grubinich's line of sight.

Tolya had been so eager to feel Nicole up he neglected the Zippo in the cargo pocket of Jake's BDU's. He thumbed the lid up, struck the wheel. The dim light of the lighter confirmed his theory about the sticks.

"Yes!" he said.

"Yes, what?" Nicole stepped out from behind him to see what he 'yessed' about.

"Torches," he said, and held the end of the stick to the flame. The 'stick' was actually a dry pinyon branch with a pitchy bole at one end. Whoever made the torches had wrapped a ball of dry sage, dry grasses, and pinyon twigs around the bole, and bound it with a length of braided sage bark. Once it was ignited by the tinder, the pitchy center might burn for as long as an hour.

Jake held the torch aloft and counted the remaining torches: they had eleven left.

Earlier, he had reasoned that since ancient people had used the lava tube caves to store meat in their ice-filled depths, they must have had torches to light their way. They couldn't see in the dark any better than he could.

If he had reasoned correctly, somewhere in this tunnel there would be ice, which meant water, even if they had no way of carrying it. How he was going to get them out of the cave, he had no idea.

"Jake, look." Nicole bent over to finger the pinyon needles on one of the torches. *The needles were still green.*

She straightened up. They stared at each other a moment, trying to digest the meaning of what they saw.

Jake broke the eye contact. He wasn't ready to forgive her yet.

"Carry the torches," he said, and moved off down the tunnel. He withdrew the diamond knife, let it dangle within easy reach.

Chapter 24

The Man was mopping up the last of his eggs with a wad of toast when the sharp rap on the backdoor of his office came. He swiveled around in his chair, away from the rolltop that served as credenza and breakfast table, opened the top drawer of his desk and withdrew a Colt .45. He chambered a round, cocked it, and held it in his lap, covered with a napkin.

"Come!" he yelled.

A short, stocky man stepped though the door. He wore his hair flat-topped and white-sidewalled. A black leather patch hid the socket of his right eye. Small white scars seamed and puckered the right side of his face around the patch. Biceps strained against the black tee shirt. His cammo BDU trousers flared above black canvas boots.

He took two steps into the room, assumed a parade rest position, hands clasped behind him.

The Man sized him up, opened his desk drawer, rummaged around until he found a used toothpick, lay the .45 on the desk top and said, "Well, come on over'n set down." He picked the ham out of his teeth.

Patch didn't move, gazed calmly at the Man.

"Standard fee is fifteen thousand in advance."

The Man swiveled around to the credenza, unlocked one of the doors, withdrew a ten thousand dollar stack of hundreds. He tossed it on the desk. "There's ten thousand; you get the other five when the job is done."

Patch remained motionless, impassive, calm. "Standard fee is fifteen thousand in advance. Paid in full."

The Man leaned forward, resting his meaty, clasped hands near the .45. "Well, hell," he said, faintly smiling. "'At don't sound like much of a deal t'me. What if you don't git the job done? What if you jest waltz outta here with my money an' I don't never lay eyes on ya agin?"

Later, when he thought about it, he couldn't understand how it happened so quickly. One minute Patch was standing quietly ten feet away, the next, he was pointing the barrel of the .45 at the Man's nose. How did he do that?

"You piece of shit. If I have to come back here to collect, I will take it all and gut you like the pig you are."

Patch neatly dropped the clip out of the .45, ejected the chambered round, and caught it with his left hand. He pocketed the clip and the round, threw the pistol on the desk. He leaned over the desk until his face was scant inches from the Man's.

"Fifteen thousand. Now."

"O.K., O.K., no needed to get riled." The Man swiveled to the credenza, extracted another bundle of hundreds, counted out five thou, and lay the remaining five aside.

"That's better," Patch said, pocketing the money. He assumed a parade rest stance in front of the desk. "Who, when and where?" he asked.

The Man shuffled through some papers, tossed two eight by ten black and white glossies across the desk. One was a picture of Rick Sanchez; the other was Tom Curdy. "These two officers and everyone in the cabin. No one escapes."

Although the explosion shook the ground and they staggered, Vassili kept on walking, and didn't look back. Tolya, however, paused to admire the cloud of dust rising in the early morning air. The amount of C-4 they packed around the cave entrance could have easily leveled a two-storey building. Enraged at the disappearance of his captives, Vassili himself had shaped the charges so that most of the blast focused into the tunnel. But it sealed the cave, too, just in case Jake and Nicole weren't killed by rockfall. If they weren't already dead, they soon would be. The cave had become their tomb: no air, no water, no food, no light. Tolya shrugged and trudged after Vassili, shaking his head. Waste of a good piece of ass.

Nicole awoke to absolute darkness. The acrid bite of dust stung her nose and burned her lungs.

"Jake?" Silence.

All she remembered was that they had been trudging, for what seemed like hours, along the wall of the tunnel when the shock wave from the blast flattened her in the dust.

"Jake?" Silence.

She tried to stand up, but realized she couldn't feel her legs. She felt around and discovered them pinned between two slabs of rock.

"Oh, God," she moaned. She screamed at the blackness surrounding her: "Jaaake!" Silence.

Then she heard a small grating sound, like bricks sliding across bricks.

"Nicole! Nick!"

"Here! I'm right here! I'm trapped."

"Just a minute. Ouch! Son of a bitch!" More sounds of rock clattering against rock.

The Zippo sparked once, twice, and the torch burst into flames, producing an eerie, haloed light, yellow in the thick dust.

Jake came to her, torch aloft. The bloody red gash on his forehead aside, he looked aboriginal, his face a ghastly white, coated with flour-fine dust. He jammed the torch down between the fallen rocks.

"Are you hurt? Any pain?"

She lay, twisted, propped up on her elbow, but she was actually pinned on her tummy. The huge slab of basalt, weighing many hundreds of pounds, lay at a fifteen degree angle across the back of her thighs and legs. The only reason her legs hadn't been crushed flat was that the slab was held up at one end by another block of basalt, creating a rough triangle. Her legs lay in the triangle.

"No, no pain. I can't feel anything in my legs."

Jake reached for her hand. "I'll get you out," he said simply. He studied the situation for a moment.

After a moment, he said, "O.K. I'm not going to be able to lift it very much, so be ready to scramble. And she did. He was only able to lift it a couple of inches, but Nicole dug her way out with her hands and elbows, dragging her dead legs behind her.

Jake dropped the slab with a crash, and knelt beside her, massaging her legs.

"Feel anything yet?"

"Oh, ow! Yes. They're tingling."

Jake laughed. "I think that rock just cut the circulation off." He stared at her legs. "Better your circulation than your legs."

Nicole sat, back up against the wall, exercising her legs. When the torch began to gutter, Jake lit another, jammed it down in the fallen rock.

Nick looked around. "Now what?"

Jake sat down, his back against the cold wall of the tunnel.

"Keep moving; that's all we can do." The ancient knife still hung from his neck. He held it up in the torchlight, studied it. "Is this what they're after?"

Nick squirmed. "Yes. No, not exactly. I *don't* know."

"What do you mean, 'You don't know?'"

She hugged her knees, looked sideways at Jake.

"Just that, Jake. I don't know. The Mexican who sold those artifacts had no clue what the blade was made of. Dad suspected it wasn't just quartz, and had it tested.

She stood up to test her legs, sat back down. "The Russians must be working for the Diamond Consortium. I don't know how they found out, or whether they think there must be more big diamonds. Dad thought there were. Anyway, the Consortium has a reputation when it comes to controlling diamond supply. A couple of murders here or there don't matter."

"Jake," she took his hands in hers, looked earnestly at him. "I didn't know—Dad didn't know—about the Russians."

"But you knew about the diamonds! Why weren't you honest with me?" He shook her hands off.

"Jake," she said, hands on his shoulders, "think. We didn't know you. We don't even know if there *are* any diamonds out there. All Dad knew was that there was an archeological site somewhere. And he thought he could use it to prove his theory. Diamonds were icing, if they existed." She removed her hands, stared a the dust between her boots. Nick shrugged. "That's it."

Jake stared at her profile, yellow in the torchlight. "Doesn't wash, Nick. Only diamond can shape diamond. Diamonds are brittle; they shatter if they aren't cut properly. These people didn't have that kind of knowledge; they didn't know squat about diamonds—even what they were. Hell, they wouldn't even have a word for them."

"But it does make sense, Jake. They've been using diamond technology in India and China for thousands of years. The Chinese made sapphire-corundum axe-heads, shaping them with diamonds over five thousand years ago. The Solutreans made quantum leaps in blade technology. They were the greatest flintknappers the world has ever seen. They weren't stupid, Jake. If they found a material as hard as diamond, they would try to find a way to use it."

Jake grunted and stood up. "Speaking of finding a way, we'd better do just that. If you can walk, that is."

She stood up, shook it out. "I can," she said, gathering up the fallen torches.

"You want me to carry some of those?"

"No, I carry my own weight," she said.

"That's it," Bob Duncan said. "I think those boys probably mean to fight it out, and we think there is a high probability of significant fire power up there." He finished briefing Phil Jenkins of the DEA, as well as Tom and Hal Lindsay, on the 'tactical situation' they faced.

The conference room of the Python County Law Enforcement Complex was typical of such conference rooms: harsh fluorescent lights, muted green walls, institutional stainless and plastic chairs, beige carpet, a long, simulated wood-grain formica conference table, except this table still provided a row of ashtrays spaced down the center.

Bob sat down, looked to Tom. Smoke curled languidly up from Tom's Camel.

At the head of the table, Jenkins shoved himself back, strode to the chalkboard where the USGS topographical map of the Caldera Quadrant hung.

"Let me get this right," he said. Jenkins tended toward chubbiness, which showed in the two inches of fat that bulged over his belt buckle and rounded his face. He looked like a rosy-cheeked cherub in an official U.S. government-issue dark suit. A short man, not over five-six, he gloried in his position as regional director of the DEA. Short, mousey-brown hair, pale blue eyes, yellow power tie, spit-shined Florsheims. A take-charge federal kind of guy.

As he swaggered to the map, his suit jacket fell open and Tom glimpsed the twin Glocks, one for each side, in shoulder holsters. "Must have some really dangerous secretaries at the regional headquarters," he thought.

"Now let me get this right," Jenkins said again. He extracted a silver telescoping pointer from his jacket pocket, extended it, and tapped a meandering red line on the map. "This is what you call the Red Road. And the bust is going to take place up this side road here." He tapped a broken grey line.

Tom nodded.

"It's marked 'Kettle Line Cabin' on the map," Duncan said.

"Oh, yeah. I see it now." Jenkins cocked his head first to one side, then the other, studying the map. He took a step back.

"Judging from the contour lines," he said over his shoulder, "this is a pretty steep box canyon with only one road in."

"That's what Bob said." Lindsay lit up a Marlboro Light with his Zippo, tilted his chair back on two legs.

Jenkins frowned. "I don't allow smoking at my briefings."

Lindsay returned the frown. "Ain't your briefing."

Tom leaned forward, both hands clasped on the table. "We believe there may be anywhere from five to ten suspects. Our informant said something big was going down, about eight."

"Right," Jenkins said. "Meet you here about six tomorrow evening. We'll take credit for the bust, of course."

"Oh, of course," Tom said.

After Jenkins left Tom sat back in his chair, shook his head. "No wonder the country's in the mess it is."

Duncan and Lindsay exhaled sighs of disgust.

"It's just as well," Tom said. "We'll let them take credit for the bust, and any casualties, too, if Ol' Zeb has a couple of fifties stashed up there." He paused. "I'll want you two and Rick."

"Sanchez has called in sick the last two days."

Tom stood up. "Well, Bob, call his ass up and tell him I want him here at six sharp tomorrow. Boy's gotta stop moping sometime. He ain't the first man ever had a woman cheat on him. Won't be the last, either." He grabbed his Stetson and marched out.

Chapter 25

Patch crouched at the edge of the canyon wall that overlooked the line shack. From his vantage point, he had a clear view of the shack, hidden in the cul de sac of trees, and the gate below, the same gate Zeb had hung the skull and crossbones sign on.

He eased himself into a prone firing position, studied the area through the M3A 10x Leupold scope of the M24 rifle. He made the gate at just over 500 yards. The gate that Tom and the others would have to come through.

The shack was a piece of cake. It lay about 300 yards from his position, an easy distance for his M79 "Thumper." The HE rounds would ignite the dry, ancient cabin instantly in a killing conflagration. And he could easily pick off any runners, if they should escape the blaze. By the time the Feds figured out there was another shooter besides the boys in the cabin, he'd be long gone.

Satisfied that everything was as it should be, he eased ten yards back from the edge before he stood up, and started back to his hide.

The Russians had plotted a course toward a line of low black cinder cones that lay north by northwest of the cave they dynamited. The agony of a land birthed by a violent volcanic mother became more and more apparent as they approached the hills. The collapsed lava domes grew wider and plunged deeper; some of them ran a hundred yards across and sixty feet deep. Where their path was not pocked by craters, acres of sharp, rubble-like a'a lava lay like fields of black teeth. And where lava solidified into rivers of ropy pahoehoe lava, it, too, was scarred by deep ravines and crevasses that sometimes required arduous detours or scaling slick walls of basalt.

Occasionally they encountered deep ravines choked with sage, pinyon, and towering wild rye grasses. It was along the edge of such a ravine when Tolya, who had taken the lead from Vassili, shouted, raised his Uzi, and fired a six-round burst.

About fifty yards behind, and still laboring through the treacherous a'a lava field, Vassili could only stand and watch as Tolya ran along the edge of the ravine, occasionally raising his Uzi as if to fire. Grubinich couldn't see what Tolya shot at. Then Tolya jerked, stopped suddenly, and turned back toward Vassil. Two slim spears, about five feet long, had appeared suddenly, as if by magic, piercing his chest. The Uzi hung at the end of a limp arm. He took two steps toward Vassili, collapsed.

By the time Vassili got to him, a bloody froth dribbled from Tolya's lips; his chest heaved a couple of times, and then he was dead. Kneeling beside the body, Vassili screamed.

The blast had brought down more rockfall than was immediately apparent. The deeper Jake and Nicole plunged into the lava tube, they were often forced to scramble up over unstable piles of basalt blocks that had fallen from the roof. They moved carefully, with an agonizing slowness. Their mounting thirst was all the more unbearable by thick dust. First one torch burnt out, then another, and another. They spoke very little, as they picked their way along, until finally, they reached a point where the tunnel was plugged completely.

Jake clambered up on the pile, holding the torch aloft, trying to see a way through. He clambered back down, and sat next to Nicole.

She leaned against the smooth wall, eyes closed, resting. "Well?" she asked.

"Nope." He relaxed against the wall, and stared at the wall opposite.

She stirred beside him. "Now what?"

The torch began to gutter, and Nick lit a fresh one off the old. She jabbed it down between some stones, and sat back, staring at the flames. The old torch fluttered, went out, and smoked.

Jake reached over, took Nick's hand.

"We could die here," he said.

"I thought you strong macho-Rambo Ranger Special Forces types were supposed to say things like, 'We're not gonna die; I will not let us die'—stuff like that."

"This ain't the movies, and we're trapped. This could be our last day of life."

She wrenched her hand free and slapped him on the shoulder. "Jake! Stop it! We've got to be positive. There must be something we can do. What can we do?"

"We could get married."

"Married? Have you gone crazy? Married!"

"Yeah. You don't want to spend your last night on earth without sex, do you?" Jake grinned.

"I'm not spending my last night on earth and I'm definitely not having sex with you, not unless you get us out of this."

Jake sat back against the wall, crossed his arms and closed his eyes. "No sex, no escape; that's it." He opened his eyes and smiled at her. *Hecetu waylo.* That's the way it is." He closed his eyes again, apparently dozing.

Nick stared at him, aghast. She couldn't figure out if he had popped his cork, or if he knew something she didn't.

"Jake." She shook him. "Jake, c'mon; you're scaring me." She slumped, momentarily, unsure what to do, fear rising in her throat. What if he really had flipped out? It wouldn't be the first time one of these guys disappeared over the edge. "You know the way out, don't you? Don't you?"

Jake stirred, opened his eyes, and kissed her. "Relax. I don't know the way out, but they do," he said pointing.

Half a dozen rattlesnakes, of various lengths, slithered at the base of the wall across the cave. The black tongues flickered, hesitated, then the snakes disappeared, one by one into the rockfall that plugged the cave. He stood up, grabbed the torch and stepped across the cave floor to the wall at the base of the rockfall. He held the torch up, revealing a crack about three feet wide. He turned to Nick and grinned. "I don't know where it goes, but it does go. C'mon. Wait." He turned back around. "What about the sex?"

She slapped him again. "We aren't out of this, yet, and not if you were the last man on earth. Extortion will get you nowhere. Prick."

Jake laughed. "Bitch." And then he squeezed into the crack.

He didn't feel nearly light-hearted as he acted. But the stress, the darkness, the thirst, and the danger of their situation were beginning to take their toll on Nicole. He could see the fatigue, and mounting fear in the lines of her face.

Actually, he had no idea where the crevasse they squeezed along in led. Chances are, it led nowhere, and would soon become too tight to negotiate. But it was important to keep her moving, and not thinking.

True, the snakes might be able to use the crevasse to find their way to the surface, but then they could easily slip through cracks that Jake and Nicole couldn't. He hoped they stayed ahead of them. In these close quarters, neither he or Nicole would be able to avoid a strike from a coiled and frightened rattler. He pushed grimly forward, resisting the claustrophobia of the darkness, and the weight of the basalt pressing in on them.

And, as he suspected, after they had squeezed along for about a hundred yards, the crevasse narrowed to where Jake could no longer squeak through.

"What is it," Nicole croaked.

"Too narrow," he answered, "can't get through."

Nick buried her face against the wall, began sobbing. "Oh, Jake. I'm so scared! Oh, God," she screamed. "Get me out of this!" She beat her fists against the cold, black basalt. "I don't want to die like this!"

Jake turned back and held her tightly. "We're not going to die. There's a way out and we will find it." He kissed her. "We just have to suck it up until we do." His torch guttered.

"Nick, hand me another torch."

She did. One torch remained.

He held the new torch up high, hoping to find a wider space nearer the ceiling. No such luck. Nick had to back up a couple of steps so he could kneel down to inspect the crevasse at floor level. There, it widened into an arch about two and a half feet off the floor. Jake figured he could barely squeeze through.

"Jake…"

"Nick, it will be O.K. I'm not going to leave you alone here long. I'll just go a little way to see if the passage opens up on the other side of the bottleneck."

She moaned a little bit, but took a couple of steps back so he could lie on his belly to begin the crawl.

"God, Jake! I'm afraid of being left alone in this dark."

"You're not going to be alone," he said, squeezing under the arch. "You will be able to see me all the way. I need you to hang on to it, Nick. Now, c'mon. We're a team, and we're going to make it. I won't leave you behind."

Thrusting the torch before him, Jake crawled along on his elbows, coughing from the bitter smoke that quickly fouled the air.

Just as he breathed a silent prayer to the Snake People, saying if there were any in the crawl space, he meant them no harm, buzzing shattered the silence and the darkness just beyond the ring of his torchlight. "Shit!" he muttered, and moved forward swinging the torch back and forth in front of him.

"Jake, what's that sound? Nicole called.

"Rattlesnake," he called back.

He held the torch as high as he could. Just beyond the reach of the torch, but within its dim circle of light lay a large rattler. It's black tongue flicked in and out, obsidian eyes glittered; the rattles buzzed menacingly.

Jake called out. *"Hau, kola! Miciye. Isnala Mani le miye ca. Omakiyayo!"* Hello, friend. My brother. It is I, Walks Alone. Help me!"

Nicole called out: "Jake, what's going on? Who are you talking to?"

"The snake," he called back. The snake and the man eyed each other for a long moment in the flickering yellow light of the torch. The rattler reared up like a cobra, lunged backward into the darkness. After a moment, he heard a soft "thump." Jake crawled forward.

After he had gone about ten yards, he wasn't sure, but he thought he felt the slight movement of air, not a breeze, but a brush. He crawled forward; the crushing weight of the basalt above his head disappeared, and he stood up on a basalt ledge. It was actually the topmost ledge of a series of ledges that ringed the inside of a lava dome like an amphitheatre. He stepped to the edge, held the torch high. The rattler, along with several others lay on the sandy bench below.

He stood at the inside edge of a basalt lava dome, an immense bubble of basalt, created when trapped gasses in red hot oozing lava expanded. Only this lava dome had not collapsed inward on itself, like most of them had. Twenty feet above his head, part of the ceiling had buckled and dropped to the floor beneath, creating a skylight. A shaft of sunlight streamed in, illuminating a natural amphitheatre large as a high school auditorium. What he saw raised the hackles on his neck and the hair on his arms.

Chapter 26

"What time did the swarm begin?" Desh stood, staring at a computer monitor, looking over the shoulder of a graduate student. He peered at a series of red, jagged lines that only a seismologist could understand. A "swarm" is many, many small earthquakes happening over a period of time, usually confined to one area. They are too slight to be felt, except by seismographs.

The lanky, sandy-haired student, whose name was Montgomery, after the British World War Two general, swiveled his chair, and peered up at Desh through thick lenses. He wore an unironed, yellow short-sleeved shirt, packed with red, green, black and blue pens and pencils. Taco droppings stained the front.

The remains of the offending tacos lay wadded up in the paper they arrived in. Monty's cubicle smelled faintly Hispanic: spiced hamburger, tomatoes, and hot sauce.

"Actually," Monty said, swiveling back around, punching computer keys, "there has been a gradual increase in phenomenon since the 4.9 recorded at Greeno a day and a half ago. In the last 24 hours we have recorded over 300 occurrences ranging from 1.0 to 2.9."

"Where?" Desh demanded.

The kid punched some keys. "Looks like about 40 kilometers southwest of Greeno, or about 25 miles out in the desert."

"How deep?"

The kid punched some more keys, swiveled back to face Desh. "They began about 7 kilometers down. The latest ones are...." He swiveled back around, fingers dancing on the keyboard. "...three kilometers."

"Oh, God," Desh moaned. "How far is it from Python?"

"Just a sec." The kid's fingers flew over the keyboard. A new screen appeared on the monitor. The animated program zoomed into a circle of low, black cinder cones. "The swarms are centered here, sir, at this location, called Black Butte. It is...ummm...." He paused, converting kilometers to miles in his head. "...approximately 155 miles west and north of Python."

"O.K.," Desh said, get me hard copies of all of this and bring it to my office. Good work!"

He fumed back to his office and sat, trying to figure out what to do. With no GPS and no tilt meters to measure ground deformation, he could not definitely conclude that an eruption was imminent. And it was probably too late to get sensors out there, even if he could persuade the powers to be of the necessity. But his gut told him there would be an eruption. He looked up a number on his cell phone and dialed it.

Tom had just walked in the door when the phone rang. Unbuckling his gun belt as he went, he stepped into the living room and picked up.

"Curdy." A pause. "Oh, hi, Desh." Another pause while he listened. The door to the bedroom opened, and Ellie stepped into the room wearing a black bikini that was little more than black string and tiny triangular thingies. Tom's jaw dropped.

"What? I'm sorry, Desh. Say that again." He flopped on the couch, ogling Ellie, who executed a series of modeling poses. She looked sunburned.

"So what are you telling me?" Pause. "Desh, I can't mobilize the entire emergency management system of the city, county, and state on a hunch." Pause. "You're sure?" Pause. "You're not sure."

He waved Ellie over, who sat on his lap.

"Well, Desh, I can't do that, and you know it. Call me back when you get something solid I can go to EMS with." Pause. "Yeah. Right. Keep in touch." He hung up.

"Geez, lady," he said, putting his arms around Ellie, "lewd and lascivious behavior will land you in my jail."

"Will I get handcuffed and everything?"

"Especially the 'everything'."

"Oh, boy!" She held up her wrists.

Tom grinned. "So what's up with the bikini and the sunburn?"

"Honey, we're going to Mexico, remember? I'm just getting ready."

"El, we're not going until September. This is June."

"I know. I just don't want to be white and rural."

"White and rural?"

"Yeah. You know. Deadfish white from Stixville. Soooo, bikini — latest fashion — and tanning bed." She rose, sylph-like, from his

lap. "Pot roast is in the oven. Get it out, will you? I'll go change."
She disappeared into the bedroom.

"Rural and white," he whispered, tracking Ellie's ass with his
eyes. He had no interest in pot roast.

After he shot Haraldsen, Anatoly struggled back to base camp,
spitting blood and bone splinters. Intense pain savaged his jaw and
the left side of his face. He passed out once on the way back. He
crawled the last hundred yards, managed to flop on a cot before a
blinding pain exploded in his brain, and he passed mercifully into
unconsciousness.

The sun set, then rose, set and rose again with blistering
intensity. Anatoly awoke to a red world of searing pain and
shriveling thirst. He managed to find a water bottle, but couldn't
get his lips to form a seal around the bottle. He couldn't swallow,
either. So he gave up and tried to pour the water down his throat, but
succeeded only in drenching himself. He lay back down, feverish,
sweating.

He slipped in and out of consciousness, dream, and delirium. On
the farm in the Ukraine, his mother scolded him for chasing the
chickens, and wringing their necks. He moaned and writhed as his
father beat him with an axe-handle for the offense.

His boyhood love, Marika, heavy-thighed and potato-shaped, came
and went through the tent, dogged by the heavy boots of Stalin's troops,
who eventually raped her, shipped her East in a cattle car.

Finally, Tolya came for him at dusk, beckoning him out onto the
desert. Tolya, his friend and comrade at arms for many years,
wraith-like and translucent, beckoned him to follow, saying it would
be all right. Soon everything would be all right, just follow. Tolya
disappeared into a crevasse, and Anatoly, too, stepped into the
abyss. Dimly, he was aware he was falling, but he didn't care, Tolya
would take care of him.

Jake stepped back to the crawl space.

"Nick, come on through! He kneeled by the opening, and
helped her out. Together, they turned. Nick walked to the edge, and
gasped, momentarily forgetting her thirst.

The sun poured through the skylight at the top of the dome,
creating a pillar of light illuminating the circle of mammoth skulls at

the center of the cavern. Twenty or more of the skulls lay there and the great ivory tusks, now brown with age, curved outward and upward for ten or twelve feet, creating a smaller circle. There, eight more tusks had been stacked, tipi-like, to make a shrine within. There sat three figures, enrobed in mammoth hides, cross-legged, slightly hunched, facing West.

"The Mothers," Jake whispered.

"What?" Nicole whispered back.

"The Mothers," he whispered ."Those are the Mothers of the First Clans. They are also *the Mother*."

"How do you know that?"

Jake shrugged. "I just know." He made his way down the steps to the sandy floor of the dome. Nick followed. At ground level, they both saw the low arch across the cavern. In ancient times, it could have easily been covered with a single mammoth hide. A short tunnel connected the arch to the blinding sunlight outside.

Nicole stood up and made for the inner shrine.

"Nick, no!" He whispered harshly.

Puzzled, she came back to him.

He began unlacing his boots. "Take your boots off," he whispered. "This is the most sacred of sacred ground. We don't want to offend the spirits."

"Jake, you don't really believe—."

"Yes, I do. Take them off, please." She sat, began unlacing her boots.

When they were barefoot, Jake led them sun-wise, from East to West around the outer perimeter of the dome. It lay deep in shadows, but they could make out what looked like bundles of fur lining the back wall. These bundles formed the outermost ring of concentric circles. Jake and Nicole crept silently, gingerly, on a narrow, sandy pathway between the wall and the bundles, and the next circle of skulls.

"Hand me your torch," Jake said quietly.

She handed him the last of the torches. When it flared and Jake held it aloft, they both gasped and took a step back, at least as "back" as they could without stepping into the next ring of skulls.

The bundles had faces—the shriveled, leathery, bony faces of the long dead, mummified by the dry climate, freezing in winter, blistering in summer. They had been bound into cross-legged sitting positions, bundled in mammoth, camel, or elk hide and bound with strips of rawhide. Though the arms had been tightly bound next to the torso inside the fur, the hands protruded, palms open in supplication. Sometimes the open palms held the dusty, crumbling remains of vegetation, which Jake assumed were the remains of flowers. Occasionally, a cheek glowed red with ochre, rubbed lovingly on the dead face.

They walked, barefoot and silent, Jake holding Nicole's hand, until they had almost come back to where they began. But not quite. They stood one row over from where they started.

Jake held the torch aloft, again, and studied the layout of the skulls. To his right, lay the shrine of tusks and the Mothers, still spotlighted by the pillar of light. Then he understood.

"Look," he said, gesturing at the room.

Nicole stepped closer. "What?" she whispered.

"It's a spiral. We're standing in a spiral that leads out from the Mother's or back to them, depending on how you see it. C'mon." He took her hand and they continued walking, spiraling past hundreds of skulls.

They seemed to be grouped by species. Small mammals, rabbits, various rodents, some very large marmots lay fartherest out from the shrine. Small skulls had been stacked in neat pyramids, side by side, all staring inward.

Next came the predators. Jake and Nicole padded silently past, paying homage to the fox, the coyote, the wolf, and the long extinct dire wolf with its scimitar fangs.

They encountered a smooth arc of bear skulls next: the huge ancestor of the grizzly, the skull nearly a yard across, the terrible short-faced bear, that stood as tall as a horse and could run nearly as fast, and numerous smaller skulls of their cousins.

Then came the snarling skulls of the great cats: the American lion, and a smaller species of cougar. But Jake and Nicole were the most impressed by the massive array of saber-toothed tiger skulls—a hundred or more—terrifying even as skulls in death.

The inner rings seem to be preserved for the great herbivores upon whom life depended: various kinds of antelope, camel, species of elk and deer, as well as hundreds of bison, formidable with their ten foot spans of scimitar horns.

Finally, the spiral led them past the massive domes of mammoth skulls, to the inner shrine and the Mothers. Jake and Nick stood in the shaft of light at the entrance to the tipi of mammoth tusks.

"Oh, Jake," Nicole whispered.

Jake nodded. Instinctively, they kneeled, though they weren't sure why.

The Three Mothers sat in a slight arc, shoulder to shoulder, robed in mammoth fur. The robes lay open at the front, revealing the long, soft buckskin dresses that covered the bodies to the ankles. Arm holes had been cut in the fur; withered sticks of arms protruded; the hands lay peacefully in their laps.

The left hands clutched bouquets of dried flowers; the right hands of all but one grasped a diamond knife—identical to the one Jake wore around his neck.

He removed the blade from his neck and examined it more closely. He stared at Nicole; she back at him. There was no denying it.

The old women wore small venuses at their throats, identical to the ones Jake and Nicole wore, only smaller. Finally, each wore a cape of eagle feathers, signifying their intimacy with the spirit world.

Directly behind them, a thin slab of basalt had been planted, now tilting slightly to the left, and unknown hands had etched the Shaman of the Hunt: the head of a man with the horns of a stag, the legs of a buffalo, the wolf-skin cape with the tail dangling, and the massive penis in front. He appeared to be dancing.

But as compelling as all this was, it did not compare to what lay in front of the Mothers: directly at their feet lay four laurel-leaf spear points, each an inch and a half wide and over twelve inches long—far too big, too fragile to be actually used in a hunt. Two more similar blades lay diagonally crossing the four. Exquisitely knapped from red and black obsidian, white chert, a red, blue and grey agate, and a sort of chocolate flint, they lay before the Three as clean and sharp as the day they were made.

And directly in front of the blades lay a small ivory dome, now brown with age, that showed the seams where the sutures of the skull had not yet closed. Perhaps it was the skull of an unborn mammoth. But whatever it was, it had been used as a bowl to hold the hundred or more raw diamond crystals, some as large as plums.

Diamond crystals occur in many different shapes, with many different facets, anywhere from four to forty-eight. All of them appeared to be represented in the calvarium. Why the old Mexican took the Mother's knife and not the diamonds is anybody's guess; perhaps he didn't know what they were.

Nicole reached out to touch one, hesitated, drew back her hand. Jake inched his way into the ivory tipi on his knees.

"*Hau! Unci Maka!* Grandmother," he whispered. "I am ashamed, for I have nothing to offer you, except the blood in my body." He nicked his wrist, dropped a couple of scarlet drops in the sand.

"This," he elevated the knife, "belongs to you, and I now return it." He lay the blade in the empty right hand of the Mother.

A faint rustling, like a slight breeze across fallen leaves swept through the room.

"I beg you to have pity on us, to look upon us in a good way, and preserve out lives." He inched his way back out of the tipi.

Nicole had been staring at the ivory tusks. "My God! Jake, look!"

"What?"

"Look at the tusks!"

Row after row of tiny stick figures, divided into scenes by the spacing, spiraled around the entire length of each tusk.

"It's like a winter count," Jake said after a moment. "It's a history of the clans." He took her hand. "C'mon, Nick. We gotta get out of here. We don't belong here. It's too much. It's just too much."

Jake retrieved their boots and they picked their way toward the low arch and the way out. They stopped in the tunnel to put their boots on. Nicole sat with her head cradled in her hands.

"Jake, I don't know how much longer I can go on."

He draped his arm across her shoulders. "I know, Nick, but you've got to. Alpha has to be just around the corner."

"I know," she said, "but it's got to be a hundred and ten, maybe fifteen out there. I just don't know if I can do it."

Jake looked out into the brilliant white light. Heat waves shimmered up from the lava field. "Yeah. I know," he said finally.

She looked back from where they had come. "Let's rest a minute. Can we?"

"Yeah, O.K., but not too long, or we won't be able to move." He leaned his head against the wall, closed his eyes. He wasn't sure how much longer he could go on, either. His tongue felt the size of a shoe. He was beginning to notice disorientation and confusion in himself.

"Jake?"

"What?" he said, without opening his eyes.

"Did you notice anything strange in there?"

With an effort, he picked his head up and looked at her. "What do you mean, 'strange?' The whole damn place is strange."

"No, Jake." She lay a hand on his arm. The skulls—did you notice anything about the skulls, and the Mothers, especially their capes?"

He thought for a moment. "No, not really. They're skulls, eagle feathers." He shrugged.

"Jake, think. Some of those skulls are thousands of years old, but did you see any dust on any of them? Did you see any dust coating the Mothers, or their capes? There should have been a couple of inches of dust on everything. And the flowers! Flowers can't last a thousand years; they'd crumble away to nothing. Those dried flowers didn't look any older than a month—maybe two. Somebody is caring for that shrine, Jake. They have to be."

She stared at him. "My God. Maybe there is a tribe of indians out here."

He stared back. "Well, if there is, let's hope we find them, and they have water." He stood up, and extended his hand. "C'mon, we'll die sitting here."

When they stepped out into the sunlight, they discovered the tunnel opened fifteen feet above a dry wash. Like an empty canal, the wash hugged a low bluff of basalt and cinder cones, curving out of sight, to the right, northward.

They slid, slithered, and finally, fell down the embankment, raising a cloud of dry, sandy dust. Jake sat up, tried to spit out a mouthful of dust. Nicole lay inert, groaning.

"Great start," she said.

He helped her up, and they set out grimly northward. They struggled along the wash, struggled against the incandescent sun, and the rocky, boulder-strewn river bed, for it *looked* as though a small river had once flowed here, though Jake couldn't imagine how or when that might have been.

The way was further complicated by thick, woody hedges of sage that grew in low places where snow melt puddled in the spring. The tough, woody branches growing thickly together forced them to crawl on their hands and knees. And rattlesnakes were virtually invisible in the mottled play of sunlight and shadow.

They had just emerged from such a thicket when Jake realized that the bluffs encompassing the wash had gradually risen until they towered over the wash some thirty feet. The wash, too, had narrowed until it was little more than a stream bed, twenty feet wide. They walked in a canyon of smooth, unscalable basalt walls. Behind him, Nicole stumbled, went down.

She landed on her hands and knees. "Jake, I can't. I can't any more." She hung her head, panting. She flopped on her side, curling up in a fetal position.

"Get up!" he said harshly. "Get up!" Angry now. He marched back to where she lay. "Goddamn it! Get up. You give up, you die." He jerked her upright into a sitting position, helped her to her feet, slung one of her arms over his shoulder.

"Look," he said, pointing with his chin. Up ahead, the canyon took a sharp turn to the right. At the turn, a huge slab of basalt had fallen, creating a lean-to against the canyon wall.

"We're gonna to where we can see what's around the corner. You can rest in the shade of that boulder."

He half-carried, half-dragged her to the turn, lay her in the shade, propped up against the canyon wall. He flopped down beside her, waited until the black spots before his eyes disappeared. Then he stepped out to where he could see what lay before them. His heart sank.

The way ahead of them was blocked by an jumble of monolithic basalt boulders which lay at the foot of a six foot high slick wall. He climbed the boulders, peered over the wall to see what lay beyond. His heart sank again.

The high, black basalt bluffs opened into a ring of black and red cinder cones, each resembling a small volcano. A mile of burning, black, glittering sand lay between him and the most distant cinder cone, which he assumed was point Alpha. The dry wash they had followed continued beyond the wall, straight as a spear-cast to the largest of cones. Nothing lived in the caldera created by the circle of cones, and for the first time, Jake became aware of the absolute silence surrounding them: not a bird chirping, nor cricket, nor whine of wind. Silence as absolute as the abyss of deep space.

The silence affirmed what he knew in his heart: without water, he and Nicole would never make it across the incandescent anvil of the caldera. Before they made the hills, they would collapse in the roasting heat, and lie, fully exposed to the beating sun, until they perished. And no living thing, not snake, or lizard, or vulture would note their passing.

Gingerly, for the strength in his legs ebbed quickly, he clambered down the boulders. He dropped to his knees in the black sand and began scooping it out with his hands, hoping against all reason that some water might seep into the hole he dug.

At six inches deep, he dug out a cubic crystal, three inches square, with a grayish, greasy luster. He leaned back against the boulders, and laughed, and laughed, and laughed. His laughter echoed against the canyon walls, and back again. He tossed the crystal up and down, like a golf ball, and stuck it in his pocket, chuckling.

The Venus fell out of his shirt and swung back and forth as he continued digging. At eight inches, he found another crystal, an octahedral crystal, about as large as an apricot. Moments later, he found another, the size of a grape. He kept digging until he had scooped out a depression about two feet deep. He had stuffed eight grayish, greasy crystals in the cargo pocket of his BDU's. But there was no water, only black, dusty sand.

He crawled back to where Nicole lay beneath the slab of basalt. She had toppled over, and lay in a fetal position. Jake shook her.

"Look, Nick! We're rich," he said, holding up one of he crystals. "We're going to die of thirst, but we found your father's diamonds. Nick, c'mon!" He shook her again. She didn't move. Then he felt nausea and vertigo, and a blackness reached up from the sand and enveloped him.

Chapter 27

The 11.3 gram, 7.62 x 51 NATO hollow point round slammed into Tom Curdy's collar bone at a steep downward angle traveling at two thousand seven hundred fifty-six feet per second. Simultaneously, both the round and the collarbone shattered, disintegrating into hundreds of razor-sharp projectiles of lead and bone.

The shrapnel severed the subclavian artery, the subclavian vein, and the maxillary artery. The force of the combined projectiles hurtled downward shredding the upper lobe of the right lung, the right auricle and puncturing the pulmonary artery, the superior vena cava, and the aortic arch. A 3.6 gram fragment of the bullet ripped on downward, piercing the left ventricle, finally lodging itself between the eleventh and twelfth ribs near the spine.

The impact knocked Tom's Stetson off, knocked him two feet backward, spun him around once, and dropped him. Thomas Wilson Curdy, "Mack," was dead before his Stetson quit rolling, dead before he could take Ellie to Mexico.

Rick Sanchez had pulled the cruiser he and Tom had ridden in off to one side of the track so the three black Suburbans, four agents to a vehicle, could assemble and charge though the gate first. He had just finished peeling the gate open when the crack of the rifle broke the silence, and reverberated through the canyon. He turned, surprised, in time to see Tom spin and fall.

He had just taken a step forward toward Tom's body when another round slammed into his fifth cervical vertebra severing the spinal chord. Bone and bullet fragments blew out his larynx, as well as all the major veins and arteries in his neck, including both branches of the aorta. The hollow point very nearly severed his head from his body, which came to rest three feet from the point of impact, spread-eagled and face down.

Jeannette Sanchez would later tear the house apart, searching for a non-existent life insurance policy.

Phil Jenkins had dismounted the lead Suburban and had stood, hands on hips, watching, as Sanchez opened the gate. He wore his SWAT outfit: black BDU's, trousers bloused into black canvas combat boots, black Kevlar vest and helmet, complete with goggles.

His twin Glocks peeked out from under either arm. He looked magnificent.

Jenkins did not see Tom hit. At the "boom" of the first shot, he looked around, confused, as if he didn't know what it was. When the second round, the round that killed Sanchez, blew flecks of tissue and blood back on his face, he dropped beside the Suburban in a fetal position, covering his helmet with his arms. He might have stayed that way had not his driver, a grizzled Viet Nam veteran, and DEA agent of thirty years' experience, tapped the horn twice and revved the engine. Jenkins came to his senses, jumped in the GMC and yelled "Go! Go! Go!" Three black Suburbans tore through the gate, following the track across the meadow.

Two additional sheriff's cars had completed the caravan to Five Mile Canyon and the Kettle line shack. Bob Duncan and Hal Lindsay manned one, and Nick Greenwood and Sheri MacDougal rode in the other. The plan was for the DEA to charge in and make the bust, and the Sheriff and his deputies were to follow to help secure the prisoners and the evidence. Consequently, all four deputies had dismounted their vehicles and had stood, watching, while Sanchez opened the gate. All four of them watched in horror as first, Tom, then Sanchez, were gunned down. Three of them immediately took cover behind open cruiser doors; Greenwood sprinted toward Tom. Sheri MacDougal grabbed the law enforcement version of the M-16 carbine from its rack in her cruiser.

All four of them later remembered hearing a "thump" as the Suburbans charged through the gate, and then the "cruuump" of the explosion behind the finger of trees that concealed the cabin. In the ensuing melee, they did not hear the two additional "thumps" but heard the explosions and the firecracker popping of rounds cooking off.

At approximately twenty yards past the gate, the right front tire of the lead vehicle carrying Phil Jenkins and three other DEA agents ran over the trigger mechanism of the M-15 "track-breaker" anti-tank mine, exerting the required three hundred fifty pounds of downward pressure. Twenty-two pounds of high-explosive detonated instantly, simultaneously blowing Phil Jenkins upward and to the left, into the ceiling of the Suburban, blowing the engine block through the firewall and into the driver. A massive, searing fireball accompanied the blast, incinerating all four occupants. Death came so quickly they were unaware of the event.

Of the two remaining Suburbans, one peeled left and the other peeled right to avoid the wreckage. Each vehicle quickly detonated similar mines, with the same devastating consequences. In less than thirty seconds, three vehicles lay twisted, charred, and burning. Twelve agents lay dead in them.

Hal Lindsay, a veteran of the First Gulf War, swore, "Goddamn it! Goddamn it! Fuckin' Zeb mined the road!" He stared through the open cruiser for a long moment at Bob Duncan, who stared back, speechless. Then they both ducked again as Zeb, naked to the waist, and wearing an olive drab dew rag charged from trees screaming, spraying the meadow with his M-16.

Sheri MacDougal calmly lay the carbine across the top of her cruiser, sighted, and fired a single round. The shot was true, smashing into Zeb's skull just above the supraorbital ridge of his right eye. He dropped, mid-scream, into a silent heap of bones and olive drab rags.

Later, when Sheri was finally able to go home, she sat on the edge of the bed, calmly recited the litany of the day's events to her husband, Joey, including her part in the death of Zebulon Kettle. Then she sprinted into the bathroom, threw up, and lay curled around the toilet, sobbing. Joey called his sister, Wanda.

Sheri's shot finally shocked Bob Duncan into action. He reached into the cruiser and keyed the mike.

Bennie Juarez responded instantly: "Dispatch."

"Jesus Christ, Bennie! We need some help out here! Call the state and get as many guys out here as you can. And get as many ambulances as you can. We got multiple casualties. And call the hospital! And the National Guard! We got a mine field out here." And then he began to sob: "Oh, God, Bennie, I think Tom's dead."

In the morning, Shirley would search through the top drawer of her desk until she found the pink slip of paper Tom had written Shota's number on. She delivered the news. After a long interval of silence, a tightly controlled voice responded: "Thank you." Then the line went dead.

Chapter 28

Nicole awoke choking. Someone poured water down her throat. She inhaled about half of it, sat up and coughed. Felt like the top of her head had blown off.

Jake sat back on his haunches, watching, helped her to a couple of sips from an old canvas water bag, then handed her the bag.

"Where'd this come from?" She spoke with a rasp, her voice like a file on wood.

"We had visitors. It was here when I came to, along with that." He nodded toward a sheet of pinyon bark. Assorted dried berries, roots, and dried meat lay on it. The meat looked greasy and rancid.

"Well, who were they?"

Jake looked away, then back at Nicole. "I don't know. I didn't really see them."

"This is your grandfather's water bag, isn't it." Nick held the bag up.

"Yes, Nick, it is."

She gave him the "Well?" look.

"I didn't see much. Someone pouring water down my throat. Strange voices. Someone whispered my name."

"What name?"

"Isnala Mani."

"That's your name?"

Jake stared at her a long time, looked away. "That's the name the spirits call me."

"The name the spirits call you." She shook her head, sucked greedily on the sack of water.

"Take it easy, Nick; little sips at a time."

She shook her head "O.K.," scooted back to the basalt wall, sat against it, head between her knees. Jake scooted back to sit beside her. She handed him the wet bag. He took a couple of sips. They rested. The sun climbed in the East.

He picked up the bark platter. "I suppose we should try to eat some of this." He picked a piece of dark, greasy meat—looked more like a lardy twig—and tasted it tentatively.

"A little on the strong side, but O.K."

"What is it?" Nicole asked.

Jake shrugged. "Woodchuck, for all I know. Eat. We gotta move soon."

Nicole tasted a stick of meat, made a face. "This must be what road kill tastes like."

"It's protein. Eat," he said, crunching through a woody root.

Nick wiped her hands on her pants, sat back. She felt better. Amazing what a little water will do. The headache was diminishing.

She stared at Jake. "O.K. You're not going to tell me, so I guess I'll have to ask."

"Ask what," he said.

"The waterbag. The name. The food. The people who brought it. What the hell do you think I mean? A living tribe of paleoindians — possibly the greatest archeological find in the history of science? What do you know you're not telling me?"

Jake shifted uneasily. "That's just it, Nick. I *don't know*. I don't know what it means. You know about my grandfather's water bag and the Venus left in its place. *Isnala Mani* is the name the spirits have called me. It's the name Wilma called me.

"What does it mean? *Isnala Mani*, what does it mean?

"It means "Walks Alone."

"And who is Wilma?" He told her about the healing ceremony at the hospital and what Wilma had said about his going West. He crawled out from under the over hang. Nick followed him.

"We've got to find them, Jake."

He walked to the middle of the stream bed, Nicole in tow.

"I know," he said. "Look." he pointed at an atlatl shaft stuck in the sand. The two Venuses—his and Nick's—hung from the nocked end of the shaft. Someone had drawn an arrow in the sand pointing toward the buttes that lay beyond the barricade of boulders, across the anvil. "They left us directions."

Nicole grabbed her Venus, put it back around her neck, and said, "Well, let's go. Do you know what this means, Jake?" She walked away. "My God! Think of it! We have just made contact with a living tribe of prehistoric Indians. Think of what this will mean to archaeology. To anthropology. To the world!" She stopped, turned around. "Jake?"

He stood where she left him, fingering the leather thong of his own Venus.

"Jake?"

He replaced the Venus around his neck and walked slowly toward her, shouldering the canvas water bag.

"They can't be found, Nick. The world can't know they're here."

She stood, mouth agape. "You're kidding, right?"

"No, I'm not." He walked on past, jaw set, eyes flinty.

She laughed a nervous little laugh, hurried to catch up with him. "You're not serious. This is why we came out here."

Jake marched on. "No, it isn't."

She stopped in her tracks, hands on hips, angry now. "O.K. Why did we come out here then?"

He stopped, pivoted, boots grating in the gravel.

"We came out here to find your father's archaeological site. We came out here to find out if these people really do exist. **I came out here** because the spirits want me to help them. **I came out here** because they need to be protected, not exploited.

"Protected from whom? My father? Me?"

He retraced his steps to where she stood. "No, Nick. Think. If word of the diamonds ever got out, the people would be destroyed. Their culture, their lifestyle, their beliefs would be destroyed. If the Russians have their way, they will probably be hunted down and killed. Eradicated. And all evidence of their ever having been, bulldozed. The Consortium would have to, or they would never get the mining rights."

"But Jake, we could learn so much. They're the last of their kind—."

"That's what She said. She also said it was up to me." He turned and stalked off.

"Jake! Wait!" Nick ran after him. "Who is 'She?'"

"Never mind," he flung over his shoulder. "You wouldn't believe me, anyway."

She grabbed his arm, stopped him. "At least give me a chance."

He shook himself free, began climbing the boulders that barricaded the canyon.

"Jake! Wait!" Her voice echoed up and down the canyon, and out onto the slopes of the cinder cones that encircled the anvil of black sand they would have to cross. Vassili, slipping and sliding down one of them, stopped in his tracks, hit the ground, praying his black BDU's would blend into the surrounding sand.

When Bob Duncan walked through the doors of the Python County Law Enforcement Center early the next morning, Shirley wordlessly rose from behind her desk and hugged him. They clung together, choking back tears.

"You talk to Ellie?"

"Yeah."

"She ain't alone, is she?"

"No." Shirley took a step back. "Bobby, you should know she was working last night. She was in the ER when they brought Tom in."

Duncan groaned. "Oh, God."

"There's hospital staff with her now; her kids are supposed to be in later today. I'm going over with something to eat later."

Duncan leaned back against the counter, crossed his arms across a belly that slopped over his gun belt. He wore a black straw cowboy hat. A gold Python County Sheriff's Department badge had been printed in the center of the crown, with PCSD arching over it.

He shook his head mournfully. "I'll tell ya, Shir, in fifteen years of service, I ain't ever seen nuthin' like what happened. Sanchez was openin' th' gate, an' bam! Tom was down. Then three or four seconds later, bam! Rick was down. Then them DEA boys charged through th' gate an' blam! blam! blam!. All three uh them Surburbans blew up an' was burnin.' Then, *then,* Kettle's ol' shack blew up. Christ—'x'cuse me—it was just like the damn movies." He shook his head again, looked at the floor. "It was a goddamn—'x'cuse my French—war zone."

Shirley waited.

Bob looked up. "Mo 'n crime lab boys out there?"

"Yeah, Bobby, they are."

"How 'bout th' Army?"

"116th Engineers are already out there."

Duncan started to walk down the hall toward his cubicle. "Good. Can't do much until we get them mines swept up." Duncan's radio squawked.

"Bobby? This is Mo."

Duncan withdrew his mobile from its worn black leather holster, keyed the mike.

"Go ahead, Mo."

"What's going on, Bob? Some FBI dick just said to clear out. Says it's their jurisdiction now. You know anything about that?"

"Just a sec." He looked at Shirley. "You know anything about the FBI?"

She nodded toward Tom's office. "There's two suits in Tom's office waiting for you."

Duncan swore under his breath, keyed the mike again.

"Mo, who's out there with you?"

"Landski, Amil, some state guys."

"The Feds are here at the office. I haven't talked to them yet. Don't let anybody touch anything 'til I get back to you."

"That's a rodge. Out."

Bob yanked his hat down a little more firmly on his head, marched to Tom's office, opened the closed door.

The first thing he saw was the guy sitting at Tom's desk. The Fed wore a charcoal Italian suit, white shirt, red power tie. Olive-skinned, blow-dried silver hair, huge Mediterranean nose. He looked up at Duncan over his readers, crossed his hands briefly over whatever he had been reading on Tom's desk, stood up and extended his hand.

"Sal Puntura, Special Agent in Charge, Salt Lake Division, FBI."

Duncan stood still, rigid, choking the doorknob still in his hand. He ignored the man's hand.

"You're behind Tom's desk. Get the hell out from behind Tom's desk."

"Ahh, sure." The agent adjusted his tie, slipped his readers in his jacket pocket, slid out from behind the desk.

"No disrespect intended." He smiled an oily smile, revealing rows of perfect porcelain teeth. He gestured toward the other man, kid, really, in the room.

"This is special agent Michael Watson."

The kid was a cherub in a dark blue suit, except for the hair. No golden ringlets, just regulation blonde hair, watery blue eyes, rosy, pudgy cheeks. The kid extended his hand.

Duncan ignored it, leaned back against the door jam.

"What kin I do for you boys?"

"Well, can we sit down?" Sal asked.

Duncan flashed a thin smile. "Sure. But don't get too comfortable, 'cause I'm leavin'." While the Feds fiddled with turning the two chairs facing Tom's desk around, Duncan called Mo: "Mo, you there?"

"Yeah, Bobby. Go."

"The Feds are takin' over jurisdiction—murder of Federal officers, stolen munitions, an' alla that. But Mo, I want you boys t'stay there an' make sure the evidence is handled right. If you catch any flack, call me."

"You got it. Out."

Sal looked up, sharply. "You're not thinking of interfering in a Federal investigation, are you Sheriff?"

"I ain't the Sheriff, an' no, I ain't. Just makin' sure all the "i's" are dotted an' th' "t's" are crossed, so whatever scumbag killed Tom gets what he's got coming."

"Surely you understand we have a job to do here, too, Deputy."

Duncan stood up straight, hitched his gun belt up over his portly self. "It ain't the job you got that bothers me, *Special Agent in Charge*, it's the way you do it." Duncan gestured the men out of the office.

"Now if you'll excuse me, I got a couple of widows to visit."

Chapter 29

Duncan didn't recognize the somber, willow-thin woman with stringy blonde hair who answered Ellie's door.

"Is Ellie receiving visitors?" Then he heard Ellie call out from the depths of the house: "Who is it, Jamie?"

"Bob Duncan," Bobby said.

"Bob Duncan!" Jamie yelled back.

Ellie appeared in the hall behind the stringy blonde.

"Come on back, Bob." Then she disappeared through a doorway at the back of the hall.

Jamie led the way.

Ellie sat at the kitchen table. A cigarette burned in the ashtray. She stood up when he came into the room, gave him a hug, sat back down again. She gestured at a chair, "Sit down, Bob."

But he didn't. He stood there, awkwardly, clutching his hat to his pot belly. A long moment passed. Ellie looked up.

Duncan tried to speak, but the words just wouldn't come. He stood on one foot, then the other, gazed out the window beyond Ellie's shoulder, stared at the linoleum beneath his boots. Tears rolled down his plump, rosy cheeks. He just stood there, clutching his hat, silently sobbing, silently shaking.

Ellie jumped up, embraced his bulk, and held him.

"Oh, Bobby," she said. "It will be alright. Somehow, it will."

In the long journey between the womb and the grave, men labor and sweat, toil and carry, break rock, clear fields, plow their furrows in the deep fields of life.

Where there is harvest, there also is loss; where there is life, there also is blood and death, and strong though a man may be in back and arm, even the strongest stumble, weaken, and fail, in the fallow lands of sorrow.

It is women who gather the bitter fruit of battered flesh, heal and preserve it for another Spring.

Duncan broke away from Ellie, sniffled, wiped his nose on the back of his hand.

"Shoot, Ellie, I came over here to comfort you, not th' other way around.

Jamie handed him a paper towel. He blew loudly, wadded the paper up in a ball, clenched in his fist. They sat down.

Ellie reached across the table, lay a hand on one of his.

"Tell me, Bobby. Tell me how he died."

When Duncan finished telling it, he sat back, picking at the kitchen table cloth.

After a while, Ellie lay a hand on Bobbie's. "Thanks," she said quietly.

"Anything I can do for you, Ellie?" Bob asked.

She cleared her throat. "Yeah, Bobby, there is. Jake Two Feathers is Tom's best friend. I'm sure he would want to know. Would you find him for me?"

"Well, yeah," he said, glad to have a job to do. "He's out at his place, ain't he?"

"No, Bob, he's not. He's out on the desert with those two archaeologists. Ram would know. He flew them out there."

Bob stood up. "I'll go find him and tell him, Ellie. Don't you worry none. I'll do that right now." Then he left, glad to breathe light, sunlit air, free of the weight and darkness of grief. He drove out to Blackhorse Aviation.

The Quonset hut that was Ram's office and hangar sat in the sage flats about half a mile out of Python on the edge of the Anvil. A tiny, dusty office took up about a tenth of the cavernous space. The rest was hangar and maintenance area for the Huey.

The front door was locked, so Duncan trudged all the way around to the other end of the huge building. He was surprised to find the hangar doors rolled open.

"Anybody here?" Silence. He walked toward the tool lockers and several heavy work benches in the rear of the building. A wrench or two, and some oily rags littered one of the benches. The place smelled of grease, kerosene, and oil. He walked around the benches toward the back door to the office.

"Ram! Anybody here?" As he passed the last bench, he stopped dead. Bobbie Duncan might be a small town, farm boy deputy, but he knew a puddle of dried blood when he saw it. He yanked his Glock out and keyed his shoulder mike.

Nicole had to scramble up the boulders to catch up with Jake. When she crawled over the last boulder she found him standing a little way out on the sand, hands on hips, staring across the black expanse before him.

They stood in a caldera, ringed on the left by a series of black and red cinder cones about a hundred meters high. Directly across from them, about a kilometer away, towered the largest cinder cone, two hundred meters above the plain. The land sloped gently upward toward the cone. A series of black sand dunes undulated toward it. Silver roundels of dwarf buckwheat dotted the expanse.

Directly to their right, the ancient stream bed had carved a channel fifteen feet deep and twenty yards wide. It was partially choked with sage and drifts of black sand winds had blown in.

Nicole drew up beside Jake.

"What is it?"

"Listen," he said.

She listened a moment. "I don't hear anything."

"That's the point. It's still. Too still. C'mon," he said, taking her hand, "we gotta get across this before something happens." He started across, dragging her behind.

"But what's going to happen?"

"I don't know, but something is. I can feel it." He broke into a jog.

Jake struck out on a course roughly parallel to the wash. It was heavy slogging in the sand; after a quarter of a mile, he slowed to a walk, to let Nicole catch up.

"Jake," she wheezed, hands on knees, " I can't keep this up in this heat."

"Yeah. I know," he said, scanning three hundred and sixty degree arc around them.

Even in the most remote, the most hostile deserts, there is life: birds in the air, heard, if not seen, lizards, snakes, small mammals, even insects. Where Jake and Nicole now stood, all life had fled. The sand, the ancient cinder cones waited, even the moving air paused, and listened.

"C'mon," he said. "We gotta get some cover: head for that tall cinder cone; don't stop 'til you get there!" He took off jogging.

Wearily, Nicole followed his sweat-stained back. They almost made it.

When Jake topped the last of the dunes before the cinder cone, he dropped to his knees, heaving, and waited for Nicole, who was about fifty yards behind. Just as she crossed the low ground between the dunes, the earth vibrated like a cable stretched too tightly. It moaned, shuddered. Sand from the slope of the dune behind her, and from the one Jake rested on hissed downward, filling in the dip where Nicole stood. She froze, stared helplessly at Jake while the sand quickly covered her boots, then her knees.

Jake jumped up, took two steps down the sliding dune and yelled, gesturing wildly: "Move! Get out of there."

Then the earth snapped like a broken plate, opening a rift three feet wide and waist deep. Nicole dropped into it. Sand poured into the crevasse like a waterfall. Jake watched in horror as the rift ripped toward the cinder cones in the distance at the speed of lightening. The earth roared, leapt, threw him rolling down the slope toward the open jaws of the rift. He kicked, swam against the heavy current of sand. He dropped into into the crack with a heavy "thud" anyway.

"Oh, God," he thought, "don't let this thing snap shut." Sand poured in on top of him.

He fought his way up, spitting sand, choking.

Then it stopped.

He looked wildly around. "Nick! Nick!"

She lay about six feet away, doubled over at the waist, face down.

"Nick!" He called again. She stirred, looked up.

"I can't move, Jake." She struggled weakly. She had been buried, standing up, to the waist.

He got around behind her, dropped to his knees, and began digging like a dog.

"Dig, Nick! Push the sand away from in front of you."

After about ten minutes, they had cleared a funnel-shaped hole down to her knees. Jake grabbed her from behind, jerked her out. They scrambled to the top of the dune, threw themselves down, panting, out of breath.

Jake suddenly sat up, looked around. "Shit!" he said.

Nicole lay flat on her belly, propped up on her elbows. "What?"

"The water bag—it's gone."

Nicole grunted. "Yeah, but we're still alive." She rolled over and kissed him. "Thanks, Jake. That's twice."

"Well, let's hope there's not a third." He stared at the panorama in front of them. "We're still in deep shit, you know." He pointed at the butte. "There's your 'sickle-shaped' island."

A quarter mile away, and fifty feet below them, the prevailing south westerly winds had scoured the base of the butte down to bedrock basalt. It had also sculpted two huge sand dunes, one on each side, that curved outward like horns.

Nicole sat up. "Jake, I don't think that's site Alpha." She gestured with a sweeping arm. "I flew with Ram to Alpha. I don't remember any of this—these cones, the caldera—hell, we could have set up camp, here. I don't think this is it." She nibbled the tips of her fingers.

Jake stood up. "Well, wherever we are, we have to get the hell away from this quake zone. C'mon." He helped her up. A low arch at the base of the cinder cone beckoned. "We'll head for that," he said.

They slipped and slithered down the dune to the basalt below. Although the wind had scoured it bare, a few scraggly sage had taken root, and clawed the rock for survival. Curtains of dust still hung in the air, slightly obscuring and haloing the sun. They sweated grit. Jake stopped abruptly. "Can you smell it?"

Nick nodded. "Woodsmoke."

What they couldn't see from the top of the dune was that the bedrock basalt ended abruptly in a bare ledge fifteen feet above the streambed. In fact, the ancient stream had boiled up out of the cave and carved a cul de sac.

The entrance itself was a vast arc—a sickle-shaped bite out of the base of the cone—that was fifty yards from edge to edge, and twenty feet from pinnacle to pit. A small grove of pinions had grown up in front of it, and hid most of what lay behind.

Jake held his hand up, halting them as they walked along the ledge. "Listen."

Nicole stopped and listened. She heard a faint roar, like a jet taking off in the distance. "What is it?" she asked.

"Let's go find out," he answered, leaping down to a small outcropping, to another below it, and then to the sand of the stream bed. Nicole followed. As soon as his boots hit black sand, he bent over and scooped something up. He turned to Nick.

"Look," he said. He handed her a greasy-looking grey cube almost as big as a hardball.

She hefted it. "Oh, my God. This isn't a diamond, is it?"

"I think it is," he said. "C'mon." He made for the cave.

They threaded their way through a dense stand of pinions, and broke out into a small clearing.

"Oh, my God," Jake whispered.

"What?" Nicole asked sharply and stepped out around him to look.

Ten or twelve low dome-shaped huts dotted the clearing. They were simple structures, shaped like inverted tortoise shells, pinyon branches stacked over a frame of bent limbs. The remains of a fire smoldered in front of one of them, slowly drying a rack of bloody meat.

Nick gave Jake the "What now?" look.

He cupped a hand to his mouth, and called out, "*Hau, kola! Le miceya Isnala Mani.*" "Hello, friend. It is I, Walks Alone."

Utter silence.

A myriad of thin trails spiderwebbed the camp, but merged into one well-used path leading into the cave. It cut through a lush stand of ferns. As they crossed the threshold into the cave, they flushed a flight of barn swallows from their nests high up on the wall. A low, rumbling roar grew louder. They crunched down a gentle, gravelly slope, and stopped, awestruck.

They stood in what had once been the magma chamber of a small volcano. A column of white light streamed down through the open vent of the cinder cone high above. Like a spotlight, it illuminated the small river that spilled from a tunnel directly across from them, and fell fifteen feet to a pool below. Veils of mist rainbowed the pool and the encircling graveled beach. Ledges on both sides of the pool curved up to the waterfall.

Nick slipped her hand into Jake's. They peered at the pool, emerald at the edges, gradually fading to the darkness of abyssal depth. They stared down the throat of an ancient volcano.

Nicole shuddered, involuntarily, and shuffled her feet. The thought of how deep the water might actually be, frightened her.

She bent down, scooped up a handful of gravel. The pebbles ranged in size from peas to cherries, all glistening with the same greasy grey luster. She held them out to Jake. "Jake, look," she said solemnly. He looked.

"Yeah," he said, "I saw." The gravel in Nick's hand and under their feet were diamonds. She held several million dollars in a single hand.

"What should I do?" she whispered.

In spite of himself, Jake laughed, walking toward the water. "That's a first: a woman who doesn't know what to do with a handful of diamonds—I'm getting a drink."

Nick quickly stuffed the diamonds in her pocket and followed.

They slaked their thirst, then Jake led them a couple of steps up the ledge leading to the waterfall. He called out again: *"Hau! Le miyeca, Isnala Mani!"*

After a moment, a head peeked shyly from a hidden gallery to the left of the river. The original river that cut the tunnel must have once been a much larger and more violent river, for there was a thirty foot margin of basalt on both sides the present flow, creating a platform at the river's edge.

"Isnala Mani!" Jake called, and held up his empty hands.

An adult male stepped into full view. Long black hair cascaded down his shoulders. A full beard hid most of his face, except the high cheek bones and the obsidian eyes—eyes that flicked from Jake to Nicole, lingered a moment, back to Jake.

Standing close to six feet tall, he was not at all squat and brutish, as one might expect. A bare chest revealed bulging pectorals and biceps; it tapered to a trim, ropy abdomen. He wore knee-high boots, wrapped with leather thongs, and a tanned leather kilt. His right hand grasped the throwing lever of his atlatl, his left, three or four feathered spears, about five feet long. He stood wary, but not frightened, studying Nicole and Jake.

A hidden voice questioned him from the gallery. He answered with one guttural word. His eyes never left Jake.

First one, then another, then another, of the People emerged from the gallery to stand beside the man Nicole had already named "Alpha." There were thirty or more, mostly men, a smattering of women, and five or six children. They stared silently at the pair below them.

Then the crowd parted as the last figure tottered out, supported by two young women. The Shaman wore a full-length bear skin, and a bear skull hat. Small bones and assorted feathers had been woven into a grizzled, tattered beard. A necklace of small animal bones and skulls clacked as he teetered, stooped, along.

When he drew abreast of Alpha, the wizened old man straightened himself up, shook off the girls, and peered in Jake and Nicole's general direction.

"Isnala Mani," he croaked, pointing a thin, bony arm.

"Hau!" Jake answered.

Then Alpha flinched, dropped all but one of his spears, struggled to nock it and raise it to throwing position.

Jake turned in time to see Vassili burst into the cave, Uzi at the hip. The silenced weapon spit like a trapped cat. One, two, three of the People went down.

Jake launched himself off the ledge at Grubinich, screaming, "NOOOOO!"

Chapter 30

Jake's flying tackle knocked Grubinich flat on his back and sent the Uzi skittering. But before he could disentangle himself, the Russian grabbed a handful of Jakes's hair in his left hand and punched him savagely with his right: "I. Take. Now. Two. Lives. You. Owe. Me."

Only when Jake kneed him in the balls, did Grubinich let go. Jake rolled left, came up on two feet. Grubinich was on his knees, coughing. Jake kicked him in the solar plexus, then the face. But the Russian, thick as a rhinocerous, absorbed the blows, levered himself up, and whipped the bayonet from his boot.

Then the cavern floor rumbled, tilted fifteen degrees to the left, fell back, tilted fifteen degrees to the right, shook like a dog shaking water, and fell back again. Water sloshed from the pool. A ten ton block fell from the ceiling drenching Jake and the ex-KGB officer with a curtain of water. Nicole flipped off the ledge like a tiddly-wink and rolled perilously close to the frothing pool. Above, near the river, the People rolled around like marbles. Only Alpha stayed on his feet, swaying gracefully with the bucking Earth, atlatl cocked, ready for a throw.

Outside, on the caldera, the quake unzipped the trench that almost buried Nick, opening a ravine thirty yards wide and fifty feet deep. A curtain of lava a hundred feet high and the length of the caldera exploded from it, showering the area with lava bombs. Two of the smaller cinder cones disappeared entirely, replaced by a fountain of fire fifty feet in diameter. A river of lava soon flowed toward Python. The sulphurous stench choked the wind; billowing grey clouds blanked the sun. Steam vents shrieked.

Nearer the cave, the ancient stream bed hemorrhaged scarlet lava like a severed limb. But where the stream ran away from the cave, the lava poured toward it. Hot gasses exploded like mortar rounds, blowing lava bombs hundreds of feet in the air. Tendrils of yellow and white gas slid like spectral snakes through the sage and across naked basalt. The land bellowed, bucked, and bled.

The Russian closed on Jake; the wicked blade cut a glittering arc that would have disemboweled him. Deftly, he spun sideways at the last second, stepped toward the knife, karate chopped the wrist, knocking the blade from the Russian's hand. Vassili retreated two steps, swept the Uzi up from the gravel, swung it to bear on Jake's chest, pulled the trigger.

Nicole, crouching nearby, pitched a fist-full of sand and gravel at the Russian's face. The three round burst went wild, ricocheted around the cavern. Nick threw another handful. Gravel clattered off the weapon. Grubinich pulled the trigger. Jammed.

Jake rushed in. Grubinich reversed the weapon, swung it like a baseball bat, whacked Jake in the temple. The Indian collapsed like a blown bridge. And lay still, nose and ears leaking blood.

Incandescent lava pooled at the lip of the cave, swelled, and spilled over. Wide as a sidewalk and eight inches thick, it oozed toward the pool like red-hot concrete. A lava bomb whistled in, thumped, rolled, and wobbled to a stop. Grubinich glanced over his shoulder at the lava, back to Nick, who charged, screaming, clawing, kicking.

He casually backhanded her, knocked her to the ground, advanced a step, and grunted as the five foot spear punched through the meaty part of his shoulder, just above the clavicle. He glowered up at Alpha, who looked wildly about for another spear. Contemptuously, he yanked the spear out, threw it aside. Nick lay flat on her back, shaking her head, trying to regain her senses.

"You want to play with me, *zaichic*? O.K., we play." He ripped her blouse open, yanked her to her feet by the shirt.

He fondled her for a moment. "Very nice," he said. "But beauty *is* only skin deep." Then he backhanded her again, knocking her to the gravel. She rolled next to the lava bomb.

"You like it hot, *zaichic*? I'll bet you do." He grabbed a handful of hair, dragged her a couple of feet to the smoldering rock. As he pushed her face toward it, she kicked, pummeled his chest with pathetically small fists.

She screamed when her cheek touched the incandescent rock.

Grubinich sat back on his haunches, piggy eyes glittering.

"Good. I like a woman who screams."

Nicole sobbed, kicked the gravel weakly.

"You like that? Here, let's make it hotter." He grabbed her by the shirt collar, drug her to where the lava oozed, dropped her six feet from the creeping flow. When he ripped her pants open, she tried to resist, but he smashed her again.

"Let's see what you got," he said, yanking her trousers down. Her boot and her pant legs began to smoke.

He undid his belt, unzipped his BDU's. "You will like—." Then he gurgled, surprised at the feathered shaft that blossomed, like a poisonous flower, from his neck. He clawed his throat, leapt up, coughed a scarlet spray, and fell.

Nicole's boot and trousers burst into flames. She screamed, tried to roll away. The last face she saw was Alpha's as he snatched her up and leapt toward the pool.

FIVE DAYS LATER

*"**Isnala Mani**! Come back! You are not finished. **Hokahey!**" The Grandmother tapped Jake's inert chest with an eagle wing fan. The body lay on a pile of furs on a massive basalt plinth. A broad strap bound a soft, blood-stained leather pad to his temple.*

*Jake's **ni**, his life spirit, watched, curiously detached, from a crack in the cave it had hidden itself in. The Grandmother, the shrunken old shaman, the massive bear, and the lovely dark-haired woman, stood in a ring around the plinth. Behind them stood a ring of People. Somewhere out of sight, a fire burned, casting their shadows on the cavern wall.*

*Nicole lay on another deep pile of furs next to the cave wall. A younger woman, one of the Shaman's attendants, knelt and removed the leather dressing on her face. The **ni** cringed at the thick, black crust that had been her cheek. The second attendant uncovered Nick's right foot and leg, carefully folding the furs back, gingerly peeling the leather dressings from the blistered, weeping flesh. The **ni** recoiled, retreated into its crack.*

*"**Isnala Mani! Hokahey!**" The Grandmother carved an elegant, flourishing circle above Jake's body with the eagle wing. The tip of the wing stopped, pointing at the crack. "**Wanna!**" She stamped her foot. A peal of thunder boomed, rolled outside the cave. Reluctantly, the **ni** emerged, a white light no larger than a firefly. It settled on the tip of the fan. She slapped Jake's chest with the wing; the light disappeared; a small moan escaped his lips. The bear*

stepped forward, lay its massive head on Jake's chest. Then, the great brown form dissolved, disappeared into the chest, like water funneling down a drain. Jake heaved a great breath, coughed, and slept.

A sudden commotion disrupted the hush of the cave. A young man broke into the circle of the Grandmother and the Shaman, breathless, chest heaving. Outside, in the distance, a Huey, "whop", "whop", "whopped", slowly drawing near.

The boy spit a strangling stream of gutturals and clicks. The gnarled old man hacked an order, litters appeared, Jake and Nicole were loaded on them, and whisked out of the cavern. As Nicole's litter passed, Alpha dropped the atlatl spear that killed Vassili on it.

Jake clawed his way toward light from darkness of unfathomable depth. He opened his eyes to the sunlight of a hospital room in Python.

Chapter 31

Like a deep sleeper jabbed awake, his first reaction to light was anger. He vaguely remembered a deep and simple grace, a floating in a warm, profound darkness, buoyed up by an encompassing Presence. The light of waking consciousness jolted harshly, renewing the weight of flesh, that often seemed so impossibly heavy.

Nicole. What happened to Nick? He wasn't sure if he merely dreamed her burns, or if he had actually seen them.

How did I get here? Again, he could not distinguish between vision, dream, or reality. He had the sense that he had been lifted up, hurried through deep, maternal chambers, scorched by heat, choked by stench, transfixed by blinding, nauseating pain. And the woman. The mysterious, the vaguely familiar dark-haired woman who cradled his head against her breasts, once again forcing the bitter brew down his throat. She kissed him fully on the lips. Then, the blessed peace of warm, immeasurable darkness.

He tried his legs experimentally. They seemed to work O.K. But when he used his arms to sit up, he discovered the pinch of an I.V. He levered himself up anyway, sat back against the headboard. A wave of nausea nearly swamped him; his skull hammered. He raised a hand to his head, felt heavy bandaging.

Then the door swung open, Sheila froze at the threshold open-mouthed. "Oh, my God. You're awake! Wait a minute… ." Then she disappeared.

A minute later, Bones pounded into the room, followed by Sheila. Within seconds, a small knot of hospital staff gathered outside Jake's door, craning to catch a glimpse of him. Olivia Haglund stood on her tip toes. Sensing them, Bones turned and closed the door.

"Alright, people, back to work," he said.

Sheila stepped behind the bed, studying the bewildering array of monitors, tubes, and readouts. Jake tried, but he couldn't see what she was doing.

Bones stepped up to the bed, gingerly took Jake's hand, unnecessarily feeling for a pulse. The monitor, just out of Jake's sight, behind him, recorded a strong, steady beat.

"You're in ICU at the hospital, Jake," Bones said, looking at his watch. "They brought you in yesterday."

Jake squirmed, took his hand back. Sheila stepped back into view. "I know where I am, Bones. Where's Nick? Nicole — Ms. Haraldsen?"

The doctor held a pen up. "Just follow the pen, if you can."

"Goddamn it, Bones. I don't need to follow the pen. Where's Nick?"

Bones to Sheila: "Go call Mo and Bob, will ya? They wanted to know." To Jake: "Just stay calm, Jake. Ms. Haraldsen is in Utah, at the University of Utah Burn Center."

Jake's eyes teared up. He looked away, then back again. "How is she?"

Bones studied Jake for a moment, then pulled a chair up to the bed. "She was badly burned—second and third degree—but stable when we transported her yesterday. She'll need grafts on her foot, part of her right leg—most certainly on her face." Bones hesitated. "What happened, Jake?"

Jake shrugged, gestured helplessly. "I don't know. I was knocked out."

Sheila re-entered the room. "On the way," she said.

"I don't even remember how I got here," Jake said.

Bones cleared his throat, crossed his legs, picked imaginary lint off his chinos. "Joe Landski spotted you and Ms. Haraldsen from the Search and Rescue helicopter about five miles from your base camp. Bob Duncan sent a team in on foot, to haul the both of you out. Closest place they could land a chopper was the base camp."

The doctor lifted a chin toward the closet. "Sheila, would you mind?"

She stepped to the closet, pulled out a stack of heavy furs. A long, thin shaft lay across the top of them. Jake noted the dark stains on the shaft, smelled wood smoke emanating from the fur.

"When they found you," Bones said, "you and Ms. Haraldsen were wrapped up in these. The spear, arrow, whatever it is, lay across her. These things mean anything to you, Jake?"

They did, but he shook his head "No."

"Do you have any idea what happened?"

"No, Bones, I don't. Like I said, I was out. What's the big deal? I got hit on the head."

The room grew very quiet. Bones stood up. "Yes, Jake, you did. But you got more than that: somebody did a trephination on your skull."

"Trephination? What's that?"

Bones stood up, began unwrapping Jake's head. "Somebody cut a hole in your skull, Jake. Probably to relieve the pressure of a hematoma. Judging from the size of the hole, I'd say they removed a clot, a pretty good one, too." Bones continued unwrapping the dressing. "Sheila, would you bring us a hand mirror, please?"

"Sure," she said, disappeared, and returned momentarily with the mirror.

Bones carefully removed the four by four pad covering the hole in Jake's skull, wrapped it fastidiously in the center of the bundle of wrappings, handed it to Sheila. "That's not all. They put a plate of something in your skull. We need to know what it is. I don't know if we can leave it there." He handed Jake the mirror.

Someone had shaved a patch of scalp just above his temple on the left side. Wide as a quarter, but square, the hole had been hacked into his skull. Something smooth, shiny, and transparent, had been inserted between the scalp and the bone. Looked like someone installed a window in his head. His first impulse was to reach up and touch it, but Bones stopped him.

"Don't touch it!" he barked. "Sorry, Jake. That came out harder than I meant it to. Infection. We don't want to get it infected."

The doctor sat back down. "Here's the big deal, Jake: Yesterday, when they brought you in, you were in a coma, a drug-induced coma. That," he nodded at Jake's wound, "looks like crude work. It isn't. Whoever did it knew exactly what they were doing and why. Not only that, they put you to sleep so the body could begin to heal. And, here's the deal, whatever they used didn't lower your blood pressure, didn't impede respiration or heart rate. And not only that," he said, leaning forward in his chair, "there's no sign of infection. None. Not even around the edges, in the scalp." Bones leaned back, nailed Jake with his eyes. "Bottom line is, somebody out there knows a hell of a lot more pharmacy than we do. Frankly, Jake, I'd like to know what they used. What I can't figure out is why they didn't suture the scalp closed. And what the hell is that plate they put in your head?"

Someone tapped lightly on the door. Bones nodded to Sheila, who admitted Mo Creighton and Bob Duncan. Duncan carried his hat in his hand. They pulled chairs up closer to the bed. Duncan fiddled with his hat: he didn't seem to know what to do with it when it wasn't on his head. Sheila took it from him and set it on the counter near the sink. After the small talk, they got down to business.

Bob cleared his throat, clearly uncomfortable. He looked over at Sheila, then at Bones.

"Sheila," Bones said. She took the hint and left.

"We gotta ask you some questions," Bob said, "if you're up to it, that is."

"Shoot."

"When was the last time you saw Harlow Ramsay?"

"What's today?"

"Friday."

Jake stared up at the ceiling, thought for a moment. "Well, then, last time I saw him would have been a week ago Tuesday or Wednesday, the day before Nicole and I left for the archaeological site we were looking for. Why?"

Bob looked at Mo, who stared back. "Jake," Mo said softly, "Somebody shot Ram and Cherie. Looks like somebody machine gunned 'em down."

Jake stared at his hands. "Oh, Christ," he said. "Oh, no." He looked up. "Cherie, too?"

Mo nodded affirmatively.

Jake looked up. "Where?"

"Joe Landski spotted you from the Search and Rescue Chopper. The closest place to land was your base camp. All we found was Ram's chopper, and their bodies down the draw. Some blood on a cot in one of the tents."

"Dr. Haraldsen?" Jake asked.

Duncan shook his head. "All we found was the chopper and the bodies. Can you tell us anything, Jake? Do you know what happened?"

The Indian thought deeply for what seemed interminable minutes. The men in the room waited patiently. Jake looked up, made eye-contact with each of them. "I think I do know what happened. But we need to keep a lid on this, at least for now. Deal?"

"So far as we can, Jake. You know that."

"Fair enough." Then he told them of the Russians, the diamonds and the archaic People he and Nicole encountered, and why they needed to be protected. He told them his theory about why the Russians tried to kill him. He told them of his fight with Grubinich and of being knocked out.

"I don't know what happened after that. I don't know how Nicole got burnt, what happened to the big Russian or his two buddies. Nick got away somehow." He looked at the atlatl shaft. "You can bet that's human blood on the spear. I think the Indians killed the Russian and got Nick and I out of there. How, with the volcano erupting, I don't know, or why."

"So, you think there's still four people out there, including the archaeologist?" Duncan shifted uneasily in his seat.

"Well, I don't *know* if the Russians are still out there," Jake answered, "but Haraldsen certainly is. He had no reason to leave."

The Coroner looked at the Chief Deputy, shaking his head, and stared back at Jake. "If they're out there, they're probably dead and we'll never find them—can't really even go looking."

"Why?"

"The lava flow, Jake," Duncan said, "it's pretty much covered the whole damn desert, and still coming. Don't see how anything could survive. Do you?" This to Creighton.

"I don't see how," Mo said, looking down at his feet.

A silence fell on the room, each man occupied with his own thought.

Jake slid down in the bed, obviously tiring.

Bones stood up. "Time to go, boys. Let our patient get some rest." The two other men stood up.

"Wait. Why?" Jake asked. Why were you looking for us?"

They all sat back down.

"Ellie asked me to find you," Duncan said quietly.

Jake sat back up. "*Ellie?*" The heart monitor blipped a little faster. "You mean Tom's Ellie?"

Duncan nodded.

"Why?"

Duncan and Creighton both looked to Bones. Figured he was better at it than they were.

Bones stood up, put a hand on Jake's shoulder. "Tom was killed last Wednesday, Jake."

"Killed? How?"

"We was out to the old Kettle line shack. Tom got a tip about some drug dealers—"

"It was like they was waitin' for us," Duncan interrupted; "Tom wasn't killed, Jake; more like he was assassinated. It was a bushwhack. Got Rick Sanchez, too." Duncan told the rest of the story while Jake sat, paler than before. Bones kept an eye on the monitors.

When Duncan finished, he said, "I'm sorry, Jake. I know you two were close."

Jake looked away. "Fuck! It was a sniper, had to be. But why?"

Creighton stirred in his chair. "It was a set-up, Jake. We figured whoever was running the dealers decided to get rid of them. We found the bodies—Roscoe, Hebrew and the others—what we can't figure is why anybody would want Tom dead—unless he knew something no one else did. He say anything to you?"

Jake shook his head "No," lost in the shock of the news.

Creighton stood up, Bob followed his lead.

"So whoever engineered this is still out there?"

"That's our best guess," Duncan answered.

"Any clue who it is?"

The deputy shook his head sadly. "No a one, Jake. Nothing. Listen, you get some rest, we'll talk more tomorrow. We got a lot t' think about." They shook hands and the men left. Bones turned to leave, too.

"Bones!" Jake stopped him. "How soon can I get outta here?"

"Well," he said walking back toward the bed. "We need to decide what to do with that plate, whatever it is, and—"

"It's fine, Jake said. "It's made of diamond."

"Diamond!"

"Trust me," Jake said, "it's diamond."

"Well, we still need to close the scalp over it—"

"Will it heal the way it is?"

"Well, yeah. I imagine. In time."

"They didn't close it, Bones, so the bad spirits could get out. We'll leave it."

The doctor stared, trying to think of something to say. He knew better than to argue with the Indian.

"Well, you still need to stay here four or five days so we can monitor your condition—make sure you're O.K."

"Two days, Bones. Two days. I got things to do."

Chapter 32

Two days later, Jake sat at Ellie's kitchen table, lighting a Marlboro.

Bones had ranted on about the possibility of infection, and other physical calamities, but Jake left the hospital anyway. Meij drove him home.

The first thing he did was carry an offering down to the sweat lodge in thanks for his and Nicole's lives. He said a prayer for Harald.

Then he made a vow to take vengeance on whomever was behind Tom's death, appealing to the spirits, and *Tunkasila*, the grandfather, for help. He drove a chokecherry stake in the earth outside the sweat lodge. It would stay there until Tom's death was avenged.

Jake knew the terrible *geas* to which he had just committed. It was a vow that must be fulfilled, even if it meant his own death. He permitted the simmering rage to boil through him, hot, molten, as the liquid rock flooding the desert.

There is Justice, and there is human law: the two are not always the same. Nothing would stop him: not circumstance, not other men, not the slick-faced, cologned law of attorneys.

It is one thing to kill another man in honorable combat. It is another to take life like a thief skulking in the night, by treachery, or betrayal. The sniper who pulled the trigger that sent the bullet into Tom's heart was coward enough, but the man who paid him to do it was the worst coward of all: he did not earn the death of a brave enemy by strength, and skill, and courage; he bought it, like a woman buys a pound of hamburger. Tom Curdy deserved a better end. Jake Two Feathers swore to redeem his death.

Then he marched up to the house, took a shower, traded the turban of dressings for a 3 x 3 band aid, donned a black watch cap, and ate the ham sandwich Meij fixed for him.

By two, he was sitting at Ellie's kitchen table. She burst into tears when she saw him. He simply held her, saying nothing. No words could prevail against the absolute of death; against the wasteland of grief, none would comfort.

They clung to each other, hoping for endurance.

Ellie's two children, Gary, 31, and Ginny, 29, sat for a while at the table, polite, mildly interested in the dark, strange, vaguely threatening Indian, whom their mother so obviously trusted. After a while, they drifted off, answering their cell phones and text messages.

Ellie and Jake relaxed into the comfort of her thick, black coffee, her Camels, his Marlboros. A peace descended on the sunlit kitchen like doves to evening water. They reminisced, managed a giddy laugh or two, shared sorrow like a loaf of new bread.

The sun slipped toward the rim of earth. The doorbell rang, Ginny appeared at the kitchen threshold to ask if her mother were receiving visitors. Brusquely, Ellie shook her head "No." She smiled at Jake, embarrassed. "They mean well, but… ." Ellie shook her head sadly. She looked down at her hands, out the kitchen window. "This is a good town, Jake, filled with good people."

"Yes, it is," Jake agreed, "and Tom was the best of them."

Then she brightened. "You hungry, Jake?" She nodded toward the kitchen counter, piled with tin-foil covered pies, roasting pans, Tupperware tubs of salad, plastic bags of dinner rolls.

"So, what do you want? I have roast beef, ham, turkey with all the trimmings."

Jake grinned. "Well, then, I'll have turkey. Did they make dressing and giblet gravy?"

"Yeah. They did."

"Sounds good to me."

Ellie jumped up, busied herself unloading plastic containers from the fridge; dumping gravy, mashed potatoes, creamed corn into pots and pans.

She reached into a cup on the window sill, withdrew a hair tie, tied her hair in a short ponytail. To Jake's eye, she looked young, curvaceous, despite the black pools beneath her eyes. His heart ached for her and Tom.

"I heard," she said, peeling tin foil off a flat dish filled with dressing, "they found Roscoe and Hebrew Kettle's bodies in the old shack." She stuck the dish in the microwave, set the timer. "You want the turkey cold or hot?"

"Cold's fine."

Ellie sat back down. "So they got 'em all, then—the men who killed Tom?"

Jake picked up a Zippo lying on the table. It was Tom's old Zippo, dinged and scratched. He had carried it since Vietnam. A copy of the Ranger shoulder patch, the black and red scroll, with white lettering that read "75th Ranger Inf" was enameled on the lighter. He lit a cigarette, stared over the lighter at Ellie.

"No, Ellie, they haven't." Jake sat back in the chair, exhaled a cloud of blue smoke.

"What do you mean?" She sat rigid in the chair.

He leaned forward. "Bob Duncan told me he thought the whole thing was a set-up, a double-cross and a set up. Whoever was behind the drugs wanted the dealers dead and he wanted Tom dead. Apparently Rick Sanchez, too. Those old boys out there didn't shoot the gun that killed Tom. Somebody else did, probably a sniper."

"But why? Why would they want to kill Tom? You talk like he was assassinated."

"I think he was, Ellie. I think he knew or saw something the kingpin didn't want him to know. Tom probably didn't even know he knew it. Had to be something connected with Roscoe and Hebrew. Did he ever say anything to you?"

She stood up, went to the stove, and stirred the gravy, thinking. She turned to face Jake.

"He *did* mention something. The night you were shot. He came home late from the hospital and talked about a strange meeting behind Hector's bar. They were sitting behind the bar—must have been two-thirty, three o'clock in the morning."

"Did he say who it was?"

"Roscoe Kettle and Hootie Gillespie."

Jake looked down at the lighter in his hand, flipped the lid back, flicked the striker wheel.

"What are you thinking, Jake?"

"I'm going to check it out." He snapped the lid shut, extinguishing the flame.

"You do that," she said, and went back to stirring the gravy. Rather vigorously, Jake thought.

At twilight, he gave Ellie a last hug, and left. He drove the Hummer thoughtfully home. When he got home, he changed into black BDU's, a long-sleeved black tee shirt, and his old combat boots. He gathered the few tools he needed: a World War II vintage K-Bar, a jimmy, a penlight, and just in case, a small roll of duct tape.

As he passed the kitchen counter, he grabbed the Benchmade M-WG 701 switchblade, clipped it in his trouser pocket. On his way out the back door, he lifted a set of keys off the peg.

Jake kept the old '78 Ford F-150 around for the chores he didn't want to use the Hummer to do: hauling trash, rocks for the sweat lodge, fire wood. Occasionally, he drove it to Dillon, Montana, to pick up a load of soapstone.

When it was new, the truck had been painted what Ford called "Light Jade," a variation of what most people would look at and call "aqua." Twenty-seven years later, it was basically a rez truck: faded and rusting paint, one fender primed, but not painted, the other three dinged and dented. Jake kept the engine, and transmission tweaked, though. Once in a while, he drove it out on the Anvil, just to give the four wheel drive a workout. It was nondescript, unmemorable, like fifty other trucks in Python.

He unlocked the truck, started it. While he waited for it to warm up, he tucked his hair under the watch cap, pulled it down over his ears.

Once in town, he cruised slowly past Hootie's Motel. The office was dark, the parking lot empty, and the marquee read,

Hootie's Motel
For Sale

A Larry Whitcomb Real Estate "For Sale" sign had been hammered into the grass along the parking. Jake turned the corner, and parked in the alley behind the office. A brand new red GMC Sierra 2500 with a matching camper shell sat next to the building.

Jake looked at the sky, settled in to watch, and wait for absolute darkness.

After about a half an hour, Hootie emerged from the door, dragging a handcart stacked with smallish cardboard boxes, about the size of shoeboxes. He looked all around, unlocked the lift gate of the camper shell, and muscled the boxes into the back of the truck.

Either Hootie was pathetically weak, or the small boxes were incredibly heavy. When he finished, he leaned on the handcart, rested a minute, locked the camper shell up, disappeared inside, dragging the cart behind. Seconds later the light bulb above the door switched on, casting a weak circle of light.

Jake eased out of his truck, and, no more than a moving shadow himself, followed patches of darkness to the back door. In one swift motion, he unscrewed the light bulb, crouched down listening at the door. When no alarm was raised, he tried the knob. To his surprise, the door swung open on an empty office.

An old roll top served as credenza for the desk stacked with styrofoam "to go" cartons. A banker's lamp painted the cardboard boxes stacked along the walls a sickly green hue. Across the room from the desk, a closet door stood open. The room smelled like a garbage dump: putrefying food, stale smoke, something unwashed, unclean.

He darted through the door, eased it shut behind him. He waited for a challenge, but none came. He crept to the desk, silently began going through the drawers. He wasn't sure what he looked for—anything that tied Hootie to Roscoe and the drug dealers.

Two of the desk drawers produced stacks of porn magazines, edges grimy with thumbing, covers missing or loose. In the bottom drawer, under yet more porn, a stash of Neo-Nazi brochures, magazines, and e-mail newsletters. Jake quickly scanned some of it; it turned his stomach.

His penlight caught a shine in the trash can. He discovered the eight by tens of Tom and Rick Sanchez, ripped in half. A yellow sticky with a phone number hid Sanchez's face. Jake's gut knotted. He forced himself to control his breathing.

A grating noise sounded from the closet, like a door sliding open. A beam of light splashed across the floor. Jake ducked behind the desk.

The floor creaked as Hootie emerged from the closet, dragging the handcart with another heavy load. Jake heard him swear when he discovered the light out, heard the bulb squeaking as he screwed it back in.

Jake slid around the far end of the desk, darted into Hootie's concealed room. He saw empty shelves that lined three walls, gun racks with the M-16's, the familiar rope-handled olive drab wooden crates of ordinance. 50's crouched in the corners. Smelled gun oil, cosmoline. The steel table running almost the length of the room lay bare, except for four remaining stacks of one ounce gold ingots, and a .45.

He picked up the .45, racked the slide far enough back to see it was loaded. He flipped the safety on, held the gun along the seam of his BDU's.

"Hey! What th' hell you doin' in here? Get the hell outta my bidness!"

Jake whirled, backhanding Hootie with he heavy gun. The fat man reeled, crashed to his knees, spitting blood. His glasses flew through the doorway.

Jake kicked the cart out of the way, stepped behind Hootie, slipped the .45 in his pocket, grabbed a handful of hair, jerked the head back. He held the torn glossies up to Gillespie's bleeding nose.

"That the phone number of the shooter, you fat maggot? You know, the one you hired to kill Tom and Rick."

"My glasses. Cain't see without m'glasses."

Jake stuffed the photos back in his cargo pocket, retrieved the .45, jammed it in Hootie's ear, cocked the hammer. "You're not gonna need 'em, Hootie."

"Now, hold on! Hold on, here. We kin talk about this, cain't we? Whut's done is done, but there's plenty for ev'rybody. See 'at gold there? Go on, take it. It's yourn. Jest don't hurt me."

Jake jerked the hair upward, forcing Hootie to stand up. "Outside, you piece of shit. And Hootie, you so much as twitch, I will blow your fucking head off." He pressed the muzzle to the base of Gillespie's skull.

"You gonna kill me?"

"No, Hootie. *I'm* not going to kill you. I'm going to take you for a ride."

Chapter 33

ONE WEEK LATER

Jake was sitting on the deck playing *Gabriel's Oboe* from *The Mission*, when Meij showed Bob Duncan and Joe Landski out to the deck. They waited politely, hats in hand, until Jake finished the last haunting note.

Jake stood. "Hey, Bob! Joe!" He handed Meij the cello and the bow. "You guys want coffee? No? Well, have a seat."

The men sat around the glass table on the deck.

Duncan began. "Jake, we need your help."

The Indian smiled. "Ask, Bob. You know I'll help anyway I can."

Duncan handed Jake an evidence envelope containing several thin, black blades. "You know what these are? Go ahead. Open it."

He opened the bag, dumped the contents on the table, held one of them up to the light. "Yeah," he said. "These are obsidian blanks."

Duncan and Landski stared at him.

Jake explained: "When you make an arrowhead, first you take the node of chert, or obsidian, whatever you're using and shape it into a cylinder, called a core. Then, with a hammer stone, you knock these blades off the core. Then you take these blanks, and knap them into whatever you want: arrowheads, knives, scrapers—whatever."

He held one of the blades up. "These are too thin to make points, but they'll cut like hell. They're a hundred times sharper than a surgeon's scalpel."

"Yeah, we know," Duncan said.

"What do you mean?"

Bob gathered the blanks up carefully, put them back in the bag. "A USGS helicopter over-flying the Anvil spotted Hootie Gillespie's body. Somebody murdered him, Jake."

"No shit." The Indian shook his head. "Who'd want to do that?"

"Somebody who was plenty pissed," Landski said.

"Why do you say that, Joe?"

"Because," Duncan said, "whoever did it stripped Hootie's clothes off him, staked him out naked, n' cut his eyelids off." Pause. "Then left him to th' sun, 'n th' ants."

"That ain't all," Landski said. "Whoever did it sat right out there by Hootie—still alive—an' chipped them blanks, just like you said. We found the chips an' the core. He used a couple of them blades to cut the eyelids off. We got a couple with Hootie's blood on 'em."

"If that wasn't enough," Duncan said, "must uh been two or three hundred little tiny cuts all over th' body. Not too deep, just enough to bleed an' get the scent of blood in th' air, attracting ants, blow flies, coyotes."

Jake shook his head. "Must have been a hard way to die."

"Was," Landski said. "Ravens got his eyes."

Jake looked up. Said nothing.

Duncan: "You know anybody who makes arrowheads, Jake?"

"No, not personally. But there's a lot of mountain man types who probably do."

"Well, anyway," Bobby said, opening a large manila envelope, "we searched the office at the Motel and found these in Hootie's trash." He slid the torn pictures of Rick and Tom across the table.

"These were in Hootie's trash?"

"Yeah. They were."

"Trace the phone number?"

"Doing it now. We also found a hidden room with stacks of M-16's, a couple of .50 caliber machine guns, and a desk drawer full of Neo-Nazi shit."

Jake looked up thoughtfully. "So you telling me you think Hootie was the one who planned Tom's death?"

"Looks that way don't it?"

"Yeah, but it's all circumstantial. Never hold up in court."

"Proves it good enough for me," Duncan said.

The men fell silent for several moments. Finally, Landski spoke up. He fidgeted in his chair. "Jake I gotta ask ya. I was drivin' back into town late last week, an' I coulda sworn I saw you drivin" Hootie's new truck out on th' Red Road. Wasn't you, was it?"

Jake laughed. "Me? I just got out of the hospital, Joe. I'm not in any shape to manhandle a 350-400 pound man."

Landski shook his head. "Musta been somebody else."

"Musta been," Duncan agreed.

The three men talked small talk for a few more minutes, then they shook hands. Joe and Bobby left.

Jake walked down to the sweatlodge, pulled the chokecherry stake out of the earth. He'd burn it next time he had a sweat.

SIX MONTHS LATER

After dealing with Hootie, and while Nick was still in the hospital, Jake went back to the Motel, recovered her and her father's luggage. Haraldsen's he put in one of the guest rooms; he left Nicole's at the foot of the bed in his master bedroom. Let her choose.

When he brought her home, she hung her things in his closet, cleaned out one of his drawers and folded in her lingerie.

Although the burns were healing, Jake wondered about her heart. Each day the thick cicatrice of scar on the left side of her face, where Grubinich touched it to the lava, seemed to harden. He never spoke of it, and she didn't bring it up.

They seemed to be two stars locked in orbit around each other, held by the gravity of their shared ordeal. Once, he found her in his study, holding the atlatl shaft that had suddenly appeared in Grubinich's throat and allowed them to escape. They hadn't talked about that, either. But both of them gazed often toward the Anvil and wondered. "Were they still there? Did they survive the eruption and the miles of new, hot lava?"

They drove out to the cinder bluff to see the new flows and Joe Landski stopped them at a road block.

"We just want to go a little closer for a look," Jake said.

"Yeah, hell, go ahead," Joe said. "Ain't like you don't know what you're doing." He paused for a moment, staring at the sky. "It's fucked about Tom, ain't it."

"Yeah, Joe, it is," Jake said, and drove to a place where they could see across the Anvil. They got out of the Hummer and walked a few feet off the road. The air was noticeably warmer as they looked at the new lava flow: three hundred square miles of black, smoking scab on the face of the desert.

"Jesus, Jake," Nicole said, stepping closer to him.

"Yeah," he said, putting his arm around her. "Yeah."

Their days passed in tranquility at *Makoce Waste*, their nights in love. Jake's nightmares of war faded, but were replaced with dreams of his dead children and wife. He carried within himself a vast emptiness from lifetimes ago, but real nonetheless. He had loved *Cante Wohitika Wi* as he had loved no other and he could not seem to give her up.

Nicole sensed his grief, and often touched him with a caress when a shadow crossed his face, but she did not ask, and he did not share it with her. There seemed to be a bridge between them that could not be crossed, something hanging in the air, a waiting.

One afternoon he roused himself, stood up from the couch where they had been reading.

"What are you doing?" she asked.

"I'm going to sweat," he said.

She stood up and went to him. "I want to go in with you."

"Are you sure" he asked. "It's awfully hot in there." He kissed her on the scar.

"Don't." She pushed him away, drew him to her again, kissed him fully on the lips.

"I'm sure," she said.

Jake made the preparations, and at dusk, they went in. The heat was intense, and the lodge swelled in the blood-red light. Nicole sat across from him, eyes wild with fear and near panic. He began the first song, drumming softly, closing his eyes. When he finished, and looked at her again, the rocks had cooled a little. She smiled a small, curious smile.

He was about to ask "What?" when the woman he knew as Nicole Haraldsen reached out with both arms toward the rocks. Blonde hair turned black, and began growing toward her waist. Blue eyes turned brown; a tee shirt and long skirt transformed themselves into a long elk hide dress decorated with elk teeth. *Cante Wohitika Wi*—the woman of the cave—sat smiling at him.

She reached across the rocks and took one of his hands in hers. "My husband," she smiled. "I love you. I will always love you—until the earth and stars are no more. But you must find a way out of your pain. This woman loves you, needs you. See...." She waved her hand, and he saw three small children playing in the sunlight. "Your children wait for you."

When he looked again, he saw Nicole, confused.

"Wow," she said. "I think I just went someplace."

Jake scooted around the sweat lodge until he sat by her. "I love you," he said.

Printed in the United States
149301LV00002BA/81/P